Drops of Glass

A Tale of Magic in the Great War

The Shards of Lafayette
Book 1

Kenneth A. Baldwin

EBURNEAN
BOOKS

EBURNEAN
BOOKS

Drops of Glass

To Massimiliano
You were a friend when the world was dark.

Chapter 1
The Curse
Marcus

Now heaven be praised
That in that hour that most imperiled her,
Menaced her liberty who foremost raised
Europe's bright flag of freedom, some there were
Who, not unmindful of the antique debt,
Came back the generous path of Lafayette.
-Alan Seeger-

He hadn't heard me, he hadn't seen me, and with a squeeze of my finger, he would fall from the sky.

Sweat beaded under my leather flight helmet. I'd trained for these moments. A German single-seat pursuit plane, sitting defenseless under my nose, and the new Vickers twin machine guns rested in front of my cockpit, just offset, begging to be put to use.

Pull the trigger a quarter of an inch—that was all it took—and I'd open my scorecard at long last. The boys on the ground would welcome me back a hero.

But I had never killed a man, even after two years at war. I was cursed.

At first, it was natural. Every soldier enters the war without a kill, and each man looked forward to the day, macabre and twisted as it may sound. Some, the foolish ones, looked forward to it like a birthday or a ballgame. Others looked forward to it with dread like a trip to the dentist, but we all looked forward to it in some way.

Because we all wondered. The questions were relentless: *Will I freeze up? How will I do it? What will it feel like when I stick a bayonet through a German and save the world?*

Precious few of us wondered whether we'd be the ones left dying slowly in a trench or trying to crawl from a ravaged tank or burning fuselage.

And now, with a pull of my trigger, I could wonder no longer. I only had to bring myself to squeeze my finger a quarter inch.

After a time, it got awkward for those of us still unsullied. New boys coming over to the war would ask how long we'd been out here—then inevitably for our number. This was especially true among pilots, who reveled in their records of downed planes. Every pilot knew two numbers: their confirmed kills and the true number of their kills.

My two numbers were the same. Zero.

I shifted my hands nervously on the joystick. *Come on, Marcus. Take the shot, already.*

Soon, the other soldiers talked about me as if I had the influenza, and each had their own prescription for me to bag my first Boche. *Lead your gun to take distance and speed into account. A swig of bourbon didn't do any harm. Wait to shoot until you're sure your rounds will strike the kill box on the enemy's fuselage.*

As if I didn't know.

Then the tips melted away, replaced with clumsy explanations that somewhere I'd been cursed. And that belief inspired them to see me with rage-inducing reverence.

The Curse

Marcus, take the damn shot.

Descending from above as Luf had taught me, cloaking my Nieuport single-seater in the sunlight, I had settled in behind this poor German pilot like a cat in the night.

But like always, my brain would not stop thinking.

Why hadn't he seen me? The idiot. The foolish idiot. Was he a new pilot? Had he not been trained properly? Didn't he know that you must always look about you, scan the sky, pay close attention to those terrible blind spots?

My rudder pedals protested against my feet, and the joystick jostled as the wind caught my wings and rudder. Nature tried to pull me off course, tried to stop the violence before it happened.

Just a squeeze, little German. That's all it will take, and you will die. If you're lucky, one of the machine gun rounds will hit you, so you don't fall in flames with your machine. The flames would lick your skin and bubble it and the worst fate you could imagine would be to survive the crash.

A quarter inch. That's all.

But I had never killed a man, no, not after two years at war.

Suddenly, the pilot shifted his head back and forth. He seemed to mock me. His engine screamed in my direction, taunting me, daring me.

It was all getting dangerous now. Every moment I hesitated, the risk grew. He was unlikely to be the only plane nearby. Even if he didn't take evasive action, his comrades would find him and open fire on his pursuer.

The German pilot dipped into a gentle bank. He turned his head and must have seen the tip of my wing, because he turned again, fast now, panicked. His eyes met mine. I should have pulled the trigger then, in that moment when our eyes locked across the clouds and he knew I was there.

But I didn't. For some reason, I couldn't.

The German Pfalz dove and banked hard, giving me a brief

glimpse of the two black crosses on its wings. I had missed the easy shot. If another presented itself, I could not hesitate again, but now it would be different. Now there would be honor in the kill. He had a sporting chance to beat me.

The plane flipped over several times, curving under me, changing direction before making its climb to get above my machine. I jammed hard on the stick and my Nieuport gave chase. The pull of gravity tugged at my face and insides as the diving speed of my aircraft built so I could propel it upward again. The Pfalz darted so quickly without fear, and it had already twisted around to climb beyond the aim of my machine guns.

We circled one another. I tried to match his movements, but I struggled against the hardiness of the nimble German machine. The Pfalz D.III was known for its sturdiness, its reliability in a dive and sharp turns. My Nieuport 28, new at the front, was a model thrown to the Americans because the French didn't want it. My turns could not be as sharp as his, for fear the linen on my plane would pull away from the wing's leading edge and fail.

Yet, I could not risk falling too far behind in this contest to get well above the other. Already he had begun firing his Spandau machine gun to prevent me from taking certain maneuvers. They all went wide as I clung to the strategic defense I'd been taught. These fighters could only shoot forward. If I could just stay clear of his nose...

But with every turn, the Pfalz's heavy wings cut away pieces of my escape route. This couldn't go on for too long. Though I hadn't yet shot down a German, I had logged plenty of flying hours. But even experienced pilots could knock themselves unconscious from too much maneuvering.

I spiraled down and dove quickly, trying to sweep beneath him, but he followed me deftly. When I pulled up from the dive he was gone.

Gone?

The Curse

No. I glanced now at a bank of clouds. He had disappeared into them. A dare and a peace offering. *Follow me or go home.* I stared at the white plumed wall. I had given this man his chance for a gentleman's duel. The game was on. To turn back now—

I put a hand to my neck, grasping for a glass marble suspended there on a small chain, but I could hardly feel it through the padding of my flight suit and gloves. The movement was automatic, superstitious. What was it pilots said? *When it's your time, there's no stopping it.* Magic marble or no.

It was time for me to get my first.

I flew into the clouds after him.

When I emerged on the other side, I saw them. My quarry with two other German fighters, death waiting. They seemed to be laughing at me. *Greedy American. You could have gone home.*

Instinct took the controls, and I squeezed my trigger. But my guns hardly had time to sing before they jammed. I was defenseless.

No, no, no.

The three planes seemed to hang in the air, as if pausing to comprehend my dilemma. Then in a flash, they closed in.

I flipped my nose downward again and spiraled back into the bank of clouds for cover. I didn't need to check if they were following. I knew they would be.

I only hoped I could get back to my squad mates. But between my chase with the Pfalz and my scramble to escape its reinforcements, I'd lost significant altitude. Unless my boys were searching for me below our assigned patrol, they might not see me. And besides, they might be busy with their own German warbirds.

The terrible sound erupted. The mechanical, uncaring rat-tat-tat of the German guns. Rounds came zipping through the air. I rolled and banked and clutched at the glass marble around my neck.

My hands shook. Gravity and terror assaulted my stomach.

The Germans sailed after me, taking turns shooting off rounds. Ten. Twenty. Fifty. One hundred rounds. Any bullet could end my life. I could not stay clear of all their guns, so I crossed their noses in a sporadic pattern of twists and slides. Could I outmaneuver them long enough to exhaust their ammunition? Their fuel?

Psssht.

The sound of a round piercing the canvas of my plane was anti-climactic. There was no explosion. No fanfare. Just a hole now in the wing with air whistling through it.

My gut climbed into my throat, condensation clouding on my flight goggles. I tried to wipe them, but my training was running out my ears. Fear, a recurring and unwelcome guest, evicted the smooth, smart evasive maneuvers I'd been taught, and now I let the animalistic instinct of survival take control. My swerves grew more daring, pushing the Nieuport to its limits, unconcerned about how much the wings could take.

I needed to get back to the Allied line. If I could fly low enough, perhaps our anti-air guns could help me, or even our artillery or infantry machine gunners.

My panicked maneuvering impeded my forward progress, though, and it was slow going, punctuated with the zips of the German rounds piercing the howl of the wind.

Two years at war. I could not die here.

A jolt on my right wing. Glancing over revealed the trail of holes in the canvas, not so neat as the first, less graceful. I felt that impact as if the French oak frames in the wings were my own bones.

I noticed the effect on the plane almost immediately. It did not respond as it had before, and now pushing the Nieuport's limits wasn't dangerous—it was suicide. But what else could I do? The Germans were competing now, each jockeying for position to claim my death on his scorecard.

The Curse

The panic was as deadly as the German guns. It could not end here. My number was still zero. I had not yet claimed that hero's honor I'd left home to achieve.

Could I stomach a crash landing on rough terrain? Perhaps they would count the downed plane and leave me alone. But I could not crash yet. I was still in German territory. The line was visible, but I was flying dangerously low.

My vision soon clouded with the explosive rounds of anti-aircraft fire.

Rounds from behind. Rounds from below.

I had no choice. I had to climb or Archie on the ground would blow the Allied colors on my wings to bits.

I yanked back on the stick and adjusted my angle before banking into a wide turn away from the approaching battery. Forty-five degrees to the left and shallow enough so as not to flash the tops of my wings at my pursuers. It'd be an easy target.

A round fizzed by my head, close enough to take my breath away, but soon they had flown straight past. They split in different directions on their re-approach.

Climb, Marcus. Climb. At least enough to give yourself a better chance against the ground fire.

My plane jerked behind me as another burst of fire poked a few holes in my fuselage. My thoughts drifted to my mother. The little stack of my father's unopened letters in my luggage.

Their boy downed in God-forsaken Toulon without so much as a single victory, not a single bad guy nabbed in all his time away.

Ahead of me, I thought I saw my reflection, my plane climbing into a suspended pool of still water, breaching the veil separating life and death.

But no. It was Campbell!

His propellor dove straight toward me, and I barely had the sense to alter course before the two machine guns mounted in front of his cockpit blazed to life.

I swung my plane around just in time to see Uncle Sam's top hat painted on the side of Campbell's plane. I regurgitated a burst of air, sweet relief. I had unknowingly masked his attack, and the Germans scattered. I took advantage of the opportunity to continue gaining altitude and circle back to give him some much-needed help. Surprise or no, one pilot against three weren't odds anyone liked.

Not that it stopped men like Campbell or Luf from trying.

A flash of light burst to my left, and I glanced over in time to see a Pfalz, *my* Pfalz, the one I had so thoughtfully refused to engage, catch fire—a terrible and awesome byproduct of Campbell's enthusiasm. The plane dropped as the pilot panicked. I banked to see it play out, watching the man's desperate dive unquestionably lose control and spiral to the earth.

A victory for Campbell.

My breath caught in my chest. Ironically, being in the air made it harder to breathe, and the relief hardly had fuel to swell.

Two on two now, and that changed everything. The Germans resorted quickly to evasive team maneuvers. I recognized the patterns we saw in many German pilots. The machine gun fire calmed, the pilots now reserving rounds for sure shots. We didn't give them any.

As we danced around one another in the sky, a few more of our boys joined the fight from their nearby patrol. In less than a minute, the remaining Huns turned away to retreat.

We lined up to pursue. If we closed the distance quickly, we could count two more German planes out of the Kaiser's service. But as I settled in between Campbell and Winslow, they glanced over and noticed the state of my aircraft. There was no hesitation. They signaled to turn home immediately.

I flushed bright red but followed.

Service in the air was nothing like what I'd seen on the ground. Each machine, each pilot, was precious, and it wouldn't do to take unnecessary risks. After all, Campbell had already claimed a victory. Better to bring home the whole squadron and fix up a plane to fight another day under more favorable circumstances.

But no one—not a single pilot I knew—ever liked his comrades to make up for his lack.

I glanced at my guns. Jammed and harmless. My heart still hammered at over a hundred rounds per minute, but I had a good half hour to calm it down before we landed at Gengoult—thirty minutes to convince myself I'd never been afraid.

Chapter 2
Enhanced Repair Measures
Jane

In dreary doubtful waiting hours,
Before the brazen frenzy starts,
The horses show him nobler powers; —
O patient eyes, courageous hearts!
-Julian Grenfell-

No one else wanted my step ladder.

The other mechanics jealously guarded theirs as if they were made of gold. The one left to me, the first woman to work alongside them fixing up planes in Croix de Metz, was said to wobble. In fact, several mechanics had fallen over and earned nasty bumps and bruises that made the physically demanding job of fixing things all the more difficult.

None of them wanted a woman to succeed beside them. It would make them look less proficient, earn them even greater scorn from the pilots who took their projects into the sky.

So they gave me the wobbly step ladder.

But the thing about wobbly step ladders is that they simply need some good advice from someone who cares. So, for the first week I came into possession of my step ladder, I cleaned it for a half an hour each night and spoke to it the way no one speaks to step ladders.

Eventually, its confidence grew, and its wobbles decreased until it was mostly reliable.

But as I worked away under the cowling of one the 94th Squadron's Nieuport 28 single seat fighters, my step ladder regressed into bad habits.

"Steady now, Beatrice," I said calmly. "At times, we're all tempted to revert to old ways. But we cannot fit into past flaws any better than we can wear worn out boots."

And with my comments, I either balanced myself better, or my step ladder stopped wobbling on its own accord. It's difficult to say which happened.

"Hey, Jane! How's it going over there?" A voice drifted from the ground behind me up and into my work. I took a steadying breath.

"Just fine, thank you," I called back without turning.

"Will you be much longer?" The voice belonged to another new mechanic: given name Steve, surname A-Perpetual-Pain-in-My-Side.

"I'm working on the fuel line. This one has cracked, so it might be some time still while I fix it."

"How do you plan to fix a cracked fuel line? Magic powder?" That was Steve's friend, Brady. His ugly laugh was a testament to his facial features.

"Hey, now," Steve replied, "she's not going to use magic powder. She'll probably just ask the fuel line to *stop being cracked, please*." Steve tried to adopt an accent older than the American state he hailed from. It sounded like a drunk Welsh teenager doing his best at first year of preparatory school. But they both laughed all the same.

11

"If you could move along, I would appreciate it. I have a lot to do here." I turned on them with a glare.

"Aw, come on, Steve. You've got her all upset." Brady ran a hand through his wavy hair. There wasn't much to like about his face, but his hair was his pride and joy. He kept it a little longer than he was allowed and took every opportunity to show it off.

"She's only sore because her boy is up in the air," Steve replied. My face flushed. Beatrice wobbled in anger.

"She sure knows how to pick a fella. Who knows? Maybe Gun-shy Markie will finally get a kill—or maybe he'll finally *be* a kill. Hard to say."

I clenched my jaw and descended from Beatrice, wrench grasped firmly in one fist. I approached them with all the menace I could muster.

"Marcus will come back," I said with rigid jaw. I stared directly up into Brady's shrewish face. "And he has more courage flying up there than you will ever have."

Brady's lips twisted into a smile.

"You see how riled up you gotta get to give me a lick of attention?" he asked with a mischievous grin. He nodded. "Tell me, now. You and Marcus, you got something there of a romantical sort?"

"Of course not," I replied, still considering how I might use the wrench to worsen his knobby cheekbones.

"Then why not come into town with me this weekend? I'd love to take you for a spin. I'm about tired of all the weepy-eyed widows waiting for us over there."

"How dare you," I growled.

"Watch it now, Brady. She might cast a spell on you," Steve said with a chuckle.

I let the comment sink in, watched his eyes as he slowly worked himself up into believing I might. It had taken me some time to embrace the benefits of my reputation, but they were there. After many long seconds, Brady lost his courage.

"Invitation stands, Jane," he muttered. He gave a not-so-subtle thumbs up to Steve, and they started off toward the mess. Then, he called over his shoulder, "Maybe a little loving would solve that frowny face."

I dropped the wrench and satisfied myself with pulling out a clump of his beautiful hair.

I was late to lunch. When I walked in, I ignored Brady, Steve, and their cohorts scowling in the corner and collected my food quickly before looking for a spot to eat by myself. I was used to eating alone, at least when Marcus was on duty. My mother would be surprised to learn that the seclusion didn't bother me. I had come to the aerodrome on request of Major Raoul Lufbery as a *specially* skilled mechanic, arriving with eyes wide open to how I would be received.

Still, I found the social groups that naturally formed around the airbase amusing. Mechanics tended to eat with other mechanics. Pilots ate with pilots. But today, the women at a table in the corner beckoned me over to join them.

For me, solitude was expected. This invitation was not.

I paused before heading in their direction. I was friendly with the girls that worked at the base, but rarely had it earned me an invitation to sit with them. There weren't scores of us at the aerodrome—only a handful. Some worked as cleaners, some as cooks, the petulant one with the raised nose worked in intelligence.

I was the only mechanic of my gender, at least here.

"Jane, sit down," said the hen. Flora was her name, from Cornwall. "We women must stick together."

I swallowed a snort. Rarely had I seen women truly stick

together. And seeing as this was one of Flora's rare, irregular invitations to converse, her comment did nothing to warm me.

"That's very kind of you," I managed as I sat down.

"Oh, it's nothing. Isn't it, ladies?" The gaggle beside her nodded and clucked. Lunch with ladies meant questions and talking. Under different circumstances, I'd hesitate to accept this invitation. But Marcus was still on patrol in the sky, and I'd welcome any distraction. I gently touched the glass marble hanging around my neck beneath my jumpsuit.

"They don't do you any favors in the wardrobe department, do they?" Flora said. The other women returned to their sets of private conversations.

"Blouses, skirts, and grease don't get along well," I replied, dropping my hand to pick up my spoon.

"I can't imagine they do," Flora replied. "I have to commend you, Jane. I'm embarrassed at my luxury working in the intelligence office when I see the muck under your fingernails."

My mucky fingernails brought soup to my mouth before I replied.

"Well, sadly, not all of us can help the war effort by talking on the telephone."

Flora smiled tartly.

"No, some of us have to go about servicing the planes and the men that fly them."

I tried to ignore Flora's comment. Inside, I knew what women were capable of—how quickly we could turn on each other when threatened somehow. I tried to turn this cynicism into a shield. But Flora lived to sit atop the social ladder, and her opinion reflected the belief to which the others likely subscribed.

So despite myself, her quips pierced my defenses. It was too much. Every time Marcus went into the air (and he did so often) it was too much. But not for the reasons everyone assumed. I stared down at my bowl, unwilling to give Flora the satisfaction of seeing me cry.

"Oh, don't be like that," Flora said. "I didn't mean to get nasty. You don't do yourself any favors, you know. Rumors circulate that you've taken to witchcraft. And being attached at the hip with one of the pilots isn't an endearing look, either. The truth is most of these women are afraid of you. They wouldn't know what to say at all if they found themselves alone with you for a stretch of five minutes."

"I see," I replied. "It must be your responsibility as an intelligence operative that has gifted you the social savvy to speak with me so freely."

She scowled, and we fell into uneasy silence. I wasn't the only one that experienced the stress of war. We all struggled with fear when a pilot went up. Dread. Anxiety. A whole patrol had been gone since late that morning. We mourned even the pilots we disliked.

People like Flora used this pain as a motivator to distance herself from everyone. Part of me envied her that wisdom.

I clutched the glass marble around my neck.

"Turner!"

A voice called to me across the mess. The compacted figure of Major Lufbery beckoned to me, hand ever at an acute angle, holding a phantom cigarette when a real one was unavailable.

"Excuse me," I said, happy to have a reason to leave Flora and her flock for a real distraction. Without glancing backward, I knew they stared as I walked away.

"Yes, Major?" I asked when within earshot. He turned with an invitation to follow him out of the mess.

"Do you have that fuel line crack fixed?" he asked.

"Not yet, sir. It will likely need to be replaced. Do we have a spare?"

He grimaced. "Jane, if we had a spare, I'd have asked another mechanic to look at it."

"I see, sir. You are hoping I can..."

"Come up with something creative," Lufbery finished.

I turned the idea over in my head.

"You may overestimate my abilities, Major. I can't simply conjure up magical weldings."

He smiled, his eyes squinting.

"You can't, huh?"

"You know I can't. Whose plane is it?" I asked.

"Huffer."

I paused. Most of my time went to patching up Marcus's plane. Lufbery had officially assigned me to him. But occasionally, he requested that I work on other discreet repair jobs. It didn't endear me to the assigned mechanics. But Lufbery had discovered my peculiar aptitude and method for repairs back at Villeneuve-les-Virtus aerodrome, the training base for the 94th.

Major Huffer was the official commander of the unit, but Lufbery was a war hero, having flown with the Lafayette Escadrille since the early days of wartime aviation. Most of the pilots looked to him for leadership.

"I see. And the commander being without a plane is never a nice thing," I said carefully.

"Well, I'm not giving him mine. If he's not going to be careful about how he uses his switch to control his engine, let him be grounded."

"You think the fuel line cracked because of misuse?" I asked.

"Don't make me say it out loud, Jane. But if one of the younger pilots cracked his line by switching cylinders the way he does, I'd have a serious conversation with him."

We stopped as we neared my motorcycle, a Royal Enfield that I used to get around the base quickly. It made me grateful that I was assigned a jumpsuit and not a skirt.

"Well, as I've told you, magic—"

"Enhanced repair measures."

"Very well, enhanced repair measures have a great deal more to do with the relationship between the pilot and his machine than some silly words one might say to try and fuse a cracked copper tubing."

Lufbery nodded and searched for a cigarette. I waited for him to dismiss me. He didn't.

"But you already knew that," I said.

He lit his cigarette and took a leisurely drag. "I may remember you saying something about it."

I smiled. "And you know that Major Huffer's capacity to effectuate any enhanced repair measures is... limited."

"I suspected as much." He shrugged.

I swung a leg over the Enfield. "Thank you for the assignment," I said. "It was an effective distraction while Marcus was out. Officially, I know that is beyond the scope of your concern and had nothing to do with why you assigned it to me."

"Nothing at all." Lufbery's smile was contagious. There was no doubt as to why his pilots liked him. He cared about his friends and wasn't afraid to turn protocol on its head to ensure safety, efficacy, and respect.

I went to start my engine, but the major put a hand on my arm.

"You and Marcus are close," he said.

I nodded. Since Villes-les-Virtus, I'd been afraid that command would separate Marcus and me. The romantic rumors that circulated about us did very little to ease that anxiety.

"He's important to me, too. He's different, you know, from the others."

"I know."

"He doesn't go into town. He doesn't talk about the Germans the way the others do. He still hasn't opened his scorecard."

"There are plenty of pilots who haven't yet downed a plane," I retorted, unaccustomed to having to defend Marcus from Lufbery.

"I'm not critiquing him," the major said. "The opposite. You know, Jane, this war has cost so much. Taken the lives of so many men. Some of them were never meant to be soldiers, and there's nothing wrong with that. In fact, it's something worth protecting."

I furrowed my brows.

"May I speak candidly?" I asked.

"I have. You can, too."

"That notion is ridiculous. You can't protect anyone at war, and you know that much better than I do."

Luf slack lips tightened across his face.

"Still, it might be worth trying," he said. I must have rolled my eyes because he continued in a hurry. "How old do you think I am?"

"What kind of question—"

"How old?"

I studied his features and puzzled. He had creases in his face. His eyes sat deeply, and they habitually cast themselves about lazily the way my father's did in the morning before tea. His body moved sluggishly, fatigued even when rested.

"Perhaps high thirties. Maybe forty," I said.

"I just had my thirtieth birthday."

I blushed.

"War ages people differently than during peace time," I stammered, trying to correct my social stumble. "You've been at combat for years."

He watched me scramble to recover before responding, "I met Marcus when he was nineteen years old. Before he joined up with the Lafayette, they had him driving ambulances at the front where he saw things that'll peel the skin from your eyes."

He put his cigarette to his lips, perhaps pushing away similar horrors. I ignored the smoke, even though it had always made my eyes burn. Marcus was only three years my junior.

"He wants to be the next great combat pilot. He was a teenager when the war started, and I don't have to tell you what the stories newspaper men write can do to young kids who don't know any better."

I fanned the smoke gently away from my face.

"You don't want him to be the next great combat ace?" I asked. He dropped the rest of his cigarette on the ground and ground it into the dirt with a crunch.

"Maybe I'm just tired of seeing the war have its way with the boys it seduced," he said. "If something deep inside of Marcus won't let him shoot another man—now wouldn't there be something strangely pretty about that? If he went the whole war and never had to take a life?"

"If you feel that way, why did you recruit him for America's first pursuit squadron?"

"Because he's a good pilot, and he deserves to become a combat ace if he wants to. We need combat aces, and for the sake of the war, I have to put my personal feelings aside and treat him like I would anyone else. It might cost him his life. It might cost him something more. That's the price of leadership. But if it were possible to protect him, I think there might be something in that."

If anyone in the world understood my friendship with Marcus, it was Lufbery. But he'd never spoken about his understanding so openly. I found a great relief flooding into my chest on hearing his words.

"Why are you telling me this?" I asked.

"There's something rumbling from command. Something's coming. I just wanted to warn you." He squeezed my arm. "Better see what you can do about Huffer's plane. At least let me tell him we've tried to fix his fuel line. And don't worry. Marcus will be down within the hour. I'm sure of it."

He turned and walked off, puffs of smoke from a newly lit cigarette marking his pathway in the air behind him.

Chapter 3
Polished Rounds
Marcus

To these I turn, in these I trust—
Brother Lead and Sister Steel.
To his blind power I make appeal,
I guard her beauty clean from rust.
-Siegfried Sassoon-

The aerodrome buzzed alive when I landed at Croix de Metz. Mechanics ran to our planes immediately after we touched down, and when they saw our machines polka-dotted with gunfire, swears about the damned cabbage eaters droned like humming bees.

My legs shook more than usual as I descended from the cockpit. Fortunately, my heavy fur flying suit had enough girth to hide it. Although Spring had warmed the French air on the ground, it was still cold enough in the sky that we'd never think to fly without the heavy jackets.

With a few steps, the shaking slowed, but the misery clung to me.

Polished Rounds

I had failed more than once that afternoon. Not only had I failed to open my scorecard again, I'd almost given that enemy Bosch a reason to drink with his comrades tonight.

I patted the glass marble resting under my flight suit. I'd almost died up there. It wasn't the first time, and it wouldn't be the last. An almost daily dance with death should have desensitized me to the risk. But my legs still shook every time I got out of my plane as I considered how close I'd come to being another tally among hundreds of thousands.

I eyed the mechanics dutifully at work. Did any of them long to go up into the air aboard the machines they spent their days and nights repairing?

When I was a mechanic, I hadn't dreamed of it. When I first joined the aero squadrons, we were still calling them escadrilles, still under French command, and I was just happy to get away from driving the ambulances—emotionally and physically exhausted of ferrying a never-ending stream of wounded and dying from the front.

The screams. The stench. The choices.

I squeezed my eyes shut.

If the Germans had shot me down today, there'd likely be no ambulance ride, just a new permanent address in German-occupied France or perhaps a cozy wreckage in the middle of no man's land.

"Looks like it was hairy out there," one man mumbled as he helped push my plane off the landing strip and toward the hanger.

A part of me longed for the safety of the mechanic's uniform again. Machines can be fixed or scrapped and salvaged. The work was straightforward, optimistic even when infuriating. Tightening bolts and testing cables reminded me of my first job fixing up bicycles at the ripe age of fifteen.

But there was little honor in being a mechanic—at least, not the honor that drew me to the war in the first place. I came looking for medals, stories my father could share with his customers, scars I could show everyone when I came back. I needed souvenirs that would prove my family belonged in our community.

When I'd first arrived, they had me fixing ambulance cars. Then, as the need for drivers increased, they put me behind the wheel. I soon learned there was no glory to be found in the trenches, only death. I was ashamed to say that the death got to me.

But in the air, especially among the early pilots, things were different. It was like King Arthur, chivalry and all. That's how the papers talked about them. Those boys in the young Lafayette Escadrille, the volunteers who couldn't stand Great Bully Kaiser, who gave up perfectly good lives full of Ivy League potential to dance the honorable dance in the sky.

Lufbery. Rockwell. Chapman. They were knights of the air, bringing honor back to the war God had turned His back on. On the ground, the meat-grinding guns laid waste to so many lives, but they had adhered to a code that defied the senseless violence.

In the air, there was still honor to be won.

Or at least there should be.

Maybe that's why I didn't unleash my rounds when I should have—why I hesitated. My first victory wouldn't come from a hiding spot against an opponent who had no idea I was right behind him. It would be earned the old way or not at all.

It would be earned the way my opponent would appreciate, attached to a story I could share in crowded bars of interested listeners.

A heavily gloved hand clapped me on the shoulder. I turned to see a toothily grinning Campbell.

"Thought we'd lost you back there, Marcus," he said in a boastful, good-ole-boy type of way. His youthful smiled radiated an awful gluttony, fishing for my gratitude.

I swallowed and plastered a pleasantry across my own features.

"What? You mean the German plane you stole from me?" I joked, poking him in the ribs.

He threw his head back and let out a single, barking laugh that extended his prominent jaw.

"Stole from you? Did you hear that, Winslow?"

I turned to find Winslow beside me, his eyebrows raised in that kind, claylike expression he often wore.

"Hear what?"

"Mark here didn't want our help after all. Said we stole his German bird," Campbell went on.

"Oh, is that right? Best not to be too greedy now, Markie." Winslow said, a little bit sternly. His face was sturdier, fuller in shape and concern.

"That's right," Campbell went on. "France is littered with the planes of ambitious pilots. That's some free advice, Markie boy."

They prattled on like a well-rehearsed radio play. I bit my tongue, wishing I hadn't made a wise crack to begin with.

Contrary to the time-tested heroes of the war, Douglas Campbell and Alan Winslow were newly discovered legends, claiming the first kills from any American-trained air squadron just a week or so before, an affair that cost only a few minutes and a generous helping of sheer dumb luck.

Yes. Dumb luck.

How else do you explain two completely inexperienced pilots downing an Albatross D.V and a Pfalz D.III at under a thousand feet? Campbell and Winslow didn't know the danger they were in. They hadn't seen the evolution of the German planes like I had, and even I could hardly appreciate the terrors of the early years of the war, back when some German genius was first to discover how to shoot a machine gun directly through a propellor. The Fokker Scourge. The rain of metal and fire and devastation. Bloody April.

No. They were just two green boys happy to give the Kaiser a good licking.

But whatever serendipity Campbell and Winslow enjoyed, they had done so in full view of the city of Toul, and now, the war-ragged French people all but considered American pilots gods of the air.

It didn't matter. Luf would meticulously train their dumb luck into competence.

Major Raoul Lufbery. A damn aviating genius with an under-rated official record, he was the true leader of the 94th and an even better friend. About ten years his junior, I worked under him as a mechanic in the Lafayette. When he'd asked me to come along and be a pilot in one of the first American air squadrons, I could not turn him down. There was something about him that inspired in me a sense of kinship I hadn't known since leaving home. Hell, perhaps even before I'd left home. I'd do anything for Luf.

As we walked toward the hangar, I saw him leaning against the doorway, a cigarette hung from his lips, his hands busy polishing a glint of metal, calmly waiting for the lumbering fur-suited pilots to arrive for a debrief.

"What happened out there?" Lufbery asked after plucking his cigarette from its resting place. "Mark's plane is riddled."

"If you ask him, Major, he had everything 'under control,'" Campbell said.

"I don't think he meant that," Winslow corrected, giving me a congenial squeeze around the shoulders. "Gun jammed. Isn't that right, Mark?"

Technically, that was correct even if it didn't tell the whole story. Still, it was a welcome way out. I nodded without raising my gaze from the ground.

Even though I couldn't see it, Lufbery's scrutinizing glance settled on me. I couldn't bear the thought that I'd failed him.

"You two go get cleaned up," he said to Campbell and Winslow. "Marcus, a word."

My two comrades exchanged a knowing glance, Campbell even daring to allow a mockingly sympathetic expression to tug at the corners of his mouth before heading toward the barracks to clean the grime and oil from their face and hair before dinner.

I watched them shrink into the bustling chaos of the aerodrome and wished I could follow. Luf's mustache pulled tight across his upper lip as it did whenever he had to give a talking down to someone, a duty I knew he dreaded.

Men like him ended up in positions of leadership; they never aspired to them. I think if he had his way, he'd still be flying with the old Escadrille. Just one of the boys in those early Nieuport aircraft, scuffling with the cabbage eaters in frigid winds.

He still flew out with his pilots, in most actions, but even so, I sensed a type of bridling restraint in the way he handled his plane, as though his wings had sandbags tied beneath them.

I'd have given one arm to see him open all cylinders and really go again.

"Mark, what really happened up there?" He inclined his forehead and leveled his eyes at me like an elder brother.

I shifted on my feet.

"It's like Winslow said," I muttered. "Gun jammed."

"That happen to you a lot?" Lufbery asked. His English had a French, foreign tilt to it that made more colloquial expressions like "a lot" stand out for their oddity.

"Jane and I will take it apart and check its components. Might have a faulty flange or something."

"Maybe you should polish your bullets," he said sardonically. He tossed a shining machine gun round to me. I caught it awkwardly, encumbered by my flying suit.

"You still polish all your rounds before going up?" I asked.

25

"I'm not the only one," he said, making me blush.

"I'm not as disciplined, but I've been trying to follow your lead. That's all," I replied.

"I know. I know that about you. You take the time to prepare, even on stuff that might not matter. That's why I'm confused that your guns jam more often than usual."

He took a drag on his cigarette but didn't take his eyes from me. He might as well have stuck its lit end right on my face for how it burned.

Lufbery's disappointment held a magnifying glass up to my failures. Two years here. No victory. Not in the air. Not on the ground. We both knew I'd had chances.

"I want to show you something," Luf declared, flicking what was left of his smoke to the ground and smothering it with his boot. He turned and walked back into the hangar. A handful of planes had already been wheeled in for repairs, repainting, or safety from the threatening rain. Some were ours; some were in transit and headed to other squadrons at different airbases.

"Pick one." He jutted his chin at the line when I'd caught up.

"What do you mean?" I asked.

"Am I speaking French or English? *Pick one.*"

My eyes swept across the aircraft until they rested on an old Nieuport 17 sitting in the corner. It was among the first single seat pursuit planes for our side with large V-struts at the end of the wings and a Lewis machine gun mounted above the cockpit. I pointed at it.

Our unit was blessed with enough 28s, but Luf kept this old 17 around "should something go wrong." I didn't care to think what would go wrong enough to make us fly an old 17 into battle against the new Pfalz or Albatross.

He crossed the hangar to the old bird, shooing away nearby mechanics before climbing into the cockpit. I followed close behind.

"You would choose an old one," he said. "But all the better."

"What are you doing?" I called as his head ducked out of view. I didn't get a verbal response, but my hands shot out by reflex to catch a flask. It clinked against the machine gun round still cradled in my palm.

I weighed it in my hands and spun off the top. The scent of bourbon assailed my nostrils.

"Whiskey?" I asked as Luf hopped back down to the ground.

"Yes. And not the lion cub either," Luff said.

I couldn't help but laugh. Whiskey was the name of one of two lion cub mascots for the old Lafayette Escadrille. Keeping a lion was exactly the wild, inane type of thing those boys were known for, and the French military wasn't about to tell them no—not while they were shooting down planes as American volunteers. The lions loved no one as much as they loved Luf. They followed him around the aerodrome as if they were nothing more extraordinary than family dogs. To me, the three of them were icons of an older era, before everything became official and stamped and starched. Bureaucracy killed some of the romance in the service, and it sent the two lion cubs to a zoo in Paris that past November.

"You think I was drinking up there?" I asked.

"No," he said pulling out another cigarette. "But maybe you should have been."

"Sir?"

He sighed and rolled an idea around his mouth before exhaling.

"Why did you become a pilot?" he asked.

"You asked me to be one. You said mechanics sometimes make the best pilots."

He furrowed his brows.

"Alright, then why did you come to the war in the first place? You weren't forced to. You were a volunteer."

I nodded.

"I wanted to give it to the ole Kaiser," I recited. That was the canned good-soldier response to this type of question. It had the seal of approval by nearly every soldier on our side.

But not Luf. He'd known me too well for too long by now. Over the course of long repair jobs, I'd shared with him how the patina of the headlines demeaning the Kaiser had worked on me. My Scottish parents had traveled all the way to California on a dream, but as is the case with many immigrants, the community didn't exactly welcome us with open arms. Some of my schoolmates, the same ones that teased me for the Scotch Pies my mom sent me to school with, volunteered to fight for the French Foreign Legion. The whole town came to life talking about their bravery and sense of honor. That was an idea that rooted deep inside me. This war was the chance to make something of myself and my family's name.

At the start of the war, a lot of boys had similar stories about why they volunteered. But we didn't simply share them at the drop of a hat. We all agreed that we were her to give it to the 'ole Kaiser, and that was plenty.

Of course, now the reasons American boys were out here didn't matter. They had to be.

"Given' it to the Kaiser, huh?" He shrugged. "Is that why you didn't have the stomach for the front line?"

I bristled.

"No one has the stomach for the front line," I said coldly.

"That's why you volunteered to drive ambulances, then? To fix them? An indirect way of sticking it to the Kaiser?"

Suddenly, I wanted to take a long swig from the flask.

"What are you trying to say, Luf?"

"Guns don't jam until you try to shoot them. That's all."

I chewed on my lip and stared at the old, weathered paint on the Nieuport 17.

"It's gotta be right," I finally said.

He let out a deep, pained sigh, as though I confirmed a suspicion he held. I hurried on to explain myself.

"The victory. It's gotta be right. The German never even saw me up there."

Luf scoffed. "You think that matters?"

"It's my first, Luf. I left the ambulances because I wanted this war to mean something. If my first victory is some cheap kill from a hiding spot, what's the difference between that and mowing down a line of infantry with a Spandau?"

"Sometimes, I wish you hadn't worked with the Lafayette," Lufbery said. "It ruined you. You heard the stories, the legends, saw how the people treated us. Saw the code among the early airmen."

"That's not a bad thing."

"It rewrites history. You think all the boys in the Escadrille only earned 'honorable' kills?" His eyebrows knit quizzically.

"I'm not *that* naive. But they weren't happy about them."

"No. They weren't, and that's healthy. But none of us were so stuck up as to pretend we wouldn't do the job unless it was exactly to our liking either."

My hands fell to my sides.

"Is that what you think of me?" I set my jaw hard.

"You risked your life and the lives of our other pilots because you wanted your first victory to be special. If it's going to take hard words from your superior to clear your head of that, I'll use them. Don't be stupid."

"Well, if that's what you think, then take me out of the sky."

I bored my frustration directly into his eyes, and to my surprise, he shied away.

"I will not."

I scowled. I wanted to yell at him and fight back, but I wasn't

29

about to make a scene, not after Winslow and Campbell were already gloating. "Why not?"

"Get over it, Marcus. Plenty of those boys going up will get at most one or two victories in their life. Even if you don't shoot planes down, you can still chase planes off, assist other pilots in sorties, deter attacks…"

"You mean you want me to be one of those free-loading pilots?" I spat.

"A free-loading pilot does more for his country than a dead one."

"Am I appropriately dressed down, Major?" I asked through gritted teeth.

"Don't be so sour. Go get washed up. Jane will want to see you."

"She'll see me when she sees me."

"You know, it's important to care for your friends as well as you do your aircraft. Besides, I don't want whatever witchcraft she used to keep your fabric from shedding to wear off. Go on."

I turned on my heel and headed out of the hangar. My blood churned and bubbled into my cheeks. It wasn't fair for him to treat me like a child. Luf knew what I was talking about. He knew that honor existed above and beyond the needs of the war. Odds were all of us would be dead by month's end, and if we died after compromising the morals that distinguished us from our enemies, what then?

But maybe his comments rattled me for another reason. Luf had a way of seeing through whatever guise I put up, and that made me nervous. I'd been testing him when I asked why he kept me in the sky.

Truth was I needed to be up there. I wished my curse was just a case of being gun-shy, but it went deeper, more paradoxical. I kept the truth in a secret pocket in my heart. I needed to fly because I needed redemption.

Polished Rounds

I tossed the flask of whiskey to a mechanic and stuffed the machine gun bullet in my pocket.

I'd show him. My first victory would be right. And, just to spite the major, I'd do it on his bullet.

Chapter 4
Drops of Glass
Jane

Can you recall the midnights, and the footsteps of night watchers,
Men who came from darkness and went back to dark again,
And the shadows on the rail-lines and the all inglorious labour,
And the promise of the daylight firing blue the window-pane?
-May Wedderburn Cannan-

I stood beside the mess near my Enfield motorbike, twisting my fingers in knots.

I made it a habit not to be present at his landings. The anxiety was too much. I'd heard of course that Marcus touched down, but rumor had it that his plane was the worse for wear. I hadn't yet looked at it. I would later, and I would use every bit of mechanical and arcane knowledge I possessed to fix it up and keep him safe for another flight.

How many more flights would it take? How many more evenings would I stand beside this mess hall waiting for him?

I glanced up and saw his square shoulders approaching in a clean uniform. A scratch ran along one side of his face. I closed my eyes and bit back concern. It was only a scratch. When I opened them again, Marcus had stopped. He'd seen me, and now he fought a smile as he always did. The smile was the signpost. It said he was back, that I was pathetic for being worried, that he found joy in my concern.

It was bothersome enough that it replaced my concern with eye-rolling frustration.

We'd met only months before at Villeneuve-les-Vertus during air combat training. Lufbery assigned me to Marcus's mechanical team, and it took no less than a few hours to feel right at home one with another.

Both of us were peculiar, outcasts of our own making. He reminded me of life before the war, somehow. Curious how some people make you remember things they have no business reminding you of.

Marcus was an odd little duck, different from the other pilots.

Most of the American pilots at our aerodrome were newly arrived, full of gusto and enthusiasm. They seemed interested only in their attempts to shoot down German planes or evening excursions in rooms adorned with billiard tables and cigarette smoke in one of the nearby open houses. The French were welcoming and overly generous to Americans. They showered them with meals and drinks and invitations to lights-off affairs I was quite certain they would not be writing home about.

But Marcus didn't attend those smoke-filled game rooms. He preferred to spend time working on his plane, going over flight reports, or even whiling away the afternoon by playing cards at the base with me and Lufbery, if the major had the time.

Marcus shook his head and resumed his walk toward the mess. I found myself running to greet him, closing the distance, wrapping my arms around him, saying a silent prayer of gratitude that he was alive—

"Easy, Jane. You know how they are about decorum around here," he chided, trying to push my arms away. I let him, but only so I could hit him in the arm. He laughed, so I hit him harder. "Easy there, Harry Greb."

"I heard the most terrible things," I scolded. "There was talk you'd nearly been shot down!"

"Oh, you heard about that?" he asked.

"What happened?"

He sighed and labored slowly toward dinner. I had hoped his reaction would be boyishly obnoxious, that he'd have some starry-eyed dangerous account he knew would set me on edge. His disappointment was somehow worse.

"Did you already eat?" he asked.

"Not so fast, Mr. Dewar. You tell me right now."

He rolled his eyes.

"My gun jammed. The Germans noticed I couldn't take a shot, and they swarmed me. Three Pfalz fighters."

My heart spiked. I tried not to imagine Marcus thousands of feet in the air surrounded by three German killing machines. Emotions swelled in my throat. I shoved them down and grabbed his arm tightly.

"Ow!" he cried.

"Were you wearing yours?" I asked urgently, pulling my own glass marble out from under my oil-stained jumpsuit.

"It was Campbell that saved me, not the necklace." He smirked.

I ignored his protest and put a hand to his chest, probing for a second before reaching through the buttons of his shirt to produce the marble, fastened to a chain. Inside, through a cloudy drop of glass, I could still make out a small strand of my dark brown hair.

"It still works!" I sighed, wide-eyed with relief. He tried to muss my hair with a clumsy hand.

"Don't try to downplay it!" I replied, dodging the attempt. "You must never take it off."

"Never?"

"Not until you're safe on some farm or something somewhere and the Germans have buried their guns in the dirt."

"So... never."

I hit him again.

"Don't be so daft." I peered more closely at the glass. "It has a crack."

He tucked the marble back into his shirt out of sight and glanced about. I knew he didn't like the others to see. I'd had the necklaces made by my mother's best friend, a wealthy eccentric with an unabashed passion for magical arts who I'd always known as Aunt Luella. She didn't want to make them, fearing it would raise my hopes falsely. She insisted that magic to protect living things was fickle and unreliable.

Still, in the end, she sent back two glass marbles, one with a strand of my hair, the other with a strand of his, and the instruction that so long as we managed to protect one marble, the other would remain intact.

It was immature magic, but I was so eager to have something, anything to get through the war.

I frowned, unsure of how the crack in his glass would affect its efficacy.

"Say," he said after noticing my concern, "do you think you could make a Nieuport-sized marble? The plane came back with more than just a crack."

I blinked away my fears and put on a strong face.

"Tell me you're lying."

"Shot up like a Thanksgiving turkey."

"I hate that phrase," I said, turning on my heel. "What did you do to my plane?"

I swung a leg over my Enfield.

"You're not going to make me fix it alone," I said.

"I'm famished," he replied, "and I hear the mail came in."

"You never read letters from home," I protested with a scoff.

"Who knows? Maybe I will this time," he replied. I scowled. Marcus's mother and father wrote him religiously, but I'd never known him to open and read one of their letters, at least not without pestering insistence from me. "I'll see if I can help after I'm finished eating," he added.

I revved the engine in a defiant response.

"Imagine, I get assigned one of the only pilots in the 94th capable of fixing his own aircraft and he won't help me."

"It'd be easier to help," he replied, "if you didn't insist on your weird witchcraft fixes."

"I don't see you complaining when they work." I leveled my eyes at him.

"And yet, my gun jammed," he said. "Maybe you should spend more time tending the Vickers and not just the wings and the engine."

I opened the throttle and took off, leaving Marcus to his cheeky attitude and empty stomach. But I could not stop thinking about his slumped shoulders when I had asked about the flight, couldn't help but cringe with the same anxiety he did. I circled back and chimed in again with sincerity that surprised even me.

"I'm so glad you made it back, Marcus."

Were his eyes glossing? I swallowed a lump in my throat and waited for his witty retort, but he only shrugged.

"Chin up, ace," I said riding off again.

"I'm not an ace!" he called after.

The sun already sat low in the sky, and I'd lit a few lanterns by the time Marcus joined me in the hangar. The lights cast shadows of wings onto the ceiling in dramatic stripes. The lanterns all sat nearby, as I'd need to put them out quickly should the alarm sound. German bombers now had become infamous for night raids, something that sounded like a fantasy only a couple years before. Lanterns like these lit up a hangar like a Christmas tree.

A mechanic's job was not overly dangerous. We didn't go dogfighting in the air, but bombs had claimed their fair share of non-pilot lives at airbases.

Marcus's plane was a right mess, and I was only grateful that most of the frame had escaped damage. But bullet holes had ripped through the linen on his wings. They would need to be stripped, re-lined, and re-doped. There was a hole or two in the fuselage as well, but they were far from the engine block or any other vital bit of machinery.

I was just tightening a bolt after my check of the aileron when he walked in.

"Not as bad as you made it out, if I'm honest," I said. "Most of their shots missed the frame. The longerons are all still intact. Bit of canvas, and she'll be fit to fly again in no time."

"And those ailerons? I lost a good bit of maneuverability up there."

I snorted. "I don't know why they have those cables so exposed. One errant shot and suddenly your flaps fail."

"I thought the fabric was going to shed. A couple of grouped rounds had it fraying."

I smirked.

"It might have if you had a different mechanic. Fortunately, I was wise enough to apply some of my—what does Lufbery call them? Enhanced methods?"

He watched as I hopped into the cockpit and tested the pedals, carefully monitoring the ailerons and rudder.

He shuffled his feet and shivered.

"You look like you've a bit on your mind," I said. "Was the soup that good?"

He laughed bitterly. "You know how it is. Nothing like a naval blockade and years of bleeding farmland dry when it comes to culinary achievement."

I grunted as I climbed from the cockpit.

"It wasn't that bad. I enjoyed mine well enough even while sharing company with Flora Smithfield."

"You sat next to Flora?" Marcus stopped shifting and stared.

"It wasn't pleasant," I replied. "But I think she means well."

He smiled for a moment, but it faded quickly.

"I got a letter from home," he said.

"And did you turn a new leaf and open this one?"

He rubbed the back of his neck.

"They're all the same. My mom goes on and on about exotic ideas like gardens or old friends I can't remember."

I wiped my hands on a cloth and waited for him to go on, but he swallowed his words and drew circles in the dirt with his foot.

"And your dad?"

"I'm sure he's got a new venture that will be a big success." He blew out a long breath. "Maybe he's right this time."

I never understood the way he spoke about his family. Parents, at times, can be overbearing. I'd always considered that part of their job. My father ran a restaurant. My mother helped him. Their successes were mine, and their failures were mine as well.

"Jane, what if my gun didn't jam up there?" Marcus asked abruptly

"Of course, it did."

"But what if it didn't? Why haven't I got my first victory yet? It's not for lack of opportunity."

"Does it matter?" I asked. My mind wandered to my conversation with Lufbery earlier that day. Eventually, Marcus might get his first kill. I was petrified by what it might do to him.

"How can you ask that? Of course it matters. I'm surrounded by brave men who are up there succeeding. Taking down planes."

"Is it success to shoot down Germans, or is it success to get home safely?" I asked quietly.

"Getting home safely won't win the war."

"You're right," I muttered. "Everyone knows only more rounds and munitions can do that."

He wrinkled his nose. We'd had this conversation before, and I'd always left it unsatisfied. Some terrible siren song I could not understand lured men to the war. I think they reveled in the chance to use the machinery entrusted to them, to test their bravery, or some other ridiculous notion. But even the women at home working in factories or helping the war effort elsewhere believed that just a little more force could get the job done. We all believed it once upon a time. There had to be an end, somewhere—every tunnel had a light if you walked in deeply enough.

"You sound like a pacifist," he replied.

"And yet, here I am fixing your war plane." I took a deep breath and set my wrench down. "You know I mean well. But violence has failed a thousand times. If we donated the same resources to diplomacy..."

He leaned against the Nieuport's belly.

"Hey, maybe it's just two sides of a coin. No one starts with machine guns," he suggested.

"Well, if machine guns can't end it, what good are they at all?"

"What would you do?" he asked suddenly. "If the war ended, I mean."

I sat down on a toolbox. This question lingered under all our thoughts, but we never reached for it. It was too hard to surface again from such beautiful ideas.

"*When*," I corrected, "the war ends, I imagine I'll go back home to my parents. They're getting on in years now, and someone will have to look after them. Perhaps I could convince them to move out to the country. Read my fair share of books and dance again."

"You dance?" He laughed.

"Don't sound so surprised."

"It's just... I've never seen you dance before."

I stared at him. "It's difficult to dance to the rhythm of war."

"I'd like to see it," he replied with a shrug.

"What? Me dancing?"

He nodded.

"I'm not a ballerina. I dance with partners. You know, the Grizzly Bear, things like that."

"The Grizzly Bear?" He laughed again. The sound encouraged me.

"Very well then. What will you do? Back to your parents as well?"

His jaw clenched as he considered it.

"You have any room at that country house of yours? I could chop wood for you."

"What about your home, the beautiful and exotic climate of California? Why fight in the war if not to go home after? Don't you miss your family?"

He shuffled his feet and clenched his jaw. Soldiers were fragile in the way Achilles was fragile. Touch the right spot and they come apart.

"Of course, I do. But what if they don't—" He cleared his throat and swallowed. I rarely saw him this way. "My parents died the day I left," he said quietly. He had shared this memory with me before, but only in fragments, the way people always try to explain difficult things. I had to translate it into a motion picture in my own mind, imagining how it occurred in reality.

Marcus stepping on a train, luggage in hand. His face would have been bright, filled with the enthusiasm of his enlistment. His mother and father, quietly hiding their Scottish features under hats, waving him on proudly.

Marcus looking back to wave a final goodbye. They wave

again. Then Marcus sticks his head out the window on the train, one last glance backward, an unexpected surprise for his parents. His mother sobbing into his father's arms. His father's eyes closed, mourning his son already.

The first time he'd told me, I'd understood that his leaving meant the figurative death of his parents. It took me some time to understand what Marcus truly meant—that on the day he left, his parents died to him.

I saw Marcus lost in these memories. The weight of them threatened to drag him down to a place from which recovery took significant effort and time.

I'd come to believe that he held on to the hope that if he could win a victory, a golden road back to the time before he blamed his parents for letting him leave might materialize. At the same time, he was smart enough to know that shooting down a plane would not repair that trust.

I pushed back the toolbox I'd been using a stool with a scraping sound. "All right, then. The Grizzly Bear." I wiped my hands again on a rag and approached him.

"What?"

"It's not any more difficult than flying, surely. Come, now. One hand here."

Awkwardly, step after clumsy step, I kept him from the dark. As I scolded him for improper form or stamping my foot, the gloom that hovered above him dissipated one laugh at a time.

If the war was good for anything, it was putting things on hold. But if putting things on hold meant living another day, I would happily take it.

But that night, back in the women's barracks as I prepared to attempt sleep amidst my imaginations of Marcus fighting Germans in the sky, Flora disturbed me.

"Jane," she said without an ounce of disdain or sarcasm.

"What is it?"

"It's a message for you."

"What, at this hour? Surely any repairs can wait until tomorrow."

"It just came in. Confidential."

I squinted at her.

"Then why do you appear to know what it might say?"

She frowned at me in a condescending way that made me want to poke her in the eye.

"Experience."

I took a steadying breath.

"Tell me, Flora."

She shifted on her feet and tried not suppress any type of smugness.

"You may be getting transferred."

Chapter 5
Red Eagle Fallen
Marcus

Through joy and blindness he shall know,
Not caring much to know, that still
Nor lead nor steel shall reach him, so
That it be not the Destined Will.
-Julian Grenfell-

"We have new orders." Major Huffer stood in front of all available pilots of the 94th inside a hangar. It had been two days since I'd almost been shot out of the sky. Thanks to Jane's dedication, my bird was already well on its way to being patched up.

"New orders that move us closer to the real action?" A cheerful pilot called from a seat in the back. That was Rickenbacker, a damn good pilot and already showing promise as a careful one.

"There's plenty of action here, Eddie," chimed in Campbell. "Just gotta know where to look."

As everyone laughed, Luf took a drag on his cigarette and smiled. His cool demeanor did nothing to instill confidence in

Major Huffer. Much to the commander's chagrin, we almost always deferred to Luf for the last word during briefings like these.

"Quiet down," Huffer called out. Pilots are a rowdy lot, heady and arrogant. Respect is earned in the sky. Huffer was working on that, but Luf had already earned it in spades. These jovial side conversations sent the former into fits, but only bemused America's reigning Ace of Aces.

"We are not being repositioned," Huffer went on. "Our assistance is requested for a movement by the Eighth Army. They're trying again to march toward Saint-Mihiel, flatten the bulge and reclaim the salient for France."

"What's their plan this time?" asked Winslow. He leaned against one of the hangar's support poles with his arms crossed.

"They will shell the Germans for a prolonged period, attempting to scatter anti-aircraft support, and then, they will slowly move infantry behind tanks through no-man's land."

"Tanks?" Echoed someone from the crowd. I took in a cold breath. Tanks were Britain's latest and greatest innovation, but so far, they had been a hit or miss strategy. With the proper support, the tanks were death machines and incredibly effective against infantry. But they were also slow, especially across the shell-torn earth in the dead zone. They'd be sitting ducks for experienced German artillery. And if they broke down, as they did often, the infantry escort trudging behind them would be open game for machine gun nests. The thought of being stranded in a shell hole out there beside the burning wreckage of an armored tank made me shiver.

Huffer continued.

"We will escort a bomber squadron that will run ahead of the tanks to distract, and with any luck, upend artillery. We are free to engage enemy pursuit planes and give the German infantry strafing runs to discourage machine gun fire."

Rickenbacker whistled.

"There's the ticket," he said.

"Sounds like we can expect heavy resistance," sounded a voice in the back. That was Captain Peterson, a smart flyer who earned his first victory in the Lafayette. He played the numbers and was unafraid to run from bad odds.

Most of us were simultaneously terrified and thrilled at the idea of heavy resistance. We turned, instinctively, to the man in the room with the most experience against such heavy resistance.

Luf shrugged.

"It's war. It doesn't matter if the resistance is light or heavy—you fly smart, and when it's your time, it's your time."

When it's your time, it's your time. We'd all echoed the phrase between one another so much that its chilling meaning had been transformed into a warped battle cry.

"I've told the French that we can commit all available planes to this," Huffer continued. "So I want everyone sharp and triple checking engines, guns, flight suits, everything. We'll run a few patrols to practice our group maneuvers before this weekend."

"Looks like we will have to cancel any weekend trips into town," said Campbell.

Luf smiled slyly.

"What's a weekend?" he replied.

"It happened!" A shout came from outside the hangar accompanied by the white noise of great movement. The two majors didn't wait to dismiss us before leaving the hangar to assess the commotion. We followed.

Outside in the grass, a boisterous group of pilots, mechanics, cooks, switch girls, cleaners, and other aerodrome operations crew gathered around Flora. There were British, Americans, and French, a mixed lot of Allied personnel, the type of variety we could only expect might increase now that Ferdinand Foch was taking on the role of Supreme Commander of all Allied military effort. All, of course, with an asterisk beside American efforts.

I spotted Jane, her coveralls stained with grease. I sidled my way through the crowd toward her quickly. Meanwhile, I caught bits of conversation.

"Shot down."

"By who?"

"When?"

"I just heard. They don't know for sure."

"Don't know if it's him?"

"No, they don't know who got him."

"I didn't think it was possible."

I hadn't seen our people this excited since Winslow and Campbell had shot down those first German planes. Whatever news Flora had was big, real big. I couldn't resist a balloon of hope and fear expanding in my chest. Was this how the war ended? I wasn't ready. It was insane not to be exuberant about such a thing, but I wasn't ready.

"Was it the Kaiser?" I asked, dumbly.

"The Kaiser? What? Don't be daft," Jane said while she avoiding my eye contact. She hadn't been herself the past few days.

When Luf reached the center of the group, he held up a hand and we all quieted.

"What is it? Start from the beginning." He searched Flora's flushed face. She was all brown curls and rosy cheeks, comely even in uniform, but made more beautiful by her excitement.

"Yes, major. It just came in. The Red Baron. He's been shot down."

A deafening cheer went up around me. But no cheer went up within me.

The Baron? Scourge of the Skies. They said he had more than eighty confirmed kills to his name. He was the heart and spirit of the German Air Service. His bright red triplane could rally ground troops with a simple flyover, make good pilots fly funny, and cause great pilots to scramble. There wasn't an Allied airman alive who hadn't woken from at least one nightmare about Richthofen on his tail.

Men around me were shaking hands and whooping and hollering, but I caught Luf's expression. He stared pensively at the ground, turned, and walked back toward the hangar.

I stepped to follow him when Jane nudged me in the ribs.

"You feel it, too, don't you?" she asked.

"What's that?" I pulled her by the arm out of the crowd so I could hear better.

"The sick twisting in your stomach that people should celebrate another man's death like this."

I squinted at her. "That man was a devil. He killed so many of us."

She nodded at them.

"You think they're cheering for the thought of safety, then? Justice? Vengeance?"

"It seems awfully just that a man like that meets his end," I replied.

"What about Lufbery? He has his fair share of killed pilots as well, doesn't he?" she asked. "Would it be just for him to be shot down?"

"That's different, Jane, and you know it."

"How?"

"The Baron's a German. A Hun. They're on the unholy crusade, not us. We're just trying to kick a bully back where he belongs."

She folded her arms. I threw up my hands and paced away from her.

"What, then? It's not worth cheering that one of our greatest enemies is gone?" I asked.

She smiled bitterly. She was smarter than I was, always had been, and would often take this posture when she knew something

I didn't. It wasn't mocking or condescending—it was worse than that. She looked...sad somehow.

"I only noticed that you weren't celebrating as the others are. Nor, should I mention, are your best friends."

I stared at the group of people near me, all smiles and jovial conversations, renewed with a motivation and energy that the tide of the war might be turning. Then I gazed after Luf, who retreated quietly. I didn't expect him to get loud or holler with excitement. That wasn't his way. But his shoulders had slumped.

"You're different than them," Jane said with unusual energy. "Promise me you will never forget that."

I squinted at her.

"You're acting strange, Jane."

She hugged me, took the opportunity to kiss me on the cheek, and left without another word.

I followed my feet to the hangar. It didn't take long for me to find Lufbery sniffing around my Nieuport. He stood in the cockpit examining the repair job Jane had made of the plane.

"Trying to find the mysterious cause of my recurring gun jams?" I called to him.

He polished the feedblock on my Vickers and took his time responding.

"These machines are so different now," he said. "Seems like just yesterday we were standing in our 17s, back before some engineer figured out how to shoot through the propellor."

"A lot has changed since then," I suggested.

"A lot will still change." He leaned back in the cockpit. "Why does your plane smell like herbs?"

I blushed.

"I think Jane scented the padding between some of the joints of my wings."

"Another enhanced repair job," Luf said. He smiled sadly and descended from the cockpit before crossing the hangar toward a few supply crates.

"I noticed your reaction about Richthofen going down," I called.

"My reaction?"

"Maybe lack of reaction is a better way to describe it."

He stopped and lit a cigarette.

"I don't see you celebrating out there either," he responded.

I listened to the sounds of the crowd, still loud and irreverent from outside.

"Why aren't I happier about it, Luf?"

He shrugged in a way that reminded me he was half French. Americans can't shrug like the French can. We overdo it.

"I remember when we first heard about the Baron," he said. "He was in Boelcke's group. His star pupil. I'm not sure if you can appreciate how significant his contribution to the war was."

I rubbed my neck.

"Sure, I can. Eighty planes. Can you imagine?"

"It's about more than that." He sighed. "My mentor was a famous aviator, you know. He dreamed of new horizons for airplanes. He worked tirelessly to show the world the magic in flying. I often wonder what he would think about the innovations war has required."

"I'm not connecting the dots," I admitted.

Luf leaned against a workbench.

"Some of us that fly these machines are killers first and aviators second. Some of us end up in the Air Service because we can't stand serving in some other way. But some of us were born for the sky, were born to change the whole paradigm. Baron von Richthofen changed the game, helped us understand something that is so necessary for anyone who wants to challenge the blue."

"What's that?"

"No matter how good you are, we all go down. When it's your time, it's your time."

Luf had a vacant look on his face. I struggled to find any words to comfort him.

"How many friends have we watched fall from the sky, Marcus?" He shook his head sadly. "We weren't really at war, not the way those boys in the trenches are. Even on different sides, us pilots are engineers tackling the same problem, trying to build better aircraft, develop greater techniques.

"Why should I celebrate the Baron's death? With him goes his mind, his experience, unmatched by any pilot since those first planes took flight."

I wrestled with a knot in my stomach.

"We have to shoot them down, though," I said. "That's war. And with him gone, more of our boys will be safe, right?" These were the rehearsed words I repeated to myself every time I went into the air. This is war. Killing is necessary. If I don't get the bad guys, they'll get me or more my friends. I repeated them to motivate myself to pull the trigger. I just had to start believing it first.

"Hell, Luf, you have more kills than they count for you. And they've counted a lot. I mean you've shot six planes down in a single day!"

"Yes, we have to shoot them down. I've shot them down. But part of me always hoped Richthofen would have been the one to get me. That he, if any of us, would have defied the odds and outlived the war, even with all the notoriety and fame and hundreds of thousands trying to shoot his particular plane out of the sky."

Luf's eyes shone through a layer of gloss. This wasn't like him. It mixed me all up. For so long, he had been my steady hand, even-keeled, stoic, and meticulous.

Once, when Kiffin Rockwell of the Lafayette Escadrille had been shot down, Luf lost it. Really lost it. He defied his captain's orders, got in his plane, and circled a German aerodrome daring any pursuit pilot to come up and challenge him, all but begging for a chance to settle Rockwell's score. No German birds gave him the satisfaction.

But that was Kiffin Rockwell. He was the spirit of the Lafayette Escadrille. Watching such a strong emotional response from Luf now, so much later, with so much war-hardened experience under his wings, and at the news of our greatest opponent's downfall—well, it shocked me.

But similar sentiments resided in my gut. Jealousy that I wasn't the one to take the Baron down. Unfairness that if I were to die, it wouldn't be the Baron to do it. Disappointment that he couldn't run the gauntlet. Sadness that such a talent was gone. And yes, too, there were positive emotions of vindication and safety, even hope that this would spark some new change and the tides of the war were turning.

But above all else, there was a cold dread that even the Baron went down. And if he went down, what chance did any of us have?

I slumped into a chair by the workbench.

"I'm assigning you the alert tomorrow morning with Peterson. And this time, Marcus, if you get the chance, don't jam. Shoot down a plane."

"No Hun flying through that has me too afraid," Peterson said right before taking a sip from his coffee mug. He gestured toward the sky. It was filled with a thick, impenetrable morning fog.

I shifted on my stool under the tent and pulled my flying suit closer around me. It was cold for a French spring morning. I'd indulged by layering my fuzzy coat over my horse leather jacket.

"And if they're bombers?" I asked.

"Come on, Markie. Why send bombers out in that? How could they target anything?"

"Maybe they thought it would burn off."

I poured myself more liquid warmth and put my hands around the mug. The heat radiated through the cup and up through my forearms.

I searched for little moments to appreciate warmth here on the ground where a hundred mile an hour windchill didn't nip at me. Up there, the tips of my fingers pinched and pained and my feet turned into blocks of ice strapped to my ankles.

Usually, alert duty wasn't a bad deal. You sat out in a tent right by the airstrip and kept an eye on the sky or waited for the phone to ring. Most mornings, we weren't raided. And if German birds did head our way, they had to cross a bit of our territory to get here, so usually we got advanced notice from Lironville or some other observation post with a phone line and enough common sense to give us the heads up.

But I was in a rotten mood this morning. News about the Baron had disturbed my sleep, and I hadn't seen Jane since the day before. It wasn't that unusual. At times, she and the other mechanics had to work longer hours on a rushed fix-up job and our schedules didn't connect. But no one I asked had seen her either, and a part of me started to worry.

"It was almost this bad when Campbell and Winslow got their firsts," Peterson said, sighing. "You know I was up there, too, that morning. But I turned back. Thought they were mad for flying in that weather. And they were! Had to fly so damn low that a poor French farm boy got shot through the ear during the dogfight. Can you believe that?"

"I saw him," I replied. It was the hundredth time I'd heard the story. "Little guy seemed real proud of it, too. I wouldn't be as happy if someone shot a hole through my ear."

"Who knows, maybe I'm lucky. Maybe you'll nab your first this morning, too!"

I took a sip of the coffee and scowled.

"Don't see how it's any of your business."

"Oh, don't get sour." Peterson replied. He picked up a pair of binoculars and scanned the fog. "It just defies understanding is all. I mean, when did you leave California, again?"

"Two years ago," I muttered. "To the month, actually. Spring 1916."

"Exactly."

"But it's not like I was in the infantry or on the front lines that whole time," I said, comfortably reverting to my usual defenses.

"Sure. I remember. You drove ambulances, you've told me. But never a chance to shoot a German while picking up the wounded?"

I set my jaw and took a sip.

"Look, I get it. A lot of ambulance drivers don't like talking about it. Doubt you got much opportunity when you worked for us at the Lafayette as a mechanic, though." He clicked his tongue. "For how much you talk about the Lafayette, you'd have thought you were one of the founding members."

I shook my head. A small breeze brought the smell of cold dirt through the tent. I was proud of my time with the Lafayette. It was hard work. After working on bikes as a kid, then Fords, planes were a challenging adjustment.

"I flew with you, too, for a month or so," I said vacantly. I didn't usually remind others of this fact, largely because it cut against the argument that it wasn't so unusual for me to have no kills to my record.

I had a strange set of mixed feelings for Peterson. He began his aviation career early at the Lafayette and entertained a paradoxical and maddening outlook on my life. On the one hand, he often forgot that I was more than just a mechanic for that squadron, but at the same time he touted his single victory as proof that he was, by far, my superior. I should have revered Peterson with a similar reverence as I did with Luf. But secretly, part of me considered him one of the free-loading pilots I complained to Luf about.

Peterson lowered the scopes and let them hang around his neck.

"Do you remember those early Lafayette days" he asked. "You know, it made me mad with jealously reading about their victories in the papers."

"You know how those newspaper folks inflate everything. But those guys were special. I mean—ah, forget it. You'll think it's stupid."

I buried myself deeper in my coat and kicked at a clump of grass trying to grow.

"Might be stupid, but I'm dying of boredom." He nudged me.

I took a deep breath.

"I just mean—David, the honor. The respect. You know what I'm talking about. You flew with them. They lived and breathed for shooting down Germans, but they still carried a reverence about those Bosch pilots. If I can achieve anything in this war, I want my name to be remembered the way those Lafayette heroes' names will be remembered."

Peterson sat in silence for a while, studying a thin flock of birds before stuffing his hands in his pockets.

"Big talk for a guy who hasn't gotten his first yet."

I glared at him, but he just sniffed and kicked around a pebble in the dirt.

The sound of a motorcycle distracted me from Peterson's over-abundant sensitivity. Rickenbacker was headed over, half-dressed to go up in the air. He came to an abrupt stop and swung his leg over the seat.

"I'm here to relieve you, Markie," he said, tossing me the keys.

"Relieve me? Why?"

"You've got a date back at the officers' hall."

My neck flushed with sudden heat, but I was relieved that Jane had finally surfaced from her work.

"I've told you boys already, Jane is not—"

Rickenbacker cut me off with a healthy laugh.

"Not with the witch mechanic. More important than that. Billy Mitchell sent someone for you."

I froze.

"Billy Mitchell? As in Colonel Mitchell of the Army Air Service?"

"You know any other Billy Mitchells that could relieve you of alert duty around here?" He didn't wait for me to move before pushing me off of my stool and sniffing my mug of coffee. He grimaced.

"What does he want?" I sputtered.

"You know, you won't believe this, but the Colonel didn't write me ahead of time to read me in on his strategy."

He smiled good-naturedly. I liked Eddie. He took piloting seriously and had a way of making you enjoy his ridicule.

"I wouldn't keep ole Billy waiting," Peterson said, incapable of hiding a twinge of jealousy in his voice. I hardly heard him. I had already revved the motor, hit the throttle, and kicked up a bit of dust.

When I got to the officer's quarters, I paused in front of a curtained window to make myself presentable. I was hardly dressed to meet a superior officer. I still wore my flight coat, and the motorcycle had whipped my hair around and spat mud on my face. I spit in my hands and did what I could.

My pulse fired on all cylinders. What could the colonel want with me? Was this a chance to earn the honor I came to Europe for in the first place? A high-profile assignment that would surely make the papers? Or was the Commander upset about my flight report from the other day and had come at long last to override Luf and ground the cursed pilot?

I stepped through the door. Inside, a man in dark khaki stood peering out the window at the readied planes outside. His collar rode his neck high, and a bar of medals sat above his left breast pocket. He looked pristine, out of a catalogue, but not the face I'd seen for the Army Air Service commander before. I tried not to think about my own shabby appearance.

"Colonel Mitchell?" I asked, standing at attention.

"Hell no, Dewar. Sergeant First Class Smith to you. Colonel Mitchell sent me to pick you up—instructions to leave immediately. A car is waiting outside."

I peeked out the window at an open-cabbed Cadillac I had failed to notice amidst my nerves. Half of me came alive with excitement, but a small part of me resisted. *Immediately* meant I'd have no chance to let Jane or Luf know I was leaving.

"Immediately, sir?"

"And I'm afraid you'll have to wear this." He tossed a burlap sack to me. It scratched against my hands.

"Wear how?"

"Over your head. Our destination is classified." His tone teetered between disinterest and delight.

"What about my things? Will we be coming back?"

He shrugged.

"Maybe. But if you don't, we'll make arrangements."

"What about Major Lufbery?"

"He's been made aware. Come on, now. It's a bit of a drive."

I stared at the burlap sack. Soldiers on the front filled these with dirt and used them to line their trenches.

"You're serious?" I asked.

"Major Lufbery didn't mention that you had a hard time following orders."

"Sir." I nodded, turned on my heel, and exited the building.

Once in my seat in the Cadillac, I put the sack over my head and tried to get comfortable. Despite the porous material, the burlap didn't breathe well. The seat beneath me shifted as the car took on the Sergeant's weight.

"Cozy?" he asked.

"I don't suppose you can tell me what this is all about?" I asked.

Smith only laughed and turned on the ignition.

Chapter 6
A Meeting of Strangers
Jane

Only thin smoke without flame
From the heaps of couch-grass;
Yet this will go onward the same
Though Dynasties pass.
-Thomas Hardy-

"Private Turner, are you terribly uncomfortable?"

I'd heard Lieutenant Atkins's voice through the linen sack on my head nearly a hundred times.

"Lieutenant, I'm all for Queen and Country and all that—however, I doubt the continued secrecy is necessary. I don't know the country all that well, and I'm unlikely to recognize the area we drive through now. Would you be so opposed to me removing this ridiculous covering."

Even over the engine of the car, I heard his mustache bristle.

"I shouldn't," he replied.

"Would you prefer if I arrived unconscious?"

"Oh, very well. I suppose we've gone far enough," Atkins replied. Gratefully, I pulled the sack from over my head. Around me stretched wide green meadows and gentle hills. It looked to be late afternoon, and we'd been driving the better part of the day.

"Oh, wait, I recognize this place!" I said.

"You what?" Atkins turned bright red in an instant.

"I'm teasing, Lieutenant. Come now. How else am I meant to deal with these nerves?"

Atkins took his hand from it casual position resting on the door and placed it firmly on the wheel.

"You mustn't kid around, Jane. This is serious business."

"Perhaps I'd be more understanding if you were willing to tell me anything about it," I observed. "Put yourself in my position. A strange lieutenant comes about, plucks me from my mechanic post with the 94th American Aero Squadron, puts a sack on my head, and tells me I'm uniquely suited for a confidential assignment."

"Yes," Atkins said flatly. "It all does seem odd, doesn't it?"

"Mechanics don't often receive secret assignments, do they?"

"No. In fact, they don't."

My heart skipped as I continued my audible train of logic.

"Now, the only thing I have out of common with most mechanics is what my commanding officer refers to as enhanced mechanical methods. This leads me to speculate—" I took a breath, "that the war effort might have need of my affinity for those methods."

This conclusion silenced Atkins for some time, leaving me all the peace and quiet necessary to admire the thrum of the car's engine and the crunch of its wheels on the road beneath us.

"It's quite dire, I'm afraid," he said at last.

"What is?"

"Everything will be explained," he said. "But I should warn you that this assignment kicked up quite a stir in command. You will be held to the utmost secrecy, and you will need a false name."

"A false name?"

"In the event of capture," Atkins went on, "to keep you and your loved ones safe, as it were."

Some ugly churning swell moved in my gut.

"Am I in some danger, Lieutenant?" I asked, trying my best to keep the quiver from my voice.

"The fortitude and courage of our British women in times of peril have constantly impressed us. You are the only person openly practicing, shall we say, 'unusual' methods and happenings and come what and so forth."

"You mean no other woman is carrying out her duty in an unusual way?" I asked.

He scoffed.

"It's not that. It's just— I mean— We need your, special skills, or else..."

He let out a frustrated breath as he searched for words. My eyes widened as I tried to finish his sentence.

"Or else we might lose the war?"

He looked at me sadly.

"Or else the end of the war may not matter. Go on. Put the sack back on. We're getting close."

I obeyed, but the security was only required of me for the next half hour as we wound through what felt like mountainous terrain. When bidden, I removed the sack again and was rewarded with the view of a picturesque French valley at sunset. Large hills surrounded us on most sides. Ahead of us at the end of a long straight country road sat a beautiful standalone farmhouse, cast in stone and shingled with wood. It was undamaged and appeared unbothered by the passing of time.

Near the house, a dense wood gave the valley its border.

As a whole, the scene was peaceful, lovely, and altogether foreign after the world had been so long at war. This was a place for painters, poets perhaps. Not soldiers.

But as we approached, someone might have run me over with a tank for my surprise.

Two men stood beside a Cadillac. One decorated American army sergeant, and one Marcus Dewar wearing a dashing uniform that didn't belong to him.

What was he doing here?

We pulled to a stop, and I disembarked, smoothing the uniform Atkins had provided me the night before, fully adorned with a tie, cross belt, and oversized trousers. I replaced the hat on my head in an attempt to hide my surprise, but it sank down over my brow comically as though I were a child.

"What are you doing here?" Marcus asked before anyone else could speak. His voice teetered back and forth between relief and worry. There went any pretense we didn't know one another.

"I might ask you the same thing," I replied.

"Lieutenant Atkins, is it?" The man beside him asked. His features were full and doughy, as though he'd yet to experience the hunger of war. The hand he extended to Atkins was plump.

"And Sergeant Smith, no doubt?" Atkins replied stiffly. The way he stood made me to notice just how tall the lieutenant was compared to the rest of us.

"That name will do fine." Smith smiled.

Atkins sniffed and continued.

"Allow me to introduce—"

"Jane Turner. We know each other," Marcus finished for him. Atkins coughed.

"No, Sergeant. I'm afraid you are mistaken. This is Private Melinda Doe."

I scrunched my nose and turned to my friend. The name sounded awful. It didn't fit me at all.

"For confidentiality, Marcus," I said, grudgingly. Marcus blushed.

"What the hell is going on?" he replied, trying to cover his embarrassment.

"You two got history?" asked Smith.

"Yeah. I'm sure you're aware that she's my mechanic," Marcus went on, evidently not eager to participate in the illusion of code names.

"Technically, I'm one of Major Raoul Lufbery's mechanics," I said, trying to defuse him. "I just so happen to like your plane best."

"My plane, huh?"

"Ah, is that right? Your mechanic? Hm." Smith folded his arms and leaned against the hood of his car. "Major Lufbery recommended Marcus for this specific assignment. I'm assuming..."

"Yes, the major recommended Private Doe as well."

"And what assignment is that?" Marcus demanded. "Come on, Smith. You've dragged me all over France in a burlap sack."

"Burlap? They gave me linen," I added.

"Burlap seems barbaric," Atkins said.

"It's rugged. American." Smith replied.

"It's not about the sack!" Marcus cried.

The distant hum of a motor caught our attention. Far off, I saw a cloud of dust obscure the long streaks of sunset light. I squinted down the road and saw a car without military markings making its way toward us.

"We'd better get inside," Smith said. The amused lilt left his voice. "Our other dinner guests are here."

Marcus and I shared a worried glance. His hand drifted to the handle of his pistol as we shuffled up the gravel walk and inside the house.

Right as we entered, a tantalizing smell welcomed us into a crowded room adorned by the warmth of a lit hearth. A large round table had been set for eight in the living room. I noticed sofas pushed to the walls to make room for it, a curio cabinet oddly facing the kitchen doorway, and other haphazard placements of cushions and credenzas. This home had been converted, quickly, into some type of formal meeting room.

I followed Marcus around the table, to a seat facing the door. He hated to have his back to openings or exits.

Smith and Atkins took no time settling in beside us before checking their pistols and holding them at the ready, aimed toward the entrance. I had little to no experience with a pistol, but I followed the example of the men.

"You wanted answers, Dewar?" Smith asked. "Here's one. A few Germans are about to walk through that door."

"What?" he cried. I grabbed his hand instinctively, fear sweeping into my bosom. Had we been summoned as part of an execution? An assassination? "What Germans?"

"Well, two are almost nobodies, not unlike the two of you. One, supposedly, is an envoy from the German Reichstag."

The gun in my hand weighed too much. I set it down on the table and shook my head.

"Careful, Jane," Marcus muttered. "Why even carry a gun if you're not going to use it?"

I stared back at him, weighing whether I should point out the irony in his comment, but the nightmarish heat built steadily in my throat.

How could Lufbery have recommended him for a mission like this? Had we not spoken about the importance of protecting his innocence only days before?

The heat from the fireplace, at first pleasant, now suffocated me. When we heard the slam of a car door outside, Atkins and Smith crouched by their chairs. We followed suit, and soon the makeshift banquet table had become an impromptu fort.

"Do not shoot unless ordered," Smith said.

"Or shot upon," Atkins added, "in the case Smith and I are killed before one of us can issue the order."

I shuddered. My arm shook, hand trembling under the weight of the pistol. This was wrong. I was a mechanic.

"Jane, please," Marcus whispered. "I won't let anything happen to you."

My scowl was icy.

"I'm not afraid of dying," I said.

"Then why are you shaking?"

I knit my eyebrows, but before I had time to explain, the front door creaked open. Adrenaline raced through my veins. My finger fumbled to rest on the trigger of my pistol. No one breathed. We waited for a sign of movement.

"Wait for my order," Smith growled.

Suddenly, my mind filled with terrible images, of Marcus killing a man right in front of me, of him shot and dying, of me futilely trying to help him.

The tip of a stick edged into the cracked doorway. Attached to it was a small square of white cloth. A miniature flag. White. Surrender?

"Sergeant Smith? Lieutenant Atkins?" A voice burdened with a heavy German accent called into the room from outside.

"Mustermann? Is that you?" Smith called.

"Ja. I'm here with Earnst and Lina. We are going to enter the house now. Ja?"

Atkins and Smith eyed one another quietly.

"Last chance to back out," Smith muttered.

"Why come all this way for nothing?" Atkins replied.

"We are unarmed," Mustermann called out. "If you are to shoot us, so be it. It is a risk we are willing to take for the sake of us all."

I leaned back, the strength in my legs draining. The calm in the German's voice soothed some of my fears, but his words conjured up Atkins's comments from the car.

The end of the war might not matter.

A Meeting of Strangers

Mustermann entered the door frame, his hands held in the air. He had a round face adorned with a large mustache and bushy sideburns. He wore no coat, despite the spring chill outside. Perhaps he intended to demonstrate that he did not hide any weapons on his person. I estimated him to be about fifty years old, but his age was not carved by the realities of war. Nor had his wrinkles developed under the elements. He wore reading lines, lines that I knew from my own mother's face.

"I've come for our dinner appointment," he said. He took the seat nearest the door, the seat most vulnerable to surprises and attack but also with the quickest escape. His eyes studied the barrels of the four guns pointing his way, protruding over the edge of the table like periscopes. "May I sit here?"

Smith lowered his weapon first.

"The other two?" he asked Mustermann.

"They are a little shy and a little afraid. Earnst, Lina. Come and sit with me. You can see how they did not shoot after all."

A man and woman, in their twenties as I was, filed in behind him. They tucked their heads protectively into their chest before quickly taking their seats. Even a blind man would have noticed the fear in their expressions.

When I looked at the three Germans sitting across the table, shaking despite their courage, something came over me. I lowered my gun and marveled.

They feared as I feared.

They were no different than I was.

A swelling discomfort grew in my chest like panic. I could not wrestle with a concept so large. I had never supported the violence of war, on principle. But despite that conviction, casualty reports and headlines of victory had so dehumanized our enemy that such news passed by my notice without objection. To see them in front of me now, so human, cast all that in a great upheaval.

So I stood from my crouching position and sat down across the table from them as though I were a simple dinner guest.

"Don't be rude," I chided my companions. They followed my lead, and I was awarded with a kindly appreciative smile from the older German.

When the guns were put away, the mood changed instantly. Lina's shoulders heaved with deep breaths of air. Earnst's hands relaxed, but the pinch marks on his palms took time to fade.

The young pair was attractive—handsome as couples went. Her face was draped in blonde curls, and his strong jawline supported a clear, well-shaved face. They looked like relatives from Reading.

"...Forgive the thorny welcome," Atkins said. "We have reason to fear."

"As do we," Mustermann said.

"You sure do," Smith added. "Especially the way Pershing is coming in. You have a very great reason to fear."

"We did not come here to posture with you," the older man replied. "Are we waiting for anyone else?"

"Dupont," Smith called.

The door of the curio cabinet by the kitchen swung open, and we all jumped. Atkins and Marcus had their weapons drawn in an instant.

"None of you bothered to check the house. What if I were a killer? One of Ludendorff's men?" A gruff, French voice came from inside the cabinet. A tanned, dark-haired man dressed in humble civilian pants and jacket emerged from his hiding spot. He had waited quietly inside this whole time. He tossed his pistol on the table and sat down casually.

"What? I didn't want to be on the front line if shooting broke out," he said in response to our incredulous stares.

The others relaxed and put their weapons away.

"Thank you for your hospitality," Mustermann said with a nod of his head, a bow of sorts. Dupont waved him off.

"It's not my house."

"It is your country."

"Maybe you should tell the Kaiser that," Dupont spat back. He carried a weariness I had seen in so many French soldiers. Physical, spiritual, emotional exhaustion. It had been so long since any of us had a good reason to hope for much. Even the anger was halfway dead in the troops now.

"We have tried," Mustermann said quietly. "That is, in part, why we are here."

"Dupont, please, we're all hungry," Smith said. "These British folk are just too polite to say it out loud. Can you tell the cook?"

Dupont didn't take his gaze from Mustermann while he slipped into the kitchen. A few moments later, and after a muffled bit of contentious French, he materialized with a thin, severe woman in an apron. The two of them brought platters with them, filled with all the foods I'd been smelling since we arrived, fare much more lavish than what was available in the aerodrome mess. We dove in with bridled enthusiasm, each of us harkening to an obscure sense of respect for our enemy at the table. Despite the bounty of roasted game and potatoes, we ate mostly in silence with only quiet conversations between seat mates.

"What did Luf get us into here?" Marcus asked me between bites of bread.

"Well, I know why *I'm* here. Atkins said it has something to do with magic."

"Oh, stop, Jane."

"I'm serious."

Marcus slowed his chewing and retreated into himself to think.

"Have you ever heard of anything like this?" I continued. "A meeting between low-ranking allied officers and an ambassador from the Reichstag? The secrecy? No one is using their real names."

"Except us."

"Well, whose fault is that?" I jabbed.

"This goes up, though, Jane," he said, ignoring how I scolded him. "Smith is here at the behest of Colonel Mitchell, and he's the commander for the US Army Air Service."

"They must have heard about your piloting skills."

He shot me a bothered scowl and sipped a bit of wine.

"You're a special pilot, Marcus," I protested. "Lufbery told me himself."

"Yeah, tell that to my growing list of kills."

"Must I remind you that you are on no German's list of kills either, which is more than scores of dead Allied pilots can say?"

We turned back at the Germans. Earnst and Lina approached the food cautiously, as if they suspected poison or tampering. At the very least, they seemed to have a healthy disdain for French cuisine.

A humanizing shadow fell over my understanding as I considered that the German lines probably didn't eat much better than we did. Imagine that. Hundreds of thousands of soldiers on both sides of the war eating spoiled tins for years.

"Luf would have had a reason to recommend us," Marcus murmured. "He doesn't do things without a reason. And magic might explain your involvement, but not mine."

I pursed my lips and swallowed my thought. Already, I'd speculated at several possibilities, but my mind returned to one over and over again.

If all sides of the Western Front were afraid, and they'd brought in a lowly mechanic to help, there must be some arcane threat.

The very idea made me tremble in fear.

As if Mustermann read my thoughts, he stood and gently put his napkin on the table.

"I appreciate the hospitality," he said with a gesture toward the half-eaten dishes. "We travel roughly and are now quite more comfortable. But we must also press that we are in danger the longer we stay here. Our travels have been tracked by the German Secret Police. We have been warned that no expense will be spared to discover our identities or disrupt our mission. May we get on with the business?"

Atkins nodded.

"So long as you don't mind me working on this chicken bone while you talk," Smith said. He leaned back in his chair and nibbled.

The German did not react to Smith's intimidation. He only nodded and began.

Chapter 7
Boelcke's Goggles
Marcus

"Strange friend," I said, "here is no cause to mourn."
"None," said that other, "save the undone years,
The hopelessness. Whatever hope is yours,
Was my life also."
-Wilfred Owen-

"I'm not sure how many details have already been divulged to all present, so be patient with me while I lay out my understanding. Lieutenants Atkins and Dupont, Sergeant Smith, if I omit information that you have, please add it, so we may all understand one another."

The sun had gone down out the windows, and the room drew its light from the hearth and several lit candles scattered around the room. Mustermann took a small sip from his wine glass and cleared his throat.

"Only days ago, Manfred von Richthofen was shot down. I'm sure I don't need to describe the extent of his contribution to our military efforts."

"Contribution?" Atkins scoffed. "You mean how many of our boys he killed?"

"Mighty fine word for it," Smith joined.

Mustermann halted, a pang of fear in his eyes. I sensed how delicate he must believe this arrangement to be, how much he risked to be here.

"Excuse my terminology," Mustermann amended. "I did not mean to cause offense. I only meant to say he was a prolific and lethal aviator of great importance to German High Command."

"He was the best," I said plainly. Atkins and Smith turned to me in surprise. "No pilot in the war will disagree. He shot down eighty confirmed. Eighty. That's more than both rosters for the Cubs and Yankees put together, including the benches. All of them. Objectively, that is the best."

I let a pause fill the room, reverence for both the lives lost at his hand and for the man himself, the gap between those two sentiments bridged awkwardly by the parties in the room.

"You a Yankees boy?" Smith asked. He was feigning a disaffected attitude, trying to show he was unimpressed—all posturing for the Germans, and maybe for the British and French as well.

"We've only got the Trolley League in California, but we read the papers." I shook my head. Why talk about baseball at a time like this? Why let your mind wander to home? Mom, dad, crying at the station. I blinked hard.

"Indeed," Mustermann went on. "Eighty confirmed, and more unconfirmed. But there is another pilot that may match him in superiority. I come here on behalf of the Reichstag because we fear an enemy and his technology that transcend the alliances of the war. What I am about to share with you is known only by a select few members of that legislative group and German High Command."

Smith tossed his chicken bone onto his plate and folded his arms. Mustermann ignored him.

"For the past year or so, we have had reports come from up and down the Western line of a German pilot shooting down British and French planes—a pilot no one could identify and no squad commander could claim. At first, we accredited this to the confusion of war—miscommunications. But with time, this phantom downed more and more of our enemies."

"You Huns got yourselves a rogue pilot?" Smith asked with a laugh.

"No, they don't. I'm afraid it's more than that," said Atkins. Earnst leaned forward in interest, a stark contrast to the guarded demeanor he'd carried since walking through the door. "We've seen the same," Atkins continued. "An unaccounted-for English plane shooting down Germans. And, unfortunately, on our attempts to bring him in, he turned his guns on our aircraft."

I knit my eyebrows.

"The French as well," Dupont admitted with a shrug of the shoulders. "Though, they never fired on us. We never minded. If someone wanted to shoot down Germans, why would we interfere?"

"What kinds of planes?" Jane asked, her hands settling on the table. "Are you suggesting that one man has access to pursuit planes from each of these countries?"

"No," Mustermann said. "We believe this phenomenon has occurred with several models of our air unit: the Albatross, the Fokker, the Pfalz. It's as though this pilot has an entire fleet of planes."

"Who's servicing them?" I asked. "That would take the effort of a whole aerodrome."

"Especially when you add in all the British designs we've seen as well," Atkins added. We turned to Dupont.

"Yes, yes, ours too." He grimaced as he admitted it. The fire crackled in the silence. I shared a glance with Jane, both of us disbelieving, eyebrows knit in confusion.

"So you're telling me there's a man with a whole fleet of planes from both sides of the war?" I asked.

"Likely many men," Mustermann corrected.

Smith whistled loudly. "A little gang of hidden war thieves causing mischief? Sounds like you boys have gotten pretty sloppy. So what, you want us to join forces, try to find this little aero group and work together to eliminate the threat to what we'll call the normal way of waging war? That's cute."

"I'm afraid it's not that simple, either," Mustermann said. "Lina, if you please."

The woman beside Earnst hadn't said a thing since she arrived. She glanced surreptitiously at her partner. He nodded, and she produced a bundle from under her jacket, wrapped in linen cloth and canvas.

"We attempted to get in contact with these aviators, questioning nearby towns and villages and tracking sightings. We quickly discovered that where they flew, strange occurrences followed."

"Strange occurrences?" Jane asked. I could have sworn the glass marble hanging around my neck warmed, and I could almost feel the hair on Jane's neck rise as if it were my own.

"At times, nothing more than reports of strange lights or sounds. But in some cases, there have been unusual behavior by soldiers or criminals. Public dancing. Unprovoked aggression. Prolonged screams. Unusual dreams..."

With each description Mustermann listed, Atkins and Dupont shrank into their seats. I scowled at the puzzle. Surely, there was some type of explanation. Perhaps this group had been using a new form of weaponry. It wouldn't be the first time a novel hell was released on the battlefield since the war started. Superstition ran rampant among the ranks, but I'd always tried to keep a clear and level head, even if the others considered me cursed. Beside me, though, I knew Jane drank up every word like gospel.

"What's the spilling point, here, Muster?" Smith said with a yawn. "I mean, as much as I love a good meal and ghost stories out here in the country, what does the pretty lady have in the parcel?"

Mustermann muttered something in German, and Lina carefully, quietly, unwrapped the little package on the table. Inside was a pair of airman's goggles.

"Goggles?" Smith asked incredulously.

"Not just any goggles!" Earnst cried in labored English. "These goggles belonged to Boelcke."

Smith looked around the room quizzically.

"Who?"

I might have punched him for his insolence, feigned or not. To think a member of the US Army Air Service didn't know of Boelcke made my skin crawl.

"The first great ace," I said, clarifying, not so much in an attempt to back up the aloof American shtick Smith seemed hell-bent on playing, but to honor the great pilot. "You must have read about him, Smith."

"He revolutionized the air. I've heard that even your pilots train from his methods," Earnst added. He stared at me resolutely, and I nodded his way. It didn't sit right in my stomach, but we saw eye to eye on at least the truth about Boelcke.

"You speak English pretty good." Smith chuckled. Earnst blushed. The woman beside him placed a hand on his in support.

"As a youth, I spent time in England," he replied.

"That so?" Smith continued. "On vacation?"

Mustermann came to his rescue. "Must I remind you, that though our countries are currently at war, it wasn't long ago that a German sat as King Consort of England."

"What he would have thought of your Kaiser's decision to go to war," Atkins quipped.

"Is there significance to these goggles beyond their owner?" Jane pressed with an annoyed wave of her hand. I was grateful.

These men sat on hairline triggers, ready to burst into an outrage. "You mentioned strange occurrences."

"Yes. Lina found the goggles discarded among crates of old things. As you can imagine, we have improved the design of our aviators' goggles somewhat since the beginning of the war. She gave them to Earnst, one of our pursuit pilots, as a good luck token. Earnst, can you describe your experience?"

Earnst took a deep breath, and his eyes darted about nervously. I couldn't blame him. The rest of us were skeptical with folded arms and crossed legs. Each one of us had a firearm on our side, and at any moment, if something smelled funny, we could turn those guns on him easily. But there was something in the expression of Atkins and Dupont that offered the benefit of doubt, as if they wanted answers, and Earnst might have one as plausible as any other.

"I was assigned near Cambrai. British and Canadian soldiers and tanks made strong attacks against us. Your tanks moved slowly, but our artillery was distracted, harassed by shelling and enemy planes. We had to fight your planes to let artillery fight the tanks. One morning in November, things looked bad. We'd been outnumbered in the sky, and to calm Lina's nerves, I took the goggles with me. She is my wife, you see..."

Lina blushed and cast her face down as six pairs of eyes scrutinized her.

"At first, I noticed nothing. Our squadron engaged the British. Our mission was to eliminate British bombers so our artillery could fire at the oncoming tanks. The British were determined. We lost many fighters quickly, and I was overwhelmed with the panic. But then—"

He hesitated and struggled to find words.

"Then what?" Atkins asked.

"I noticed a British single seat plane that seemed...funny. Wrong."

"Wrong how?" Atkins asked. I noticed Smith had gone strangely still beside me.

"How can I describe it? It was like the game, chess. At the end of a game, a player can see the pieces and know there is a way to win, even if he can't see exactly how. The plane looked like that. It shone a strange blue. It called to me—like a starving man smelling food he can't see."

"So that's it? You wore goggles that made a Sopwith Camel shine blue?" Dupont asked, his tone agitated with exasperation.

"More than that. I followed this call and engaged the plane. I flew badly. The enemy could have easily shot and killed me many times. But he didn't. Instead, I turned on him in my Albatross and shot him from the sky. The pilot did not survive the crash. I am sure. Then, far off, I saw another plane and experienced the same thing. 'That plane is yours,' seemed to cry a voice in my head. 'Leave these others and pursue it.' I obeyed, and when I closed the gap between us, I saw the pilot desperately trying to unjam his gun. I shot him down as well."

A creeping nausea grew in my gut, the same sickness that came when my gun jammed in the air or I woke up from a hot nightmare. If Earnst was suggesting the goggles could give some sort of advantage in a dogfight, that could change everything, especially if they could be replicated.

"So, they're lucky goggles?" Smith asked. His tone was biting. Earnst glanced up at Mustermann, and the older man gave him a promissory nod, approval to bare the relic's secret.

"I have since worn the goggles into the air many times. They have functioned the same. I don't know how they work, and it scares me to say it out loud, but they know when a gun is jammed. They let you know when and which gun is jammed. It's like—it's like—"

"Like magic?" Jane gasped. No one answered her. The wind

whistled through the dark outside, singing its eerie song through the thin windows.

"So why tell us?" asked Smith. "Sure, you may believe the goggles work like that. But if you could reproduce the effect, you would have by now. Why not just give them to your best pilot and let him use them to his advantage? Boelcke must have known their secret."

I bristled at his suggestion. Some misguided and corrupt pride in the brotherhood of the air triggered a defensive mechanism at the suggestion Boelcke may have unjustly profited from a cheater's device to earn his fame.

"Because now Richthofen has been shot down," Mustermann said in a deep voice.

"I'm not following," Smith replied.

Mustermann slowly paced the room. My hand drifted to rest lightly on the grip of my Colt pistol, just in case he tried something.

"Soon, thanks to Boelcke's goggles, Earnst earned a reputation. His superiors asked him to meet with Richthofen to discuss his methods. The meeting did not go as expected."

"What did he say?" I asked. I hoped for an answer to my liking. I hoped the Red Baron would have condemned Earnst for using them. I didn't know if I believed what Earnst claimed, but if the Baron did, I hoped that he would have condemned them in disgust.

"He would not touch them," Earnst said. "I explained how they worked. I insisted that they could make him an even better pilot. But he shook his head and threw a blanket over them like he was afraid. He seized my shoulders and made me promise not to wear them. When I laughed, he said, 'Make me that deal right now or I will shoot you myself.'"

"But why?" asked Atkins. Jane pinched my leg under the

table. But when I turned to her, she didn't say anything, only wore a thoughtful and anxious frown on her face.

"I don't know," Earnst replied. "I shook his hand, but thought the Baron had gone a little crazy. I planned to continue using the goggles. I wasn't about to give up my advantage, not when it meant safety for me or a better chance to come home to Lina."

"And the Baron didn't shoot you down?" Smith asked.

Earnst shook his head and tried to continue, but he fumbled with his words. Mustermann took over.

"About a week ago, Earnst was attacked by a German plane. He said that, somehow, instead of indicating a jammed machine gun, the goggles signaled to him that this aircraft was one of the rogue planes we hunted. He is the first of our pilots to engage one of these men and return to tell his story."

"How did they do that?" Dupont asked. Earnst took a breath.

"I saw one of our Albatross planes during a patrol. At first, the goggles worked the same way. A blue shine and a strong instinct. I was certain that the plane's gun was inoperable, but when I went closer to escort him to safety, the light changed. The whole plane glowed stronger, clearer. Strips of blue light branched from the plane like lightning. I understood something was wrong just as the Albatross turned on me and started firing. I was fortunate not to take a bullet in my chest. He shot holes in my wings, and I barely made it back to our airbase where anti-aircraft fire managed to scare him off."

The air hung spookily around Earnst as he finished. Silence stretched over us as we each decided to believe or disbelieve the story. I wanted to speak with Jane privately.

Boelcke's goggles. The glass marbles. I put a hand to Jane's gift hanging around my neck, never before believing in it as much as I did now. She noticed, and for some reason, she wrung her hands like a nervous wreck.

Boelcke's Goggles

In the quiet, we all noticed the sound of an airplane passing high overhead. Strange. It was a little late to be flying.

A clapping sound violated the quiet.

"Incredible. What a story!" Dupont stood and continued his sarcastic applause. "You found magic goggles that are totally unreliable and brought us all here to tell about it. At first, I was concerned that these goggles may actually offer you some advantage against our pilots. I confess, I considered shooting you to take them just now as you spoke. But I see that would have been rash since they are a children's fairy tale."

Lina burst to her feet, face red.

"They are not a fairy tale! They saved my husband's life!"

Smith stood up slowly and put two hands on the table as he bent over it.

"Sounds like they almost took his life, too, Lina. Now, Dupont, don't make an idiot of yourself. Let's just all calm down. Mustermann, what's your proposition? Why are we all here?"

Mustermann sucked in a big breath of air and rested his hands on his belt. His chest puffed out confidently.

"Whoever these flyers are, I propose we join forces to find them and destroy them."

"Why would we do that?" Smith asked.

"Because they have the potential to prolong the war," Mustermann replied.

Atkins scoffed.

"I hardly think any contribution to the attrition that has already occurred will delay any possible surrenders," he said.

"No?" Mustermann folded his arms. "An enemy of my enemy, Lieutenant. We don't know what motivates this radical and mysterious group. If it fights not to attain victory, then why is it fighting at all? It may be that it wants to prolong this conflict. And, if the strange occurrences continue, there is no telling how unpredictably items like Boelcke's goggles may affect either side."

"So you want to put together a joint task force that can reach both sides of the line," Smith surmised.

"Yes." Mustermann nodded. "At the very least, we need more information about this group. What if they have some greater plan? What if they are in possession of more devices? There is too much we don't know."

"Why should we trust you?" Dupont asked. "What if this is just a trick to learn Commander Foch's vital secrets?"

Mustermann sat down again beside Earnst and Lina. He finished the wine in his glass. His gaze settled on the flickering candle flame on the earth. He flexed his hand.

"Earnst, Lina, and I are here against the wishes of German High Command. This may be hard for you to believe, but there are many in Germany who do not want this war. The Reichstag is not behind the generals, nor even the Kaiser. The war will not end the way they wish. That is clear. If they fail, our nation's governance will either be crushed or radicalized. The age of Imperial Germany is coming to an end. When the smoke settles, those of us who hope for a just and productive Germany will rise. We do not want a rogue group of fighters to claim credit or cause chaos. All have suffered."

We leaned back and considered the plea for help. I couldn't help but marvel at his admission. Could Germany be as divided as they say? I couldn't comprehend what it would be like living in a country where a monarch could so blatantly disregard the will of his people. Three nationals creeping across the lines to carry out a secret cry for help on behalf of a scorned and ignored legislature. These three were brave. They were humble. They were desperate.

"We'll think about it," Smith said.

Chapter 8
Pilot Wanted
Jane

If I should die, think only this of me:
That there's some corner of a foreign field
That is for ever England.
-Rupert Brooke-

There is no darkness like that which exists in the countryside.

The Germans had left several hours ago, and Dupont instructed the men as to the bunk assignments in the house. As a woman, I would be taking up residence with the perpetually bothered cook, Annette, in a cottage about fifteen minutes' drive from the property. Atkins was about drive us there when Marcus volunteered.

"You, Sergeant?" Atkins balked.

"Trusted for top-secret missions, sir, but not to escort Private Doe and Annette home for a night's rest?" he asked.

"Of course, I didn't select you for the mission, did I?" Atkins replied. "And Private Doe is in my purview."

"They're being asked to go on a suicide mission," Dupont complained. "Why stand in the way of love?"

That we were teased even amidst such a life-altering revelation took me by surprise.

"It's not that, sir," Marcus replied wearily.

"He would be so lucky," I interjected. "I have worked on Sergeant Dewar's plane time and time again. I trust him with my life and more. I suspect he wants a private word about everything we've just discussed."

Marcus nodded.

"No offense to any of you," he said, "but Jane's the only one here I trust worth anything. Her opinion most of all."

Atkins looked around the room helplessly, but Smith shrugged his shoulders and Dupont's eyes sparkled with wine. The Frenchman walked forward and gave Atkins a large kiss on both cheeks before grasping his arms dramatically.

"You worry so much! Go on. Off to bed. They are not children."

Atkins eventually surrendered and tossed Marcus the keys to his car. I swiped them from his hand before Dupont finished explaining how to get there. Annette didn't wait. She had already staggered crookedly from the room, one hand on her back.

"We'll manage well enough," I said. "I'm sure Annette knows the area." I clapped Marcus's arm and whisked off after the poor, tired cook. Dupont's suggestive eyebrows bore a hole into our backs. In some way, it made everything feel more normal.

We didn't speak much during the drive. Occasionally, Annette let out soft French swears about her *mal au dos*. Other than that, Marcus and I soaked in the sound of the car's engine and the gentle whipping of the cold spring wind going by the windows. I loved driving any vehicle I could. The meticulous attention to the road helped me process my most difficult emotions. A small part of me had always imagined what it would be like to take the pilot's seat and fly as Marcus did.

I mentioned it once to him. He didn't like the sound of it.

When we arrived at the cottage, I cut the engine, turned off the headlights, and planned to ask Annette for a private moment with Marcus, to plead with her that we needed no chaperone. But the wheels had barely ground to a halt before she sprung quickly from the back seat and limped to the dark cottage. After the door creaked closed behind her, we sat listening to all the quiet clicks and groans of the settling automobile. It was so dark I could only catch faint reflections of moonlight off the metal finishes on the bonnet.

"Do you believe them?" I asked.

Marcus must have expected the question, but he sighed.

"Do I believe that Boelcke's goggles are magic? No."

"And why not?" I asked.

"You don't think it's a little insulting?"

"Insulting?"

"Many consider Boelcke the best pilot to ever live. If he had magic goggles that protected him in the air or gave him an unfair advantage, don't you think it's a discredit to the man?" He leaned his head back on the canvas seat.

"You cannot be serious." I let out a guttural complaint, exasperated.

"I'm very serious. Boelcke may have been German, but he deserves the honor he earned in the air."

I gaped. This man had just sat through one of the most peculiar and possibly important meetings in the entire war, and he was still caught up on the honor of pilots.

"It's not a game, Marcus!"

He blushed.

"I know that."

"Do you? Do you understand that we're not out here to score

points and make legends? Can you appreciate what Mustermann and Earnst and Lina risked in coming to speak with us? They could have been killed. What they're doing must constitute treason."

He shifted in his seat to look at me.

"Treason? Mustermann was here representing a member of the Reichstag. It's not as though he is some lone wolf on a crusade to take down his government."

"His like-minded compatriots will not defend him from the wrath of German High Command or the Kaiser. Thinking otherwise is plainly foolish." My words fell out quickly in an elevated pitch. I'd kept calm for so long, but the crushing understanding was all coming at once.

All my life, I'd been brought up to believe in magic. My mother's best friend Luella was like an aunt to me, and she took it upon herself to train me to recognize, appreciate, and even practice a strange and unbelievable method of bending nature in peculiar ways. But it had always been just that. I'd never met anyone other than her, her husband, my mother, or my father, that truly comprehended or made use of magic.

Yes, there were many so-called spiritualists and magicians and practitioners eager to make a quick dollar by convincing others with their tricks. But the magic worth protecting, worth keeping secret for how dangerous it could be—I'd never known anyone to believe in that.

But if Mustermann was right, if it had attracted the attention of the wrong people... suddenly Atkins's admission that the end of the war might not matter made sense to me.

"So you think just because they risked a lot coming to talk to us, they're telling the truth?" Marcus asked.

"That's exactly what I think," I replied. "If there is a power out there, Marcus, a power we don't fully understand, and it can be exploited as plainly as it has manifested in Boelcke's goggles, I can't stress the destruction it could wreak."

Marcus bit his lip and glowered at the gear change box.

"Well, you've been using magic to fix up our planes," he sneered. "How's that any different?"

"The magic I use is nominal. Half of the things I attempt might not even be effective at all! I only do them because I'm desperate that you—"

I bit my lip as emotion came tumbling up amidst my words. Tears would not do here. I did not want him to play along because he felt sympathy for me. I had to make him understand.

"It's just a lot to take in," he whispered.

"You believe in something, Marcus. I know you do. I see it in you when you talk about the men who flew the skies before you. You think there's a code of chivalry between pilots that transcends the violence. I'm asking you to look deeper. If such a code exists, nonsensically, unbelievably, if that magic exists, why not something more tangible?"

I put my hand on his, willing him to believe. That was the hardest part, believing. Believing in anything was so risky with the war going on. Belief gave you something that could be stolen or destroyed.

But it was too late for me. I understood about the magic. I had come into the war believing. And from that belief hope sprouted like weeds. Hope that the war would end, that I could return one day to my family, that I could somehow preserve the best parts of Marcus's heart.

He parted his lips to share something and closed them again several times before going on. It gave me the impression that he struggled to say what he wished.

"Maybe it doesn't matter," he said, finally. "I may not have to believe in magic to face some facts. Those radical pilots must exist.

Atkins and Dupont have struggled with the same. What do you think they are? Dutch nationalists or something?"

I folded my arms and rested my temple on the steering wheel.

"Who can say? Seems like quite sophisticated involvement from a country determined to stay neutral. Besides, it sounds like these pilots have uncanny skill. If you don't believe they are magically assisted, then you must believe them to be a squadron of some of the best pilots in the war. Did you notice that no one claimed to have shot down one of their planes?"

I chewed on my cheek. I had noticed. Unless the Dutch had some top-of-the-line training program that simulated tactical experience, they had no business being anywhere near as proficient as these pilots seemed to be.

"So that leaves what? Defectors?"

"Possibly."

We sat quietly and listened to crickets chirping out in the night.

"Why us?" he asked.

"Pardon?"

"I mean, it's very clear why you were chosen for this. But it's not like I'm the best pilot in the squadron. I don't have a single downed plane to my name."

"That doesn't mean you're not an incredible pilot—"

"It's not the time for encouraging talk, Jane." He cut me off too sharply, signaled that there was more to his resistance, something deeper than self-doubt.

"Well, perhaps you're here for me. They can't exactly dispatch a whole unit to protect the witch girl if they want to keep this mission confidential."

Marcus jolted upright, struck by a thought.

"What if we succeed?" he asked. "It's not like we're going to make the papers back home, are we?"

I laughed.

"Can you imagine the headline? 'Inter War Powers Team Handily Defeats Radical Defectors Chasing Magical Device.' It would sell papers, but no, I don't imagine any journalist will be catching wind of this."

"No military honors either. If we die out there, they'd cover it up. They brought me out here in a damn canvas bag."

I clicked my tongue, and disappointment dimmed my heart. He was still, even now, thinking about the honors.

"I imagine you're right."

"So what is there to gain?"

"If it's true, and this radical group does have plans, even if just to prolong the war, we could save lives. You know how attrition has served all parties thus far."

He narrowed his brows and balled his fists.

"Earnst has been using those goggles since autumn!" he said. "They didn't wait to come forward with this until the imposing American machine marched steadily toward Berlin and Ludendorff trembled beneath the shadow of Uncle Sam. They waited until now to come forward under the guise of mutual interest. What if it's a sham, Jane?"

My head throbbed. It had been such a long day, and Marcus needed time. At any rate, it didn't appear that I would convince him this evening to see my way of things.

"Does it matter?" I asked. "Orders are orders."

He let out a long hiss of air and rubbed his temples.

"I didn't sign up to die quietly in the shadows," he replied.

"It doesn't have to be that way. Please, think about what I've said."

Begrudgingly, he nodded.

Jane

Annette woke me early the next morning in a right fit, complaining that Smith was outside ready to take us back. Through my admittedly basic French, I understood that she was late to prepare breakfast for the company. Groggily, I donned my uniform and wandered outside. I offered Annette the front seat, but she waved me off and babbled off about thirty indistinguishable French mutterings.

"Good morning, Sleeping Beauty," Smith said loudly.

"How kind of you to come fetch me, Sergeant."

"Well, you know us Americans. Up and at 'em early. And I like to think our manners are better than some say."

He clearly had the benefit of at least an hour awake already. I struggled to bring my mind up to the same pace. He was impeccably uniformed and neatly groomed.

"Boy, could I use some breakfast, though. Annette, I hope you make a good breakfast!"

All he earned was another dismissive hand by Annette.

"Was Atkins still sleeping?" I asked as he pulled away from the cottage.

"You know, I wanted to take this time to have a little chat."

I furrowed my brows. So far, Atkins appeared to be easily persuaded by anyone about anything.

"I see," I replied.

"It's just a peculiar thing that we're dealing with, Miss Doe. It's sensitive. I need to know I can trust you."

"Well, I don't know how a short car ride will persuade you either way."

"Fair point, Private." Smith laughed. "Fair point. Still, how do you slice it? The whole magical device story in general? You think the Germans are trying to be funny to us?"

I shook my head.

"What does it matter? We have orders in any case, don't we?"

"Well, say we didn't. Do you think they're being funny?"

I squinted at Smith. Something in the plastered, smug smile he wore betrayed deeper information, a greater gravity to his demeanor.

"Well, I'm not sure why you'd want my opinion anyway. I'm only here because they say I'm a witch."

"See, I don't believe that," he countered. "Witches are for burning. And I don't want you to burn. Doesn't seem like Atkins or Dewar want you to, either. Golly, if you knew with what esteem Major Lufbery talked about you..."

"Then what do you think I am?" I asked.

He leveled his eyes at me over his square shoulder.

"An asset. Now will you please stop hedging and tell me what you think about the Bosch story?"

I rubbed my eyes and took a deep breath. His insistence reminded me of the seriousness of our predicament, and it chased my drowsiness away.

"I've only heard the stories, tales about how magic used to be once upon a time, before we came along and chased it out. But my teacher told me that there are still pockets of magic, strongholds that we can't chase away even with all our science. I suppose it only makes sense that with the advent of flying, we were set to collide with one of these holdouts.

"Whenever we make a new discovery, set to change the course of the world as we know it, magic resists the change, resists our understanding, and that manifests in different ways. Boelcke's goggles terrify me, but they don't surprise me. It's just evidence that we've done exactly that. We've found one of these magical holdouts."

Smith clenched his jaw several times and stared at the road. The smile had faded.

"What do you think that means for the war?"

"You know more than you're letting on," I replied. He was

testing me, but Atkins had already revealed how the English feared the magic. They concealed the extent of the risk from us.

"Why, Miss Doe. Are you accusing a military man of keeping secrets?"

It didn't take us long to arrive at the farmhouse. The morning dew still clung to the plants giving off the smell of damp earth. The early light illuminated the whole valley. A place can look so different between night and day. I noticed new details now that the novelty of our meeting had ebbed. The house itself was already old, a mix of plaster, rough stone, wooden roof tiles—all wearing an elegant coat of climbing vines just starting to leaf after winter.

The moo of a cow surprised me from around the corner while I admired the emergence of spring bulbs. Lingering daffodils. Snowdrops. Hyacinth.

I waited in the front room for Marcus, Atkins, and Dupont. But in a shockingly short amount of time, Annette had produced a table setting full of light, enriched breads and coffee. I hardly had a chance to taste much by the time Marcus emerged from the hallway and Annette was pushing her first offering to the side to make room for samplings of cured pork and juice.

"These French don't know a damn thing about breakfast," Smith said.

"Jane," Marcus said in surprise. "I didn't know you'd be here so early." He sat down and helped himself to one of the sidelined croissants. It flaked in his fingers.

"Smith was kind enough to fetch me," I said.

"Where are the rest?" he asked.

"They're busy," Smith said. "Come on, Sergeant, American bites. You need more than that."

I took a sip of milk.

"So, what do you make of it, Sergeant?" asked my friend.

"Make of what?"

"Make of what?" Marcus laughed. "I can't tell if I'm dreaming or if command is pulling some elaborate prank."

Smith smiled. "Strange times, aren't they? You two up for a walk?"

Marcus looked at me in confusion. "I've barely had anything to eat."

"I told you to take bigger bites. We're behind schedule. Come on." He stood and headed out the door before either of us managed a reply.

"Here." I stood and handed Marcus a few extra croissants. "They travel well."

We walked out of the house and took in a deep breath of the morning spring air. The valley was so quiet. The crunch of Smith's boots violated the peace, making me cringe. He walked quickly, the pace of a soldier not yet fatigued by the toll of war.

"Where are we going, Sergeant?" I asked.

"Marcus, I need your buy-in, son," Smith said, ignoring my question.

"If you're here as proxy for Colonel Mitchell, I'll obey whatever orders you give me, sir."

"That's not going to be good enough," he replied. "I'm sure we all know why Private Doe is here. She's the only chance we got of really unraveling this thing. But why do you think we pulled you from your ever-so-prolific streak at the front?"

Marcus blushed. "Well, frankly, I don't know sir."

"Attitude matters on a mission like this, kid. I don't even mean that it matters because it gets you in the right frame of mind. You two will need to transcend the barrier between reality and whatever else comes outside of reality."

"Finding the rogue pilots, sir?" I asked. The new confidence Smith used in his voice intrigued me. He had shed the skin of indifference.

"That may be what Mustermann wants, but as far as we're

concerned, that's a secondary priority." Smith spit off to the side of the trail.

"Sergeant?"

"They're still the enemy, even if they want to be friendly on this. They have one device. We happen to know for a certainty that there are others. You two have to even the arms race. We will be damned if any more magical devices end up in the hands of either the Germans or whatever rogue group is trying to find them."

"You believe in the magic?" Marcus asked. His incredulous tone offended me. Was this how he spoke about my beliefs to others?

Smith stopped several paces ahead and turned around to wait for us. He checked his watch again.

"Marcus. You are here because you, more than any other pilot alive, will fight to protect Jane Turner at all costs. But this is not for show. I need you all in."

The sound of a rotary engine drew our view to the sky, but the hill blocked any sight of a plane. Smith continued around the bend, and when we followed the hill gave way to another field, flat, open, and wide. An unmarked Nieuport made its descent. Dupont and Atkins waved receiving flags to help guide the pilot in.

"Glad you decided to join us," Atkins said wryly as we stood beside him.

"It's this dreamy country air. Thought I was back stateside," Smith replied, all alertness replaced with his aloof caricature once more.

The plane was closer now, and I recognized the smooth fuse-lage and rounded wings of a Nieuport 27, a reliable French design that had not been entrusted to American pilots.

"Who's that?" Marcus asked.

The plane came down smooth as glass, despite the field having an occasional bump or two. It taxied to a stop and cut the propellor before the pilot hopped out. Dupont gave him an enthusiastic salute.

Major Lufbery took off his flight cap and nodded his thanks before heading our way.

"What is Luf doing here?" Marcus wondered aloud.

I shrugged. At this point, nothing surprised me.

Lufbery gave us a smile and shook Smith's hand.

"Major—" he said. Smith clicked his tongue.

"Just Sergeant Smith, here." Smith smiled firmly. I peered at him. Major? Of course, if they all insisted on using fake names, why not use fake ranks, too?

"I don't see much cover for my plane," Luf said, his smile faltering. "I hope we don't have any visitors."

"A perfect site was impossible," said Dupont. "But I should hope that no German fighters come this deep into France—assuming you didn't bring one behind you."

Lufbery shook his head.

"That's a rule I don't break. No leading enemies back home. Information wins wars, they say."

Smith put a hand on his shoulder and motioned to a copse of trees across the field.

"Speaking of information, we'll bring you up to speed." We followed Smith across the field. Marcus and I took the opportunity to flank our friend.

"With all due respect, do you have any idea what sort of mess you got us into, Luf?" Marcus asked.

"You don't sound very grateful."

"He doesn't believe what's going on," I said.

"And why should he?"

"Because the Germans risked everything to tell us!" I replied.

"Of course, I don't believe it. Magic goggles?"

"Magic goggles?" The major cocked an eyebrow.

"Ten years ago, would you have believed a man could fly in the air?" I countered. "Now look at you!"

"That's completely different, and you know it."

Lufbery stopped and looked at us bickering. We quieted, embarrassed at being caught during such an outburst. He scrutinized both of us, squinting in the morning sun. He had a way of calmly reprimanding his unit, an almost fatherly attribute to inspire introspection and reflection.

He pointed a finger at Marcus.

"You wear a magic marble under your flight suit when you go in the air." He dropped the statement like a verdict and continued walking.

"Thank you!" I cried, following closely behind.

"That's—there's a reason for that. I do it as a favor for her!"

Marcus scrambled after.

Chapter 9
Where the Germans Are
Marcus

We came upon him sitting in the sun—
Blinded by war, and left. And past the fence
Wandered young soldiers form the Hand & Flower,
Asking advice of his experience.
-Margaret Postgate Cole-

L uf vacantly patted his pockets in search of a cigarette. Smith stood in front of him, smack-dab in the middle of a clearing underneath a dappled canopy. Atkins leaned against a thick-trunked ash, but Dupont, Jane, and I had taken seats on the ground.

"Now that's a story," Luf said at last before lighting up.

He had listened quietly while Smith summarized the Germans' account of the rogue flyers and Boelcke's goggles. The rest of us chimed in to add details or, in the case of Dupont and Atkins, hesitantly affirm the story's credibility.

"Have you ever seen one of the rogue flyers they're talking about?" Smith asked.

Luf raised his eyebrows but shook his head.

"Can't say I have."

Given how many times Luf had taken flight, that surprised me. After all, even I'd seen fire exchanged between two Allied planes. It wasn't always easy distinguishing friend from foe in the air. But Luf didn't bother looking at Smith during his curt response. I wondered if he might not be telling the exact truth.

"So what do you think?" I asked.

He cast me a sideways glance.

"I think it doesn't matter what I think. If command is decided..."

"It's not. That's why we're all here. My orders are to assess Mustermann's offer and, if it seems credible, to launch the mission," said Smith. "But this assignment doesn't officially exist. If this does turn out to be some kind of ghost story, no one wants that black mark on Pershing's tab as he does politics' dirty dance to coordinate with the other allied powers."

Luf glanced at Atkins.

"Worse with us, I'm afraid. At first, when I brought it to his attention, Major General Trenchard scorned the idea outright at first. When I suggested Private Doe was the only person considered suitable for the job, he almost took my head. We had no clearance to meet with Mustermann until he heard that Colonel Mitchell was willing to dispatch a pilot of his own."

I didn't like the idea of Trenchard belittling Jane like that. Jane's experience pre-dated the Women's Royal Air Force and in my eyes, that lent her the same type of credibility Luf had brought with him when the States entered the war.

But when I opened my mouth to voice her defense, she kicked me in the shin. I yelped. Everyone stared.

"What about you, Dupont?" Smith asked. "Who's running the armée de l'aire nowadays? Duval, isn't it?"

"Since August," Dupont confirmed grimly. "I must confess, we had no interest in meeting with the Germans."

"Yet here you are," Jane said. Dupont sighed and picked vacantly at the tree bark.

"My assignment was clear. Arrive early and kill the German messengers behind closed doors. If a shot was unavailable without risking the lives of our allies, I was to poison them."

A bird cawed somewhere out in the woods. We stopped to listen. I heard Jane swallow a lump in her throat.

"You didn't, though," I said. "Why?"

Dupont shrugged.

"What he said was interesting. And none of you shot them, either."

Smith chuckled.

"Well, this is a convoluted mess," he said. "No one wanted to move forward with this thing, and yet, for some reason, we're all considering it."

"What happens next?" Luf asked.

"The Germans will be coming back later today for our answer. If we say yes, Marcus and Matilda Doe here embark on an operation completely off-book. There will be no mention of it in any official briefing or record, no coverage in any newspaper. I have the strictest orders to safeguard its confidentiality."

"Safeguard?" I asked. "How do you mean to do that?"

"It's a fancy way of saying you're considered expendable if you can't keep their secrets," Jane said with a sneer. "That we're both expendable."

"What?" I stood up, an awful knot tying itself in my stomach. "You're joking."

I searched for humor in the men's faces but saw only stony stillness. I scrutinized Atkins most closely. All his concern about propriety, about Jane's reputation—would he be willing to silence her if need be?

This was real and twisted, now, but it made awful sense. Command wanted someone to quietly investigate reports of fabled rogue pilots and magical devices while Pershing, Foch, and the other brass pretended no such things existed. Completely off book.

The mission was not real, but the danger was. How could anyone live in such limbo?

What if I died? What if I got my first downed plane just to have it go unreported? What if, somehow, I outlived the war with nothing to show for it but nightmares of rogue pilots and a dear pen pal named Jane from England?

"Why would we agree to something like this?" I asked.

No one wanted to answer. There was no reasonable reply. Yet the creeping curiosity hung as palpably as the spring morning mist.

"And you need to answer Mustermann by tonight?" Luf asked. Smith nodded.

"Then we've got time for lunch first," he continued, "assuming Dupont hasn't poisoned the food."

Dupont raised his hands in surrender.

"No Germans. No poison," he said.

"In the worst-case scenario, we request additional time from Mustermann. And that scenario isn't even that bad," said Smith. "This is the closest I've come to a vacation in a long time."

"Finally a chance to enjoy some good French food again. Hasn't been quite the same since I started working for the Americans," said Luf as he clapped Dupont on the shoulder.

"French cooking? Clearly, you've forgotten all about the American breakfast," Smith chided.

"Neither of you know a thing about breakfast," added Atkins.

Jane and I watched them marching away, pluckily arguing over trivial nonsense as if they were ambassadors at a World Fair. I turned to my friend.

"They can't be serious about this," I muttered, shaking my head.

She stiffened and took a breath.

"I believe the Germans, Marcus. I think this could be the most important thing we will ever do for the war effort."

"Jane, I know you're into the whole magic thing. But this is nonsense. Do you know what happens to people who carry secrets this large?"

Jane stood and brushed off her clothes.

"I do. But we have to convince Smith to say yes. If you can't believe in it, Marcus," her voice broke, but she pushed through it, "then we can find someone else to be my protector."

She walked off without giving me a chance to argue.

J ane was unbearable at lunch, all determined expressions and quiet conversations with Atkins. I doubted she was serious. How could she be? After all her efforts to protect me, after insisting we wear matching enchanted marbles, after all her anxiety every time I went in the air— we had an understanding. Neither of us said it out loud, but it was a tacit agreement that we wouldn't separate, not unless command ordered it.

But as soon as some other folk came along and validated her beliefs in the unusual, she played tough and pretended that it'd be that simple to part ways.

I scowled through the meal. It took a good amount of self-control not to mouth, "I know what you're doing" across the table when she looked my way. It was a persuasion tactic. She wanted to go on the adventure, investigate the magic, unravel the enigmatic flyer squadron...

And that was perfectly normal. In some ways, the adventure appealed to me, too, magic or no magic. It tugged at the boy inside of me, the one who left my home to go help the French in their war against Germany. But that kid disappeared a long time ago. He disappeared on his endless trips to the front lines, where he learned just what was at stake in this conflict.

Death was not the worst thing that happened to soldiers. Getting haunted, now that was much worse.

After lunch, Luf invited me back up to the field to run a check on the Nieuport he'd flown in. I treasured this type of invitation, as even now, several years into my experience working on warbirds, Lufbery's tutelage was worth its weight in gold. His inspections were meticulous and insightful. Planes had defects, even straight from the manufacturer—and if I'm honest, especially straight from the manufacturer. It was a byproduct of the immense pressure the factories were under to produce machines as quickly as possible for the ongoing war effort. We'd seen our fair share of eager pilots go down because of industrial flaws in their newly assembled planes.

Not to mention how heavily that air travel took its toll on our machines. So, just as he polished every round that went into his twin guns, Luf relentlessly inspected his aircraft. He considered it a question of survival. It also explained his wariness at flying a plane he had not spent time configuring.

But despite their tedious nature, somehow he made the inspections exciting.

Watching him testing the tautness of the cables and the axles of the landing wheels with a borrowed set of tools was like watching the big brother I never had run finals checks on a downhill pushcart we'd thrown together from scrap.

"Sounds like you're decided against the mission," Luf said. His question drew me out of my euphoric haze.

"What? You mean trying to chase down mystery pilots and more magic goggles?"

Luf stayed quiet and continued checking the give on a line of bolts on the bottom side of the plane. He did this from time to time, asked a question and let me talk it through.

"Come on, Luf. Don't you think it's a load of junk? And a disrespectful one to boot? This Hun is trying to suggest that Boelcke managed to accomplish what he did because of some enchanted specs. You know as well as I do that that's nonsense. It's offensive. I mean, I know the man flew for the other side, but a skilled pilot is a skilled pilot and doesn't deserve to be disparaged that way."

Luf dropped his wrench in the toolbox on the grass beside him and wiped his hands.

"You always paid too close attention to the papers, Marcus."

"What do you mean?" I asked as I helped him to his feet.

"One mention of Boelcke and you get all distracted. It always had me worried about you in the air. Every time you went up I was afraid you'd get it in your head that you were fighting some respectable German ace and get so distracted by it that you'd make a fundamental mistake."

I bit my tongue. He was right, as usual. It hadn't taken a German ace to get my head turned around. I'd had opportunities to shoot down at least five of the Bosch by now, golden opportunities at that. Each one left to fight another day because of the unfair circumstance that put them in my crosshairs. The only thing that kept those men alive were whatever ghosts lived in my head.

"You think I'm missing something here?" I asked. He tossed me a rag, and we set to spot cleaning and polishing the Nieuport's exterior. This had become our customary last step. Wiping off the cables, checking for grime and build up, anything that might cause corrosion, drag, or weaken the plane's structural integrity. Of course, we gave special attention to the Vickers guns.

"It's a special mission. You're so distracted by the magic goggles that you've flown right past concerns about what three different countries have agreed on."

"The rogue flyers," I said after a moment.

Luf nodded and picked at a semi-congealed splash of gunk on

the propellor. I slipped into the cockpit and stood to inspect the top wing.

"You said you'd never seen one of them," I added. "That true?"

Luf grunted from his effort.

"I've seen a lot of strange things in the air."

"You've fought one?"

"No. I flew beside one, once. Helped me take down a two-seater. Distracted the gunner while I settled into position below and behind. I thought it was one of the French."

"What was he flying?"

"A Nieuport. I thought he was one of ours until he turned his guns on me. There wasn't much in it. I think both of us were low on fuel. A few evasive maneuvers and we called it quits. But he flew north when I flew west."

I let my hand rest on the cold steel of one of the Vickers' barrels.

"You never told me."

"Believe it or not, Marcus, I haven't shared every detail of every fight up there with you. Even if you have asked for them."

"And you didn't fly after him to see who he was? Even a short distance to see where he was going?" I asked. My breath quickened at the thought. The little boy inside of me eager for adventure again. Luf leaned against the fuselage beside me.

"I've been up there a lot of times. You develop a set of rules for yourself."

"Like 'don't get curious?'" My tone was overly playful.

"Like 'when you're low on fuel and there's no need, leave risks well enough alone.'"

"Don't chase ghosts." I sat down, rested my feet on the familiar wooden pedals. "But isn't that exactly what you're asking me to do?"

"Sounds like these ghosts have been verified three times over. Come on, Marcus. We've received worse orders than this with less chance of survival. Why are you balking at a mission like this one?"

He was right, and I felt like a child sitting in that cockpit having life and war explained to me so plainly, as if I hadn't been out here so long already.

"But there's something else, isn't there?" Luf asked.

My stomach turned. I couldn't tell it straight, even if I wanted to. There was too much shame in admitting it out loud, even if my insides were begging me to open up, to explain why I needed a victory and why I couldn't get one. Instead, I chose to go round about.

"Luf, how do you do it?"

"Do what?"

"If they could only confirm all the planes you've shot down..."

He lowered his gaze at me.

"Finish the sentence, Marcus. If they could confirm all the planes I've shot down, then..."

"Then, well, you'd be a legend! Your name would resonate with Boelcke and Richthofen. Everyone would know you're one of the best pilots the war has ever seen."

Luf smiled and searched for a cigarette.

"You know why I go across lines to shoot down German planes? All the way over where our observers can't confirm kills?"

"Why?" He had never talked about this with me. The most I ever got back was a smile and shrug of the shoulders.

"Because that's where the Germans are."

He didn't have to say more. *That's where the Germans are.* A subtle rebuke, gentle but firm. Luf wasn't here to score points. He wasn't here to become a legend. He was here to shoot down German planes and protect his squadron, me included. I'd never met anyone so dedicated to the cause, so obsessed with the process, yet so removed from it all at the same time.

Luf had become a legend in his own right, at least among those who knew him, and that was enough for him.

"I want to be like you, Luf."

"Don't get starry, kid."

"But I do." The words came tumbling out. Before the war, I could never have imagined speaking so openly to another man this way, with such naked admiration. But our time together had bonded him to me like the brother I never had, or perhaps more. Did brothers talk to one another with such affection, or were they plagued with a distant sense of competition? It wasn't like that with Luf.

"I want to be like you, but it's hard to let go of wanting some kind of recognition. I'm tired of being known as cursed or gun-shy. I want my dad to read about me in the paper and show his friends. Let their boy, a war hero, do for them what they can't do for themselves. Imagine how people would come round his shop then. Imagine how they'd pat him on the back and welcome him and my mom to dinners. I don't want to be a waste. Part of me believes I've done nothing but fail since I left home. I know the count doesn't matter, but only those who have one can say that. I know it's selfish to keep asking for more chances, but I need it, Luf. I need it."

Luf clapped me on the shoulder.

"That French spring country is making your eyes water," he said.

I tucked my head and blinked back the tears that had crept through my defenses. It wasn't uncommon to see men cry at the front. Stakes were too high. Friends going down. Your own life almost lost. The daily filling and dumping of adrenaline required emotional dues.

But I didn't cry. Speaking of rules we made for ourselves, that was mine.

I learned other ways to cope. We knew when and how to comfort the broken hearted and when and how to let them wallow in it. This was different. These tears bubbled up from a well dug before the war, muddied by my experiences since.

I didn't want the recognition I mentioned to Luf. I needed it. I wanted it when I left home to mark a new beginning for my family. Now, I needed it because of one terrible night when I had driven my ambulance for another load of wounded and dying soldiers to cart back from the front, and I'd wandered off to some bombed out shell of a house to relieve my bladder. What I found in that house, who I found... it was the first time I didn't shoot someone. And I had paid for it since.

"I'm not saying you have to believe in magic," Luf continued. "I don't think I do. But don't discount this assignment because of it. Besides, this mission will take Jane all over the war. You going to let some other pilot escort her around?"

Mention of Jane replaced my sorrow with entitlement. No one out here knew Jane like I did.

"Just something to consider," he said.

"Thanks, Luf."

"That's Private Whiskey to you."

We laughed only briefly. From the other side of the hill, a violent boom violated the serene French countryside.

"What the hell?" I asked. "That sounded like a bomb."

I scrambled from the cockpit, and we ran to the edge of the hillside. Below, past the farmhouse, far on the horizon where the road entered the valley, a car swerved down the road. Behind it, a smoking crater marred the landscape. And above, a large, heavy bomber swooped like a dragon spitting fire.

"It was a bomb," said Luf. The distant roar of the plane's engine reached our ears now. "We've been compromised."

Chapter 10
The Gotha
Jane

Mute in the glamour of shells he watched them burst
Spouting dark earth and wire with gusts from hell,
While posturing giants dissolved in drifts of smoke.
-Siegfried Sassoon-

The makeshift receiving room where we'd been hosting our meals shook. The window rattled loudly. Atkins and Smith paused their card game and peered outside. I had already crossed to the window to investigate.

At first, the cloud of dust and smoke seemed alien, the buzzing form in the air just a bee. I'd only been in the valley for a day, but its stillness had beguiled me. Such a physical upheaval came as an intruder in the night, a prowler in the children's bedroom. The nausea of fear came in swiftly on the back of understanding.

"Bomber!" I cried.

The others wanted to see for themselves and rushed across the room, abandoning the cards in a mess and edging me out of the way.

"How'd they find us?" Smith growled, all traces of his aloof bravado replaced in an instant with grit in his vocal cords. "Dupont, you said this house was remote!"

"You drove here yourself," Dupont spat back. "Was it not remote?"

"It must have been that plane we heard overhead last night. German reconnaissance plane marking our locale. I was too awestruck by Mustermann's story to check the window covers. Look there, out on the road!" Atkins said as he fished for a pair of binoculars. "Is that a car?"

"Whose? Mustermann's?" asked Smith. "See that? There's the plane. What is that? At this distance I can't tell if it's a Gotha or a damn airship!"

"It's flying round and back. If it's interested in the car, I can't imagine the pilots will take kindly to the house," Atkins said.

"Will you all stand there arguing while they blow you up, then?" I asked, door already open before me. The others filed after me, and we ran for the cover of the nearby trees. My over-sized WRAF coat and skirt did not make it easy in this terrain, but then, these uniforms weren't designed for dangerous situations.

In fact, these uniforms had hardly been designed at all.

I stopped halfway to the tree line.

"Private, keep running!" Atkins grabbed my elbow and pulled me after him. Dupont was already ahead diving over a low ridge and under a shrub.

"What about Marcus?" My breath caught. He and Lufbery must have heard the sound. I clutched at my glass marble.

"He and Whiskey know what they're about. Where's Annette?" Smith asked.

I put a hand to my forehead. "She went out foraging this morning. There's no telling where she got off to."

"She'll do just fine. Now come along before we're seen!"

I wanted to sprint up the hill beside the house to find him, and ensure he wasn't doing anything terribly stupid, but I let Atkins pull me along.

When we reached the ridge, I fell hard on the ground. A sharp pain shot through my elbow just as another blast shook the earth. Smith pulled branches over us to cover our position, and Atkins propped himself up to watch through the binoculars.

"You won't believe this, Smith," he said. "It's one of the new Gotha bombers, and that is Mustermann's car."

"I guess the man wasn't kidding about getting German High Command all riled up," Smith replied. He took the binoculars. "The car is shooting back. Some type of mounted gun through the window. All the good that will do them. And here they tried to convince us they came unarmed."

"Jane!" Marcus's voice called across the property. My eyes darted to the corner of the house where he frantically scanned the area. A sigh of release came from my lungs, and I whistled to signal our location. He rushed over and dove clumsily over the ridge, his body coming to rest beside mine. His solid tangible presence did something, at least, to calm my anxiety.

Heavens only knew if he'd been seen.

"Is it one of ours?" he asked urgently.

"It's a German bomber," I whispered back.

"What's it doing all the way out here?"

"Following his friend," said Dupont. "Mustermann."

"A German bomber bombing a German car?" Marcus stammered. "Why?"

I turned my head toward him. Even now, he resisted the truth.

"Maybe Mustermann wasn't lying about risking their lives to meet with us," I said.

Marcus's back straightened. A wave of varying emotions cycled through his expression. He had tried so hard to fit the facts into another narrative. He didn't want to believe Earnst or Lina. He didn't want to accept that the bloodiest conflict in modern history was enough to dislodge magic from its hiding places.

Another blast rattled the ground, sending vibrations through my ribcage. I had seen larger bombs, bombs intended to topple hangars or factories. But our destructive tools had come so far since the first airborne explosives, and even smaller bombs like this one, meant to incapacitate a vehicle or a tank, made its mark.

"Where is Lufbery?" Dupont asked.

"Where do you think?" Marcus replied, motioning to the heavens. With a quick glance to the sky, we saw the major's Nieuport circle upward, gaining altitude to engage the bomber. The gap between them would close quickly. Already, the German pilot had altered his bombing pattern to take note of the sudden French fighter materializing from the hills.

The tactics changed quickly. The German pilot tried to flank the major, using its gunners to spray strafing fire across the wings, but the Nieuport outmatched the plane one on one. Bombers were designed to hold off enemy pursuit planes, not engage them in a dogfight. Usually, they had an escort. I wondered what must have happened to the other planes that accompanied this Gotha. The thought chilled me. Perhaps they were still nearby.

Lufbery climbed high before twisting into a steep dive. My breath caught while I watched. I'd worked on planes for a year now. I mended the problems. Patched the holes. Strengthened the joints. But I'd never been in the air, and though I'd seen sorties when they were close enough to base, to have a front row seat to see my handiwork in action humbled me beyond measure.

The Nieuport pulled up and righted itself, taking a dangerous position below the bomber and away from the topside gunner. But as Lufbery took aim, a burst of machine gun fire reigned out of the bomber's underside, and he banked wildly off course.

"The trapdoor," Marcus muttered. "Bringing down a bomber used to be simple. Get below it and shoot through its underbelly.

Now, they're putting gunned trapdoors in the bottom. They'll be nothing but flying fortresses next."

His voice was terse, and I could tell he fought back his overwhelming nerves. I did the same whenever Marcus went in the air. The rest of us sat frozen in place, holding a collective breath. Not only did I fear for Lufbery's life, but our own as well—not to mention anything about the three Germans in the car being targeted by their own military. If he could not take down the bomber, there was no telling what it might do to the house, the cars... we'd be stranded at best.

Lufbery circled upward, barreling and sliding. More machine gun fire blazed from the Bomber, two guns lighting up at once from the rear as both of the bomber's gunners swiveled wildly to line up their quarry. The Major passed by the nose of the plane, putting the superior maneuverability of the Nieuport on display, but the pilot lit up the front guns as well.

A cold feeling crept up the back of my neck.

"Is there no weak angle?" I asked.

"Up," Marcus replied. "The weak angle is up."

As if in sync with Marcus's comment, Lufbery climbed higher in altitude. The guns on the Gotha roared in pursuit. Its pilot tried to give them a broadside opportunity. My fingernails dug deeply into my palms as I watched the upward circling climb, fearing each rattle of machine gun round might be the last.

"Why won't he fire back?" I asked.

"He's not yet desperate," Marcus said. "That's the winning strategy. Boelcke used it. Richtofen. It's come through our ranks as well. 'Don't fire until you know you have a shot.' Worst thing that can happen to you is to run out of ammunition in the middle of a fight."

Suddenly, the depth of sound changed. Amidst the roar of vacillating machine gun volleys, a piece of the sonorous buzzing went silent. I gasped as Lufbery's plane stopped its climb and slid sideways, its tail swinging unnaturally to the right and spinning.

His plane twirled and dropped. The machine guns sputtered and stopped as the gunners watched the Nieuport fall. My heart fell with it. Lufbery's plane spun round and round, as if someone had stuck a pole through the middle and blown on the wings like a pinwheel.

"Well, I'll be," Smith cursed quietly. I glanced over. He looked through the binoculars from behind a pair of aviator goggles: Boelcke's goggles. I turned back, hardly noticing, consumed by the apparent doom that rushed to greet my friend. There was nothing I could do but watch him plummet.

"Now's your chance, Whiskey," Smith said again.

The buzzing of the Nieuport's engine hummed back to life, and Lufbery stopped spinning, pushing the plane down into a dive, half-looping upward, and spiraling just below the tail wing of the bomber.

He was dangerously close. No gunner could miss at that range. I expected fire from that underbelly tunnel, but the world paused in the discordant harmonies of the dissonant engines, a moment suspended on a line that might rebound or snap.

Then it was awful.

Lufbery perked up his nose and let loose a loud, air-ripping volley from his double Vickers, and he didn't let off. The bomber dipped. He fired. The bomber slid. He fired.

He fired and fired until the fuselage of the great Gotha burst into flame. The German plane came down like a stone from the air. Its wings had been riddled with holes, its struts splintered, and the great weight of such a machine reached for the gravity of Earth like a child for its mother.

"He got him!" Marcus shouted. "That's Lufbery! Major Raoul Lufbery! There's no better pilot! What a maneuver. They can't teach that!"

"That's a thing of beauty," Smith said, his eyes tracing the falling wreckage of flame.

Marcus hollered in victory. I blinked. Tears had pooled in my eyes, but I wasn't sure which of my emotions caused them. Fear. Relief. Pride. Sorrow. Could such clumsy words ever do justice to the multi-dimensional spectrum of what I experienced?

But though Atkins and Dupont clapped one another on the shoulders with broad smiles, the relief perished prematurely. The falling Gotha was headed in our direction. From within its belly, explosions sounded, the fire setting off the vestiges of the bombs it carried.

"Deeper!" Dupont called. We followed him, tripping and stumbling over roots and fallen limbs, but within moments, he had found a massive trunk lying on its side. We burrowed down beneath it, just as a devastating blow came into contact with the ground. Around us, through the canopy, bits of shrapnel, pieces of wood and burning canvas, rained down and a cloud of dust over-came us.

My hands shook. I tried to calm them, to grab on to something, but they trembled violently. Behind closed eyelids, visions of home flooded my mind—the taste of my father's fish and chips, my moth-er's snorting laugh, kisses stolen and given, dances...

I wanted nothing more than to be home.

A gentle hand on the back of my neck roused me from the pain of this nostalgia.

"Jane. Jane, are you all right?"

I opened my eyes and uncovered my ears. Marcus's eyes searched mine. They were warm and handsome, so unlike many soldiers' eyes. Between the irises hope still shone. Somewhere inside of him, it lived, and like a torch, it spread to my heart, reigniting the courage that had gone dark there.

"I'm fine," I replied. My hands still shook, but the tremors slowly waned. The fear dissipated. We would soldier on.

"Is everyone in one piece?" Smith called out.

Dupont stumbled to his feet.

"Oh no," he muttered before bolting through the trees toward the wreckage, his pistol drawn.

"Dupont, get back here!" Smith yelled. When Dupont ignored him, he snorted. "The French and their passionate, good-for-nothing..."

"I'm on him," Atkins said and gave chase. Smith shook his head. He looked at Marcus and me.

"This complicates things," he said. Marcus narrowed his eyes.

"Are those Boelcke's goggles?" he asked.

Smith nodded and took them off.

"Convinced Mustermann to leave them here as a sign of good faith." Smith's eyes glossed with a peculiar sheen. He laughed to himself and whispered. "I'll be damned, but they work."

I stared, grasping now for the first time the importance of Smith's experiment.

"You watched the fight through the goggles?" I asked.

"Hardly thought to grab them when the bomber showed up, but I'm sure glad I did."

Marcus squirmed beside me.

"What do you mean they work?" he asked, a trace of anger on the edge of his voice.

"I mean that while Private Whiskey pulled his risky spiral, it just so happened to coincide with the German's bottom gun jamming."

"How do you know?" Marcus stammered.

But we all knew, at least after the fact. The bloated pause before Lufbery opened fire—a gun jam would explain it. A flash of sympathy for the pilots raced through me. How they must have panicked when they realized...

"It's just like Mustermann said," Smith replied, tossing the goggles brusquely to Marcus. "There's something inside of you that goes off. And as you believe it, the plane gets a bit of a glow to it. Like the glow of a Christmas tree from down the hall after too many drinks. Hazy like, almost blurry. It's like you could swear someone was shining a blue flashlight on the jammed gun."

I turned to Marcus. Part of me wanted to flaunt how I'd been right, that the magic was real, but the danger of the immediate situation cut the wind from my sails. Instead, I hoped he would at least see reason. He saw red.

"Luf downed that plane because he's the best pilot we have."

Smith raised his eyebrows.

"Best American pilot, you mean."

"Best Allied pilot."

"Not by the numbers," Smith said flatly.

"Then forget the numbers," Marcus spat back, his voice raising.

I furrowed my brow.

"Marcus, you have to start believing. Why else would the Germans send a bomber after Mustermann if not to keep him quiet? These goggles are important. This mission is important. They must be on to something."

"On to what?" Marcus asked. He shook his head "What? Blue flyers and special goggles? Smith, what if this is all part of a larger cup and ball routine? If I were Ludendorff, one of my top priorities would be finding a way to make the other Allied commanders lose faith in General Pershing. Isn't this type of goose chase exactly the thing to accomplish that?"

"You think the Germans would sacrifice a Gotha in a show of pageantry? Have you lost your mind?" I asked incredulously.

"I appreciate the point you're trying to make, Marcus. But like it or not, she's right." He looked at the goggles with a faraway frown. "It's too many validations. I don't know if those goggles are some kind of military innovation or if they're the product of some devious enchantment or what, but they worked for me just now.

Could it be that the Gotha had some type of technology synched up with these goggles to show me what I expected to see? Maybe. But that's not technology our government has any idea how to replicate."

"But, sir—"

Sharp shouts from Dupont and Atkins cut short our conversation. Calls for help mixed with rudimentary commands in German.

"This day keeps getting better," Smith said as he peered through the trees toward the wreckage. "The pilot survived."

We sprang forward, pulled on by morbid curiosity and dreadful expectation. It didn't take us long to arrive at the crash site. Atkins stared down the sights of his sidearm while Dupont dragged the wounded pilot from the remains of the Gotha cockpit.

No one wanted to stay close for long. Parts of the wreckage were still ablaze, and there was no telling if explosive shells lay hidden, yet to detonate inside.

"The gunners?" Smith asked.

"Certainly dead," Atkins replied with a cold nod of his head toward the back of the wreckage.

"We'll take this one inside," Dupont said. He had yanked the German free. The pilot had a young face, marred by expressions of intense pain painted with ash. A cursory glance explained why. His leg bled profusely and part of his flight suit had burned away. His blonde hair was singed through holes of his flight cap, and the top of his ear blistered...

But bringing him inside proved more difficult than expected. A portion of the Gotha's engine had separated during its descent and rolled through the front of the farmhouse. The building's western wing had also crumbled. The explosions must have compromised the integrity of the roof's architecture, and the impact of the engine toppled the whole thing over.

Our cars looked a bit worse for the wear, as well. I prayed the damage was mostly cosmetic. There were dents on the hood, and the seats had been torn. I didn't want to end up stranded.

As Dupont manhandled the German, dragging him to the remains of the farmhouse, a sickly nausea bubbled in my stomach.

"Lieutenant Atkins," I called. He jerked his head in my direction to signal he was listening but didn't falter in his aim of the pistol. "What are you planning to do to him."

The side of Atkins's mustache twitched, and he paused.

"Ask him questions."

"Lieutenant, he's injured. He's not likely to—"

"It may be best if you stay out here, Private Doe." Atkins nodded grimly and cleared his throat. Necessary evils. I'd heard the phrase so many times. Raids. Prisoners. Justifications. Before I could protest any more, Atkins entered the building behind Dupont.

My heart beat faster, faster and faster, picking up speed like the Gotha as it fell to the earth. I turned my appeal toward Smith.

"Sergeant," I pleaded. "We cannot be monsters. Please. At the very least, give this man a chance to speak up and save himself the pain of—"

"Oh, don't worry, Private." Smith waved me off. "I don't consider torture to be very Christian, nor do I think it very effective. I'll tell ya, I had a brother once put me in a painful full-nelson, the way only brothers can, and I think I'd have said just about anything to get out of that. Funny thing, don't you think?"

His nonchalance infuriated me, but I could not scold him for seeing things my way. Here was America, come to the war late with an attitude of cold superiority and emotional detachment. God bless them for it.

Amidst the sound of the crackling flames, we didn't even notice Mustermann's car pulling up the gravel drive. He was out of the driver's seat in a moment. Behind him, Earnst helped a white-faced Lina from the seat. She kept motioning to her ears.

"Remarkable flying," Mustermann said. "Where is the marvelous pilot so I might thank him? Between the machine gun fire and the bombs, I don't think we would have lasted the straightaway."

The relief was palpable in his posture. A nervous smile danced on his flushed face.

"Mustermann, perfect timing," Smith said. "The bomber pilot survived."

The three Germans stopped where they were. The smile from Mustermann's smile fell in a heartbeat. Earnst looked at Marcus, but my friend buried his gaze in the dirt.

"The pilot survived a crash like that?" Earnst asked.

Smith whistled.

"A crash like that. Now, who wants to be our interpreter?"

Chapter 11
A Shot in the Dark
Marcus

Red fangs have torn His face.
God's blood is shed.
He mourns from His lone place
His children dead.
-Isaac Rosenberg-

The pilot's name was Johann, and it took some convincing to get him to talk.

Mustermann put on quite the display in shouting at him in German, gesticulating wildly, invading his space. Johann struggled to concentrate through the pain in his leg. A metal splinter had pierced his shin and jutted out his back calf. We'd done our best at cobbling together some field treatment, but all of us watched and waited for signs of infection. Between his burns and the puncture wound, it might only be a matter of time before we lost him.

Jane and Lina had run into the woods together to search for herbal treatments to help him manage the pain, and if I suspected correctly, to loosen his lips. We all wanted answers, and the irony

of the situation weighed on us. We had to question a German prisoner through a German interpreter, and if they were aligned, we
couldn't trust anything either of them said.

Fortunately, Dupont seemed to understand enough German
to recognize if the translation was too far from the truth. We kept
our questions simple with yes and no answers. Mustermann didn't
have enough time to get Dupont lost in a complicated sentence.

We had Johann propped up against a wall, his legs stretched
out on the ground below him.

"Did you know Germans were in the car you attacked?"

"Yes."

"Were you under orders to kill them?"

"Yes."

"Does German High Command believe there is group of
defectors in its military?"

"Yes."

When we had exhausted the simple questions, we had no
choice but to trust the old German's translation. Earnst, though,
had a hard time keeping his emotions in check, and Atkins and I
had to remove him from the room before questioning could
continue on more than one occasion.

After Jane and Lina applied their presses and wraps with
dubious combinations of wildflowers, weeds, and who-knew-what-
else they'd gathered from the forest, Smith relegated both of them
to the kitchen, where thankfully, a very shaken Annette had
survived the bombing.

The poor thing was shaking like an autumn leaf all curled up
in the stone larder. Lina and Jane helped her calm her nerves by
asking for instructions on how to prepare a simple meal for the
party.

At first, Johann spoke quietly, reluctantly, but whether he
understood his survival lay in the hands of his questioners or Jane's
healing witch brew kicked in, his tongue loosened.

He had received special assignment to fly over enemy lines to bomb the city of Nancy to disrupt a meeting between rogue German statesmen and enemy contacts. But on an information gathering trip the night before, a German recon plane had spotted a car described by German Secret Police at this farmhouse. The target shifted from Nancy to this building.

On the way over, the bomber's escort had been engaged and dismantled by French forces and ground fire, but somehow, the big Gotha made it through. In unfamiliar territory, it flew first to Nancy, and then followed the cardinal directions from German intelligence. As it so happened, they picked up the trail right as Mustermann, Earnst, and Lina made their way back. Johann figured he had the firepower to destroy the car and the farmhouse.

"But how were you sure it was the right car?" Atkins asked.

"It fit the description," Johann said, then smirked. "Besides, the French don't drive like Germans. If you know the difference, you can tell."

The women interrupted us then with a simple dish of fried potatoes, served on broken half plates. We ate in silence before having Annette sit down with a gun across the room from Johann. From the look on her face, I had no doubt she'd use it if necessary. Lina stayed with her, complaining of a migraine. The rest of us took a step outside to deliberate, but Dupont kept a watchful eye on the room through a broken window. The sun had dipped behind its battlements, and in the dark, the air grew colder.

"Allow me to apologize," Mustermann said. "I put you all in great danger."

Earnst paid only half attention, one eye on the window to ensure his wife was all right. The rest of us were tired from an emotionally overwhelming day.

"We knew the risks," Atkins said. "You put yourself in grave danger, as well."

There was something in Atkins' eyes, something I recognized

from Jane's expression, a softness and a sense of respect. He believed Mustermann, perhaps even admired him. I cast a sideways glance at Luf, who worked a cigarette a step behind the rest of us, bundled up in his flight coat. He hadn't had the time to don it before engaging the bomber earlier that day, and he came back freezing. The remains of the bomber had mostly burned out, but portions of the wreckage still radiated heat near where he stood.

"If it were not for the bravery of your pilot, I fear German Command would have had their wish. But I hope this shows you just how important our task is. Ludendorff does not want us cooperating. He does not want us to find these rogue pilots. He wants the war to continue. He believes that Germany can still outlast its enemies."

Smith clicked loudly in his cheek, but he betrayed no sign of assent.

"What do we do with the pilot?" Dupont asked.

"Well, seems like we got a bunch of good answers from him," said Smith. He nudged a small piece of debris with his foot. "If possible, I think we should take him back with us. If he remains cooperative, he could be particularly useful to the American offensive."

Mustermann stiffened.

"He will need proper medical attention, as well," said Jane.

"You mean your magical remedies can't stitch him up?" I asked, chiding her, eager for some form of levity after so much dread.

"Marcus, now's not the time. If infection sets, he won't last long."

"Do you think it's wise to bring him back with you?" Mustermann said, nervously shifting on his feet. "After all, you've attempted to keep this meeting and this mission confidential. This pilot has now seen much and might compromise that secrecy."

"You know, Muster," Smith folded his arms, "if I didn't know better, I'd think you were suggesting that we just let the boy die from his wounds. But I know that can't be true."

"No," the German replied, folding his hands sheepishly. "I am not suggesting that."

"Good," said Smith. "Atkins? Dupont? You agree? Bring him back, fix him up, and see what other intelligence he can provide?"

They both nodded stoically. Apprehension turned as a knife in my stomach. They made the decision so casually. They spoke about Johann the same way a group of people might decide what to eat for lunch. Potatoes, tinned ham, and should we let Johann live?

As we had questioned him, I couldn't help but humanize the bomber pilot. In the way he spoke about his orders, the maneuvers of his plan, the pain of loss over his fallen companions... I saw some of myself in him. Had we not both trained to take to the sky? Had we not both respected and marveled at the deadly paint strokes of tracer fire streaking through the clouds or the artistic dance of an aircraft looping and turning and spiraling.

Did Johann also get letters from home he didn't like opening?

Did Johann worry about his number?

I glanced again at Luf. He had performed magnificently today, all but wrote a poem in the air. A quick punchy bit of verse that leaves you savoring the rhyme. But he didn't smile. No euphoric glow or adrenal rush animated his features. He stared, vacantly, at a small pile of burning embers, marking the smoke as it floated into the air and vanished.

"Very well," said Mustermann. "We will take the strategic approach, then. I hope that this experience has strengthened your resolve to cooperate with us. Gentlemen, have you come to a decision?"

Atkins, Dupont, Mustermann, Earnst, Jane, and Luf all turned to Smith, but he turned to me. His gaze penetrated my conscience with a single question.

Could he rely on me to protect Jane and see this through?

I didn't know what to say. Our conversation earlier had culled my doubts about Mustermann's sincerity, but I wasn't Luf. He had scored a kill today that would never be recorded, never confirmed. That didn't bother him, but it bothered me. Heroism thrives in the sunlight. Public accountability and adoration of bravery was not something shameful. It was fuel. Even Luf could appreciate the public support of his endeavors. Sure, not all of his downed planes were confirmed, but enough were.

But me?

In my mind, I was back on that train, leaving my parents behind, off to find something to write home about. And I still hadn't found it. I wondered what the conversations must have been like for my father, who could boast that his son took part in the Lafayette Escadrille, but primarily as a machinist and only briefly as scoreless pilot. A spectator. And I imagined how his peers and betters would at first perk their ears and then summarily dismiss their interest.

My mind wandered into the forbidden corners of my memory —back to that night I had not shot a German when I should have. Back to the consequences of that failure...

I needed recognition. I needed redemption. It burned my throat to admit it, but I needed something to bring back with me, or else I could never go back at all.

"Marcus, please," Jane said, taking a step forward. I started, protests spewing from my lungs, but none of them got airborne. Jane stood like a warrior amidst the rest of them. Her bravery shone like a beacon in the dark. She looked at me, and with a flash of her eyes, somehow my fear gave way. Somehow, I took a step forward and planted my feet beside hers.

Somehow I could put what I needed on hold.

Maybe, if Jane was sure, that was enough for me. Maybe, I didn't need to believe in magic. I just needed to believe in her.

"Sergeant Dewar?" Smith asked. "You think the US Army Air Service should devote their time and resources to this joint operation?"

I glanced about and saw Luf. He nodded subtly, helping me to the finish line.

"Someone needs to investigate," I replied.

"And you're aware that you will need to keep all mission information completely secret except as instructed by me personally?"

I nodded, haltingly, and that was that. Smith closed the gap between us and shook my hand.

"The United States thanks you for what you're about to do," Smith said, the warmest I'd heard his voice since meeting him. His crisp posture cracked. A sadness tinged his eyes, but only for a moment. "Mustermann, what do you propose our next steps are?"

"Our latest reports of the Rogue Flyers come from the north, near Dunkirk," he said. "I suggest they start the search there."

"We've had similar reports," Atkins said. "We can put them in contact with a captain stationed there who reported the latest sighting. God willing, nothing happens to him before you can get there. The town has undergone significant naval bombardment."

"In the meantime, Earnst and Lina will investigate some of the leads reported by a few Jastas on our side of the line."

"Where?" Dupont asked.

Mustermann stared at him.

"If we're working together, we're sharing information," Dupont said. "Where?"

"Near Brussels."

"Very well," Dupont said. "Atkins and I can run communications. We will prepare a cipher by morning. You will deliver information on the dates we tell you, by the methods we tell you, at the places we tell you."

"It will have to be a rudimentary code, but if needed we can change it periodically," said Atkins. "With any luck, you can track down these rogues within the week."

"Happy hunting. We'll reconvene in the morning. In the meantime, I'll see what can be done about these cars so we can get little Johann to one of our hospitals," said Smith.

Everyone nodded and, understanding the dismissal, dispersed.

"I'm proud of you," Jane said. I ignored her and called after Smith.

"And what do we do exactly if we find one of those planes?" I asked.

He turned and smiled.

"Follow it home," he said. "Or, if that's not possible, shoot it down."

A gunshot woke me in the middle of the night. Instinct took over, and I had my gun in my hand before I'd even rolled out of bed. The men were all sleeping in the same room, removed from Johann and his painful moans. His condition had not improved, but until the cars were repaired, we had no option but to sit tight and do our best. We had taken to shifts watching him.

But the crack of the gun jarred all of us awake with a start. Almost all of us. Who was missing?

Luf looked across the dark room at me and answered my unspoken question.

"Dupont. It's his watch."

We stumbled to the living room. Jane, Lina, and Annette waited at the opposite door stemming the hallway to their rooms.

On the table lay a smoking Star pistol. French issue.

Johann had a gunshot wound to his chest. His eyes were vacant. Gone.

Beside him stood Mustermann. Dupont sat at the table.

The gruesome shock of the situation numbed me, silenced me. Annette took one look, crossed herself and disappeared back into the hall.

"Why?" I managed to choke out. I addressed the question to Dupont—it was his weapon on the table—but Mustermann answered.

"It was not Dupont."

His answer made the scene worse, more nightmarishly wrong. I wished I could scrub the sight from my eyes. It was too familiar, dragging me back to the muddy horrors of the ambulance rides. We had tended to the pilot, given him food. We were going to take him to a hospital. He might have lived.

"Your own countryman?" I gasped. Mustermann's gaze was hard and unmoving. The creases in his face etched with deep shadows cast by the single candle in the room.

"I cannot blame you for your desire to prolong this soldier's life," he said. "You were right, I'm sure. If your officers loosened his tongue, the information he carries might be helpful in your war effort. You may consider my actions as a means of safeguarding German military intelligence. But you would be wrong.

"Dupont or Atkins may correct me if I'm mistaken, but in the past several years, there have been countless raids yielding countless war prisoners, all questioned for vital information. Has any of that intelligence ended the war?

"This pilot, if left alive might jeopardize our joint mission, the first mission of its kind, involving cooperation between Germany, the United States, France, and Great Britain. My life and the life of many others who support my cause would be forfeit if such news surfaced. Secrecy is our most valuable weapon, and it comes at great cost."

I struggled to keep my composure. Mustermann argued with cold, unfeeling logic while the life of a young pilot who had put everything on the line to serve his country seeped out the hole in his chest. A searing surge of adrenaline lingered at the back of my throat, a sensation I considered sacred, reserved for fallen friends. It was not for German pilots. And yet...

I glanced around the room. The others stared with similar shock and disgust. Jane's face contorted, frozen into a no-man's land between sobs and righteous anger.

Even Smith—Smith with the steely cool of a United States bravo—furrowed deep creases between his brows and the corners of his frown.

"Even if you don't like it, you must see my reasoning," Mustermann insisted. "Need I remind you that there were three Germans in the plane your pilot shot down, and your feelings are not kindled against him."

"That's because there are rules to this," I said, seething and ready to defend my friend. Luf didn't budge from his space in the doorway. "And when they went into the air, they knew what those rules were. Shooting a defenseless, wounded prisoner in the middle of the night is not the same as besting an enemy pilot in aerial combat."

It couldn't be the same. If it were the same, I was a coward. Honor had to to distinguish between kills, or else...

Mustermann folded his hands behind his back, and a sad smile tugged at his cheeks.

"Not every war can be fought by putting on a uniform so the other team knows where to shoot. I do what I must so that one day, Germany might not be ruled by the whims of a Kaiser and his friends."

His meaning haunted me. A kill was a kill, whether it happened in a dark room or the brilliantly bright sky. I'd seen too many men dying in trucks to deny it. I'd been chasing my first victory all this time, but I knew what pulling the trigger would mean.

How had so many men pulled the trigger? Hundreds of thousands of choices.

Smith drew his sidearm.

"Will you shoot me now," Mustermann asked, "to avenge the life of a single German pilot?" He stood like a phantom, looming and ethereal.

"Not for vengeance," Smith replied. "But you took things into your own hands, went over our heads, and propose that we still do business together. Where I'm from, we call that a liability. Might be easier to investigate these rogue flyers on our own."

"You might have an easier time, but consider what you risk. Blueglow Pilots. Magical curiosities. If more items like Boelcke's goggles fall into the hands of German High Command, it will pose problems for your military efforts. Insurmountable? Perhaps not. But problems all the same. No. Sergeant, you know as well as I, our efforts must coalesce."

Smith stared down the sights of his gun. I struggled to breathe. How could that candle burn? There was no oxygen in the room. One gun drawn. One lying on the table. Mine in my hand by my side. Atkins a hand on his holster.

But it was Jane, Jane who likely hadn't even considered her own weapon, who broke the stalemate. She placed a hand gently on Smith's arm.

"He's right," she said, and I couldn't believe what I heard. "You used the goggles. You cannot disbelieve."

Slowly, Smith lowered his gun, but he looked like he could spit right in Mustermann's face.

"Here's a little tip for that German freedom you're after," said Smith. "If a country can justify killing its own, that ain't freedom."

He holstered the Colt and grunted.

"You shot him. You bury him. Dupont will keep an eye on you while you do it. And Dupont," the Frenchman lifted his tortured gaze, "Atkins will hold on to your gun while you do it. I'm going back to bed."

Smith turned and left, but the rest of us did not entertain any illusion of getting more sleep.

Instead, we all retreated to different corners of the damaged house. I followed Jane back to the room she shared with Lina. The German couple beat us there, huddling together, Earnst trying futilely to comfort his wife. Silent tears streaked down the woman's face.

We gave them space to grieve. Was grieve the right word? How would I have felt if an American plane had been sent to kill me, only to watch the pilot be murdered later?

"The poor girl," Jane said glancing over at her.

"She's had a fright all right. You think they're angry at what Mustermann did?"

"Of course, Marcus. It'd be inhuman to feel otherwise."

"Even though Johann flew the plane that tried to kill them?"

She stared at me hard, and in the cramped hallway, I had nowhere to hide from it.

"Human life is sacred. It's magic. To have it violated in such a way..." She trailed off and exhaled. The incident had me so rattled that I'd hardly noticed how much it agitated Jane. She had not seen war the way I had. Perhaps the aftermath in hospitals, and there was no shortage of horror in the hospitals. But the violence of it—there was something about Johann's killing that shattered reality.

She held up one of her hands.

"Look at me, I'm shaking like a leaf."

Gently, I steadied it with my own. Her skin was like ice.

"From the cold or the nerves?" I asked.

"Who can say for sure? The new holes in the house have let a draft into our room. Perhaps the window has been forced ajar."

"I'll go see if I can find some extra blankets."

She nodded, and I turned to leave.

"Marcus," she stopped me, "thank you for coming with me. On the mission, I mean."

"You still want to go?" I asked. She nodded.

"It seems even more important now, somehow."

I agreed. Mustermann had demonstrated beyond a shadow of a doubt just how much he believed in what he was talking about. He was either right or completely crazy. But seeing Smith's conversion in real time after he'd worn the goggles did much to convince me that maybe there was more to this than met the eye.

Maybe I didn't believe there was an assortment of magical devices out there that could turn the tide of the war, but if there were, we'd find them. And we'd do it before some autodidact crackpot pilot squadron.

"I'll get those blankets."

Chapter 12
In American Hands
Jane

I feel the spring far off, far off,
The faint, far scent of bud and leaf—
Oh, how can spring take heart to come
To a world in grief,
Deep grief?
-Sara Teasdale-

T he sun didn't rise for hours, and my emotions shifted with the hand of the clock. Every time I closed my eyes, Mustermann's face flashed across the dark of my mind. Beside him lay Johann, bloody and lifeless. And adding to the haunting visage was the real trauma shown by the people in that room, the reactions to such an unapologetic violation of natural magic.

Lina most of all.

I had tried talking with her before we'd gone to bed. Simple questions, really. I asked how her life had changed since Earnst had gone to war. I wondered if she had children or other family in

Germany. She replied curtly and without much warmth, but who could blame her? Eventually, I surrendered and left her to sleep.

Then came Johann's murder. And then, Smith nearly repeated the same.

Aunt Luella had warned me about this once when I'd been precocious enough to ask. I must have been fifteen at the time. "Please, explain the magic of murder," I'd asked. She took me first to the cemetery, then to the poor house, then to the prisons, and explained it in great detail.

Some magic was so powerful, it could not be ignored without great evil. Killing was one such magic. Our race had set up systems offering sacrifices on the altar of justice to appease this magic. But the sacrifice was not always accepted, and the magic sought balance of its own accord.

For what justice is there to make up for the loss of life? There is no currency to pay such a bill. There isn't uniformity in the debt.

When morning finally came, we emerged from the mockery of sleep we attempted. The front room was empty. Where Johann lay, someone had moved a piece of furniture to cover the stains. In place of a person, sat a settee, a pathetic attempt to erase from our minds what had transpired on that spot. My memory and imagination had enough power to transform the wood and hinges into the young pilot's face and body.

Somehow, Annette found it in her to prepare a light breakfast, but I had no appetite for it. Atkins picked politely at the bread left from the morning before. But apart from him, Smith was the only one to touch the food. He ate not only a croissant, cheese, and coffee, but a good portion of what had been laid out for the rest of us.

When he had finished, he thanked Annette and Dupont for the hospitality. Marcus gaped at him in disgust.

"You're not hungry?" Smith asked. Marcus's scowl intensified, and Smith sighed. "Sergeant, I'm not an idiot. I understand my nourishment comes across as unfeeling. But we are at war. You don't know what may come at you later. There is no guarantee when another meal is coming. And if your body doesn't have the strength to fight, you can't do anything to stop bad men."

He promptly stood.

"Sergeant, Private," he nodded to Marcus and me, "if you're done with breakfast, make yourself useful and go check to see if the car is working. Dupont said he fixed it, and I want to leave within the hour."

I glanced at Atkins. He anxiously studied the bottom of his teacup.

"You mean I'll depart with you directly? This mission starts now?" I asked. Marcus's small smile warmed me from the corner of my eye.

"You've been helping out the 94th for a long time now. You comfortable in American hands?" Smith asked.

Despite the sombre mood, Dupont snorted. Atkins rolled his eyes, ostensibly regretting whatever agreement he had struck with Smith. I studied the American, trying to ascertain any tell that might signify if he was having a go at me. But Smith wore his expressions flatly, and there was no trace of the self-satisfied grin that men use when witticizing the female form. Still, if he was going to leave me an opening, I was in no mood to have my gender flaunted.

"True American hands could check their own car," I said before grabbing Marcus by the arm and exiting the house.

The sun had just tipped its crown over the eastward mountains, pulling back the cold shroud of dark that gave cover to the night's dark deeds. We stopped on our way to the car when we noticed Earnst, Lina, and Mustermann standing by the Gotha wreckage. Quietly, we joined them. Three rough mounds of earth rested between the remains of the cockpit and the tree line. Mustermann's shirt was drenched with effort. The skin around his eyes drooped, revealing the weight of his age.

He had sounded so resolute when he defended himself the night before. But the sorrow inhibiting his posture, the solemnity with which he had dug these graves betrayed some interior conflict he had buried even deeper within himself.

I put a hand on Lina's shoulder.

"I'm not sure if condolences are appropriate, but I appreciate how difficult your emotions may be at present," I said.

Lina did not acknowledge my touch, nor did she look at me.

"They tried to kill us," she murmured. "But they are soldiers. That is what they are told to do. They don't remember what it's like not to do it."

Mustermann lumbered over to me, evidently wishing to address us, but I wasn't ready to speak with him, not after what he'd done. I couldn't fault the man's logic in deciding Johann had to die. But I wasn't ready to face someone who could follow logic to such a place.

When Mustermann was close enough to hear me without raising my voice, I addressed him, "Whatever you have to say, tell Smith." Then, I quickly turned on my heel and went to the cars. Marcus lingered behind.

Dupont was not incompetent as a mechanic, and the car's engine turned over without problem. Though, on quick inspection, I suspected the alignment of the wheels might increase the difficulty of steering, the car functioned without serious issue. I slid into the driver's seat and brought the car near the front door. The gear box and breaks seemed to be working fine. We were fortunate the Gotha had landed where it did, though I suppose the owner of the farmhouse wouldn't share that optimism.

If they were still alive.

I let my head rest on the steering wheel and took a steadying breath. I had spent so much of my resolve modeling confidence in our proposed mission for Marcus that I hadn't given myself a moment to appreciate what lay in front of me.

My entire life, my parents had so cautiously spoken about magic. They'd insisted Luella teach me as if it were my attendance at a finishing school. We began in my teenage years. When the war broke out, our studies intensified.

But though she insisted that the methods were genuine, I had never seen magic—not undeniable magic. Yes, I'd coaxed step ladders to perform better and applied what I'd learned to plane repairs. Yes, I wore the glass marble around my neck.

But that was simple magic, the kind that was easily dismissed by coincidence or conjecture.

When the Germans had shared what they knew about Boelcke's goggles, it resonated in a completely new way. But when Sergeant Smith confirmed their effect, alarm bells rang in my mind. These weren't hopeful combinations of herbs on paradoxical inscriptions written on wing joint bindings. It was real magic, magic with convincing power, magic that could not be denied. The kind Aunt Luella always told me about.

The idea that such magic might fall into the hands of German High Command terrified me.

"You sure you're ready for this?"

The smell of cigarette smoke and the presence of one hand on the car door called my attention. I looked up into Lufbery's friendly countenance.

"Frankly, no." My shoulders slumped, and I leaned back into the driver's seat.

"Good," he replied. "You're never completely ready. It's better that you walk into something knowing you're underprepared."

"Do you believe in the magic, Major Lufbery?"

He squinted at me.

"I've seen a lot of things in the past few years. I'm not sure what to call them."

"What if we fail?" I asked.

"You won't. You may die, but you won't fail. I know you, and I know Marcus. We'll miss you both at the 94th. But I'm glad to see you throwing your hat in the ring. You'll take care of him for me, won't you? His head kind of gets in the clouds from time to time."

I smirked.

"He's a pilot. His head's always in the clouds."

"He's not just any pilot," Lufbery replied. "I don't know much about that witchy stuff you're going on about, but I must remind you that Marcus has something special. If you can preserve that, there might be magic in it."

I bit my lip.

"How am I to preserve his innocence on a mission like this?" I asked.

"It might not be possible. But as a friend, I have to ask you to try." He threw the butt of his cigarette into the dirt. It was an impossible and unfair request.

"Oh," he added as an afterthought, "one other thing before we get going. You ever flown before?"

I shook my head.

"Well, then make sure Marcus shows you some of the maneuvers before the Bosch come shooting at you. It can be disorienting the first few times."

I blinked.

"I'm sorry. You mean if I actually fly in a plane?"

"Sergeant, let's get moving!" Smith called to Marcus as he exited the front door and crossed to the car. "Private Doe, glad to see she's still in working order. Private Whiskey, don't you have a plane to fly?"

Lufbery gave the side of the door a pat.

"You'll do great," he whispered.

"Major. Wait, I have questions!" I called after him as he walked away. I don't know why the thought hadn't yet occurred to me that I might need to accompany Marcus in an aircraft. Perhaps because women simply didn't fly planes for the war effort. Certainly, there were a handful of women who piloted planes in exhibition events or even commercial enterprises. The RAF developed a WRAF not to man (or woman) aircraft but rather to help those who do.

I had spent so much time mending the damage done to those machines that the idea of going up myself was almost paralyzing.

Lufbery didn't turn around, but instead he stopped to share a few last words of advice with Marcus.

"Move on over, Private Doe," Smith said. "I'm sure you're a capable driver, but you don't know where we're going, do you?"

"We're not going back to Croix-de-Metz?"

"Not quite. I don't want your friends back in Gengoult to pepper you with questions, so Dupont has secured an aircraft for you in Gondreville."

I shimmied over into the passenger seat. My oversized jacket caught awkwardly on the gear shaft, and I had to push my boots against the footrest and arch my back to get past—a very graceful position to be in.

"Yes. Sergeant, about that aircraft. Is it your intention that I fix Marcus's machines after he runs missions searching for the rogue pilots?"

Smith laughed.

"Absolutely not. You're riding in back. Salmson. Ever fired a gun before, Private?"

I pursed my lips and contemplated the rhetoric of his question. Smith snickered and settled into his seat to wait for Marcus. Meanwhile, Atkins approached with an envelope.

"Right. Melinda—"

"Oh, for heavens' sake, just call me by my given name.

Everyone here knows I'm Jane Turner, and it's not an uncommon name so it will do any lurking German spies in those bushes over there little good anyway." I spat the words furiously. Atkins leaned back in alarm, a genuine grimace of social anxiety. "I'm sorry, Atkins. I just found out I'm going in a plane."

"Quite. You did volunteer for this mission, did you not Private —or rather, Jane?"

"I know. But—" I leaned closer and whispered to hide my comments from Smith. "Do you think I will have to fire a gun?"

Atkins studied my face as though he were unsure if I was attempting a lame joke. When he couldn't decide, he handed me the envelope.

"Your cipher. I made it myself. There are only two copies. This one and..." He patted his coat pocket. "Dupont designed the one for Marcus, and it's different than yours."

"I see."

"Good luck, Jane. I can honestly say that I've never been more impressed by a woman's courage and proficiency. I know you'll come home."

His complimentary candor caught me off-guard, and all I managed was a nod when he saluted me at full attention. Marcus clapped him on the back a moment later and hopped into the car.

"Sorry, you two. Luf had some final advice for me."

"Namely?" I asked.

"Oh, just that if a Hun tries to break on me to be wary of countering with a barrel attack. I agree it's predictable, but at least by then they've got to respond with a vertical maneuver, which, depending on what I'm flying, could be a good thing."

I stared.

"What will I be flying, by the way? Smith, I'm going to get my Nieuport, right?"

"A two-seater. You'll meet her in a couple of hours."

"A two-seater? Who'll be in the other seat? Wait. You don't mean Jane!"

Smith turned the engine over, and before I collected my thoughts, the farmhouse diminished behind us. I glanced back in time to see Atkins's shrinking silhouette, still standing at rigid attention.

Chapter 13
The Salmson
Marcus

There is no book
Or face of dearest look
That I would not turn from now
To go into the unknown
I must enter, and leave, alone,
I know not how.
-Edward Thomas-

T he Salmson 2 was not a bad aircraft. It just wasn't a fighter—especially if you had an untrained gunman, or gunwoman in this case, sitting in the second bay.

We stood with Smith in a hangar at the Gondreville-sur-Moselle Aerodrome, staring at the plane. The grumpy American officer that greeted us, no doubt furious that he'd been made to give up a completely serviceable Salmson, had already stomped off to prepare his squadron for its next reconnaissance mission.

The aerodrome was brand new—in fact, too new. I'd heard about its commission. There were even rumors that the 94th might be relocated here once construction was complete. Instead, the recon boys of the 91st would call it home, but by the look of it, they hadn't finished moving in yet.

Smith and Dupont had little trouble in reneging on one of the squadron's promised Salmsons and reallocating it for our mission. I doubted its pilot had even met the bird yet.

For some reason, that soothed my anxiety. I'd hate to fly another man's plane, let alone steal it from under him, and I wasn't alone. Pilots could be superstitious like that, but when your life depended on how well you could feel every tension in the wings of your machine, who could blame us?

Your time came when your time came. But that time just so happened to be less likely to come when you were in your own machine.

At least Jane and I would be discreet. I'd seen scores and scores of the Salmson 2s in service, and from what I'd overheard, reconnaissance pilots seemed to like it, apart from complaining about how hard it was to hear your gunner because of how far apart the bays sat on the fuselage. But it was armed well. I'd have to adjust to a single Vickers gun on my front, but the second seat enjoyed a swiveling double Lewis gun.

I sized Jane up. I hoped if it came down to it, she'd find it in her to pull a trigger.

Then again, I hoped the same for myself. Who was I to talk about getting trigger-shy? But this mission would be different. My gut whispered that having Jane in the plane might be exactly what my conscience needed to end my curse. Instinctively, I would have to be more protective. It wasn't just me and my honor up there. If something happened to her, what would I do?

Yes, I doubted I'd have any trouble unleashing my gun on any threat up in the blue.

Still, the thought gave me pause.

"I don't know, Smith. You want me to engage a group of mysterious fighters in a recon plane?" I asked.

"Not particularly. I'd prefer it if you, you know, *reconned*, found out where they were based. Then we can send a bomber squadron."

"Yeah, it's just that usually reconnaissance efforts don't rely on finding planes and following them home."

"Then it's a good thing you've got Private Doe here covering your tail. Private, why don't you climb up and try out the guns?"

Jane turned on him, hands in her pockets, as though still bewildered by what she had signed up for. Honestly, I was still as confused as she was, and witnessing Jane climb into the gunner's seat of a Salmson would only convince me further that I was, in fact, dreaming.

But when Smith stared her down, Jane sauntered behind the wings, climbed up and settled into her seat.

"It looks like a natural fit," Smith called. "Why don't you try hoisting the gun?"

She awkwardly swiveled the Lewis guns back and forth, as though being forced to try a loathsome vegetable. I holstered a chuckle. I'd always known Jane to be confident, sometimes arrogant, around these machines. But reversing the tables had tinted her green, and she wasn't even in the air yet. The chuckle died on my tongue when I remembered I'd be relying on her to keep German pilots off our back.

"She should be fine. They're only, what? Twenty pounds apiece?" Smith muttered to me.

"Closer to thirty," I hedged. "But I'm sure they'll feel heavier when the pressure of a half loop comes bearing down on her, too."

Smith turned to me with some gravity.

"Remember, Sergeant. You're not in a pursuit plane. Some of the maneuvers you're used to simply won't be available to you.

Plus, if you knock your gunner unconscious from too much smart acrobatics, you'll have disabled one of your greatest strengths."

"I know what I'm doing, sir." I hated the cliché arrogance of my reply. Smith narrowed his brows at me. There was no need to point out that we were all making this up as we went along.

"Will both fire at once?" Jane called to me, a hand on each gun. I closed my eyes. She knew so much about fixing planes. How could she sound so naive about using them?

"We can only hope," Smith called back. "You know how to reload those ammo drums?"

Jane scoffed audibly.

"I've completely disassembled Lewis guns and put them back together many times over. I think I'd know how to reattach a pan magazine."

"Great," said Smith. "Come on, then. Let's bring her out."

"What? You mean right now?" Jane cried.

"No time like the present," Smith replied. "Why don't you get on down and don your flight suit. I think we've got something small enough for you."

Jane shakily climbed from her seat.

"You want us to leave already, Sergeant?" I asked, following Smith to a corner of the hangar where a couple of flight suits lay on a table. "We just got here."

"We're not sitting on this one," he replied. "We've got a report of an overly superstitious pilot particularly attached to one of the trophies he claimed from a recent kill. Might be magic. And if it is, I want you both in place in case that some rogue pilot tries to find him and claim it. The faster we can unravel this knot of intelligence the better. Pershing has big plans for this spring, so you two will go now."

I gaped, trying to invent an argument to stall our takeoff. Smith shrugged.

"I told you to eat that breakfast. Go on. Better use the can while you can."

He tossed me a flight suit. It was heavy, insulated with thick fur and lined with horse leather, but even that wouldn't keep out the chill of the air.

"You've only got a few hours on that thing before you'll need more fuel. Stop at Francheville to fill up, but don't stay long. We'll telegram ahead to tell them to expect you but not to expect answers. Keep to yourselves, but if pressed you can say you're carrying vital information on behalf of the colonel up to Dunkirk to assist with the naval effort."

While he spoke, Jane joined us, awkwardly following my lead and climbing into a flight suit a bit too large for her frame.

"Francheville is not a sleepy airfield. Quick stop. Then, on to Clairmarais. We'll telegram ahead there, too, but they'll need Marcus's cipher to decode the message. Decode it only when alone with Captain Roy Brown."

Jane and I froze, suits falling around our waists over our standard uniform.

"Captain Brown, sir?" I asked.

"Is that a problem, Sergeant?" Smith asked.

"Isn't that the pilot credited with downing Baron Richthofen?"

Smith laughed gently to himself.

"Whiskey was right, you really do have a thing about who takes credit for what, don't you?"

I blushed but persisted.

"That's not just another kill, sir."

Smith leaned against the table.

"You're right. It's the type of kill hundreds of people fight over for decades. Who killed the Baron? Ground support? Captain Brown? Did the Baron finally get unlucky and crash his plane? It's hard to say. But that doesn't matter. What matters is that you talk to Captain Brown, find out what he's hoarding, and determine if he's seen any rogue pilots. Do you understand?"

Jane finished suiting up before I did, flight goggles, helmet, and all. She had to tie the strap of the goggle behind her head instead of using the clasp to get them to fit correctly. Despite the determined, courageous glint in her eyes, she looked cute as a button. I kept that observation to myself. From the smile on Smith's face, though, I could tell he thought the same.

"Shall we get her on the runway, then?" Jane asked. "Francheville, then Clairmarais to speak with Captain Roy. I assume we'll be avoiding combat zones if possible?"

"Fly west, well clear of the St. Mihiel Salient. But it goes without saying, you may very well encounter German resistance, especially the closer you get to the front. Keep that in mind. Sergeant, if I were you, I'd use this flight to calmly explore the capabilities of the Salmson and acclimatize your new gunner. Remember your first flights up. Don't take her too high. She'll be no good to you with throbbing headaches."

Smith let out a whistle, and a few mechanics came running to wheel our plane out of the hangar. They strained from the effort, but soon the wheels got rolling, and before long all thirty feet of the aircraft was in a taxi-ready position to get to the airfield.

I climbed into the cockpit and took a quick glance around. The plane wasn't that much larger than my Nieuport, and it boasted a slightly better view on the front side. Out over the wings, though, was a solid mass of eight struts and stabilizing cables blocking visibility. But, I supposed that's why they'd placed the gunner's seat so far back. Jane had a great view on all sides as she sat behind the wings.

I twisted in my seat to see her capped head, a few stray locks of hair escaping the flight helmet and falling to the side of the comically large goggles.

"You ready, Jane?" I asked.

Her hands gripped the side of her bay tightly, and she nodded. A surge of sympathy pounded my heart as I recognized her fear. She had seen her fair share of mutilated planes and not always because of German resistance.

"Hey, I'll take care of you," I said, trying to reach her hand to give it a squeeze. She extended hers to mine, and we only just touched.

"Are you wearing your marble?" she asked. I laughed and patted my chest.

"Never fly without it. You got yours?"

She nodded.

"Though, I was going to ask," I continued, "if you're in the plane, too, does that cancel out any of the magic? I mean odds are if my marble breaks, yours will as well, right?"

"Oh, shut up," she said, closing her eyes.

"Marcus!" I started at the sound of Smith's voice using my first name. "You'll need these." He tossed up a pair of flight goggles. Boelcke's goggles.

"You still have these?"

"I was supposed to give them back, but after the Johann incident, I don't think Mustermann had the gumption to bring it up. His loss. Your gain."

I hesitated.

"Listen, kid. Once you're done with this mission, you can put that pompous attitude back on, but for now, use the goggles. That's an order."

I sighed. *For Jane.* It'd be for the best.

"Switch off!" called a mechanic below.

I flicked my propellor switch.

"Switch off!" I called back.

"Brakes on!"

I could sense Jane's nervous energy palpitating from behind me, buffeting me in waves of anxiety.

The Salmson

"Brakes applied!" I shouted. The mechanic at the front of our plane worked the propellor. With each rotation, the reality of what we were about to do screwed into my understanding.

"Switch her on!"

I'd never flown a Salmson before. Sure, it had a radial engine just like the Nieuport, but this was a new plane, and I was going up for the first time with my best friend in the world sitting as a passenger.

What was Smith thinking?

"Contact!" The mechanic shouted. With a bang, a trail of combustion exhaust popped from the engine, the prop sprang to life, a buzz saw of wooden aerodynamics blurring the world through its lens. They pulled the chocks out from the wheels, and I gently gave the engine small sips of fuel through my sequencer to get us moving. The aerodrome was buzzing, but the sporadic *brraaps* of the rolling Salmson calmed the place down. There is nothing like an active plane to draw attention.

We made it to the runway, which wasn't much more than a field of grass. Poor Jane wouldn't get the luxury of a paved takeoff on her first go.

I pumped my fist in the air to let her know we were going up, then looked to Smith standing in the mouth of the hangar. He nodded and gave me a salute.

There was no turning back now.

I switched my sequencer and activated more cylinders. The engine roared to life, its deep vibrations reverberating through my body, echoing in places beyond hearing, deep in the gut. The thrill of takeoff took me over, as it always did.

The plane lurched forward, coming to life like an oversized dog on a leash. It pulled me forward. It begged to get airborne.

We picked up speed. My sense of balance felt the tail come off the Earth.

"Marcus!" Jane shouted. "Marcus! I'm not ready!"

Marcus

She sounded so afraid, but I smiled. We'd all known that fear the first time. I was about to show her a world above the clouds. So I didn't kill the engine. I didn't slow down. I gently pulled back on the stick, and the lift of my stomach told me we were off the ground.

The mission had begun.

Chapter 14
The Magic of Flight
Jane

This is the song of the Air—
The lifting, drifting air,
The eddying, steadying air,
The wine of its limitless space.
-Gordon Alchin-

F*light!*

When Smith had instructed me to test out the gunner's seat on the Salmson, I tried imagining what it would be like in the sky. How would I react to rising through the clouds, joining the birds in their heavenly travels?

But how could anyone prepare themself for this?

My fingers clenched the edge of the gunner's bay until my knuckles were white and cramping. When the engine kicked to life, I could hardly breathe. And then we were moving. The sound of it! The somersaults in my stomach. I'm ashamed to admit that I closed my eyes.

But the first ten seconds after leaving the ground, of breaking free from gravity's demands, I opened them.

Flight!

The people shrunk below us. The buildings shrunk. The very trees—trees that had defined the vertical plane of my existence since I had first noticed their height as a young, young girl—even the trees shrunk below us!

And somehow, amidst the roar of the Salmson's engine and the rushing air past my flight helmet, I found silence within me. We passed through a thin cloud—right through it! Its mists wrapped around me harmlessly and reformed in our wake.

There was reverence in the air. And though my heart beat so quickly, though I perspired from the adrenaline despite the air chill, stillness overcame me.

Tears flowed.

Had Aunt Luella only known about this kind of magic, the magic of flight, what would she have said? She warned me so often of the war between magic and technology, how technology threatened to overcome magic entirely. But what about its synergies?

What about this?

"You feel all right?" Marcus shouted from his seat in front of me. He gave me a thumbs up. "The plane's working beautifully."

"It's amazing!" I shouted. "I'm flying, Marcus! I'm flying!"

His head bobbed as though laughing, and he banked the wings of the plane about twenty degrees to dip into a turn. Instinctively, I clutched again at the edge of my seat, but the panic was short lived. The bank gave me a view of the ground, now far below us, and I laughed, small bursts at first but then overflowing into a broad overwhelming takeover. I stretched my arms out to the sides and felt the push of the air, like swimming through water.

They bumped into the ring handles of the Lewis guns, sending a dull pang through my elbow. I withdrew my arm and examined the guns, looked forward at the Vickers on the front of the plane, and the beauty of the heavens dimmed.

Aunt Luella's admonitions circled back on me. Magic and

science. The corruption of the arcane for the evil purposes of man. This was the pattern of my species, to unlock the mysteries of nature and distort them to fit their purposes.

How many pilots had experienced the same exhilaration of dancing through the air, the jubilation of physically breaking laws considered all but immutable until only a precious few years before this moment?

And in those years, how far had the great nations of the world come in its pursuit of flight? Why? Not to unlock more of the sky's mysteries, but to knock one another from the air.

My face fell. I took steadying breaths, a task more difficult this high up. Solemnly, my fingers felt the handle of the Lewis, settled on the trigger. I looked through the iron sights and found a cloud, peaceful, voluminous, and soft. If that cloud were a man in a plane? A fellow human being?

If it were Johann?

Boasts of pilots' kill count trickled through my memory, hurt my conscience. Marcus's empty scorecard endeared me to him more. He had been making excuses since his first sortie, but I knew the truth of the curse. And it wasn't because of my Aunt Luella's education.

His scorecard was empty because Marcus didn't want to kill anyone. He might lie to himself, talk whatever talk he liked to other pilots, but in the crucial moment, he could not disconnect his empathy as he could one of the cylinders in his engine.

He was a wonderful pilot and a terrible soldier, and there, in that gunner's chair on my very first flight, I understood what Lufbery understood. I appreciated in new ways how special Marcus was, how beautiful a thing it would be to preserve that part of him. Every time Marcus took to the sky, the impossibility of his existence increased.

Two years at war, and he'd never killed another man.

I found myself promising to whatever God lived in the sky that

I would do everything in my power to preserve that part of my friend.

I pulled the trigger.

The gun jerked to life, screaming. The bolt rocked back and forth with such violence it frightened me. It had one purpose, to expel the rounds in its chamber, and the gun did not care where they went, only to spit them out. And out the rounds shot, poking holes in the cloud as readily as if it were holes in the dreams of a child looking up at them to discern their shape.

At the sound, Marcus broke left, instinctively and knocked me off balance. The gun settled back to sleep.

"What is it, Jane?" Marcus shouted. His voice barely cut through the wind, like a whispering trail of cloud. I only caught a few words. "What... see?"

"Nothing." I leaned forward to make myself more audible. "I was just firing off some test rounds."

"Geez! ... next time!" Marcus shook his head and faced forward again. I settled back into my chair, but I could not shake the sound of the gun from my ears. I heard it now in the hum of the engine and the passing of the airstream.

Flight had been disfigured at such a young age. Abused.

I spent the rest of the voyage in conflict, admiring the sensations around me, wondering over magic, science, the war, and considering that perhaps our mission might be more important than even I realized.

True to Smith's advice, Marcus flew nowhere near the front line, and we arrived at Francheville in a couple of hours. Marcus motioned with his hand that we would be landing and took us down slowly. Still, as we descended and the landing strip grew beneath us, a terrible pain bothered my ears and sinuses. For all of flight's beauties, it took a terrible toll on my body. By then, my hearing had become accustomed to the howl of the wind and roar of the motor. But nothing prepared me for the cold. Despite my heavy flight suit, the nip of the air cut through to my bones. The tips of my fingers ached.

We hadn't encountered any enemy aircraft, and it was a good thing, as I wasn't sure how my hands would function appropriately when the time came. The cold robbed them of all dexterity. I winced, imagining trying to swap the ammo drum mid-flight, fingers fumbling at metal latches and levering up iron flanges.

Our plane touched down abruptly but without incident. As ordered, we didn't spend much time on the ground. Smith had notified the aerodrome to expect us, and a team of mechanics was ready to refuel the plane and make quick engine checks. I wrinkled my nose, understanding full well that checking the cylinders alone would need more time than we had to give them. We'd pushed the Salmson for several hours, and now we'd need a few more from her. At Clairmarais, I intended to give the whole machine a good inspection to make up for it.

In the meantime, hopefully we wouldn't encounter mechanical issues. When I mentioned my concerns to Marcus, he waved off the concern.

"I didn't even open the whole engine on the way over here for fear of going too fast your first time. And I've pushed birds much harder in a dogfight. I'm sure she'll last us to Dunkirk."

We dined quickly on bread and leftover tinned roast beef from the night before. It wasn't Annette's cooking, which I sadly had not appreciated due to my nerves over the circumstances of our stay at the farmhouse, but I'd eaten far worse in my time at war. In fact, the carrots still carried flavor, despite being completely drenched in a gelatinous, onion-stenched gravy.

I found the courage to keep my eyes open during my second takeoff and gave over to a fascination with its mechanics. I'd learned all about the theory of liftoff, but seeing the air split over the wings that decided, almost of their own accord, to rise into the air was enough to anthropomorphize the Salmson. I flirted with the notion of naming the plane but decided against it. It was only our second time up together, after all.

Climbing into the skies brought me only marginally less jubilation than the first time. I was dreaming, soaring through the air, again. But just as we reached a higher altitude than before, Marcus shut off the engine. The wind sounded eerie without its hum. He twisted in the cockpit to address me.

"I know it's only your second time, but I'm going to be taking the Salmson through a few maneuvers," he shouted. "Gotta see what she can do. You should see what it's like hoisting those guns while we're practicing some combat tactics."

I grit my teeth.

"You won't make it too daring, will you? It being my first time and all?"

"You'll be fine!"

"Any advice?"

"If you have to vomit, pound the fuselage three times so I can invert us first."

"Vomit?"

"Here we go!"

He tipped the nose of the plane downward into a steep dive. I clutched the sides of the bay tightly, my feet turning under me as though standing. My stomach floated into my throat, and yes, I screamed.

Marcus maintained the dive for what seemed to me a full minute, though it was likely closer to a few seconds, before pulling up and using the momentum to launch us upwards. My body tried to bend in half, and I was grateful to be harnessed to the seat. The weightlessness that buoyed my stomach a moment ago now reversed, and gravity cemented me to the bottom of the plane.

When we leveled from the climb, Marcus dipped his wing deep, running us perpendicular with the ground and banked into a wide turn. My harness strained, and I used one hand to push away from the side. At any moment, though, I feared that I would topple from the bay like a pair of dice.

I experienced a persuasive urge to pound on the fuselage, but I did not want to give Marcus the satisfaction. There might not be shame in vomiting, I'd heard that many pilots did their first time aloft, but resisting the urge might inspire greater confidence.

Unfortunately, though, we were only getting started. He pulled us up again. Up and up.

"The loop, the loop, the loop," I stammered through clenched teeth. From the moment I learned I'd be flying, I had dreaded the inversion. Now, it crept up, over, and on top of me. But instead of dangling from my seat, as I expected, the same overly heavy sensation from the climb kept me in my chair. Just as we managed to get ourselves completely upside down, Marcus rolled us, and we were right-side up again, only much higher than we were before, and now heading in an opposite direction.

That seemed useful.

And as I contemplated the frightening scenarios in which such a maneuver might become useful, my attention turned to the two Lewis guns attached by my seat. A wrenching understanding choked me. Not only would I need to keep my calm during these acrobatics, but I would also need the wherewithal to fire these weapons effectively in the midst of them.

That understanding, combined with the somersaults, and topped off with the dubiously old leftover beef could produce only one outcome.

I pounded on the fuselage frantically. Marcus's head bobbed as though in surprise, but he understood the signal.

He rolled us over. Now, without the energy of the loop to keep me in my seat, I was dangling, but it didn't scare me. It was a relief, in more ways than one.

Marcus took me through a few different acrobatic sessions. Each time, I handled it slightly better. By the third, I even tried swiveling the guns during some of our inversions and steep turns. But the rigors of an actual fight loomed over me.

How was I going to do this?

We crossed through the French countryside, and Marcus brought us down low enough to admire some of the budding forests. The war wrought havoc on certain parts of the landscape, but behind the lines, virgin land remained with wood and hill unmolested.

And France in the spring will always be France in the spring, after all.

In the far-off distance, I used a pair of binoculars to spy a small speck I hoped might be the *Tour d'Eiffel.*

We flew well clear of Paris, but the city was wide enough and magnificent enough to recognize its importance. Germany had yet to take it, and if they did, there was no telling what it would do to the morale of the Triple Entente. Paris was a jewel, a beating heart of free society, scandalous, lavish, a city nearly every Englishman pretended to despise.

We flew onward, regaining altitude, and when we were clear of Paris and west of Amiens, Marcus killed the engine and turned to me again.

"Are you ready for another session? I think we have the fuel for one more."

"Ready," I called to him, though I still suffered from lingering nausea from our latest attempts. He started to bank into a dive, but quickly righted the plane.

Something was wrong.

"What is it?" I shouted.

He pointed far to the right.

"You'll have to learn to watch for these as well as I can. Another plane. Where are your binoculars?"

Another plane. The phrase made my blood run even colder than the windchill. I fumbled for the binoculars and searched.

"Where? I don't see it."

He dipped the wing again, and there it was far below us, a small black speck, visible only as it flew over a white cloud.

How had Marcus picked it up so readily?

I looked through the binoculars and found, to my horror, a single plane adorned with two black crosses on its wings. Two seats. A reconnaissance plane, like ours, or else a bomber.

"What do we do?"

"Nothing."

"Nothing? What if they see us?"

Marcus shook his head.

"We have altitude, and the sun's behind us. They won't spot us. Besides, there are three or four aerodromes between here and the line. One of our boys will get them."

I'd been in a plane only a day, but in a moment I understood the preoccupation I'd seen in so many pilots: a sense of stewardship for the safety of others. We had the plane. We had the advantage and the opportunity. Wasn't it our responsibility to prevent the Germans from doing any damage?

"You don't think we should attack?" I could hardly believe the words exiting my own lips. Logically, attacking was the last thing I wanted to do, but for some reason, ignoring the impulse seemed all but impossible.

"We've got orders to get to Dunkirk."

"But what if they're taking back information? What if more soldiers die?"

"Welcome to the war, Jane."

Something stirred inside of me. The very reluctance to do others harm I had admired in Marcus at the beginning of the day now came across as cowardice.

"Lufbery would attack them," I found myself saying.

Marcus turned his head as though about to say something, but recalled the intent, and the weight of the insult I'd just issued registered.

"Marcus, I'm sorry," I called. "I didn't mean to—"

The engine roared back on, cutting off the conversation.

Deflated and disappointed in myself, I nestled back into my gunner's bay and watched the plane through my binoculars. Marcus was right. Before the plane was out of view, a small group of three fighters engaged it.

I stopped watching when the German plane spewed black smoke from its engine. I knew what came next. And seeing it from up here was different than seeing it from the ground.

On the ground, planes fell to their final resting place. Even when it was the enemy, it brought on a sick feeling. But here in the sky, to my own terror, when our pilots riddled that German plane with bullets, I only wondered who it was that fired the gun.

Who would get the kill?

I was already keeping score.

Chapter 15
Clairmarais
Marcus

It's well we've learned to laugh at fear—the sea has taught us how;
It's well we've shaken hands with death—we'll not be strangers
now.
-Cicely Fox Smith-

Jane's words humiliated me.

I had expected more time to pass before the pilot mentality took over her head. Maybe I took her too high too quickly. A lot of pilots experienced lapses of judgment when flying past a certain altitude. It cost some their lives. I'd even experienced it myself from time to time, this heady sensation that your ideas were all brilliant.

Jane was not a coward. I'd always known that. But a pilot that is not a coward is a pilot that could die any time they go up.

When I took off from Gondreville, I accepted the burden of being a coward at least until Clairmarais. There was no way in hell that I would fly Jane Turner into combat her first day in a gunner's seat.

And when she launched out that dare, that challenge—calling

up Lufbery's name to coax me into abandoning her own safety, she spat my care for her directly in my face.

She couldn't know how hard it was to ignore a fight. To resist doing what Lufbery might, or Kiffin Rockwell or Chapman or any of those Lafayette boys.

But so many of them were gone now, and we had a mission in Dunkirk. Jane was chosen for this because of her knowledge about some damned fool witchcraft, not her prowess on a Lewis gun.

How could she know the danger?

I stewed in the cockpit and fumed with the engine fumes.

Jane. My best friend, and after one flight, already she called me a coward.

Could I blame her? She wasn't a soldier, and she wasn't a pursuit pilot. For her, this was much more than a special assignment. It was her odyssey into the violence of war. She would undergo the same set of emotions every soldier experienced. Fear. Courage. Remorse. Longing. Emptiness. Bloodlust.

My Jane.

I had suffered down those same long roads. What available shortcuts through the pain might I show her?

I had to protect her from more than German bullets. I had to protect her from the darkness inside each of us.

Clairmarais buzzed like a hive.

Unlike Francheville, which hummed with the energy of industry, the excitement of building something new, Dunkirk was an old fortress at work—an oiled machine manufacturing defense and destruction. Sweeping rows of hangars lined the landing field, and around us towered enormous Handley bombers, twice the size of our Salmson. To think such formidable iron eagles would take to the sky and drop unholy fire down on the German ranks boggled the imagination. The Handleys were curious ships, with two huge engines on either side of the fuselage and a pointy nose tipped with an observer's machine gun. Its snout hung in the air well above the reach of any man I knew, and its teams had a series of ladders and apple crates stacked to reach the wings, which easily supported its attendants' weight.

Jane marveled, too, salivating over the mechanical logistics at work in such a huge machine.

In the empty spaces between hangars, trucks littered the area, with teams of mechanics fixing wings or fusing bombs. I spotted filled craters, mended wounds from German bombing raids. And under the smell of oil and exhaust, the scent of the distant sea lingered everywhere.

"Check that out," I pointed to a team of four mechanics under one of the Handleys. "Do you see the size of that bomb."

"It's taken them three men to lift it," Jane replied in wonder.

At Croix-de-Metz, we had seen bombers. But up here, beside the intersection of three warring countries this close to the English Channel, closer to Ypres, where hundreds of thousands had died in battle after battle after battle, bombers carried different loads. There, we hoped to flank the enemy. Here was the meat grinder and to the north a battle for naval superiority that might give Germany and its U-boats all of the momentum they needed to win the war.

A team of three British mechanics led our Salmson into an empty shelter at the end of their row of hangars.

"Sergeant Jackson, welcome to Clairmarais," said the team leader with an accent thick enough to tell Jane where he was from. "Rowan and Thomas will work on your aircraft. I believe you're expected at headquarters."

I nodded. So I was to be Sergeant Jackson. Well, it'd be anonymous, that's for certain. Hopefully we could slip in quietly, talk with Captain Brown, and act quickly on the intelligence he provided.

But when Jane took off her flight helmet, all hope of discretion died.

The three mechanics stared at Jane's locks as they tumbled out of the leather cap. Rumors would spread by dinner, and by the smell wafting over from the mess, dinner wouldn't be long in coming.

Jane paused when she noticed their staring.

"Perhaps I should have kept on my helmet," she whispered to me.

"It would have been quieter," I replied.

"Why weren't they notified and prepared that a woman would be traveling with you?"

"Even if they were, I'm not sure they put together that you'd be traveling in the gunner's bay of a Salmson 2."

She put her hands on her hips and stared the boys down.

"Well, what are you looking at?" she demanded.

"It's just," the team leader stuttered. "I mean—"

"You're a bloody girl, aren't you?" said one of the others, a ruddy-faced boy with a sunburn and brown curls stuffed in his cap.

Jane spat on the ground.

"Private Doe, Women's Royal Air Force. Am I to be blamed if you couldn't beat a woman to the gunner's seat?"

"Oi, now! Easy!" All three burst into bitter protests, but she silenced them.

"I don't want to hear it. We've had a long flight without time to even check the cylinders in Paris before getting on. We will need her ready by tomorrow morning, and I plan on inspecting your handiwork personally, from lubricant to the taut of the leading edge to the drums of my Lewis guns."

I had to stifle a laugh. The three mechanics' jaws dropped to the floor, eyes wide as though they'd just seen their first sortie.

"And yes," Jane finished, "I have shot them, obviously."

She strutted confidently out of the hangar in the direction she believed headquarters to be in. I smiled at the mechanics.

"We're in a bit of a confidential situation," I said, "so let's do this. If you don't tell anyone about seeing a girl hop out of my gunner's bay, I won't tell everyone she gave you such a good tongue lashing."

They understood the bargain. There were several British lady mechanics that had worked on motorcycles and cars, occasionally on planes as well, and I suspected for some time that an unstated rivalry between the sexes had quietly grown with their involvement.

When they nodded grimly I clapped one on the shoulder.

"Crazy war, crazy times," I said with a laugh. "Would you believe she's a better shot than me with that Lewis gun? Imagine how I felt when she proved it in front of three other pilots. I had to double take when relieving myself for a week, just to check my manhood."

I hated talking crass like that, but for better or worse, it was a dependable ice breaker for certain groups of men. The youngest mechanic smiled in surprise, and finally, all four of us laughed together, a sign I took to be acceptance and silence.

"How'd I do?" asked Jane when I joined her outside. She'd put her helmet back on. "Was that too much?"

I shrugged.

"Those boys got so sore, I doubt they'll mention it to anyone. Where was that confidence in all your spats with Flora back at Croix-de-Metz?"

"Thank heavens," Jane said, ignoring my question. "Perhaps we should develop a better cover story."

"You mean something better than Smith's 'we're carrying valuable information' masterpiece?" I mused. "Yeah, it's safe to say that might not be adequate. I liked what you just said. The key is going to be to make sure we avoid any reporters."

"Ah yes," she said, laughing. "War time reporters. As we know, they're the source of all truth, aren't they?"

I smirked. Sometimes, back when I was still with the Lafayette, we'd pin up the most outrageous stories we found in the papers, both French and American. It was nice knowing that regardless of nationality, storytellers tell stories. One time, an American paper had reported Norman Prince downing a whole score of Hun planes single-handedly all the while his gun jamming, crash landing afterward, and picking off a final Pfalz with a well-aimed shot from his pistol.

We found headquarters easily enough, beside a large hangar, but when we inquired about Captain Brown, the orderlies redirected us immediately to the Squadron Office, another hundred yards or so beyond. We passed by a vacant photographers' hut and workshop filled with machine parts from motorcycle carburetors to peeled back top wings. To our left, planes of all sizes lay at the ready.

I opened the Squadron Office door and found a gaunt man arguing with an observer, binoculars hanging around his neck.

"I suppose I'm simply not confident that audio detection is feasible this close to the sea. Surely, the buffeting waves will mask the engine of an aircraft until it's visible to the naked eye."

"But on a cloudy day, sir, or else at night?" the observer suggested.

"If you're volunteering for night duty, Private, I'd be happy to oblige."

I cleared my throat, and the man stopped.

"Back to the watch, then, Millard."

Jane hid her face as the young man sidled past us and out the door. The officer stood erectly and placed his hands behind his back.

"Sergeant Jackson, I assume," he said.

I nodded, adding, "This is Private Doe. I'm afraid you have me at a disadvantage."

"Lieutenant Paynter. Welcome to the RAF 209."

"Thank you," I said. The small, simple office filled with awkward silence.

"So what is it, then?" he asked.

"What's what?"

"We received very little information about your purpose here. Something about naval intelligence."

"Oh, right. That's right." I shifted on my feet, nervously clutching my pair of flight gloves. Something about Paynter's impatience put me on guard.

"Well, what is it? All we have is some encoded message that our intelligence officers can't make sense of with any of our known ciphers."

"Um, about that intelligence—"

"We can't tell you," interjected Jane.

Paynter scrutinized her, assessing her gender quietly, so differently than the three mechanics. No shock or threatened masculinity there. He frowned, his lips folding suspicious lines into his cheeks.

"So you've come all of this way not to share the intelligence?" he asked.

"No. I said we couldn't tell you. We are under strict instructions to speak directly to Flight Commander Roy Brown."

Paynter scoffed.

"Do you know where we can find him?" I asked.

"In the sky," he said with little hospitable effort. "Or else on his bed frame. You're lucky you arrived when you did, I'm not sure he's going to live much longer."

"Meaning?" I probed. Something lurched in me hearing that Brown might be in danger somehow. He shot down the Baron. He was a hero.

"Meaning I'm not sure I can, in good conscience, take you to him. He resists all instruction to stay in bed and recover. The Canadian must believe he could fly unconscious if necessary."

"I apologize," Jane said quietly, "but are you his superior offi-cer, then?"

Paynter's sneer darkened. Jane had an amazing talent of emas-culating lofty men. Hell, she'd done it to me in my own aircraft only an hour before.

"You must be famished after your travels," he said. "Please, retire to the mess. I'll see to sleeping arrangements for the both of you."

My stomach growled, remembering the quick, scant meal we hurried through in Francheville, but I insisted.

"Lieutenant, you must appreciate the urgency of our mission, all the more if you don't think Brown is in a good state of health."

"And you must appreciate my concern for my commander. I will check with him, the medics, assess his health, and see if he's coherent enough to meet with you."

He clicked his heels to signify his intent to end the conversa-tion, but Jane didn't let him go.

"Could we at least have the information that was telegraphed to you? We carry the code word to the cipher, you see, and I would like to get started in its translation."

Paynter lowered his eyebrows. I felt for the man. His suspi-cions weren't without merit, and Brown's condition must have had him in a state. I'd be in a sour mood, too. But the lieutenant wasn't vindictive, even if he was a little grumpy. He walked back to the desk, whipped out a pen, and scribbled something on a piece of paper.

"Take it to intelligence," he said, brusquely handing it to me. "If you're going to be here for a while, you might consider doing something useful and flying up with us. Our squadron has changed aerodromes eight times in the past few months alone for all the German advances. Every plane in the sky helps."

He left without a glance back. His words resonated in a deep part of my heart. Every plane in the air helped, all right. Especially in sorties that accompany larger troop or artillery action. I could only imagine it'd be the same for naval efforts. In actions of this magnitude, the dogfights stacked deep on both sides. One against three looked very different than two against three. And four on eight looked very different than five on twelve.

"What an idiot," Jane said once the door closed. "Clearly he knew we were coming, and if he received advanced notice, why be so suspicious? I have half a mind to start searching every barracks and medic's bed until I find Brown myself."

I grabbed her hand gently, an unexpected moment of tenderness in the middle of a war zone. It broke her concentration and paused her temper.

"You don't know how hungry you are," I said. "We've got a little time. And besides, we need to decode that message. We might as well do that before we find Brown, so he doesn't have to sit through the process."

Jane took a deep breath and turned to me. The sharpness she'd adopted for our flight, the rough edges to mask the fear, all things I recognized because I'd done the same time and time again—all softened.

"Marcus, I'm sorry for what I said up there about the German plane," she said.

"Come on, Jane," I said with a whistle. "I was just trying to get you to stop throwing a fit. I didn't want you to get all emotional on me. Let's go. The mess is this way."

Chapter 16
The Man Who Killed the Baron
Jane

Nearer and ever nearer...
My body, tired but tense,
Hovers 'twixt vague pleasure
And tremulous confidence.
-Robert Nichols-

I learned a whole new variety of anxiety at Clairmarais.

My flight suit distinguished me without mercy, and I had to continually ignore the fact that all the men stared at me. I wondered if our mechanics would keep their silence as to my gender. Marcus reassured me they would, but after Smith's admonitions about the importance of secrecy, every moment I stood in the open, I feared for our discretion.

As I passed by pilots and mechanics, all of them paused to watch me. Other women worked at the air base. I had already spotted several helping in intelligence, prepare munitions, or in other auxiliary functions. But a woman in a flight suit... I read the emotions on their faces easily. Curiosity. Resentment. Humor. Lust. Longing.

But soon, something else about these men bothered me even more than my worry that they'd start spreading rumors. On some of their faces, no emotion registered at all. Shells of human beings mechanically toiled at their never-ending assignments. This part of France recently received a heavy battering from German assault, and the combat weary faces told all. Lieutenant Paynter said the 209th Squadron had moved eight times in the past two months alone. Such uncertainty could only deteriorate the mind.

As it turned out, decoding messages, even with the proper code words, was enough to deteriorate the mind as well.

It was a simple but thorough cipher. I had been furnished a list of code words. Marcus had been entrusted a list of numbers. Each word was decoded according to a different code word, indicated by the subsequent number on Marcus's list. As I went through it, I didn't even enjoy the luxury of recognizing which letters triggered others. Instead, I slogged through a rotating mess.

Menial was one of the words on my list.

We worked while we ate at the privacy of a small table pushed into the corner of the officer's mess. I had stowed my flight suit beneath the table to deter attention. The cooks served bowls of fish stew, which were none too appetizing. I sniffed my bowl apprehensively. My father had made a living from selling fish and chips and other comforting dishes. He taught me how to identify good quality fish and distinguish it from fish from the bottom of a barrel. Or in this case, a tin. What made the old fish in this soup unforgivable was that we were so close to the ocean. I could almost recognize the scent of the sea, but the supply chain had broken down under the German spring offensive. Proximity did not decide rations. Infrastructure did.

"You get it cracked yet?" Marcus asked.

"Nearly there," I replied, putting together a few final words. "Why do you think Lieutenant Paynter received us so coldly?"

I paused to take a healthy bite of the stew. Even if the fish weren't fresh, Marcus had been right. I was famished.

"Politics," Marcus replied, wiping his mouth with the back of his hand. "You know how it is, Jane. We've received stupid orders in the past. The chain of command is a fickle, ever-moving thing. How many times has Luf had to put up a stink about something command asked the 94th to do? Even Thenault dealt with it back at the Lafayette. Paynter's up here sitting with the guy who shot down the Baron. I can only imagine they've had all kinds of numbskull requests and communications coming in? I'm surprised one of the reporters hasn't noticed you yet. There certainly is a lot of foot traffic around here. The base is over capacity."

He drained his cup of water and grimaced. I missed the taste of pure fresh water. It took a good week to grow accustomed to the peculiarities of water on any given air base. Traces of tin from the water tanks, chlorination—there were any number of contributing characteristics. Potability took priority over palatability. A spot of tea or wine went a long way in masking the flavor.

"Then," he continued, "some American pilot walks into the Squadron Office with a lady decked out in full flight gear, insisting they have a secret message for Brown and Brown alone."

I scratched out another letter and slapped my hands on the table.

"Finished." I took a drink from my own glass and winced. Chlorine for certain.

"Sorry," Marcus grinned. "They were out of coffee."

"No tea?" I asked. "This is a British aerodrome, after all."

"Plenty of tea. But I don't care for it."

I leveled my gaze at him and scoffed.

"I might hit you."

"Let's see what you got." He leaned over the table, and I spun the decoded message around.

The Man Who Killed the Baron

---

*Flight Commander Roy Brown. Special mission clearance for
Sergeant Marcus Jackson and Private Melinda Doe. Full briefing
authorized. Clearance: Nun Yunu Wi. Priority: Critical. Top Secret.*

"I see they didn't bother to change my first name," Marcus said, leaning back in his chair.

I scrunched my nose.

"Nun Yunu Wi? How infuriating! I thought I decoded it correctly, but that can't be right."

"It's only three words. We can try again," Marcus said. "I can try if you need a break."

A looming figure with a trim mustache approached us confidently, bowl of soup in his hands. I quickly swept our cipher into my pocket. Marcus snatched what we'd decoded so far.

"Is it true?" the man asked, his accent staunchly American. He appeared to have come directly from a flight, his helmet and goggles sat perched on his forehead. Under them, his nose featured prominently on his face and deep-set wrinkles betrayed wisdom gained not only by combat. He appeared to be close to my own age, if not my elder. He stopped beside our table and put his hands on his hips. Marcus eyed him carefully. I buried my attention in what was left of my bowl of stew.

"Is what true?" Marcus asked. I felt the man's eyes turn on me.

"Is what true? Come on, now. A lady pilot?"

"I'm not a pilot," I said, looking up. He grinned, bright teeth and all, and inclined his head to inspect under the table.

"This man just wears two flight suits, then?"

"She was a passenger," Marcus chimed in. The man swiveled to scrutinize Marcus.

"And where are you from, pilot?"

"Los Angeles."

"Oh. We got ourselves a silent film actor over here?" He sat down. "Welcome to the 209, Charlie Chaplin."

"Charlie Chaplin? Please," I said. "If anything, he resembles Douglas Fairbanks." I regretted my words immediately after saying them.

"Say, I think you're right." He plopped his bowl down beside Marcus and gave him an elbow to the arm.

"And here the WREN girls are always telling me they can't kiss me because it's not allowed. You get to take one on a plane!" He laughed. I waited for Marcus to correct him, but to my surprise, he only joined in with hearty peals of his own.

"How many WREN girls tell you that?" Marcus asked.

"All of them."

More laughter. I frowned, watching them. I'd grown accustomed to this type of language from other pilots, but I had come to expect more from Marcus, at least in my presence. Jokes about decoding the fairer sex were exclusionary at best and demeaning at a close second best.

"How's the soup, you two?" The pilot stirred his own with a greasy spoon.

"It's fine," I said.

He peered at me and laughed again.

"You're a beautiful liar, and that's a dangerous combination."

"What's your name, lieutenant?" Marcus asked.

"Sub-lieutenant," he corrected. "Sub-lieutenant Oliver Le Boutillier. What about you two?"

"I'm Sergeant Jackson. This is Private Doe."

Oliver paused and scrunched up his eyebrows, feigning deep thought.

"Hmm, have we already met? I could have sworn I've met a Mr. Jackson and a Miss Doe before."

My heart skipped a beat. Was he being playful, or were our monikers too obvious? What a foolish question. Of course, they were obvious. They weren't intended to fool anyone. They were intended to tell others to stop asking. And if Oliver wanted to play along in a congenial way, that was his prerogative.

"What are you doing here?" Oliver asked, his tone darkening. "Come to back us up against the onslaught of flying Bosch?"

"I'm afraid not," Marcus replied. "We're here to see Captain Roy Brown."

"Come to see the man who shot down the Baron." Oliver sounded almost disappointed.

"Did he really do it?" Marcus asked. "I heard the kill was disputed."

Oliver smacked his lips between bites of stew and winced. His lips were chapped badly in parts, a condition I'd noticed on many pilots. Flying dehydrated men as surely as it froze them.

"He did. I saw it with my own eyes. Tracers went right into Richthofen's fuselage. The Baron got it in his mind to go after one of our new pilots—a kid wasn't even supposed to have entered the fight, said his guns jammed—and wouldn't let off. Followed him down into dangerously low altitude. Brown dove after and caught him distracted."

Marcus gaped.

"But is that all? What happened?"

Oliver shrugged.

"Brown dove and fired. That's it."

Marcus clenched his hands and searched around himself as though the story—the true story—was wriggling its way underground.

"That can't be it," he insisted. "What maneuvers were involved? What—"

Oliver put a hand on Marcus's shoulder.

"Listen, if there was any impressive flying, it was sheer dumb luck from that kid with the Baron on his tail. But he didn't even have much experience out of flight school. A simple dive and a simple shot. Richthofen was a man just like you or me. And I'm sure you know, when your time comes, your time comes."

Marcus struggled for words. I watched him for a moment, sympathy swelling in my bosom for the dissonance he fought. The Red Baron was the greatest pilot in the world. Marcus, surely, would have wanted a death more fitting.

"Where is Captain Brown now?" I asked gently.

"He's in his bed, sick. Well, we think he's sick. He insists he's fine. But he keeps throwing up and his head feels like a furnace. You two just waiting for him to come down and talk to you or what?"

"No. We met Lieutenant Paynter. He wasn't too keen on seeing us. You see, we have a secret message to deliver to Captain Brown, and I'm not sure he was happy being left out."

"Bah!" Oliver grunted. "Look, don't be too shook up about Paynter. All of us have reacted to Brown killing the Baron differently. And it doesn't help that Brown's being hailed like the hero of the war, all from his sickbed. Between reporters swarming the place and the shifting front lines pushing Allied personnel through airbases like motels, we're a bit on edge around here. Hard to know who you can trust. I can take you to the captain, if you want."

A little while later, just as the sun was setting on the far side of the landing field, we stood outside the medical unit, listening to an argument between Paynter and Oliver. The shouts were muffled through the canvas walls, and more so as Paynter kept remembering he didn't want us to hear him.

He launched accusations about poor communication, possible harm, and even fame-hungry leeches, but in the end, he stormed out directly past us toward the hangars. Oliver, smiling, appeared in the doorway.

"Captain Roy's ready for you," he said. I followed behind. Inside, the stench of sickness hung like wet, molding clothes on a line. The captain sat on the edge of a canvas stretcher bed, a scratchy blanket bunched around his midsection. He had dressed down to his undershirt. As the daylight disappeared through a small window, we relied on a small lamp on the stool beside his bed to illuminate his sweating face. He swayed slightly, but he seemed eager to put on a good appearance.

"Sergeant Jackson. Paynter tells me that you and your companion have important naval intelligence for me."

Marcus stared silently back at the captain, taking him in with a curious reverence, no doubt trying to decide if he should worship the man or despise him. But such a social paralysis had no place here. We had a job to do.

"Of a sort, sir," I cut in. "Earlier today, you received this encoded telegram. Sergeant Jackson has the keywords to decode it, and we've taken the liberty of doing so to save you time. If you desire, I can demonstrate how the message and keywords work together to prove the message's authenticity."

I started laying out the messages but stopped when I remembered Oliver standing nearby. I glanced toward him.

"Rest at ease, Private. Boots there is a walking paradox. An American pilot with a French name flying for the British. You might say he was built for this war. He is loyal and discreet."

Still, I hesitated and didn't continue until Marcus nodded me onward.

"Right. Here, see? It is a rotating cipher with these keywords. You can see how the first word lines up for *Flight*. Then *Commander*."

His eyes glossed over my scribbled notes as though not seeing them at all. He used his shoulder to dab at the beads of perspiration dotting his brow.

"You are adequately trustworthy," he said. I handed him the note, but he waved his hand. "Please, read it to me. I'm trying to give my eyes a bit of rest."

"Of course. It says 'Flight Commander Roy Brown, Special mission clearance for Sergeant Marcus Jackson and Private Jane Doe. Full briefing authorized. Clearance: Nun Yunu Wi.'" I put the paper down. "We believe we may have decoded that last part incorrectly."

Oliver chuckled.

"Well, Captain, sounds Cherokee to me. That'll explain your other telegram," he said.

"Cherokee?" I asked.

Captain Brown cradled his head in his hands.

"Yes. The United States has been using code words from the language of its indigenous tribes."

"That's smart," Marcus said. "The Lafayette used the brave as its squadron symbol. Painted it on the sides of all its planes. I don't think the Huns have had much experience with Cherokees or Navajos."

I dug for a pencil in my pocket.

"You think Nun Yunu Wi is another code word?"

"And a deceptive one at that," said Oliver. "You'll spend ages wondering if you got all the letters right, when really the code breaks down to NUY for the alphabet displacement. Of course, the only way to tell for sure is to plug it in and see if it plays."

"You received another telegram, Captain?" Marcus asked. "May we see it?"

"Of course. Its contents were never intended for any eyes here at the 209. We were instructed to give it to you to assist your mission." He shifted again and took a sip of water from a small jug beneath his bed. It dribbled down his chin. Oliver tossed a handkerchief gently onto his lap. "You're not here with naval intelligence, are you?"

"No, sir," Marcus said. "It's a little more complicated than that. We understand you may know something about planes with rogue pilots—unaccounted for allied planes turning their guns on our boys. We also hear—"

"We hear that you've possibly engaged with one of these pilots." I cut Marcus off before he could ask about Captain Brown's special trophy. Marcus didn't know magic devices, but if Brown had one, I couldn't imagine he'd be eager to share it with us, at least not until we'd earned his trust.

Brown stopped dabbing at the water on his uniform.

"Maybe I do," he said. We waited for him to elaborate.

"Do you need further clearance to share what you know?" I asked. "I thought the message we decoded for you was quite clear."

Brown looked at Oliver, and the congenial American's face cooled. He disappeared for a moment, closed the door, and returned. Whatever remaining light and fresh air that blew through the room dissipated, and now we were trapped with the solitary lantern and the smell of Brown's unwashed body.

"We didn't report it," Brown said.

"Didn't report what?" I asked.

"I better start from the beginning. After the Baron went down, I went by to see for myself. The sight was terrible. His great, red, three-winged Fokker was smashed to pieces. Its fuselage and gas tank were bashed in like a tin can. The man's famous face had smashed into the back of his machine guns, and he was nearly unrecognizable."

Brown sighed deeply.

"I was completely unprepared for the emotional toll it would take on me. Seeing his body was like witnessing the corpse of a close friend. It made me physically ill. I would not doubt if that blow was what put me in this bed. I lost control of myself, in some ways, my actions automatic as they sometimes are in a dogfight.

"Every pilot respected him, even if they hated to admit it. It was like seeing a great eagle shot down. The waste. There would be a funeral the next day, I knew. All the honors as if he were one of ours. But the pageantry behind it sounded hollow. I was bonded to him in a unique way."

"How so?" asked Marcus.

"Because he let me kill him. I don't understand it. Not five minutes before he went down, he flew marvelously. But when he went after our new pilot, swooping so low, so straight and direct, it was as if he wanted to be done. Like he needed someone to do it for him. And they were my rounds that did it. So, when I saw him, I admit I took a trophy."

My hands clenched, heart beating steadily. Oliver folded his arms and blew through flat lips.

"Of course, he did," Oliver quickly added. "Who wouldn't? The Baron himself took trophies from his kills. It's only natural to reciprocate. Lots of pilots do it, and I for one consider it a form of respect."

"What trophy?" I asked.

"His flight scarf," Brown replied. "It was splattered with his blood, but I thought it must be sacred or something. The next day, after his funeral, Boots and I went up on patrol. I was in a peculiar mood, a contemplative stupor. That's when it happened. Soon, we were joined by a third plane."

"Scared the hell out of me," Oliver added. "Thought it was a D.VII at first, and I was about to barrel over the Bosch and start firing. But it was just another Camel, same as ours."

Marcus knit his eyebrows.

"Did you know another pilot was joining you?"

"No," Brown replied. "He was just below us, and we couldn't make out who was flying. That's when I noticed something strange. You're familiar with the cocarde painted on the wings of our planes?"

"Of course," I said. "Three colored rings one on another. The way the red, white, and blue is configured tells the country of the pilot."

"Exactly. At first, I thought it was a French plane due to the blue inner circle on the wing. The Sopwith Camel is an English plane, but it's not unheard of for our pursuit planes to exchange hands as Allied needs require. But as I looked closer, I noticed something unusual."

I leaned forward with nervous anticipation.

"It was all blue," Oliver said, simply. "No red. No white. Just blue on blue on blue."

Captain Brown nodded.

"I'd heard the rumors, discounted stories about the rogue group of pilots wreaking havoc on both sides of the line. I'm not sure why, but as soon as I noticed that marking, those stories came rushing to my head. I dipped my wings to signal to Oliver that something was wrong just as the Camel eased off the engine and climbed to an elevated position above us. Above and behind."

"We dove," Oliver said. "Right into a vrille, both of us. Corkscrewing downward just as he opened fire. Tracer paths streaking everywhere between our wings."

Brown nodded absently.

"We tried splitting him, sandwiching him, but he flew like a demon possessed, spitting fire all the while. I kept hoping his gun would jam or his endless spray would exhaust his ammunition, give us some window to make an attack. But despite all our maneuvering, I never once felt like I was on the offensive."

Oliver and Brown fell silent. Behind their blank expressions replayed the sequence of the sortie, and from the haunted vacancy in their eyes, I could discern that they still had no satisfactory explanation for what they'd encountered.

"How'd it end?" Marcus asked quietly.

"I didn't want to give up," Brown said. "If these mongrels wanted fame, I'd give it to them by legitimizing their legend with a downed plane. So, we kept trying."

"Minutes stacked up. Before we knew it, our fuel tank was nearly empty. Neither of us had scored a hit on him. I waved my arms at Brown like an idiot to signal my intent to disengage. He reluctantly followed me in another dive."

"But the blue Sopwith followed," Brown said. "We had to run evasive tactics until we found our anti-aircraft battery near base. As soon as we came in view, he stopped firing, pretending to be a friend, falling into formation. How could the ground battery know that one of our own Camels had taken the offensive against us?"

"No one fired at him, and we didn't have the machine power to start up the fight again. We set down and before getting near enough to give anyone else on base a good view, he steered off in the direction of Petite Synth."

"Surely, you must have been questioned. Were there no holes in your aircraft?"

Brown shook his head.

"Not one. An hour later, I wondered if I'd dreamed the whole thing up. Others asked who we'd been flying with, but we didn't tell anyone but Colonel Collishaw."

"Why not?" Marcus asked.

"Come on." Oliver groaned. "His kill of the baron was up for debate. The last thing we wanted was for others to think he'd gone crazy. If he invented an encounter with a rogue blue flyer, that might hurt the credibility of his claim on Richthofen."

"As it so happens," Brown said, "Oliver is the one who most adamantly claims I shot the Baron. I dove, fired, and had to pull up before crashing into the ground."

"I'll die before saying otherwise. I saw it with my own eyes."

Oliver folded his arms. "Your tracers in the Baron's triplane and a blue-marked Sopwith Camel firing on us."

"But why?" Marcus asked. "Why would he attack you like that? Just to cause a little bit of chaos?"

I froze, the realization straightening my back like a posture rod.

"The scarf," I gasped. Captain Brown peered at me and slowly closed his eyes. "He wanted the scarf." Our mission. The attack was just like the rogue attack on Earnst for the goggles.

"I can't explain it." He nodded, agreeing with my supposition. "I took that scarf up in the plane with me as a good luck charm. I didn't want to be parted from it, you know? But all through the dogfight, my mind kept returning to it, even when I should have been completely focused. Somehow, in my heart, I came to the belief that if I were willing to toss the scarf out of the plane, that pilot would have disengaged and gone after it."

I stared at the goggles around Marcus's neck. *Boelcke's goggles. Richthofen's mentor.* If Boelcke's goggles had some kind of enchantment on them, harnessed some form of magic, why not Richthofen's scarf?

And if Boelcke and Richthofen, why not others? The weight of our assignment collapsed on me. There could be scores of magical devices out there, and if they fell into the wrong hands, if one side made a coordinated effort to collect them all...

"You didn't wear the scarf?" I asked.

Brown grimaced.

"No. I told you. Some of the man's blood got on it. And even if it hadn't, it seems awfully poor taste to wear the clothing of the man I killed."

"Where is the scarf now?" I asked.

Brown pointed outside.

"It's hidden with my things." He shook his head morosely. "No one other than the three of you even knows I have it. Again, I'm not proud to say I took it, but something compelled me."

Oliver crossed to his captain and sat down beside him.

"Come on now, Roy. You can't beat yourself up about that. Geez, Louise, you're sweating something awful. Let's get you something. What do you need? Sleep? Brandy? Morphine? All three?"

Brown bounced his fist on Oliver's knee.

"I've got a patrol tomorrow morning, better not hit anything too heavy. Just a small bit of morphine."

"Yeah, we'll see about that patrol," Oliver muttered as he fumbled with some pills on the table.

"Is that all you have to tell us?" I asked.

"I'm sorry. I wish I was in better health," Brown sighed as he lay down on the bed. "Let's talk again in the morning. Maybe I'll remember more. In the meantime, why don't you get to work on decoding that message I've been sitting on? Oliver, do you know where it is?"

"Yeah, don't you worry, captain. I'll show them where to find it. You just get some sleep now."

"Right. Great idea. I'm sorry, Sergeant, Private."

I thanked him and the three of us turned to go, but as we reached the door, Marcus turned back.

"Captain Brown," he said, kneeling by the bed. "Do you regret it? Shooting down the Baron, I mean."

Brown didn't turn his head, instead staring blankly at the ceiling. His voice was barely audible.

"I do, Sergeant. Damn it, I do."

Chapter 17
Thief in the Night
Marcus

Hark! 'Tis the rush of the horses,
The crash of the galloping gun!
The stars are out of their courses;
The hour of Doom has begun.
-Francis William Bourdillon-

Oliver escorted us back to the Officer's Quarters. He didn't bother pausing before opening the door and waltzing in to rummage through Brown's personal effects. I held a hand in front of Jane as we entered, hesitating a moment in case we'd caught some officer with his pants down or in some other indecent state.

She swatted my hand away, and we followed him to a canvas bag tucked beside a bed that looked much more comfortable than the one in medical. It didn't surprise me that they'd confined the captain to separate quarters. The influenza could be just as deadly as an enemy bullet, and it seemed to be showing up more and more often, taking boys out of service for recovery.

Marcus

When it first started sweeping through the ranks, the influenza used to scare me to death. No one wanted to go out that way. But barring reasonable precautions, I'd needed to come to terms with the risk. Even the most careful sometimes contracted the disease, and there was no point in getting all anxious about what you couldn't control.

"Here we are," Oliver said, producing a folded telegram paper. He handed it to Jane. "From what I gather, you're the one who does most of the work between the two of you," he said to her.

"Thank you for noticing," Jane smirked.

"What's that supposed to mean?"

"You tell me, Marcus," she said. "Is it more work *flying* a plane or *fixing* a plane?"

"I don't see you working on the Salmson right now," I countered.

"Didn't mean to poke a bear," Oliver said. He glanced around nervously, contenting himself that no one else was in the building. "Here, you'll want to see this."

Tenderly, he reached deeper into the sack and took out a folded bunch of linen. He extended it to us reverently, and he nodded at me to unfold it.

When I did, we saw what lay inside. A black silk scarf. It shimmered, the satin surface catching stray lantern light and the last rays of sunset, punctuated by streaks and blots of a matte substance that dimmed its luster.

"Richthofen's scarf," Jane gasped. I set my jaw and reached out my hand to touch it. A piece of the Baron's uniform. I rubbed my finger over a spot of the dried blood, blood that ran through the veins of the man who shot down more than eighty planes. An urge came over me to grab the scarf and run to my plane, to take it back up to its home in the sky. My ears played tricks on me, faintly hearing the sound of engines bursting into flame, of planes

184

whistling and screaming as they plummeted to the earth. The strap on Boelcke's Goggles warmed on my neck. And it might have been my imagination, but I thought my glass marble warmed, too.

Oliver jolted and retracted the scarf, startled at the sound of conversation passing outside the window. I snapped from my daze, but too late. Jane had noticed, and I already knew she'd have questions for me later.

"Better put it back," he said. "It's like Brown said, only a few people know he has it. And a relic like this from the Baron might try the honesty of some of the military men, not to mention these blood-sucking reporters."

"Sure," I muttered, fighting back an impulse to stuff it in my pocket. "Makes sense." I traced his movements as he delicately folded the linen over the scarf again and put it back in the bag.

"Anyway, I'm sure the two of you are tired. Let's go see where Paynter has you situated."

As it so happened, Paynter didn't manage to find us anything, and Oliver took it upon himself to set me up a cot in the Squadron Office. Jane bunked in the women's barracks. A handful of the girls seemed all too eager to offer a space, curiosity dripping from their smiles. Jane looked at me enviously, no doubt wishing she could also enjoy the peace of a night spent alone.

But as it happened, my night of solitude was anything but peaceful.

We agreed to work on decoding the new telegram the next morning, and I settled in, drawing the shades and setting down my meager pack.

There wasn't an abundance of storage space on the Salmson, and Smith had assured us our needs would be taken care of. I packed my toothbrush and little else. Jane managed to stuff a few more odds and ends inside the pockets of her flight suit and in the ammo tray between our seats, but it wasn't much.

That was the nature of the mission, though. Smith, Atkins, Dupont... they all seemed to think things should go quickly. Fly in, find the rogue flyers, fly back out. We'd already made great progress, arriving at Clairmarais in one piece and successfully getting Brown's story from him.

We'd already seen Richthofen's scarf. I hardly believed in the magic, but even I knew it was special.

I tossed and turned in my bed, as I struggled to reconcile all the things I'd heard and seen in the past couple of days. The rogue flyers terrorizing two experienced pilots. The Baron breaking his own pattern of excellence and all but letting himself get shot. Mustermann's killing of Johann. Smith's belief in Boelcke's goggles.

And Jane's sharp criticism in the plane on the way here.

Jane had never come after me like that before. Just the other night, she'd gone out of her way to put me at ease, teaching me how to dance the Grizzly Bear for goodness' sakes. All it took was a single German speck, flying far below and far away to raise in her the spectral doom of the soldier. The kill or die impulse.

Maybe it hit me so hard because I'd placed Jane on a pedestal. Since we'd met, she'd been a shining star in a dark world. I protected her like a match against the wind. To think that she could be brought down to that level so quickly threatened to diminish her unique goodness.

She'd apologized immediately after. She'd recognized what came over her.

From far away in the recesses of my memory came my father's advice. He believed that evil came for all men, and the measure of a man was only what he made of evil, that opportunities to do good marked the quality of an individual.

I hated the maxim. At war, opportunities to do good earned no rewards. No good deed went unpunished. I learned those lessons through despair.

But Jane? Did I put too many expectations on her? My father's advice lived inside of her. The love of my mother lived inside of her. Keeping her alive was my way of maintaining that small ember in my soul so that one day I'd find the courage to write home. If Jane was not destroyed for her goodness, perhaps one day, if the war ended, I could return home despite everything.

And yet, Jane had come after me in that plane. I wished I remembered how to cry.

The sound of far-off artillery shelling eventually lulled me to sleep.

The next morning, I made my groggy way to the mess, looking like a mess. The French had a word for their armed service members: the *poilu*. I asked one what the word meant once, he just scratched the whiskers under my chin. "It means this." Over time, I understood. *Poilu* meant men who had gotten in touch with the baser physical appearance. Unshorn. Unclean.

Me, that morning.

When I got there, I was surprised to see Jane groomed and beautiful, as if somewhere in the Salmson, she'd hidden everything she needed to prepare herself for a silent film audition.

"Good morning," she said as I sat down beside her, plate full of bacon, beans, and brown bread. One of the girls from the intelligence office walked by with a bouquet of colorful radishes and greens on her plate, and my stomach groaned with envy.

"They have fresh radishes?" I asked.

"And fresh turnips."

"Where was all this yesterday when we choked down that fish stew?"

"One of the few remaining residents in town apparently tends the gardens of his neighbors' abandoned homes just so he has something to offer the servicemen," Jane explained. "He came by this morning."

I paused. Old men—men that were beyond the conscription age—found ways to help the war effort. But that group got smaller and smaller all the time. Apparently, Britain was sending their fifty-five-year-olds to the lines now. Young men now fought beside brothers old enough to be their fathers. It wasn't that way when I first came out. The memory of my father hadn't left me since last night. I tried to imagine him in uniform.

"How do you look so good?" I asked, shaking my head out of the war logistics humdrum.

"Is that meant to be a compliment?" she asked.

"If you want it to be. Is there a storage drum on our plane I don't know about?"

"Some of the younger girls insisted. I didn't even touch my face. Apparently, my flight cap did a number on my hair that was not suitable for their standards."

"Really? I didn't consider the WREN girls so vain." I dug into my meal. The beans lacked salt, but the bacon was meaty and greasy, satisfying to the tongue and stomach. Still, I longed for the flavor of those garden-fresh radishes. "Did you make any headway on decoding that message?"

"And risk some of the girls from the intelligence office seeing what I was up to? Definitely not."

"That's all right. I've got more questions for Captain Brown, anyway. We can work on everything today. Did you see the color drain from their faces when they talked about that rogue flyer?"

Jane nodded and dotted her mouth with a napkin.

"He fought the Baron's Jasta," I continued. "They're not green pilots, but you'd have thought they fought the devil himself."

"Perhaps they did."

"What do you mean?"

Jane hedged, the corner of her mouth dropping into a slant the way it did when she had bad news to share. But before she could elaborate, Oliver planted himself right beside me.

"Where is it?" The jovial energy of his features was gone. He stared holes in my forehead.

"Where's what?"

He pounded the table with his fist.

"You know *what*. You're going to play dumb?"

Jane and I exchanged stupefied expressions.

"I see how it is. Shoulda seen it from the start. They put you up to it. Command. Somehow, they heard about the flyer, and the scarf, and they've got you out here to take it away. But it's not right. He earned it."

I swallowed my mouthful of beans without chewing adequately. It hurt down my throat as I searched for a response. Oliver's accusation had us pegged. Jane and I both knew it. And when Smith and Mustermann heard about the scarf, I had zero doubts that they'd be asking us to claim it.

But I stopped puzzling when I grasped the implications of Oliver's question. Jane beat me there.

"The scarf is missing?" Jane asked, lowering her head between her shoulders.

"Roy asked me to bring it to him this morning, but I found nothing but an empty mess of linen at the foot of his bed. Nobody knew he had it."

Jane kicked me under the table, one her subtle ways of making sure I was paying attention. She covered my wince with a profuse promise.

"Oliver, we didn't take it."

"I know you didn't," he said leveling a finger at Jane. "I dropped you off at the women's barracks. But this man, Sergeant Jackson, spent the night alone. And I saw the way he stared at the scarf last night."

I rubbed my knee.

"Strip me naked here and search me if you want," I said. "I don't have it."

"You could have hidden it anywhere last night," he said.

"Oliver, come on. You said it yourself. This base is over capacity. Reporters are crawling everywhere. Other pilots. Anyone interested in Brown's story could have come up with the bright idea to break into his things to poke around. Besides, Jane and I still need to work with you. Why would we hurt your trust like that?"

Oliver shook his head. My argument silenced but didn't satisfy him. Jane jumped in.

"And why are you in such fury? It's not yours, either, is it Oliver? Have you told the captain, yet?" she asked.

Oliver scowled and shook his head at her menacingly.

"I wasn't ever supposed to take it out in the first place. All right. Fine. If you didn't take it, help me find out who did. Otherwise, I'm afraid..." He wrung his hands, blowing hot air on them for warmth.

"Afraid of what?" I asked.

"Afraid that a shock like this might finish Brown off. You saw him last night. He's no better this morning. But he went up there on patrol anyway, over the sea."

I tried to conceal my shock. Pilots often went up when they shouldn't, but in Brown's condition, flying was all but suicidal. Poor Oliver's age showed through his stress. I patted his shoulder.

"Yeah. Of course, we'll help. Where do you think we should look?"

"I'll distract Paynter," he said. "He had access to the Officer's Quarters, and you saw how he was acting funny last night. While I keep him busy, you go into his stuff and check."

I worked my shoulders in a circular motion and cocked my head to the side.

"Maybe we should distract Paynter, since we don't know where his stuff is."

"Better idea. I'll go wait by the door. Let me know when it's time." Oliver tapped his nose at us, a signal suggestion, and departed from the table.

"The scarf is missing?" I asked Jane in a hushed voice.

"Yes. And, I don't think Paynter has it either. Come on." She stood abruptly and pulled me after. "Oliver said no one knew the captain had the scarf, other than the three of us. Correct?"

"Yeah."

"Brown didn't believe that though, did he? He believed the rogue flyer, a squadron with access to British planes, tried to shoot him down for it."

"I'm not following," I said, trying to keep up with her. She'd already bounded from the mess hall. She skipped across the muddy road and stopped on the edge of the flight field. Squadrons of aircraft lay before us, some undergoing repairs, some waiting for their pilots so they could take the skies again.

"That scarf didn't stand up and walk off. Oliver said that only you, I, Brown, and he knew where it was. None of us took it, which means someone else did. How hard do you think it would be to hide a plane amongst fifty?" She asked, grabbing me by the shoulders and making me face the airfield.

Suddenly, her idea hit me.

"You think the rogue flyer snuck in and stole it?"

"And I think he might still be here. He certainly didn't leave last night, or we'd have all heard him take off."

"We have to search through these planes."

"A blue-on-blue-on-blue cocarde."

I stopped.

"Jane, if they had the smarts to come down here, I'm sure they'd have painted the cocarde to match. And that's if he flew his own plane in, which would be pretty hard to do without attracting attention."

"Well, we have to start somewhere!"

She was already running toward one group of pursuit aircraft. I took off toward another. Clairmarais wasn't that large of an aerodrome. Even with the added traffic, could a strange pilot truly sneak on base and break into the Officer's Quarters without getting stopped or questioned? After we landed, we had hardly made it ten feet before the crew was berating us about Jane.

Mechanics shouted after me as I ran and jumped to catch a glimpse not just of the side markings on the planes but the ones on top as well. I only saw red-centered cocardes. Nothing strange. I emerged on the other end of one group of parked Camels and looked across the field. Jane popped out of another grouping and shook her head at me.

We continued. Maybe she was wrong. After all, what were the odds that the very night we arrived was the same night one of these radicals planned to sneak in and take off with the Baron's scarf? Then again, Brown had only had the scarf for a few days, and they'd already targeted him in the sky.

I reflected on Smith's urgency in getting us off the ground. The longer I was at war, the more I learned that last-minute commands often walked hand-in-hand with terrible coincidences.

My heart pounded and my lungs labored after my run through the airfield. Spots of rain spattered against my face, and I turned to the sky to see darkening clouds rolling in from the direction of the sea. If the pilot were here, he'd be grounded by an incoming storm same as anyone else. That would at least buy us some time.

I jogged over to Jane.

"Anything?" I asked.

"Nothing. At least not on the pursuit planes. I haven't checked the Handleys. We'd need to use the ladders. It would take twice as long, and we'd look three times as suspicious."

I rubbed my neck and squinted against the scattered raindrops.

"A Handley? I don't know, Jane. These fellas having a handful of pursuit aircraft is one thing, but them stealing bombers? Seems unlikely."

"Then go distract Paynter if you must, and I'll check the Handleys alone."

"Come on. I can't let you do that. What if you find this guy?"

"Then, I'll scream to get your attention."

I shook my head emphatically.

"It's too dangerous."

Across the field, the roar of a plane's propellor came to life, and the hum of a Camel's Bentley engine droned through the air. We both turned.

Red center. English cocarde.

"How about this?" I asked, turning back to Jane. "Why don't we go distract Paynter like we told Oliver we would. Then, we can come up with a plan to find this pilot before he can escape. After all, there are other ways of getting to and from the aerodrome other than from the sky. And with the storm, don't you think they'd be more likely to travel out by ground than air."

Jane stared past me, furrowing her brows. Her cheeks were flushed like mine, but on her it looked like rouge.

"Marcus, how are you so thick? Are you truly discounting the Camel taking off at the very same moment you're telling me that these storms make flying impossible?"

I turned again, a little embarrassed.

"Well, not impossible, just plain stupid. Jane, it's a red-centered insignia. What do you want to do? Fly up after a plane we have no solid reason to believe is anything but an English pursuit pilot probably going to the aid of some naval vessel?"

"Oh, just stop talking and—" Her eyes settled on the goggles hanging around my neck. Boelcke's allegedly magical goggles. She lashed out, pulled them off me, and held them to her face. Behind their lenses, her eyes grew wide. "Blue! If you would just listen to me instead of—just, come on!"

She threw the goggles at my chest and sprinted toward our hangar.

Dumbly, I put the goggles on, and the Sopwith Camel, which to all naked eyes appeared as standard issue as though it were right out of the factory, lit up in blue light. Forget the cocarde, the entire plane appeared to light up in bioluminescent rays, tendrils of light snaking off the top wing like vines, dangling from the fuselage, dragging behind the rudder like streamers, all with a mind of their own, as animated as the limbs of an octopus.

I blinked. I froze.

Magic. Or some new military technology. But no. There was no tech like this. This was beyond—

Magic.

Instinctively, I clutched the marble hanging around my neck.

In a moment, I understood Jane better, I could make sense of Smith's sudden change of heart at the farmhouse. My view through those goggles changed me in a heartbeat, and nothing— not my reverence for the great aces of the war nor my faltering faith—could make me deny it to myself.

This whole time. *Magic.*

"Marcus!"

Jane's voice, strained from shouting across the field, unlocked my feet. I ran after her as quickly as my legs would allow, trying to make up for lost time. Adrenaline fueled me, both from the thrill of the chase but also the otherworldly vertigo that came with doubting everything you'd come to understand about the world.

"They work," I stammered as I fell in beside her.

"I told you they worked!"

"No, but I mean, they really work."

"I told you they worked!

I nearly tripped when we cleared the corner of our hangar. One of our mechanics was polishing an ammo drum and nearly jumped when we came in.

"Why so hasty? Are we being raided?" he asked peering up at the sky.

"We need to get up in the air. Now!" I shouted. A couple of flight suits were strewn across a stool. They were worn, missing the lining in some parts, holed in others. I threw one to Jane, and we donned it quickly as we boarded.

"Have you lost your mind? Have you seen the weather?"

"I don't care about the weather. Is there an ammo drum in there already? Fuel?"

"Well, yes. No. I mean, no, but yes."

"Just get this propellor moving!"

We'd both taken our seat by now, and he stared dumbly at the plane, caught flat-footed both from the urgency of our request and seeing a woman climbing into the gunners' seat. Jane scoffed from her perch.

"Oh, for heaven's sake. Do I need to get down there and show you how to be a mechanic?"

Something about Jane's derision got him moving. The hangar was shallow, and we didn't share it with other aircraft, so the kid set straight to work on the propeller, working it slowly in a circle.

By the time I shouted "Contact!" and the Salmson sprung to life, I was worried the blue flyer would be long gone. He pulled the chocks from the wheels, and we taxied forward, me giving more fuel to the engine and rolling along at a clip faster than I normally would to get to the runway.

As soon as we had grass in front of us, I fed the engine and it roared to life, happy to see us. I missed the extra layer I usually wore beneath my heavy flight suit before we were even airborne, but at least the clouds overhead kept all the warmth in the air from going out to sea. I pulled Boelcke's goggles over my eyes and pulled back on the stick. We climbed as fast as I dared to push the Salmson.

Above us, ominous gray clouds warned of the danger we attempted. Rain would make flying even more deadly than it was already. But even if we got above the storm, if the rain didn't cause engine failure or we weren't struck by lightning, the real danger came in navigation above a blanket of clouds, finding our way home, and eventually landing.

"—see him?" Jane screamed from behind me, her voice barely audible over the whoosh of wind and snarl of the Salmson engine, two hundred and thirty horse power fighting her for my attention.

I scanned the horizon. We'd already climbed to the cloud floor, and there was no sign of him. I frowned. Pursuing an enemy above a blanket like this could make for a tricky return to Clairmarais, unless we could catch him quickly enough for me to duck back under the clouds and get my bearings. I was unfamiliar with the terrain. But at least the sea bordered our northern side. If all else failed, we could try to find the sea.

"Hold tight!" I cried back.

"What—" The air whipped her voice from my ears.

I pulled back and we entered the thick condensation. The moisture seeped right through my clothes, chilling me like cold bath water, and I coughed trying to breathe for all the droplets of moisture entering my lungs. It took us half a minute to overcome the cloud, and when we emerged, I was relieved beyond anything to have my sight again.

And what a sight it was. A billowing gray sea stretched out as a carpet underneath us. We glided through an otherworldly dream-scape, polka dotted with wispy tendrils of fluff. I scanned the skies, leaning into my new faith in Boelcke's goggles. Finally, far ahead, blue tendrils lit up my vision.

"There!" I wasn't sure Jane could hear me, but I shouted all the same. The unearthly blue glow radiated from his plane, and the task before us daunted me. The Sopwith was faster than our Salmson by far, and he'd had a good head start with most of his climb behind him. We'd never catch up. But if I could keep him in view, we might follow him home. Maybe he wouldn't push his engine and try to conserve fuel.

It was likely for the best, anyway. As my adrenaline waned, I remembered that Jane had no experience on those guns, and getting into a fight with a pilot that Brown described as the devil incarnate might not be in our best interest.

So I settled below him and put my nose along his trajectory. After about ten minutes, I was almost sure that the plane appeared larger than before. Maybe we were getting closer.

But just as the anxiety of losing him wore off, and I managed to take a breath, the Camel did something I didn't expect.

A renversement.

It curved upward and rolled back on itself at the apex of its loop to turn and face us.

As if with a sixth sense, the pilot knew we were following him.

"He couldn't have seen me back here," I muttered to myself. But a thousand feet above us and a half mile ahead, the blue-glow Sopwith pursuit plane had turned over and dove.

I froze, an ironclad grip on the joystick. There was little to be done. The Camel was the superior plane in a sortie. But shooting down or following this pilot home was why we came in the first place. Following him quietly had just failed, but to fight him?

And Jane—my Jane—sitting behind me, just learning those Lewis Guns. She'd never tried to hit a target before, let alone one moving through combat maneuvers.

A panic unlike any I'd experienced crept over me. Jane who had saved me from the gloom of myself. Jane whom I had sworn to protect from the war. I wanted to meet her family, see what life beyond the war could do for her, watch her get married, find fulfillment.

Marcus

Jane who, more than anyone else, might understand my story if I was brave enough to tell her.

As the Camel dropped, my heart dropped with it.

Jane must live.

Our only hope was the Aerodrome. He had his quarry; he wouldn't risk now flying back to Clairmarais.

I pushed the stick forward, and we dove back into the clouds.

Chapter 18
The Blue Flyer
Jane

Grown more loving-kind and warm
We'll grasp firm hands and laugh at the old pain,
When it is peace. But until peace, the storm
The darkness and the thunder and the rain.
-Charles Hamilton Sorley-

I noticed the Sopwith just before clouds enveloped us again.

I didn't even have the opportunity to recover. The first time we flew through the stormy cloud bank, I'd nearly held my breath all the way through the clouds, rather than breathe in the water-rich vapor. This time, I was unprepared.

I gulped in a fleeting gasp, and it pained my lungs. My sinuses, which already wracked me with pain from changes in the air pressure, rebelled as though I'd tried to breathe in river water.

We passed through the cloud much faster than we'd climbed, though, and soon enough we'd come through on the bottom. The rain had grown stronger, from scattered droplets to a gentle, steady drizzle. But from the state of the sky around us, the rain would only get worse. Already, my borrowed, oversized flight coat took on an unpleasant damp quality that amplified the air rushing the chilling wind. The rain itself, light as it was, barraged my face like needles. I wished now that I'd found a flight cap in that hangar. I must have looked like a wet flagpole with my hair flapping ridiculously behind me.

"What are you doing?" I shouted, after twisting to face Marcus. "The blue flyer is the other way!"

He either didn't hear me or didn't acknowledge my question.

And who could hear in a moment like that? Beyond the thrum of the engine, under the whistling wind, the rain sang white noise as it fell to the earth. Marcus pushed the plane harder, more steeply, and I wondered at the durability of the Salmson's wings. Did it, too, suffer from the same design flaws that ripped the lining off of Nieuport frames? Or worse? Some planes had lost wings altogether under the stress of flight.

I had no intention of dying my third time in the air.

I turned away from the incoming Earth, trying to ignore my stomach's churning, gazing back up at the sky into the gray ceiling, the raindrops raced downward beside us, appearing to me to be moving half of their normal speed. Just as Marcus curved out of the dive, my eyes went wide.

The Camel burst from the clouds above with tremendous speed.

Something came over me, a primal, dark, lusty warrior instinct, and I seized the handles of the Lewis guns with all my strength, peered down the iron sights, and fired.

The guns blazed furiously. The action shook back and forth like a locomotive, and tracer rounds carved through the wind up at the Camel. I didn't let off. My hair whipped around the edges of my vision. My body quivered in protest against the elements, but as the vestigial warmth from the gun radiated toward me in waves, I continued.

The recoil, the vibration, the explosive reaction all found a home in me. Here was power. Here was protection.

The Camel banked to the right, and I followed with the guns, hefting them on their ring to keep up with our agile foe, but I couldn't move it fast enough, and it dived past us and beyond my reach.

The engine pulsed. In the deafening absence of its roar, Marcus's voice came fragmented through the slipstream.

"Don't waste...drums."

Then the engine roared back to life.

I swore to myself. Of course, Marcus was correct. Our mechanic had been tinkering with an ammunition drum when we arrived at our hangar. I had just unleashed a spray of fire without a second thought of our limited ammunition, and glancing in the well beside me, we had only one drum to spare. At about a hundred rounds per drum, I could fire through all our rounds quickly if I weren't careful.

Vague memories of Marcus droning on about Boelcke's tactics, "only shooting when you have a sure shot," made sense. From the ground, even as a mechanic, it was so easy to ignore the logistics, to boil the entire affair down to fly and shoot.

My first real-time lesson in air combat strategy, and hopefully not the last.

The Camel flew below us, and with its position came new dangers. We were exposed from the underside. My guns could only arc so far along the downward angle, and we'd be easy prey if the Camel could line us up correctly. Marcus would be forced to engage with defensive maneuvers at the very least.

He knew it as well. He pitched the plane upward, before rolling over our right wing and plunging, corkscrewing, toward the Earth. My stomach jumped up my throat, but I caught a glimpse of the Camel on each revolution. It was a scene from a poorly cranked motion picture, one image stuttering at a time.

I heard a Vickers gun rattle off rounds. Was it his or ours? No tracer paths came near me. And the next I could see, the Camel swooped into a rising helix and out from beneath Marcus's nose. As we leveled from our own dive, I had a brief window.

I yanked on the guns, my arms protesting their unnatural weight, and pulled the trigger again. There was only a quick burst this time, not the prolonged, amateurish volley from before, but the shots went wide.

I followed the Camel with my eyes, and nearly jumped in my seat.

We were flying low. So low that the Camel had no chance to get beneath us without risking a crash. Trees whipped past below, and I could nearly smell the wet branches.

What was Marcus thinking? He broke left and gave me another view of the Camel. It barreled into another turn, taking its time to put some distance between us. I shot again, but the force of the turn made it immensely difficult to pull the Lewis guns where I wanted. The shots rattled off harmlessly. My arms burned. I had relied too much on my own strength to aim and hadn't taken smart advantage of the rigging.

The Camel climbed, picked up altitude, and came down at us. Its twin Vickers sparked to life, and for the first time since joining the war, I was truly afraid of dying. I fired back, help-lessly, the empty, creeping panic robbing my arms of more strength. Marcus rolled our wings almost a full ninety degrees, narrowing our target, but also effectively ruining my chances to hit the Camel.

I tried anyway.

After our enemy passed us, we flipped back and broke the other direction. My vision swam, reality spinning even when the plane took a steady pass. So much twirling back and forth.

When the Camel dived again, Marcus pulled the same trick of rolling us onto our side. Wild, inaccurately, desperately, I tried shooting. But to my dismay, the guns only let out a quick burst then fell silent. My first drum of ammunition had run out.

"I'm empty!" I cried. "I have to reload!"

Wide grassy fields now spread out around us, and Marcus attempted to gain altitude. The rain came down harder, pelting my face. My hands trembled as I removed the empty ammo drum atop the Lewis. My fingers slipped down the flange. The metal tore a small gash in my skin. The pain would come later. I pulled the drum free and tossed it into the ammo well, feeling the vulnerable seconds chew away at me. The new drum was much heavier, but with the heft came a delicious feeling of safety.

As I settled the drum atop my guns, the Sopwith let out a sharp *rat tat tat*. A line of ugly holes passed through our right wing, larger and more menacing than a nightmare.

Marcus banked again, and between my start at the sound of the enemy's Vickers guns and the jolting movement, our last ammo drum went whirling out of my hands, falling to the ground below.

My breath caught in my chest.

Vainly, I searched the ammo well again, but found only the empty drum I'd just removed. My heart hammered. My breaths came too quickly to be of any use. I was out of rounds. My thoughts raced back to the mechanic in our hangar, lazily toiling over one of the drums. The fool must have removed them all.

"Marcus!" I shouted. "We're empty! There's no more ammunition. Bullets gone!"

He must have understood something, because his strategy changed. He banked again, but this time, he pulled us into a deep turn, attempting to face the Camel.

His sudden offensive took the rogue pilot by surprise, and he slipped on his turn, his nose facing one direction, while the plane skid through the air in another. I felt our own plane crank, experienced a peculiar sensation of plummeting in one direction while seeing forward, and saw our movement change. We skid right across the Camel's path. The Vickers guns screamed. I ducked into my bay.

"Come on! Fire!" Marcus's voice came over the wind like a howling ghost.

Whose guns were they? If Marcus wanted a close shot, that would have given him ample opportunity. I peered over the gun well and noted, in terror, the splintering of one of our wing struts. Big holes had been blown into our fuselage right behind me. But we were still flying.

Marcus corrected our direction, the Camel did the same, and the awful dance went on.

My dread only increased. As I looked closer at our aircraft, I found other holes, bits of shrapnel, flapping tears of canvas. It was a miracle that none of the shots had connected with Marcus or me already.

I noticed the change in our maneuverability almost instantly. Marcus went back to his sweeping evasive attempts, but without the Lewis guns to ward off our attacker and with our reduced flight capacity, the Sopwith took sweeping passes across our plane. Riddling us all the more with rounds. A section of our rudder burst. Another woodpecker trail along our right wing.

The rogue pilot easily outflew us now, settling directly at our rear. I recognized now the risk Marcus took in his offensive maneuver. He sacrificed positioning to take one good shot at the enemy. Now, the Sopwith was on our tail, facing me, its unfeeling blade sawing through the air. Its guns lit up, and rounds streaked past us.

Marcus tried to climb, to dive what little he could, to evade, to roll over, but in his desperate attempts to survive, he had cut off any tactical room he might have used in a moment like this. His strategy had been to avoid this very scenario. He had needed me not to be so foolhardy with the limited ammunition.

I ducked low in the gunner's bay and prayed. Bullets sprayed overhead. A round burst through one of the struts behind me, poked holes right beside me. I grasped through my flight coat and took hold of my glass marble. A protection charm, fashioned by my Aunt Luella by using a lock of Marcus's hair. It was a charm she warned me may not work, but she had fashioned it because I wrote my mother about Marcus, about how he reminded me of home, about how afraid I felt every time he took to the sky. My mother had taken it to her friend.

My mother. Aunt Luella. My father. Marcus. A vision of their memories circulated around the marble in the dark of the gunner's bay.

And then a wild idea struck me. And if we were to die, I would die fresh out of those ideas.

I yanked the marble off its chain and thrust my hand upward, poking my head out of my seat as bravely as thoughts of my family allowed. When my eyes cleared the edge of the bay, the Camel was nearly on top of us. Even Boelcke or the Baron would have fired now.

But the blue flyer didn't. The menacing guns behind the whirring propellor lay quietly at rest. I was close enough to see his face. It was painted with awe and confusion, but something else as well, something dangerous.

Marcus didn't wait for him to recover. He broke right and barreled us over out of the flyer's direct line of flight.

In our wake, I saw double. The Sopwith had split in two, a perfect copy of itself now.

No. That wasn't right. There was another Sopwith, but this one had three wings. It fired at our attacker furiously. The rogue pilot veered off-course.

We circled round below, Marcus daring to bring the Salmson into the fight, trying to tempt the rogue flyer into coming after us.

But he did not take the bait. In a matter of minutes, the blue flyer abandoned his intentions and flew back up toward the clouds.

The new Camel chased him until the enemy vanished into the weather. Then it came round to accompany us home. When he pulled up beside us, I recognized a furious Oliver LeBoutillier.

The rain did its work on us. I was drenched. Our Salmson was soaking and barely holding together.

But somehow, we survived my first combat.

Chapter 19
Mistakes
Marcus

The drab street stares to see them row on row
On the high tram-tops, singing like the lark.
Too careless-gay for courage, singing they go
Into the dark.
-Katharine Tynan-

I gulped air. Large heaving empty lungfuls. The air would not come, despite how I tried.

Everything was upside down. Not figuratively. The sky was where the ground should be.

I hung in the cockpit just off the airfield at Clairmarais. Around me, the world blurred in disconcerted motion, nothing managed to pull my attention into focus. The engine was off. We may have run out of fuel, I wasn't sure. The dial read empty. Vaguely, Jane's voice called to me, like from under a blanket, smothered by a pillow, enveloped by the down of gray clouds.

Jane, who I had nearly gotten killed.

Two hands pulled at my shoulders. I turned and saw her face. Her hair hung toward the ground, brows furrowed, eyes wild. She leaned across the fuselage from her gunner's bay, crossing the gap that was insurmountable while airborne. Her mouth moved, but the sound came late.

She lived. This was real.

The sortie came back to me in fragments. The storm. The Camel looping up in the renversement. The vrille, corkscrewing down. All but skimming the ground to eliminate our underside as a potential target. The Immelmans. Breaking back and forth. Hearing Jane's guns go out. The desperate slip slide. And then panic.

The slip slide.

I'd had a shot. He was right in front of my guns not ten feet off. I didn't fire. But he did.

The shame pierced my gut like a hot, twisting bayonet. What was wrong with me? I wasn't cursed. I was broken. I had always been broken. If I'd wanted glory, it was there. If I'd wanted Jane's safety, it was there. If I wanted to prove that I wasn't a pathetic, cowardly, disappointment to all around me...

After that, the blue flyer predicted my every maneuver. I couldn't even remember what I'd done. I had no space to dive. I must have zoom climbed to get some altitude. Yes, leveraged the speed from the vrille.

And the storm. No wonder I was so wet. My hands shook. They were numb. Other hands now grabbed at me. Strong hands, and I was getting out of the plane. Why was I upside down? Why was our plane upside down in the mud?

And Jane? Yes. Somehow, she was already out of the plane, had abandoned her flight suit, blended in among the others trying to help me. Now we all rushed for cover, out of the rain. Propping me up. And then, Oliver was putting a bottle to my lips. It burned. I sputtered and spat, but it jarred me. A stinging liquid slap to the face. I shook my head as the world came into focus again. The sound snapping back like a rubber band. A breath caught traction, brought welcome air. Then another. And another. Each breath working more.

And Jane sat in front of me, holding my hand in both of hers. Her fingers were cold and clammy. Blood ran down the back of one. Had she been shot? No. It was too small. A wound. A scratch.

"Jane?" I asked.

"Yes, Marcus. It's me. We made it through. Breathe. You're alive. You're unharmed."

But something in my eyes said what my tongue failed to communicate, and more softly she added to me quietly.

"I am alive. I am unharmed."

I nodded and let her words sink in. She was alive. Despite my cowardice, she was unharmed. The meaning steadied me, calmed my nerves, and slowly, one breath at a time, I returned to a state of stability. But there, I found self-loathing.

I was a scrap of a man, worse than a deserter. The sight of Jane made my muscles shrivel and wither. Around her hung the ghostly faces of soldiers gone, soldiers who had funded my second chances with a mortal reckoning. She had nearly become one of them. How could I have lived with myself if Jane had joined their phantom ranks? Jane, in whom I placed so much trust. I had sworn to protect her, but more, I had found hope in her. She had offered understanding to me sufficient nearly to break me out of the tomb I made for myself.

"What happened up there?" That was Captain Brown's voice, and it sounded thin and weak.

"Roy, what are you doing? It's pouring out here. You're sick enough as it is!" Oliver protested.

"What happened?" Brown insisted.

Jane glanced about. Mechanics and orderlies buzzed around, some examining Oliver's Sopwith tucked safely in a hangar. Others slipped, trying to lift our plane from the mud. I caught sight of it and shivered. It was so battered I'd have thought we ran straight through a wall of anti-aircraft fire. Holes lined the wings, riddled the back end of the fuselage. The struts were splintered to toothpicks. One aileron was damaged, and it was a miracle the elevator had worked at all on our return.

That plane should never have made it back.

"We should bring Marcus inside," Jane said, staring at the captain coldly. I understood her expression. She used it whenever she meant something other than what she said. "There are so many people running about, and we've both had such a shock."

"And you as well, Captain," said Oliver, grabbing Roy by the arm and leading him back to the medical unit.

"Can you stand?" Jane asked.

I nodded and blushed. There was so much to be ashamed of. I'd never had such a reaction after a flight, and the embarrassment of falling to pieces in front of Jane and the others hit me hard. But that was nothing compared to the searing hot realization that I didn't fire my guns.

I clumsily got to my feet.

"Your hand," I said.

"Trying to reload. I slipped in the rain and scraped it. Nothing more."

The last remains of my immediate concern for her physical welfare melted, and I took her in. I wanted to cry, but I fought it. The care with which the other women had prepared her for the day was a joke running down her face. Her hair was matted down in a wet mess, her lipstick smeared like blood, and her sopping wet clothes accentuated a figure slimmed by war time.

We hurried through the rain after Oliver and Brown. But before we joined them inside, I grabbed Jane's arm.

"I'm sorry, I—" I couldn't finish. To say it out loud would make it more true, more than just my dark secret.

To my surprise, Jane's jaw clenched and her eyes narrowed. Had my apology bothered her?

"For what? It was my idea to go after him."

"That may be, but I nearly got you killed. If his gun hadn't jammed at the end."

"It jammed?" She asked. "Did you see it in the goggles?"

I bit my tongue. I had wracked my head back and forth desperately in order to peek the Sopwith when it was on our tail, but if there was some magic signal in Boelcke's goggles that indicated a jammed gun, I hadn't seen it.

"Why else didn't he shoot?" I asked.

Jane pursed her lips.

"Let's get inside."

I followed her in to the medical tent. Captain Brown sat on the bed and coughed weakly. Oliver, meanwhile, attempted to help him take medicine. The captain waved him off.

"Here we are, Private Doe," he said. "Away from prying ears. What is it?"

Jane glanced at Oliver.

"Will you tell him?"

Oliver's shoulders sank, and he took a deep breath.

"It was the scarf, Roy."

"The scarf? What do you mean?"

"When I gave these two the telegram last night, I took out the Baron's scarf so they could see it. This morning, it was gone."

"It wasn't Oliver's fault," I said, relieved to have something to distract me from the fight. "If the blue flyer knew it was here, he'd have found it anyway. And I don't remember seeing anyone spy on us last night."

Brown leaned back against the wall.

"You mean he took it?"

"We tried to pursue him," Jane added quickly. "That's our mission, you see. To find him and his base. Command believes he leads a group of radical pilots trying to prolong the war. But, somehow he, well, he—"

"He spotted us," I interrupted. "And he must have figured the math of one Sopwith Camel against a Salmson 2 gave him pretty good odds. We didn't stand a chance, especially because we rushed takeoff, and our plane was not combat ready."

"Marcus flew brilliantly," said Jane after a moment's silence. "We almost had him at the end."

Her words hit me like a Vickers' round in the gut.

"Almost doesn't cut it," Brown said bitterly. "Do you know how many 'almost aces' we have on our side?"

He put his head in his hands and coughed again, this time a deep guttural moan betraying his weariness.

"It's gone," he whispered. I sympathized, but something in the way he said it gave me goosebumps, perhaps because I'd also felt its pull the night before. I wondered what type of bond Roy had made with his trophy, even during the short time he'd had it in his possession.

He didn't say anything else to us, only laid down and closed his eyes. Oliver nudged him, insisting he submit and take some medicine, but Captain Brown had lost the energy to respond.

"Come on, Oliver," Jane said quietly. "Best to let him rest."

Oliver nodded glumly, and the three of us retired to wash up and change.

M y bones were wet even in dry clothes. I borrowed a uniform after entrusting mine to a couple of the girls on cleaning duty. When I asked how long it would take to dry, they replied, "In a day or two."

The rain let up soon enough, and despite my reservations, I took the opportunity to inspect the Salmson. I needed to face how bad it got, how close we were to catastrophe. When I reached the hangar, I was relieved not to find Jane at work on repairs beside our team of mechanics.

But then, no one was working on repairs. Three mechanics stared at the plane vacantly, overwhelmed. And I couldn't blame them. The machine lay there like a tattered bit of paper mâché, shot to pieces in so many places it was a miracle we made it home. I could stick my hand straight through some of the holes.

"Don't know where to start?" I asked sheepishly while walking up from behind. They turned.

"What are you doing here? Shouldn't you be resting or having a stiff drink somewhere?" The lead mechanic asked. "What was it like seeing your life flash before your eyes, Sergeant?"

"Just wanted to assess the damage. You know we've only had this bird for about forty-eight hours."

He folded his arms and sized up the propellor shaft.

"I've heard worse. Seen some boys go down on their first flight."

"No one likes to see that," I said.

"What did you find up there, a flying tank?" he continued. I knit my brows.

"What are you talking about?"

"It's just all a bit irregular. Feel these bullet holes. They're mismatched. You can stick a pinky through one, a thumb through another, and an entire fist through this one. It suggests all sorts of different caliber weapons."

"It was just a pair of guns on a pursuit plane," I said, taking in the details he indicated.

"Well, that pair of guns hit you like anti-aircraft incendiaries, and worse. I mean look at this here!"

A large chunk was missing from the tip of the left wing, as if some giant had taken a bite off of it. My heart dropped. I'd never seen a pursuit plane deal out this kind of punishment before. And I hadn't seen any unusual armament from the enemy Sopwith. I hadn't even noticed incendiary rounds. If he'd used them, we'd have caught fire for certain—unless the rain dulled their efficacy.

But an answer wriggled into my mind as I inspected the unnatural network of injury.

The Baron's scarf.

The rogue flyer had stolen it before takeoff, and Brown never had the guts to try it on. We had no idea what the scarf could do. Then again, it wasn't as though all Richthofen's kills had similar holes on their planes.

A sick bubbling in my stomach made me grimace. I hadn't taken the shot. And the idea that somehow these flyers were more dangerous, were magically favored in their sorties, made me shrink all the more.

I'd had *one* job.

Suddenly, the mechanic turned to me, hushed concern written across his mouth.

"Is she all right?" he asked.

"Who? Ja—Private Doe?"

He nodded and looked back at one of his sullen teammates sitting on a stool beside the worktable in the corner.

"Word around the base is you went up alone, that she was the first one by your side after you came down because she has strong feelings for you."

"Is that what they're saying?" I asked.

"Only makes sense, doesn't it? A single-gunned Salmson wouldn't have much fight in it if it got into trouble. But Liam here has been pretty beat up about it, blaming himself for leaving you high and dry without Lewis drums."

"Yeah, that didn't help any," I muttered. "Has he said anything to anyone? You know, about Private Doe?"

The man shook his head.

"I don't know what you two are mixed up in, but our job is to patch you up, not bring you down."

I clapped the man on the shoulder before walking the length of the plane. Unconsciously, I let my fingers trace their way along the fuselage and the wing fabric. They staggered as they caught on bullet holes and splintered wood. I tried not to think about it being Jane's skin or bones. I shut my eyes hard and willed the image away, instead turning to the mechanic on the stool.

He was the same one who had helped us get the Salmson started before the flight, young and covered in grease stains.

"Liam, isn't it?" I asked.

He nodded without meeting my eyes.

"You know I started as a mechanic, too, Liam. At home, far away in California." The boy couldn't hide his curiosity, and I smiled. I'd often faced friendly jabs or even ridicule about where I was from. Comments about cowboys, the gold rush, or silent movies usually dominated those conversations. "Bike mechanic to start. Then, of course, transferred to automobiles. I came over here not long after the war started as a volunteer. I wanted to fight the Kaiser. They put me in an ambulance, going back and forth from the front line."

Talking was a balm for my nerves after that morning and for this poor kid's conscience, as well. I feared speaking too much, but the words were fluid and difficult to stem once they'd started.

"You volunteered? Foreign legion?" he asked.

"The French." I nodded. "You see, my dad came from Scotland, and he was a terrible businessman. For some reason, he thought people in California might enjoy imported Scottish wares. He insisted there were enough Englanders out in the west that he'd find success."

I fiddled with my hands and smirked.

"Imported Scottish wares, sir?" Liam asked, forgetting himself. "What, like haggis and shortbreads and the like?"

I laughed.

"Exactly the like. I know. Who the hell in California wants to import haggis? Of course, the whisky didn't do too poorly. We didn't starve. But safe to say, it didn't go as he planned. I spent my youth watching my father try so hard to be something, someone, noteworthy. But it's not easy earning the respect of those around you. When I saw the opportunity to go, noticed how the rich automobile owners that came into the shop talked about the war, how they thought the Kaiser was a bully that needed to be stopped, how brave the American boys going over were, I jumped. I considered it my great opportunity to make our family respectable in the way he always wanted."

My gaze wandered, lingering on the trails of damage in the rear of the fuselage. I'd flown these missions many times. My plane had been on the receiving end of handfuls of bullet holes. I never took a plane down. I hid behind this idea that I was waiting for the right shot.

But what if there was no right shot?

"Your dad must be right proud of you," Liam said.

"For what?" I asked. "I'm two years deep at war."

I tried to remember when I'd last seen my father proud. Still frames came into my mind's eye, memories with more destructive power than artillery shells. I didn't allow myself to revisit these scenes, frozen moments in time full of love and pride. My mother's joyful face hard at work, doing double time at home and in the shop. My father's beaming eyes when he bragged about me to his friends.

At some point, maybe after that first ambulance drive, my love for him soured. He struck me as a bumbling fool. He hadn't seen the horrors of war as I had. His pride dropped in value, outpacing even the plummeting wartime economy. And to validate him, I needed stronger approval.

Lufbery's. But when Lufbery gave it, despite my failures in the air, I needed someone else's.

Jane's approval came too freely. Even the enemy's approval came too freely.

"Sir?" Liam said.

I clenched my jaw, keeping the emotions in check, and shifted in my unfamiliar uniform, a British standard issue. I'd not even bothered with the tie. The side slip played in my memory. We'd passed so closely by the Camel. If I'd had the courage, I could have blown him from the sky.

"You're going to make mistakes, kid. And your mistakes might get someone killed. It's hard to come to grips with that."

I had no business being on this mission. I'd come so I could protect Jane. I'd convinced myself that I could trust no one else with the task.

"I'll be more careful, sir," Liam said. His earnest commitment drew me out of myself. I clapped him on the shoulder and stood. "And sir, thank you."

The emotions tugged at my throat, painful and swelling. But even now, I couldn't get the bubble to burst. I couldn't cry, not in front of Liam. Not in front of anyone. If I started, what then? And who could I trust to collect the pieces after? I glanced at the plane instead.

"I'm not sure what hope we have for this thing," I said. "But see what you can do. For now, it looks like we're grounded."

Chapter 20
Reprimand
Jane

Show me the two so closely bound
As we, by the wet bond of blood,
By friendship blossoming from mud.
-Robert Graves-

I took a walk down the airstrip. One of the WREN girls had offered to lend me some clothes, but I hated the sight of them. The skirt and naval jacket stifled me on sight. Instead, I stole a spare mechanic's coverall, too large and excessively baggy, but more comforting. The coverall helped me disappear, at least from myself.

Now, I tried to clear my head one step after another.

It had been days since our pursuit of the blue flyer. We had failed our mission, failed to track him to his base, failed to secure the magical device Richthofen left behind. I took one glance at our Salmson before giving it up. It would take weeks to repair, if it were even possible. I didn't have the stomach to think about how close we'd come to death.

The pilot had wanted to kill us. He had the shot lined up, but he withheld. I could not forget his face when I held up the marble.

It was almost as though he were afraid of it.

The sky was tranquil above me, clear in the way only spring can provide, painted by crystal blue and splotched by goose down clouds. The smell of wet earth mingled with exhaust and oil and the cookeries and the hundred other scents that combined into the unique atmosphere of an aerodrome.

I skirted large puddles of mud, hands in my pockets. We'd decoded the supplementary telegram, and thanks to some of the friendlier WRENs in the intelligence office, I'd even learned to speed up the process.

But if we hoped for some insight to aid our mission, we found only disappointment. It was nothing more than instructions on how to communicate back to the team. We were to telegram directly to the airbase at Toul, encoded through a new list of code words provided. For some reason, I resented the obsession with secrecy. It hadn't been much of a secret when our Salmson toppled back into Clairmarais in so many pieces.

At the very least, with Brown's help, we managed to keep me out of the official story, even if it cost me my reputation. Rumors circulated, of course. Rumors that there were two flight suits at the crash site, insights that I'd arrived on the scene impossibly quickly.

But officially, the story went that Marcus, in an attempt to impress me, took up a flight in the rain. But once in the air, he encountered a German reconnaissance plane and barely made it back alive. Marcus had to withstand a well-staged dress down from Paynter and Brown—though Paynter looked all too eager to play the part. And the word around base now marked me as a lovesick hopeful of the American daredevil.

But if gossip about my relationship with Marcus bothered me, I'd have quit him a long time ago. No. What troubled me more was the nature of our assignment.

We'd found a blue flyer. We'd found a magical device. But

we'd pursued him and failed miserably. I retraced my steps from that day over and over in my head. From eating to checking the airfield to running to our plane.

We weren't prepared. Our plane was not prepared.

Had I been so stupid to think this would be easier? I cursed myself for volunteering my best friend. I'd almost lost him up there.

The daunting challenge we were up against materialized the more I considered it. These blue flyers were collecting magical devices. From the way I saw it, we understood two known magical benefits to Boelcke's goggles. It identified a jammed gun and that was a significant advantage. A gunner discovers a jam upon failure when firing. But the goggles knew before. They detected the faulty alignment of the action or a defect in the following round or some other problem with the gun.

But they did something else, as well. For Earnst, for me and Marcus, they identified a blue flyer, as if they had a mark on their plane, as if the goggles could see magic. We identified the flyer after he'd stolen the scarf. I wondered if the flyer Earnst engaged also carried a magical device with him.

If so, what advantages did the other devices provide? And if the rogue flyers had more devices, what were they capable of? What did they wait for?

What, exactly, did the scarf do?

The concept recast the very nature of this radical group of pilots. Smith, Mustermann, Atkins, Dupont all feared them. But no one knew what they played at. No one knew how many devices there were.

If they had enough planes equipped with such magic, what if they were waiting to swoop in and take power? They might gather up the void in the post-war vacuum.

The sound of a motorbike broke my concentration, splattering mud in its wake before coming to a stop. Marcus sat astride it.

Reprimand

"Hey," he said in a stilted voice.

"Hello," I replied. We hadn't spoken much since the incident. Between us lay a mountain of emotions and fears that we were both, perhaps, afraid to acknowledge and address. We'd failed one another but also tested just how important our friendship was. The outcome was sobering.

"You'd better hop on," he said without ceremony.

"Where are we going?"

"It's Brown."

The sight of the parked ambulance perturbed Marcus. I knew, of course, that he'd driven them at the start of the war. He didn't talk much about that time of his life, and when our conversations touched on his experiences as a driver, something haunted his eyes.

A few men hoisted Brown, lying weakly on his cot, into the back of the covered truck. Oliver stood beside him, whispering words of encouragement and support.

But we all knew the grim truth. The captain's condition had worsened. Influenza had started creeping up and down the lines, and precautions against cross-contamination this deep in the war were sparse and difficult. Life was too short to accommodate the sick the way they deserved or to protect the healthy. As soon as the costs of prevention outweighed the perceived benefit, command relinquished their support.

The quiet in the small group of onlookers spoke of the truth we all recognized. This could be the start of the end of Captain Roy Brown.

And to think this man had bested the unconquerable Red Baron. Did fate call him now to the grave? Did some cosmic balance demand a sacrifice for the felled eagle?

I expected Marcus to approach him before the car drove away, to exchange some final words of promise or advice with the man he'd revered. But he just stood beside the motorbike, arms crossed, studying the gravel and mud at his feet. He hardly even glanced up to see the ambulance depart.

The mood at the aerodrome was solemn the rest of the day. Brown was loved, respected, even hailed as a hero of the war. There was discussion that the whole squadron would adopt a new sigil of a falling red eagle to commemorate his historic kill.

Yet, he would not wear such a sigil. At least not for now.

The news reporters that had lingered on to follow Brown's next exploits soon vacated Clairmarais, and in their absence was a peculiar calm. Yes, men still flew off for their patrols and sorties, but it was just the well-rehearsed grinding of the war machine that by now was constant as the sunrise.

I had expected Marcus to speak with me at greater length after we watched the captain carted off. After all, he'd come to retrieve me to witness the parting.

But he didn't speak to me until dinner that night.

"May I?" he asked. I nodded.

"I checked on the plane today," he said, lowering his bowl to the table.

"And? Will she fly again?"

Marcus shook his head and blew on a spoonful of soup.

"No. At first, they thought they could rebuild it, but they kept finding more damage in the structure. They made the call today, officially unfit for flying, off for salvage."

He put the steaming spoonful to his lips and winced, then added, "A few rounds busted up one of the Lewis guns, too."

I swallowed. If a round had hit the Lewis gun, it was only a few feet from striking me. A question burned inside of me about that moment from our fight. When we had slid across the face of the Sopwith. How had he missed from so close?

"What does that mean for the mission?" I asked instead.

"It means we might be here for a little while. Not sure we have any leads right now, anyway," he replied. "They said someone is on the way tomorrow to issue my reprimand."

I nodded. We hadn't heard directly from our superiors since we'd messaged them about our incident with the scarf. Smith would not be happy.

We did expect further instructions, though. Perhaps another target, or another sector to investigate, another plane.

But that would require Marcus's willingness to fly it—to fly with me.

"Marcus, about what happened—"

"I better go check on the Salmson again." His voice strained and cracked. He set his jaw and turned his head away from me. "They might need some help sorting through what can be salvaged for other machines."

A part of me wanted to follow him, or at least challenge his leaving me. I even wanted to go with him to see how I could help with the Salmson's dismantling. Both of us were able mechanics, after all. At least that would give me something more to do.

But he needed space. And perhaps I did as well.

A few days later, soon after breakfast, I was summoned to the Squadron Office. Marcus waited for me outside, standing beside a motorcar adorned with a battered Union Jack painted on its door

"You waited for me?" I asked.

"Didn't want to get reprimanded all by myself."

We tucked through the door and found Lieutenant Atkins speaking with Paynter. The latter's face burned red with a terse, tight frown spanning his chin, and Atkins reciprocated the severity of his mood.

He dismissed Paynter and called Marcus and me into a small office in the back of the building. When the door was closed, and he had listened for several seconds to satisfy himself that we were alone, he finally addressed us.

"What did you do to Lieutenant Paynter?" he asked.

I shared a glance with Marcus and shrugged.

"I'm not sure he liked the idea of Jane being so involved in my mission. It also seemed like our instructions to meet solely with Captain Brown rubbed him the wrong way."

Atkins frowned but nodded.

"And Captain Brown?"

"Carted off to a hospital, as I'm sure you are already well aware," I replied. "Can we get to business?"

Atkins stiffly assessed my frankness.

"No disrespect, Lieutenant. We've just been sitting here for days with nothing to do," I added. "I'm quite anxious.'

He settled into a chair behind the writing desk and looked back and forth between us.

"I trust I need not remind you that your, shall we say, cohesive nature is one of the major strengths we considered when selecting you for this assignment. I trust that connection is not waning."

"We're fine," Marcus said.

I stopped the impulse to contradict him right at my lips. Atkins must have noticed.

"I'm afraid we had a bit of a shock during our encounter with the blue flyer. That's all," I said.

"A bit of a shock?" Atkins raised an eyebrow. "There's an understatement."

"We had to take off in a hurry, and our mechanics didn't have the plane as ready as they should have." Marcus shifted uncomfortably. "We didn't have the ammunition to fight him. Or the maneuverability. How can you expect us to pursue these rogue flyers when you give us a reconnaissance biplane and not a pursuit single seater?"

Atkins drummed his fingers on the desk.

"If you'll recall, your first priority was not to engage, but to follow him back to his base."

"Well, we tried to follow him, but the man was flying a Sopwith Camel. He could outrun us easily."

"And the goggles?" Atkins asked. "Did not they help you identify and track him?"

Marcus rolled his eyes. "Atkins, have you ever flown an airplane?"

I put a hand on Marcus's shoulder.

"It's possible the flyers are more sophisticated than we anticipated. He managed to enter Clairmarais unnoticed and leave with Richthofen's scarf, all without drawing attention to himself. Had we not the goggles, we wouldn't have discovered him either."

"And the Salmson?" Atkins asked. "Have they managed to repair it?"

"No," Marcus said, slouching in his seat. "It's a complete loss."

Atkins stood and sauntered to a notice pinned to the wall, tallies of the pilots' recent sorties. "Are the two of you prepared to move forward?"

"Yes," I said after an uncomfortably long pause. Marcus turned to me, eyes wild and pleading.

"Sergeant Jackson?" Atkins asked.

I shook my head at my friend, begging him to find courage or faith or whatever he needed to move forward.

"I have some...concerns," Marcus muttered.

"Concerns?" Atkins asked.

I bristled.

"Yes. The truth of the matter, Atkins, is that we almost died up there. It wasn't even close. It is no secret that I have no kill count to my record, but I do have my fair share of hours logged. You are asking me to engage a mysterious enemy with a woman in my gunner's bay who, until a few days ago, had never flown, let alone shot a plane-mounted pair of Lewis guns—or any Lewis gun for that matter. I'm not confident in my ability to train Private Turner—"

"Private Doe," Atkins corrected. "You don't know who's listening."

"It doesn't matter what name you give her if she's a tangled mess in a plane crash!" Marcus balled his hands into fists. I blushed feverishly. "I've seen those messes, Atkins! I've smelled them and driven them to the hospitals. It is too dangerous, and you can't ask me to recklessly put her in harm's way. I won't do it. I can't stop her from finding someone else to fly with—I promise I will maintain the secrecy you swore me too, but I won't kill her."

Atkins's expression did not betray even a flicker of surprise at Marcus's outbreak. He calmly turned from the report on the wall.

"And the Baron's scarf?" he asked. "Can we infer anything?"

"They're collecting them, sir," I said. "Sergeant Jackson misses the point. If Boelcke's goggles produce the effect they do, it is only reasonable to conclude the Baron's scarf may also house an enchantment of some kind. And if those two relics give pilots some benefit, why not believe others exist and do the same?"

My confidence built as I spoke, and I cut Marcus off before he could add any rebuff.

"This mission, in my view, has only become more important as suddenly a rival squadron of pilots, all adorned with magical devices granting them combat advantages, could prove to be a decisive, if not controlling force in the air."

"One squadron is not dispositive in the greater picture of—"

"One squadron could mean the difference between effective

reconnaissance, the protection of key buildings or units from aerial bombing, or, and call me a sentimental woman if you must, but the preservation of Allied lives."

My friend stammered but found no further words.

"Marcus is correct. The blue flyer almost shot us down, but we almost got him as well. I saw my own tracers miss him by inches. Marcus, with some brilliant flying in an underpowered aircraft, likewise, nearly managed a victory."

Marcus shook his head, but I continued.

"His concern for me is kind, but shortsighted. I am willing to die to protect my home. That's why I signed up. It's why I'm here."

Marcus stared at the floor. My heart pounded, my cheeks were flushed. Atkins let the moment mature before continuing.

"Earnst and Lina have uncovered a new lead. There are rumors of another artifact and reports of rogue planes. It follows the pattern. But its investigation will require Allied personnel, and I will not divulge further detail unless I can be sure this is the team that will carry out the mission. So do what you must. Take the day. Take my car, for heaven's sake. Go into town and do whatever it is you two must do to clear this bad air, and bring me back an answer."

We both nodded, Marcus in defeat.

"In any event, we've come to terms that this may take longer than we initially planned. And we are not cruel. I have your mail. You may write your families as you always have, but you must pretend you are both still on assignment at Croix-de-Metz. Our censors will correct anything otherwise. Here. For each of you. Now go. You're dismissed."

Marcus snatched the pack of letters from Atkins's hand and wheeled out of the room before the lieutenant had finished dismissing us. I had the wherewithal to take my own letters and the keys to Atkins's car before following him out the door.

"Jane," Atkins said on my way out. "It may not be my place,

but I'd be remiss not to say that having someone who wants to keep you safe so desperately is not such a terrible thing."

I clenched my jaw and replied.

"It is when he thinks he's cursed."

Chapter 21
Broken Soldier
Marcus

That this is not the judgment-hour
For some of them's a blessed thing,
For if it were they'd have to scour
Hell's floor for so much threatening...
-Thomas Hardy-

I marched beside a quiet road leading out of the aerodrome. Furious, humiliated, and downright scared, I needed the air.

It took less than a mile to realize that I was being overly sensitive, and that Jane hadn't attacked me personally. But I'd done what every wise pilot does in the middle of a fight they know they can't win, I dove and headed back to my lines.

The trouble was, I didn't even know where my lines were anymore. Since we'd been shot up, I'd been toppling, careening on the edge of a crevasse, waiting for someone or something to drop the straw that would unhinge me. I'd hoped that I could quietly disengage, but Jane's insistence on the mission's importance had nearly cut me to pieces in front of Atkins.

This mission was too much. Mystery enemies. Magical devices. Jane in a gunner's seat. It was simply too much.

But then, I'd had the shot. It was me who didn't take it. I'd already seen so many peculiar things at war. Was this mission any more dangerous than the desperate advances at the front lines?

No. The mission was outlandish, but it was I who lacked.

Not even my concern for Jane's life inspired the courage necessary to do what needed to be done.

One question repeated itself in my head. What if I had lost her? If my cowardice brought her downfall, brought the ugly news to her family's doorstep, that their daughter, their beautiful, special girl joined the hundreds of thousands of others that left home never to come back.

How much would my cowardice cost others? How many times would it take me to learn?

The cold truth finally rang clear. I would never learn. When I got back to the 94th, I'd request Lufbery to ground me.

I took a deep breath and filled my lungs with country air. It calmed my nerves and strengthened my resolve. I welcomed the smell of wet dirt and damp and new grass. This close to the sea, the air had more volume, just like home in California. It reminded me of nights driving our clients' Fords down the street to test our repairs, carefree nights burdened only by my ambitions.

What I'd give for a night like that.

I made it halfway to Clairmarais town before Jane found me. She pulled up in Atkins's motorcar and puttered at my pace.

"Where are you going?" she asked.

"To town."

"You never go to town. We stay and play cards and talk while those other pilots go to town. You've never approved of what happens in town." She leaned one arm casually on the car door as she drove and talked.

"Well, maybe it's time I give it a shot."

"And what is it exactly you expect to give a shot?"

I frowned.

"I'm sure there's a bar. Or maybe some French folk who welcome American pilots to play billiards or something like that."

"Ah, yes," she said. "That sounds exactly like good 'ole Marcus. Billiards and drinks. Practically your nickname, isn't it?"

I turned on the car, brimming with annoyance.

"How do you know what I want to do?" I demanded. She didn't laugh, but a smirk peeked from behind her poker face, a slight wrinkle around the eyes.

"Marcus, get in the car."

"I'm fine walking, thanks."

"Get in the car, and I'll drive you to one of those bars you're going on about. What? Afraid of me now, are you?"

I was. There was a struggle inside me all but impossible to reconcile. I'd always known that our friendship was important, but I hadn't appreciated exactly how much until it reduced me to a soaking wreck stuck in a muddy airfield. And yet, I hadn't found it in me to tell her the truth. She didn't know. She thought I'd tried.

"I can't do it, Jane."

"What? Go to a bar? Of course you can't. You wouldn't even know what to order."

"I can't do the mission."

The car's motor cycled loudly, complaining about the slow speed.

"Because of me?" she asked.

I was ashamed to say it out loud, but I managed a nod.

"Because you're afraid I may die?"

"You're better than all this," I said. "You don't deserve any of it. Another man shot at you. I didn't—"

"I put myself in that position."

"Did you? Really? Did you fly that plane up there? Hell, Jane!

You don't believe in violence, but you were firing off a Lewis gun like a hungry green gunner out of academy. Meanwhile, I—"

"You what? What do you keep trying to say?"

"I didn't take the shot!" I yelled.

The car came to a stop. I did, too. I stood there, wishing I could avoid her searching, piercing gaze. I wanted to hide somewhere. But the only thing worse than not knowing what lay behind those candid, innocent eyes now would be to let them go. In my heart, I feared that if she stopped looking at me now, she'd never look at me the same again.

She pursed her lips and put her hand back on the steering wheel. Her eyes glossed. Every part of me wanted to reach out to her, to somehow take back the secret and bury it as I had. But she knew.

"Why?" she asked.

"I don't know." I shook my head. The answer was honest, even if I knew there was a better one. But that required me to search deep down in those hellish holes in my memory.

"You put the mission on the line. You put me on the line."

"I know."

"Has this happened before?"

I faced the way ahead. Down the road, fog stood between me and whatever I was hoping to find in town. The smell of the car's exhaust overpowered the gentle, welcoming aroma of the country-side that had brought me peace a moment before.

Her question pulled me down into the pit. I'd spent so long avoiding the breakdown, but deep in my heart, I knew it'd be Jane to unravel it. I just needed her in the pilot's seat.

She didn't have to speak again. I opened the door and climbed into the passenger seat.

"I can't talk about it here," I said quietly. "Or now."

"Why not?"

"It isn't right."

"When will the time be right, Marcus?"

"I don't know— just, it's—"

She revved the engine violently, handling the car as if it were her Enfield motorbike. The tires kicked up rocks and gravel in their wake, and for a moment, I was pinned against the seat as if I were accelerating in an airplane. She quickly found a gentle stretch of land just off the road and turned in. We bumped along the field until we found a copse of trees. She pulled inside. Between the cover of the canopy and the overcast sky, an intimate shade filled the sheltered hideaway.

"I put my life on the line because I believed in you," she said. Finally, the barrage I'd been expecting, the dressing down I'd deserved. Her words hurt in the best way possible, they reaffirmed every terrible opinion I'd made of myself.

"I'm sorry."

"Shut up and listen," she replied. "Marcus, you're special. I see it. Lufbery sees it. You think your inability to pull the trigger is a defect, but I see it as the greatest evidence of humanity—that despite all the Germans have taken, how much they've hurt you, how much even the other soldiers may deserve their fate, you resist."

I wrung my hands. Even now, she tried to protect me, but she didn't know.

"I'm a coward, Jane. Are you trying to tell me being a coward is a good thing?"

"No," she replied. "You are not a coward."

"I am."

"Refusing to take another man's life is not cowardice. It's bravery. Especially now."

She was wrong, so utterly wrong.

"You don't understand anything."

"Don't I? You don't appreciate how wonderful it is that even when surrounded by darkness for so long, even when you have

233

every motivation, every justifiable expectation to kill, you haven't done it."

I threw my head back in exasperation.

"It's a curse on everyone around me."

"I knew the risks," she said.

"I'm costing lives." The memories came swarming in. I gritted my teeth to ward them off, shut my eyes tightly. My weakness killed men. My weakness almost killed Jane. The memories were expanding like the air in a balloon, I couldn't hold it back any longer.

Her gentle hand broke through the dark to rest on mine. I opened my eyes, and she was there, stern and tender.

"Tell me. When have I ever hurt you?"

So there, in that small copse of trees south of Clairmarais, the dam burst.

"It was a summer night, early in the war," I started. "I'd been driving ambulances for a few months to and from the front. In the good times, we didn't have to drive too close to the action. When our boys advanced, the wounded stayed well behind. But when Germany had their way, we had to drive in closer to pick up the wounded.

"One night, I'd been driving all day, and I had another round to make. I was headed back to the line, but I made a stop in a shell-torn town to stretch, relieve my bladder, and just take a second to gather myself. I can't describe what it was like, hearing those screams all day long. Dealing with the painful moaning and the smell of blood. One second, I was a kid fixing up cars in California. The next, not only had I seen death, I was its driver."

I swallowed, painfully. The memories were like a thick lump of overcooked meat inadequately chewed.

"I should never have stopped there. It wasn't on the route. And when I ducked into what remained of some French cottage to hide for a while, I saw him. He hid in the corner, curled up like some rat hiding in the walls, a German kid. He looked so young, blonde-haired and bright-eyed. He was probably eighteen, a year younger than me at the time, but I'd already seen so much while he hadn't grown into his face all the way. His uniform hardly fit right around his small shoulders.

"I pulled my pistol faster than he did and found myself with custody of a German prisoner. We stared at one another for a long time. He shook with fear. He begged me not to shoot. I didn't understand the words, but some things supersede any language barrier. And I thought of my parents, thought of some parents waiting at home for him. He was just lost. His helmet too big. The binoculars around his neck almost comically large for his frame. He just ended up hiding out for safety in the wrong cottage. The worst choice of his life. It didn't seem right. So I didn't do it. I didn't shoot."

Jane held my hand tight, as if she were squeezing the story from me, distilling it out one drop at a time.

"I let him go. He scrambled so fast off across the field. I lost him in the tall grass after only a couple of minutes before I clambered back into my ambulance and continued back to the wounded. The platoon I'd been working with the whole week complained about my tardiness because one of their riflemen had taken a bad shot to the shoulder. That drive back was horrible enough to push the German from my mind."

The next part was the hardest. The next part was the part I never let myself review.

"He wasn't just a lost boy, was he?" Jane asked gently.

I clenched my jaw. He might have been. I had prayed to God asking if had just been a lost kid or not. I prayed for a long time before hating the answer.

"When I drove back the next day, the whole platoon was gone. Cratered. Hit hard by an artillery shell, then picked off by machine gunners. There were no wounded to drive back."

I turned to Jane, pathetic as a child, and after so long, the tears fell down my cheeks.

"They had relocated, but the Germans knew exactly where to fire. I didn't shoot, so they did. I got them killed, Jane. All of them."

I was a mess now. Jane's concerned face had blurred over. My chest heaved in and out, monstrous ugly noises escaped my gut. She wrapped her arms around me and pulled my head to her chest, rocking me like a baby. I'd never told anyone. I'd been most afraid of telling her. But she squeezed me tighter and rocked me for the better space of an hour.

Eventually, the staccato sobs ebbed away. My breathing stabilized. My throat ached as if it'd done too many pushups, and I didn't even have the strength to raise my arms.

"But it didn't fix me, either. I've carried the ghosts of those men with me since that day, desperate to show myself and them that there was another reason I didn't shoot. That I wasn't simply a coward, but that honor and mercy mattered, and their deaths would be avenged the right way by a man who understood the difference."

Someone finally knew. Not just someone. Jane knew. And she didn't try to reason it away or tell me it was fine. But she was still here. The trees around us were still there. Everything was different, but nothing had changed.

"I brought our letters," Jane said quietly after a long, respectful pause. "The ones Atkins brought with him."

I nodded, the mundane nature of the statement reeling me back to shore.

"I was thinking we might drive up to Calais and find something to eat," she said.

"That's a bit of a drive isn't it?" I replied hoarsely.

"It's a lovely spring day, and we've been given leave. I intend to use it."

When I had no answer, she finally allowed herself a smile. Reluctantly, then helplessly, I joined her.

"All right," I said. "Let's go."

"And if you really, truly want to, I'll even let you get drunk in some bar somewhere."

I snorted. But she smiled. In that smile, I found strength.

"Just no bedding an elderly widow farmer or anything. Do you understand?"

From Major Raoul Lufbery:

M*arcus,*

You'll be happy to know that Rick scored a kill while out on a two-plane patrol. I think he's got the makings of a fine pilot. Smart and lucky. I'm not sure which is more important. It seems like just yesterday I was taking him over the lines for the first time, and he came back unaware that his plane was riddled with shrapnel from Archie.

I imagine that you might be having a spell getting used to a new machine and a new gunner. I know it's a strange set of circumstances, but stick with it. Sometimes mechanics make the best pilots, and I don't see why that shouldn't apply to gunners, too. In any case, I don't think anyone has the qualifications our girl does for this specific assignment.

Huffer is in a state, all nervous and worried. Command has something big coming our way. Seems like Pershing was serious when he came over here, and now the colonel is hell-bent on taking the fight to the Kaiser in the air. Everyone's eager to throw their hat in the ring, and we may very well be the aerial vanguard. I can't write you about it, but when you get back, let's just say if you haven't scored your first by then, it'll be all but impossible for you not to score one soon after.

Smith told me you had a bad time of things with those strange pilots up north and that you learned the ins and outs of a Camel the hard way. That's funny business. Some fights shake you more than others, but I'm sure you'll do us proud before long. Remember to look after your machine and your team.

That's why we're here, after all.

Hope to see you soon. The boys send their regards.

Luf

A few hours later, we sat on a hillside overlooking the English Channel with a small picnic of bread, cheese, and preserved meats. Calais stood well behind the front lines and had still preserved much of its citizen population and character. The whole town pulsed with vibrant, energetic industry. But what was more important, its beauty had not been compromised by the war. Lush sandy beaches stretched out on the coast, and the sea buffeted the shoreline in its rhythmic, steady hush.

Hush. Don't worry. Hush.

Luf's letter lay open on my lap. It did me good to hear from him. Luf always had a way of calming everyone down with his steady demeanor and quietly confident air. As I read, I could envision Rickenbacker coming back after his first kill. Everyone at Croix-de-Metz would have been waiting, surrounding him as soon as he put down. Every American success mattered. The world was watching the United States, eager to know if Germany had to take the red, white, and blue seriously.

After what had just happened, I had to admit Eddie's first success stung, but I contented myself with his victory. I'd seen others climb up the score sheet past me. The way things were going, I'd see many more.

But it was Luf's conclusion that hurt most. *Look after my machine and my team.*

I'd failed in both respects. He hadn't. Not since I'd known him. Luf shone as America's Ace of Aces, the exemplary paragon of ensuring his machine was in top shape and taking care of the boys flying with him. That included me.

And yet, he hadn't grounded me either. He didn't protect me by keeping me on base or getting me reassigned to a safer zone of the war. He flew better and understood that of all the places to be in the sky, his wing provided safest cover.

"From Lufbery?" Jane asked as she put down the several pages of handwritten scribbles she'd been reading.

"How could you tell?"

"You mean apart from its brevity and that tough guy smug attitude you've just embodied?" she asked. Her mentioning it made me notice that I'd sat up taller. That was classic pilot stuff. When we were together, it was difficult not to pretend to be unaffected and cool in the face of danger or complication.

After laying myself bare to Jane, the attitude embarrassed me. My bravado was a candle made of tissue paper.

"Rickenbacker got a plane," I said.

"It's about time," she replied. "He's been all but inventing opportunities to go look for one."

I stared out at the sea. Somewhere above the depths pilots flew to protect and attack war ships on the water. I wondered what type of courage it must take to fly over an expanse of water like that. No place to crash land without sinking. I wondered which scared me more, falling into the deep blue, or sending a man to such an unforgiving grave.

"Are you going to open the others?" Jane asked softly, nodding to the remaining envelopes on my lap. Familiar handwriting had spelled my name. One from my mother. One from my father.

"I can't," I said.

"Marcus..."

"Jane, don't start this right now."

She nibbled on a bit of cheese, both of her legs tucked beneath her.

"How's your family?" I asked.

"They're all right," she said, reluctantly letting go of the thread she'd been pulling on. "There have been night raids in some of the larger cities across England, and rumors circulate that the Germans are gaining enough ground to set up artillery to reach across the channel."

"You said they live on the west side?"

She nodded absent-mindedly.

"But they're still afraid."

"I understand."

"No, Marcus. I don't think you do."

I furrowed my brow and turned to face her. She hadn't used a harsh tone, but bold words sometimes have a tone of their own.

"Jane?" I shifted my weight, suddenly uncomfortable. "I've told you already what I'm feeling."

"Yes, you have. And I'm honored. I can never express how sacred that part of you is to me. And now, I need to share as well."

"You made your feelings very clear back at the Squadron Office."

"No, I did not. I argued, logically, what made perfect sense. But there are arguments about the mission, and there are irrefutable facts about ourselves."

She looked outward over the city and gestured with a hand at the water.

"Right over there, across that water, is my family. My father is just now finishing up a day of work in his restaurant. My mother will be assisting him, and tonight they will listen to the radio for notice of the war. Then my mother will read a novel out loud to my father so they can both try to forget they have a daughter out here standing in their place to stop the Germans from reaching our home.

"You have a complicated relationship with your family." She nodded at the unopened letters on my lap. "But they're on the other side of the world. And the war won't reach them. Even if it claims the lives of millions more, it still won't reach them like it will London and eventually Gloucestershire."

She clutched her letters reverently. Tears welled in her eyes.

"This is the first time I've been able to do more, and I don't have a choice, Marcus. What we know now, stakes as high as they are, I must help. That requires me to compromise some of my own personal principles. I abhor the violence, but I believe in keeping the people I love safe. My parents. You. There are magical devices out there, and no one can appreciate their power the way I can. This is my set of wings, Marcus."

I grimaced, stared at the grass beneath my knees, and swallowed down a lump rising in my throat. I'd never heard her speak so passionately. So often, I'd taken comfort in her British indifference. The waves of the sea continued their relentless barrage. Hush. Hush.

But now, they brought with them new understanding. Hush and carry on. Hush and fight. Hush there is work to be done.

"You could die, Jane," I said sadly. "I can't trust myself to protect you. I plan on hanging up my flight suit as soon as we're back at Croix-de-Metz."

"You could die, too," she replied. "And I've faced that every time you got in your airplane."

"But if I were the pilot—"

"We can manage your situation when we get back. I don't trust someone else with this. You don't have to shoot down a plane.

You've survived this long without doing so." She smiled and put a hand on my knee.

I shook my head. It defied reason. She was choosing to go into the fight with faulty equipment.

"But what if—"

"We will sort it out. I'm on the guns, remember? I promise, I will take the guns. You need only fly me into the action or avoid the action altogether. Things are going to get worse, and I need you. Don't make me ask Oliver."

I bristled at the thought of that east coast lunk flying around as Jane's escort. But when I failed against the blue flyer, he'd swooped in and saved her once. Why not let him do it again?

"You know, I saw Oliver watching you at breakfast this morning," I said.

"Marcus," she said politely, "he's been watching me like that for a week. Don't you dare strand me with him. Come along, now. You've managed your curse for this long. Let me help you manage it a little longer."

I wiped my eyes. She was the better between us. Stronger. More courageous. She'd been my support for so long. It was only right that I stand up for her now. She offered me a different kind of redemption. I looked at my parents' letters.

"I don't know, Jane," I muttered with a hesitant grin. "Maybe it'd do you good to have a more romantic mission partner."

"Stop it."

"I'm serious. I think you two might really go well together. You're from Gloucestershire. He's from... New Jersey."

"I will take that as a yes. Let's get back."

She stood and wiped the back of her skirt, sweeping off the dampness from the ground. She offered a hand and helped me up.

"Thanks," I said, wrapping her in a grateful embrace. She squeezed me across the shoulders hard and we headed to the motorcar. "Let's go magic hunting."

Chapter 22
The Albatross
Jane

The blackbird sings to him: "Brother, brother,
If this be the last song you shall sing,
Sing well, for you may not sing another;
Brother, sing."
-Julian Grenfell-

A tkins drove us eastward toward the line. I rode in the front seat, wedged between my friend and my commanding officer.

"Ghent?" Marcus asked. "But Ghent is well behind enemy lines. The Germans took it a long time ago, and we've never come close to taking it back."

"Right you are, Sergeant Jackson."

Marcus gaped at me.

After a few days messaging back and forth about our renewed commitment, Atkins finally received the clearance necessary to move our mission ahead. We were eager to leave Clairmarais and its awful ghosts behind, so we bid farewell to Oliver—who gave me an overly enthusiastic kiss goodbye—and collected what few things we had.

Now, in transit, Atkins finally divulged the details of Earnst and Lina's report.

They had received a coded message by carrier pigeon at their station in Nancy. Our German companions uncovered rumors about strange happenings in the city of Ghent and its surrounding airspace. According to Earnst, the reports had grown in frequency over the past year, but recently ceased altogether.

As it turned out, Ghent had once been one of Europe's cultural and artistic jewels, and allegedly movements existed within the occupied city to preserve some of their more treasured artifacts from German looting and confiscation. Earnst believed that someone had either stolen or traded for whatever device attracted the blue pilots, and now it rested somewhere in the city.

"How do you expect us to get to Ghent?" I asked. "I doubt the Huns will just part and let us pass."

Atkins clicked his mouth, making his mustache twitch.

"Jackson, can you read German?" he asked.

Marcus shook his head.

"Not much. Why?"

"A pity. It may have helped somewhat," he said.

Marcus went quiet just as Atkins pulled off the main road onto a small dirt path through the countryside. The area would have been sparsely populated even before the Germans came through, but now the small settlements and farmhouses around us came across ghostly in their defiant existence.

A certain reverence filled the motorcar as we passed abandoned homes. Atkins drove us through a small village, past a vacant church, through the empty plaza, all eerily quiet. I shuddered to think how many villages like this one had gone silent since the beginning of the war. How many would still go silent?

We pulled away from the town center and continued until we

came to a haphazard field of wheat, grown from reseeded remains from a hasty cleanup of what may once have been a cultivated harvest. A small wood bordered the field on one side, and a dilapidated stone barn stood nearby the ruins of an old home.

As we got close to the barn, Atkins turned off the engine and exited the vehicle. Marcus stood in his seat.

"You have to be kidding me," he muttered as he gaped past the crumbling side of the building's near wall.

Between old, smashed stalls waited a pristine and undamaged German two-seater, an Albatross reconnaissance machine.

"Have you ever flown one of those?" I asked Marcus under my breath.

He stared forward and shook his head.

"What? No. Of course not. When would I have flown one of those?"

"Have you ever had the chance to study the inside of its cockpit?" I tried.

"Briefly," he whispered. I swallowed and put on a good face, remembering the positive encouragement I'd given him only the day before. I trusted him to keep me safe. He had so far—barely. He would yet.

"Are you wearing your marble?"

This moved him to look down on me and smile.

"Are you kidding? I'm never taking this thing off again."

On our drive back from Calais, I'd relayed to him my desperate gesture in our dogfight with the Camel, how I'd raised the marble in the air just as the pilot should have used his advantage to shoot us down.

Oliver had come to our rescue, yes, and my actions may have only confused the blue flyer, but given the nature of our assignment, perhaps there was something more to it. I wished desperately I could speak with my Aunt Luella face to face.

"She flies well, for being German," Atkins said with a shrug.

"An Albatross C.XII. Fortunately, Mustermann managed to get us one of the newer models. You'll be a little more conspicuous, but in a pinch, I think you'll appreciate the modern amenities. It moves quickly and compares, somewhat, to the Salmson, even with its good-for-nothing German engineering attached."

Marcus and I followed him to the barn. The long, rounded wings of the Albatross barely fit inside the building and bore the distinctive, dreaded pair of black crosses every Allied pilot had come to fear. I wondered how Marcus, with his idealistic set of principles, would take a request to fly one of the enemy's airplanes.

I put a hand on the wing and felt the smooth, tight fabric, doped and solid.

"They've put a radiator right below the gun?" I marveled, examining the engine in front of the cockpit. A tentacled cooling unit sat behind the propellor, snubbing the front of a fuselage that inspired a profile the shape of a Zeppelin balloon—if a Zeppelin were made in part by plywood. The enlarged rudder behind would make a lovely target for enemy fire.

"Water-cooled Mercedes engine," Atkins confirmed. "Only one gun in back, and a Parabellum at that, I'm afraid. I hope you haven't become too accustomed to the twin Lewis guns, Jane."

"We were turning into fast friends," I replied. Marcus climbed up into the cockpit, and I peeked in beside him.

"What exactly do you want us to do, Atkins?" Marcus asked, a thick line of concern on his forehead. "Even if we can fly this thing, it will take a long time before I could fight effectively with it."

Atkins leaned against the engine and lit a cigarette.

"Well, fortunately, we don't want you to bang it up in a dogfight," he said casually. "It wasn't cheap."

"You can't expect us to land at a German airbase?" I scoffed.

"No, no. We want you to land in a field, hide the plane, then walk into Ghent."

Marcus laughed. I hit him.

"How are we supposed to walk into a German-occupied city?" he asked.

"Unfortunately, I don't expect it to be very pleasant. We have a network, of course, one that's been growing more effective as the war waxes on. You will meet with a contact on the northwest side of the city, before you reach its bordering canals.

"We have some civilian clothing for you that should match the condition and appearance of the locals. I imagine you'll pretend to be farmers or mechanics at work on some of the German machinery, or you'll come up with something, I'm sure. Time is of the essence, I'm afraid. You'll need to get inside the city and locate this ruddy bit of magic before the rogue flyers manage to. There is a contact there, Gervais le Clercq. Le Clercq has the information you need and knowledge enough about the city to get you in and out."

I crossed to the gunner's seat and hoisted myself inside. The Parabellum machine gun was mounted on a ring rig, similar to the Salmson's Lewis guns. Instantly, I missed the presence of the second gun, and the belt feed, compared to the large ammo drums, made me feel more exposed.

"Ok. So, say we find Le Clercq, how do you expect us to get back?" Marcus asked.

"It's under occupation, Jackson. It's not a prison camp." Atkins's tone took a sharp edge, startling me. "I asked if you were committed, and you said yes. This is the assignment."

Marcus sulked in the cockpit for a moment before answering.

"Sorry, Atkins. I'm just surprised is all. My on-foot combat experience is limited. Jane's is non-existent."

Atkins took a nervous drag on his cigarette and neared the cockpit, looking squarely up in Marcus's face. He seemed different to me somehow, even from when I'd seen him a week or so before. I wondered what information he withheld from us.

"Let me make something clear, Sergeant. You are here to protect her. Your skills are ordinary. You have no accolades other than a good recommendation by Major Lufbery. We might have found anyone better to do this job than you. You are here to protect this woman."

Overhearing this conversation, I grew suddenly uncomfortable, protective even. I wanted to pounce on Atkins, but I forced myself instead to face the tail of the aircraft and pretend to inspect the gun.

"We could not see eye to eye more than we do on that issue, Lieutenant," Marcus said in a calm voice that chilled me.

"Good. Jane, get down here and help me get her started."

I balked. "You mean we're leaving now?"

"The drive took longer than I thought it would," Atkins said plainly, "and you may have noticed there are no real accommodations nearby. If you leave now, you'll arrive near Ghent just as dark is falling and use it for cover when entering the city."

Marcus jumped out of the plane.

"No. Atkins, this is crazy. I don't know the land. I don't know the terrain. I need time to study. We'll get lost and stranded without fuel."

Atkins headed back to the motorcar, Marcus on his heels. I descended from the gunner's bay and tried to keep up.

"Ghent is east, northeast nearly seventy miles. Fly over the line, past Ypres. Northwest of Ghent is Bruges. It's only twenty-five miles off. If you see Brussels, you've gone far too southward. Follow the Lys, it will take you there. If you get lost, use the sister cities as your guide."

Atkins pulled a small chest from the back of the car and opened it.

"Here are identification papers. Be careful with these. You'd be surprised how difficult it was to manufacture them. The Germans are quite thorough in their regulation of photography in

Belgium. And your clothes. Put them on now, so you need only stow your flight suits when you land."

"German flight suits, I presume," I asked, eyeing the tattered skirt and shawl he gave me.

"Of course," Atkins said. He slapped a folded piece of paper on Marcus's chest. "A map, if you must. But be very careful. Expect to be detained and searched. Neither of you speak French or Dutch. If they question you, the jig's up."

"I speak a little French," I said. The German flight suit was heavy, but not much different from ours. It was fur-lined and strapped down on the wrists and ankles.

"Good. You'll need it. Now hurry getting changed and warm up your engine. Pressure is mounting on the two of you. Your encounter at Clairmarais is making some uneasy."

"Who? Smith?" Marcus asked. Atkins sighed and puffed out a cloud of smoke.

"I'll tell you once we've brought the blue flyers to their knees."

Atkins crossed back to the barn, leaving us to change. Marcus graciously volunteered the side of the motorcar closest to the barn, allowing me some privacy from all but the meager wheat field and whatever lived in the wood beyond. I changed quickly. Abandoned or not, disrobing in such an open area made me uncomfortable, and I was grateful to put on the protective warmth of the flight suit. I did not look forward to our trek into Ghent with nothing but my skirt, shawl, and blouse.

I poked around on the other side just as Marcus was getting his shirt on.

"How do I look? German?" I asked him.

"Positively *fraulein*," he said, unable to keep a grin from his face. It tempered quickly. "Are we really about to do this?"

"I'm not about to let another magical device get into the hands of those radicals. Or the Germans. If Earnst and Lina could have picked up the device themselves, they would have. It must be in Allied-friendly hands."

Marcus stepped into his own suit and peered over his shoulder at the barn.

"And Atkins? Do you trust him?"

I put a hand on my hip.

"About as much as you trust Smith."

We joined Atkins at the barn, and Marcus took his place again in the cockpit, this time performing his usual checks of the airplane's mechanics. Despite the foreign machine, he blew out a thick breath of anxious air and nodded.

"Seems close enough," he said. "To Ghent."

I helped Atkins start the propellor, and the Mercedes engine kicked to life with a loud belch. He helped me clamber back up into the gunner's bay before issuing final instructions and yanking the chocks.

"Remember, once you're airborne, you'll be in the most danger on our side of the line. But when you cross, don't assume that you're in the clear. The Germans may pick up that you're flying a peculiar route. Or it's possible those rogue pilots will be drawn to those goggles somehow. Avoid populated areas as much as you can. Try to find somewhere remote to put it down, and hike into the house designated on your map. Your best bet to making it back alive is this machine. God save the king!"

He saluted.

"Sure thing!" Marcus shouted. "Right after He blesses America."

I scoffed. It might have been audible if not for the plane's engine revving to taxi us to the wheat field. As Marcus lined us up for takeoff, he shifted around to see me.

"Last chance to call it off," he shouted.

"You have the marble?" I called back.

"I told you I did."

"And the goggles?"

He slipped Boelcke's goggles down over his eyes and gave me a thumbs up.

"I believe in you, Marcus!" I cried.

He nodded.

"Jane," he said.

"Yes?"

He hesitated a moment, as though he wrestled to share what was on his mind. Strangely, my heart warmed, and though he didn't say anything, a shared understanding resonated between us, as solid as the reverberations of the engine shaking the plane.

But he broke off the sentiment and cocked his head.

"Don't run out of ammunition this time!"

He turned back around before I could reply and sped forward.

We took off and climbed steeply into the blue. I had hoped that by now, I'd have grown used to the somersaulting whirls of my stomach as we rose through the clouds. Spring winds buffeted us about more than the flight to Clairmarais, and I gripped the edge of my seat.

Fortunately, the clouds held no menace, instead showing off white, playful puffs that we ducked around or burst through. The Albatross powered across the sky differently than the Salmson, in some ways more smoothly, in others with more aggression. But from my seat, mostly I noticed the large tail plane jutting out like a dorsal fin and flippers from the rounded fuselage.

The black crosses appeared in many places on the plane, and I prayed that no allied forces would chase us down.

Soon, we leveled out at an altitude higher than Marcus had yet taken me. Above us, the blue of the sky darkened, and the earth appeared as a distant landmark below. I craned my neck to catch a glimpse of our heading. We flew this way for not much more than fifteen minutes before Marcus turned off the engine to speak through the whistling wind.

"I'm going to have to go lower to recognize anything," he shouted. "Be careful, and watch out for Allied Archie!"

"Very well!" I called back. He gave a thumbs up and tipped the nose downward in a steady descent.

Archie. It was a nickname British pilots adopted for anti-aircraft gunnery. I'd yet to face such a thing. A pilot like Marcus should have no trouble evading them. Indeed, I'd come to learn Archie was at its most dangerous while pilots flew low and weren't paying close attention.

As we dropped, the green beauty of France came into clearer detail. Despite the ruined buildings this close to the front, at this height the structures scattered across fields and hills, punctuated by woods, still made for a picturesque scene. But that beauty suddenly, abruptly, violently ended.

Ahead of us, an enormous scar stretched across the earth. An acne-riddled, gaping wound that no force of nature had power to hide away.

I'd heard of no-man's land, but I'd never understood. No one could understand unless they'd seen it. The landscape was another world. It was Pompeii after the ash settled. Earth never existed to hold such nothingness.

In the stories I'd heard, I imagined no man's land to be a small stretch of cratered nature holding the distance between trenches like a dam. For some reason, I never appreciated that it stretched on and on and on, for no man's land had been—created was the wrong word—carved time and time again. It was the amalgamation of building blocks made of razed earth, marked only by ditches in which men waited to die.

There was no sound in my ears as we crossed it. I did not notice the black clouds bursting below us, fire reaching up from Archie's guns. We had entered a realm of destruction, and I would never breathe the same.

Marcus dipped and bobbed, light evasive maneuvers. Below, to my horror, a small group of ants climbed from one of the ditches. Plumes of smoke popped in front of them, obscuring my view. Some of the ants stopped progressing forward. I squinted as we flew past. Only a small remainder of them made it to the other trench. They climbed inside. Lights flashed. Then all went still once more.

Before long, the Earth transformed again, turned its face to hide its ugly scar, and pretended that nothing was at all the matter. The trees reappeared. The meadows turned green.

The sun bowed in the sky behind us, and Marcus flew on, into Belgium toward the enemy, far away from any safe place I'd ever known.

Chapter 23
Far From Home
Marcus

What do you see in our eyes
At the shrieking iron and flame
Hurled through still heavens?
-Isaac Rosenberg-

I gritted my teeth and fought back the memories. Fortunately, we'd crossed the lines with little resistance. Archie failed to reach us, and we didn't bump into any British or French patrols. Those were my greatest worry, especially after our fight against the Camel.

But all the concern meant I wasn't emotionally prepared to fly over the front lines. I'd flown over no man's land before, but never so far north. And besides, I always knew that at the end of a pair of hours, I'd return to the comforting arms of the aerodrome back home.

But this was far different, and memories of driving to pick up the wounded swarmed me like a full squadron of enemy pursuit craft. The rattling sounds of the dying. The copper smells. Their burdens on my shoulders. Pushing the capabilities of those cars, understanding that I could only go as fast as the engine would allow. The fastest route was not the fastest speed, and the mud sucking at our wheels was just as dangerous as the Germans.

I shook my head and surveyed the sky. The yellow of our wings and their bold black crosses spiked my heart rate. In the air, it was too simple to forget what we were, how our mission had evolved into spycraft.

We flew past other planes. Albatrosses, Fokkers, Gothas, Pfalzes, all proudly bearing the black paint of Germany. I'd spent years dreaming of shooting these planes down, watched them destroy my friends and comrades.

My knuckles grew white as I gripped the joystick. How far had we come since the beginning? If only those Lafayette boys could see the war now. Chapman. Rockwell. Prince. McConnell. How they'd marvel at how far the Nieuports had come, how easily the old Fokker models—those infamous planes that reigned in the air—were dispatched.

And here I was flying an Albatross into Belgium.

One Pfalz had investigated our plane as we passed Ypres, but Jane smartly kept her head low and hid any signs of her feminine build. I dipped my wings to say *guten abend* and the Pfalz went on its way.

I flew east and almost got us lost, but I picked up the Lys river while flying past Kortrijk. From there, navigation was simple, and we flew uncontested.

Ghent rose on the horizon. Far on its left, in the distance, I saw the lights of Bruges fading into the blur where ground met sky. Opposite, on our right horizon, Brussels, Belgium's shining star loomed from far away. But Ghent lay at twelve o'clock. At this distance I could make out its time-honored structures. The sharp spires of towering cathedrals, the looming angles of its Gothic churches, and the outline of its castle forts, now made a mockery by its foreign invaders. In the fading light, Ghent appeared to me as a forest of stone, tall trees reaching up with giant arms made by man, and I wondered how the city had survived its occupancy. How did the towers still stand? Had the Germans not used their mighty artillery to lay them flat? Did the permanence and history of the place stay even the Kaiser's ambitious shells?

Atkins had marked an airfield on his map, just southwest of the city. But at this hour, thankfully, I saw little air traffic.

I banked left and remembered the lieutenant's instructions. Find a remote field, put the plane down and hike in. Find a place to hide the Albatross. I searched the ground for a gentle wood with towering branches, but the fields were open and wide, limiting my choices. With the city off my right wing and the sun dipping behind us, the fading light forced me to make a choice. Soon, it would be too dark for a safe landing.

I pushed the nose down, and we descended into occupied territory. If anyone watched, hopefully they'd figure we were nothing but a bomber escort experiencing engine trouble. I'd known all too well that finding a pilot that went to ground took time and wasn't always easy.

We touched down smoothly on a grass field beside a copse of trees. Not far off stood a scattered handful of small houses. They were cottages and modest farm homes. I prayed their inhabitants weren't at home or didn't mind the noise belching from our engine as I taxied and searched for an opening large enough for cover under the trees. I didn't find much. The canopy above would not hide the whole plane, but large shrubs and at least one leafing ash would cover us from direct line of sight on the ground.

I powered off the engine and sat quietly, listening. Usually, setting down meant home. It meant getting warm again and congratulations or heckling by my fellows. This was different. Leaving the plane meant entering the dragon's lair, surrendering my freedom to walk into Germany's net. If the plane was discovered, or we were discovered... No military looked kindly on spies.

"Marcus, are you all right?" Jane whispered behind me.

"Yeah."

"Do you think anyone heard us? Do you think someone's coming?"

"I don't know. We'd better move, just in case." I unlatched and hopped down, feet landing with a thump in Belgian soil. I helped Jane down, too. When she landed, her shaking hands and wide eyes all but compelled me to wrap her in a hug.

"I'm not afraid," she whispered, but she hugged me back so tightly it tugged at my heart.

"Me neither. My hands aren't even quivering."

She let out a laugh, hot breath seeping through the fabric on my shoulder.

"My legs aren't wobbly," she replied.

"My knees aren't buckling."

She took a deep breath, in and out and considered the plane.

"Do you think we should do something to it? Disable it? Make it appear as though we had to force a landing?"

I checked my watch.

"What are you thinking? I don't know enough about the Albatross to suggest something, and we've got a hike ahead of us."

"I suppose you're right. We'll want to have it ready for a quick escape, in any event," she said.

I nudged her with my elbow.

"Don't worry. We won't be gone long enough for them to find it."

We quit our flight suits and stowed them inside the two-seater. I tucked Boelcke's goggles inside my coat pocket. They'd be impossible to hide if we were searched, but I couldn't just leave them behind either. Jane folded her arms tightly across her chest.

"Are you cold?"

"I won't be once we get moving."

"All the more reason to start. Come on."

We didn't bother using a compass. The city's profile guided us, and some of the towers I'd seen aloft were recognizable even on the ground at this distance. The moon rose bright and full, useful for navigation, but it would be downright problematic if we needed to hide. As we walked, the parked plane irritated my brain like a thistle thorn in my sock. Had I hidden it well enough? I could just visualize the reflecting sun off those black crosses the next day, curious farmers reporting the aircraft, a passing German patrol investigating—there were a thousand ways for us to lose access to that plane.

We scrambled from cover to cover, ducking in and out of trees, behind fences, and using the gentle slopes in the area to block views from afar. After a half hour of walking, Jane took my hand, and I was happy to hold it. For one, it'd be easier to pretend to be a couple walking back in from working the fields. But more importantly, there's something strengthening, steadying, in the physical touch of someone you trust.

Some comfort evolved from the physical exertion, our heartbeats working not to rattle our nerves but to power our legs. But in place of the paralyzing fear, my memory threatened to unstop scenes and thoughts I didn't want to face at a time like this. My parents' faces. Old friends killed in action. The hellish ambulance drives. My silent pistol trained on that German kid.

"Tell me about magic," I said to Jane abruptly.

"Magic?" Jane repeated in labored breath. Our boots echoed rhythmically.

"Yeah. Magic. Come on. You've wanted me to believe in this stuff since we met. This question should be a slowball for you."

"What do you wish to know?"

"How does it work? Why does it work? Why now?"

We crested a swell of earth to find more fields and a patchwork of small irrigation ditches branching off from a large canal. Scattered pockets of trees broke up the land, but far ahead we saw lights, some adorning moving vehicles, others more akin to spot-lights. Soon, we'd have to contend with German patrols.

"It didn't start working now," Jane said. "It's always worked. It's just that some types of magic are stronger than others."

I helped her down an embankment and over a running stream.

"That's a good start," I said. "Is flying a kind of magic?"

"In a way, I suppose. The relationship between what tethers us to the earth, gravity, lift, and buoyancy, it all ties its way into a certain kind of magic."

"So what magic do you use when you're fixing planes?"

"Have you never listened to me while I worked?" she asked, exasperated. She often talked to me while she did repairs, explaining her process. I'd always thought it was a bit of nonsense. She rattled about encouraging wings and inspiring trust in weld joints and silly things like that.

"Pretend I never did," I replied, suppressing a grin.

"You cheeky rascal. I should punch you."

"If it would make you feel better."

We ducked into a small grove and peered out. Ahead, a motorcar drove in our direction, but it turned northward long before its lights might have discovered us.

"It depends on what's wrong with the plane of course," she said. "You know as well as I do that every plane has its deficiencies. Some of them are trade-offs. Some are design oversights. Some are just sloppy because the plane was rushed to the front. Certain systems of magic address different kinds of problems."

"So, say a top wing sheds its fabric during a dive," I suggested.

"Wonderful example, Marcus. That may seem like an attach-ment issue, and most mechanics treat it that way. They try to bind the fabric to the wing's skeleton more securely. But the defect comes from a prioritization problem."

She let go of my hand and started gesticulating as if she were a schoolteacher.

"The designers were pressed to make a pursuit plane more maneuverable, but they could only work with what designs they'd had already. The practical issues of earning a contract from the military meant the design needed a certain economic allure. The plane knows the result: it was made purposefully compromised. With a defect like that, it doesn't take much for the wind to find a foothold and pull the fabric from the ribs. A small rip, a big slip."

"What does this have to do with magic?" I asked. She glanced at me askew, as though I'd missed something right in front of my eyes.

"You need to recast the priority, obviously. Make the plane believe it has no defects, that its design was top priority."

A quiet, breathy laugh escaped from my lips. It got lost in the trees around us. Jane hissed at me to stay quiet.

"What are you doing?"

"You're pulling my leg, Jane. How on earth do you trick a plane into thinking it can't shed its fabric?"

"There are several ways. Usually, I try to incorporate something into the repair that is absolutely ostentatious and unnecessary."

"Something valuable?" I raised my eyebrows. "To stoke its vanity?"

"Is it vain for something to believe in itself? Yes. Something valuable. I might prepare the material in a way that takes a luxurious amount of time."

"You're trying to tell me that if I used a gold cable instead of a steel one on the trailing edge of my wing that it might not shed its fabric?"

"Not exactly. But if you chose to spend extra care repairing the wire of your trailing edge instead of spending your time doing something else you really wanted to do, and you knew how to communicate that sacrifice to the plane, it might just believe it shouldn't let go of the fabric."

The spring night breeze chilled the perspiration on my neck. The air came off the water in the canals with an extra bite.

"And how does one communicate that to the plane?" I asked.

"Unreliably, unfortunately," she said. I smiled. Apparently, the specific process was either a closely held secret or beyond my understanding, otherwise she'd have told me more details.

"And Boelcke's goggles, then?"

She took her time responding. Her silence drew my attention to chirping crickets buzzing around us.

"Boelcke either did something to the goggles, or, alternatively, his death had a spontaneous magical impact on them," she said.

I wrestled with the concept that Boelcke cheated. It didn't sit right. He might have taught his magical secret to Richthofen. After all, the baron had a magic scarf. But if their successes were due to magic, how had Boelcke's legacy been so effective? All the other pilots who followed his advice—it was just sound flying.

"What kind of impact?"

"I'm unsure. I think flying has ripped a latent source of magic in two. We've only seen the beginning of it. Look at what's been accomplished in such a short amount of time. When decades pass, how will flying change? There are magical consequences to such discoveries. And when men act contrary to nature's laws, strange things happen in the magical realm."

"What laws did Boelcke break?"

"The law of self-preservation, for one, as does every pilot that flies against his enemy in the skies. But Boelcke stood apart from other pilots, didn't he?"

There was something to her words. I couldn't nail down why, but her explanation filled me up like a plate of potatoes. No. It wasn't natural for men to fly, and yet, for some men, like Boelcke, Richthofen, Lufbery, and all the other remarkable top aces, they'd found a home in the impossible. Perhaps humans could attain something greater than what was intended for their mortal frames.

And if they did attain such greatness, why shouldn't the earth be bothered when they met their end?

What did it cost nature to throw its hands up and admit that some humans broke the mold?

Jane pulled me to the dirt. We bellied up against a ridge in yet another irrigation ditch and watched a motorcar go by in front of us. The city had snuck up on me while I explored my thoughts. Buildings around us had grown more frequent, and the fields faded into the amenities that served a more centralized population. Bakeries and cobblers and mechanic shops and stables and the deeper we walked, the more sophisticated they became.

I could appreciate now the majesty that grew on age. These walks and canals had been carved over time with meticulous care. The city had been built to last through centuries, and some had already. But ahead called the greater testament to Ghent's permanence, structures that might never fall, both because of their architectural wonder and the respectful care they inspired year after year after year.

"We're practically in the city now," Jane said. "Just another ten minutes or so. I don't know how Ghent is laid out, but do you think we can orient ourselves on the map and find LeClercq?"

I pulled the map from my breast pocket and unfolded it in the dirt. A man like LeClercq would either be old, wealthy, or hiding. The Germans had forced working-age Belgians into labor. The longer the war stretched, the greater grew Germany's need for more munitions, supplies, machinery, foodstuffs, everything that fueled its mighty armies. And if all of the Germans were busy fighting, who was busy working to keep the fight raging?

I squinted at a mark on the map. *Kasteel Blauwhuys.*

"Look, Kasteel Blow hoo-ee, or Blau hais or—geez, I don't even know where to begin pronouncing that. Atkins wasn't kidding. If we get stopped, we'll be dead. What is that, Dutch?"

She inched closer and peered at the map.

"And here I thought most Belgians spoke French," she said.

"Hopefully, LeClercq speaks good English." The map gave a good idea of Ghent's general layout. To the north, a large canal branched up toward the sea. To the east and south, the city melted into countryside. But to the city proper's southwest side ran a border network of running bodies of water. I glanced up and noticed a long bridge with lights. Beside it sat two German motorcars.

"I think we're here. We need to turn south," I said. "That must be the Ringvaart. Is that a river or a canal?"

"I'm not sure it makes much difference. We can't cross either way. We will be stopped and questioned for certain."

"Fortunately," I moved my finger along the worn paper. "The Kasteel we're searching for—"

"Excellent choice not trying to pronounce it again."

"—is on the outside of that river. See? It's not far. Just across that wood. Maybe another mile or two. How are you doing?"

Jane leveled her eyes at me.

"Fine. How are you? Doing well? Eager to walk through a dark wood in German occupied Belgium? Hopefully, there's no sitting machine gun nests."

"You don't have to be sarcastic. I just meant, are you ready to go again?"

She hopped into a crouch and headed off in the direction I'd pointed, trying to stay low in our ditch. She quickly made it to a grove of trees. I kept an eye on the distant German sentry and followed suit. They wouldn't be able to see well into the darkness from under those lights. I was counting on it.

Chapter 24
The Belgian
Jane

But I've a rendezvous with Death
At midnight in some flaming town,
When Spring trips north again this year,
And I to my pledged word am true,
I shall not fail that rendezvous.
-Alan Seeger-

I had no intention of letting Marcus see my fatigue. I'd already allowed my fear to poke through, and that was quite enough. So, I willed my legs forward and ignored the perspiration accumulating at the base of my hair and on the small of my back. The sweat chilled me most unpleasantly, accentuating the cold spring night wafting through the paltry shawl and vest Atkins had procured for me.

In those clothes, I'm sure I looked the part. Unfortunately, the part was grim. I reflected on how badly the Belgians must have had it, occupied now for years by the Germans. During that time, the newspapers had lambasted the Kaiser's army, inflating the atrocities committed against the good people of Flanders and Wallonia, fanning flames on the information coming through intelligence networks.

At least, I hoped they were inflated.

Mass deportations. Executions. Looting. Plundering.

Despite the brutality one heard about the front line, it was hard to imagine that in the modern age of the 1900s, such barbarism might exist in a place that did not fight back.

We traveled quietly and carefully through the darkness of the wood. It seemed to me to stretch on forever. I jumped at every sound, be it a scurrying mouse or the hoot of an owl. In the shadows cut by streaks of moonlight, anything might be a German soldier. I'd heard so many stories about machine gun nests hidden in cover like this mowing down entire teams of men in seconds.

"There," Marcus said, after an agonizingly long trek. Our cautious speed stretched the miles. But through the tree line ahead, he pointed to a stately white house, inspired in part by Georgian architecture, with thick columns lining its facade. Nearby, a small pond reflected the moon's light quietly, bordered by picturesque trees and shrubs, all grown into a state of wild neglect and disrepair. As we neared, the far side of the building revealed its red brick wall. There were no lights shining in the windows. We stopped at the edge of the wood.

"Did Atkins give us more instructions? Are we just to knock on the door?" I asked.

Marcus shrugged.

"That doesn't seem like a good idea. What if we've got the wrong place and German sympathizers answer? Or worse, what if German soldiers have quartered themselves in there?"

"What alternative do we have? We can't just wait around in the hopes of finding someone named Gervais LeClercq, shouting our passcode to anyone who will listen. We might as well walk across one of those bridges and announce we've come to spy."

"Wait!" Marcus grabbed me by the shoulders and pulled me

behind a tangle of branches, deeper into the shadow of the forest. A small figure had opened the front door silently. No light shone from inside the entrance, and had we not been paying close attention, we would have missed it altogether.

The figure wandered from the house and toward the pond, clutching at a thick shawl draped over a night gown. I figured her for a woman, and when she stepped from the shadow of the house, the pale evening's light illuminated her hair. The way she stood staring at the reflection of the sky in the pond struck me with a deep reverence, so regal and graceful was she. A dame in white.

"Now what?" Marcus asked.

"Perhaps she could help us," I suggested.

"Help us? Does that look like Gervais LeClercq to you? He's our contact. I don't want to trust anyone else."

"She's coming closer," I said.

She sauntered in our direction, aimless and carefree. Could she be sleepwalking? Although she neared our location, she never stopped peering into the pond. Soon, she was close enough that we dared not whisper.

I tried to hold my breath, then ease my lungs apart a fraction at a time so as not to breathe too heavily.

"Atkins," the woman said, her voice breaking the silence as if she'd cast a stone into still water. "Our friend, Atkins."

At the mention of the lieutenant's name, relief caught at my fluttering stomach. The way she swallowed the letter R gave her a distinctly French impression, no sign of the staccato, syllabic separation characteristic of the German accent. I glanced at Marcus, but his eyes still warned me to stay quiet.

"You may come out, only do so quietly, and do not linger in the moonlight."

She spoke over her shoulder, pretending to give all her attention to the pond.

Marcus still hesitated. I could all but read his thoughts. This was not the Gervais LeClercq we had come seeking. But she seemed to know all about us, including that we were hiding where we were. I didn't understand what benefit we achieved by staying outside where the Germans might see us as easily as driving by.

So, I stood. Marcus grabbed at my wrist, but I shook him off. She surveyed me in a moment, just a twist of the head, before calmly heading back to the Kasteel.

"Oh, come along," I hissed at Marcus. "She's seen me now, and there's no turning back. No password needed."

He surrendered and followed behind me, his hands casually in his pockets as though he'd been out checking on a noise in the garden.

Ahead, the woman silently cracked open the door and slipped inside, leaving it open for us. With a final breath, I pushed fear aside and went in.

It was dark in the antechamber. The only light that poked through came from the cracks in the blinds covering tall, round top windows in adjoining hallways. A staircase stood in the center of the room, stretching up and out of view. The whole room darkened further when Marcus silently closed the door behind him.

"Atkins sent you," the woman said.

"Yes," I replied. "I'm Private Doe. This is Sergeant Jackson. We flew in earlier on an—"

"Albatross C.XIII. I know. It's not every day that an Albatross lands in the middle of a Drongen farmer's field."

I stuttered, embarrassed and frightened that our landing attracted not just her attention. But she waved a hand.

"Don't worry. We see everything. The coming and goings of the trains, the way troops rearrange themselves, how many planes go up, how many come back."

"Who's 'we?'" Marcus asked gruffly. I caught the hint of a smile on her face, and she motioned us to come closer.

"Please, sit," she said as she eased into a tall-backed chair out of view of the window. I sat opposite in a similar chair and tried to stifle a moan of relief. We'd been uncomfortable since that morning, either crammed in the car, on edge in the plane, or trekking hills through the Belgian countryside. In the comfort of that chair cushion, I all but extended a Pavlovian hand expecting a cup of tea.

But there was no tea. There wasn't even a candle.

"We're looking for a man named Gervais LeClercq," I said. Marcus stood by the window curtains, nervously glancing through them.

"Don't touch the curtains," the woman scolded. "Moving curtains are suspicious. No one touches a curtain unless they're right at the window."

Marcus stuffed his hand back in his pocket with a grunt but continued to peer suspiciously through the glass.

"I'm afraid you'll have a hard time finding a Messieur LeClercq," she said.

"How's that?" Marcus asked.

"Dead? Deported?" I added, dread in my voice.

"He doesn't exist. But I sometimes go by the name of Gervaise LeClercq. Hopefully, I'm close enough to what you sought."

Marcus jerked his head from the window, and approached her.

"You're Gervais LeClercq?" he asked.

"Gervaise," she corrected. "You may call me, simply, LeClercq."

"This isn't a game we're playing here," Marcus said. "If you're our contact, say so."

Gervaise wrinkled her nose above a derisive smile.

"It's not a game?" she asked. "There aren't two sides? No one keeps score? No one wears uniforms?"

She inched forward.

"I don't know what you think you've seen in the sky, or on the lines, where the war is so different from your life at home. But here in Ghent, the place where I grew up, it's all a game. The winners stay. The losers go."

Marcus scowled but kept quiet, returning to his observation of the world outside. We were both flustered. We had not envisioned a woman like Gervaise as our contact. But on reflection, it made sense. The work-aged men would have been put to work. If women didn't populate Belgium's intelligence network, who would?

The intelligence offices needed information, and the information came from somewhere. This woman risked her life every day right under the nose of her enemy to pass on commonplace information, facts and figures that the war lent deadly importance.

"Atkins has told you about our mission, then," I said to Gervaise gently.

"Little. We usually report on train movement. The repositioning of troops. Air activity. Our network is most valuable for our ability to keep our eyes open. But you're not here for train schedules. Otherwise, they'd not have asked me to help."

"And why is that?" I asked.

"Because I am expendable. I am the bottom rung of a tall ladder."

I blinked back my surprise. Her voice carried no bitterness in such cold self-reflection.

"You don't mean that. Surely, you're not expendable," I said.

"I drop information in a box. I don't know who picks up the information. I don't know who transports the information or where it goes or if anyone ever reads it. I am an island."

I glanced at Marcus. His scowl had melted.

"If you don't even know if you're helping, why risk so much to do it?" I asked.

"Because when it's over, I want to know I did something. I believe my actions have meaning, and it is easier to adjust action, than to quit inaction."

I took a deep breath, bothered by the unusually frank conversation. We'd met this woman five minutes ago and already she imparted her most deeply held beliefs. She leaned forward.

"We don't have time to romance one another. You are my mission, and I am prepared to die for it."

I'd seen some hailed as heroes in the war, but this was the first time I'd seen such listless courage. It bordered on recklessness.

"What I'm about to tell you may come across as nonsense," I started. "But we're here looking for something—a device, that may give us an advantage and hasten the end of the war."

"It is not my place to question your mission," she said.

I pursed my lips.

"Still, you must have questions. The device is—"

"The less I know, the better," she said firmly. "I am supposed to escort you into the city, then help you return to your plane."

I folded my hands in my lap and held my tongue.

"Where are you escorting us exactly?" Marcus asked.

"It's best that you only know when necessary."

"That dangerous?"

"It's just our way." She shrugged. "If one of us is captured, the Germans have many methods to extract information. A network like ours is built on ignorance. Ignorance is the only systematic way of generating reliable, regular information. You will follow my instructions. You will do what I say."

I nodded. Marcus finally took a seat.

"The family that owns this Kasteel are away for a time. They are friends. There are beds upstairs. We will use it as our planning ground."

"Thank you," said Marcus, relenting his suspicion at last. "I don't suppose you have anything to eat around here, do you?"

Gervaise's eyebrows piqued. The moonlight cut sad, gaunt lines from them.

"It's been a difficult winter for everyone. I was unable to gather potatoes without raising suspicion."

I didn't need to see Marcus to know that he blushed. My heart, too, folded on itself.

"How bad has it been?" I asked quietly. Gervaise's defiant chin jutted out.

"Not so bad that we can't persevere."

But in the question about food, her heroic mask had slipped for a moment, and I pushed on, daring to lean forward and touch her hand.

"How bad has it been?" I repeated.

She swallowed slowly.

"It's been worse than ever. Ever since the mass migration. There were thousands and thousands of troops coming through. We heard that Russia had fallen, and Germans were moving everything west. But with more troops have come greater demands."

She applied gentle pressure back on my hand, and I saw how young she was for the first time.

"Have you eaten at all this week?" I asked.

"It's worse for the elderly," she said. "And what few children are left. The stores are empty. They've stripped us of anything of value. Even the aristocrats dine on cabbage soup now. Everyone suffers but those traitors who have sided with the Kaiser."

She squeezed my hand more tightly.

"And your family?" I asked.

She shook her head.

"My father was deported. My mother died trying to escape the electric wire across the northern border. She wasn't careful enough."

"No sisters or brothers? Relatives?" I prodded.

"There is me. And there are the Germans. And I will beat them in the end."

My mind started racing, testing machinations to protect this poor girl. There must be some way I could get her far from the war, out of Ghent. Out of Belgium. The Netherlands weren't far away. If we could get her there... Perhaps she and I could both fit in the gunner's bay of the Albatross.

I looked to Marcus, who already shook his head slowly back and forth.

I pleaded with my eyes, tears welling against my will.

He shook his head. It was a bad idea. It would endanger the mission. It would endanger me. But I couldn't cope with such unfeeling tactical resolve.

"Gervaise, when we are through in Ghent, we will take you with us. We will remove you from this situation," I said, overriding Marcus's opinion and my own understanding that it would be all but impossible.

Gervaise released my hand.

"What waits for me out there?" she asked.

"Freedom. At least, more freedom than this."

"I will not run away. The coming and going of the trains must be reported, and I will do my part."

I reached again for her hand.

"But if you're discovered—"

"Then I will die, and welcoming me beside Saint Peter at the gates of heaven will be Edith Cavell and Gabrielle Petit, true daughters of the cause, warriors for Belgium." She patted my hand as if I were a child. "Tomorrow, I will take you into the city. Now, you should both sleep. We will leave the house before sunrise."

Chapter 25
City of Noose-bearers
Marcus

Not with her ruined silver spires,
Not with her cities shamed and rent,
Perish the imperishable fires
That shape the homestead from the tent.
-Edith Wharton-

Sleep came with difficulty. We were far from the front lines, but whether I imagined it or heard it faintly in the distance, artillery fire broke the silence in the castle. We could only find one blanket, a scratchy thing that I insisted Jane use all night. Her disguise was not as warm as mine—something I'd have to take issue with Atkins for later. Instead, I'd curled tightly on myself and tried to find some warmth in the threadbare sheet Gervaise stole from another room. In truth, the home was not run down, but it appeared as though it had been stripped of its luxuries. Occasionally, a light would break through the window from a passing German motorcar, illuminating the bedroom all three of us slept in.

Once, the house would have been beautiful. I'm sure all of

Belgium had been beautiful before the Germans burned their way through it.

Ghent's humidity made staying warm even harder, and I flickered through rest, sporadically entering and exiting nightmares about Jane being taken prisoner, Lufbery mistakenly shooting down our Albatross, or my mother trying to cross no-man's land to come find me.

I finally managed to nod off when Gervaise shook me awake.

"We have to get going," she said. I glanced out the window. The sun had not yet perked over the horizon. Its dawn glow only just started to illuminate the sky.

"What time is it?" I asked.

"Five thirty," she said. "And it will take us time to get to the bridge. The closer to six we can cross the better."

"Why's that?"

"The patrol changes at six. The guards will have been there since the evening before. We've learned they are less likely to ask questions at the end of a night shift."

I nodded and forced myself from the meager warmth I'd generated. My joints cracked, muscles aching from the hike we had the day before. I winced. It had been a long time since I trekked about like that. The life of an aviator had its challenges, but it didn't stress the muscles the same way it did for infantry.

Gervaise tiptoed out of the room to survey the area and play her role for the neighbors. She was officially one of the Kasteel's caretakers. Chores to be done. Appearances to be made.

As she set herself to the mundane work, I realized I had the completely wrong understanding of what espionage was like. I'd always thought it had much more to do with daring moves and difficult escapes, but Gervaise demonstrated the bulk of it in no less than twelve hours we'd known her. Espionage was a game of pretending nothing was different. If it went well, her enemy would be so bored that they wouldn't even notice their carelessness.

I wondered how our Albatross sitting in a field somewhere threw off the daily guise of normalcy.

"Did you sleep?" Jane asked me. She stretched her arms skyward, and her hair fell in tangles. Creases lined her skirt, shirt, and the section of her face below her eyes.

"Sure did."

"Liar," she said. "You tossed and turned all night. It kept me up."

I smiled.

"My apologies."

"No need for that. Just remind me never to sleep in the same room as you again," she said with a wicked smile. For a moment, in the bedroom of that Belgian manor, stripped of its finery but still embodying the grace of its design, I didn't feel like we were on an assignment. It was like we were on a vacation, some exciting trip where we might discover a berry patch on a hike in the woods or attend a fair in a foreign country.

For a brief moment, I nearly convinced myself we might be about to embark on nothing more than a swell, fun day.

"I suppose breakfast is out of the question?" Jane said as she glanced around the room with a curious cock of her brow.

"Better not ask," I said. "The last time I did, I felt like a rotten spoiled buffoon."

"Rotten," Jane replied. "I'd take a rotten potato if they had one."

"Maybe we'll find something in the city," I said with a shrug, ignoring the doubt in my own stomach. Inside the city would be greater competition, scarcer resources. Food might be more plentiful, stored at grocers or in whatever served as a mess for the Germans, but it'd be harder to come by.

"Here." Gervais had snuck back into the room without our notice. She tossed me a small sack of cloth. I unfolded it and saw a handful of turnips and radishes before turning toward Jane, perplexed.

"Thank you, Gervaise," Jane said carefully. "We will eat these. They look delicious."

"It's not for you," Gervaise said with a roll of her eyes. "You two whine as if you haven't eaten in a week. These are for Thomas."

"Who is Thomas?" I asked.

"Your next stop, if we can sneak you into the city safely. It's never wise to come empty handed," she went on. "But be careful. If the Germans notice you trying to smuggle vegetables, they'll take you in. And you might not come back out."

I gave the pack to Jane, who stuffed the small parcel under the waistband of her skirt. Gervaise nodded.

"They're fresh from our garden here. Thomas will appreciate your courage in bringing them."

She eyed me and grimaced.

"Do I look that bad?" I asked.

"Sneaking this one in will be easy," she said, nodding at Jane. "But the Germans are suspicious of any man your age wandering around the city." She bit her lip in thought.

"Maybe you two could distract the sentries, and I could sneak in another way?" I suggested.

"There are only the bridges. The water is freezing, and it's not so remote that no one will notice you trying to cross."

"What if he's sick? Or wounded?" Jane asked. "Is it common for convalescent men to be treated in the city?"

Gervaise dipped her head to the side.

"It's not implausible." She glanced out the window. "It will have to do. It's more important that we arrive at the correct time." She tossed an old sheet to Jane. "Make him a sling, and we'll be on our way."

City of Noose-bearers

T he air outside was bitterly crisp. We walked quickly, and I was relieved to see that we weren't the only ones trying to enter the city. The bridge stood ahead of us, spanning the canal that served almost like a moat around Ghent.

The way Gervaise talked about those sentries, I'd have thought that it was a single file system where German officers checked paperwork one by one. It wasn't that. In fact, traffic flowed smoothly. A few German soldiers standing with rifles beside motorcars surveyed the crowd sleepily, but it was clear the Germans did not intend to turn Ghent into a prison—at least, not from outward appearances.

Still, as we tried to push forward through a scattered crowd of people, Gervaise's anxiousness rubbed off on me. She clenched and unclenched her bandaged hand. I winced—and not just because I was pretending my arm was broken and infectious.

After Jane had crafted the sling, Gervaise expressed that she found it too clean and ultimately unrealistic. Before Jane or I could offer a solution, she had already produced a knife and drawn it across the palm of her hand. It took no time at all for her to turn a worn, clean sheet into a grotesque, nauseating eyesore. On our way out, I applied some mud as well, to take some of the edge of the blood off.

She wasn't totally satisfied with the outcome, as my flashy sling probably drew more attention than we wished. And the guilt ate at me. I'm sure Gervaise needed that hand.

"Come on," she whispered to herself, casting furtive glances at the sentries. We were still a hundred yards off when a new motorcar drove up to a pair of bored German soldiers.

"No," Gervaise said. "We took too long."

Jane and I stared at the ground, channeling our hunger into the slouching posture of those around us.

"What does that mean?" Jane asked.

"Hopefully nothing," Gervaise replied. "If we get separated, meet at the Museum of Antiquities. Laangstreet. The north side of the city."

"Do we need to change course?" I asked through gritted teeth.

"No. We must get through. Turning back now would raise suspicion."

A couple of German soldiers stepped from the newly arrived motorcar, rifles slung over their shoulders. These two seemed older than the sentries they replaced, more tired somehow.

The sound of their grumbles reached me, echoed by the laugh of the men they replaced.

We were close enough now to see the details of their gray uniforms, the gleam of the metal on their polished guns, the shine of their boots.

What did these soldiers have to grumble about? They were not at the front. They did not face no man's land or the slowly moving tanks of the British. How dare they complain about an early morning?

Gervaise wrapped an arm around me and felt my forehead. I coughed gently. I'd never been much of an actor. Jane walked apart from us, on the other side of the crowd, furthest from the sentries. Her headscarf bobbed up and down as she tried to keep her face down.

I heard the Germans stop laughing. We were passing near them now, and Gervaise's concerned brows were placed against my forehead, her lips kissing my hair.

"Don't look. Keep walking," she whispered into the top of my head.

A disapproving, universal muttering filtered through the morning air, past the sound of the canal's water. Then the steps of boots. The protest and teasing of his companions.

"*Madame!*" The voice was youthful, likely belonging to one of the younger soldiers. Gervaise gripped my arm firmly and urged me forward. *"Madame!"* The call came again, and my heart started pounding. I wished I had my Star pistol. But what good would it do me? I'd never shot a man, and shooting a German here was as good as shooting myself, anyway.

Gervaise had to stop. Jane's step faltered, but despite my wild eyes, I managed to send her instructions. *Keep going. We will find you. Get past the sentries. Meet at the museum.*

"Speak only what I told you. And only to yourself," she said in my ear as we turned. *"Messieur?"*

The German soldier grinned and stood awkwardly in front of us.

"Sprechen zie Deutsch?" he asked.

"No," Gervaise replied. *"Francais?"*

He clicked his tongue and shook his head. I coughed quietly, and Gervaise took the language barrier as a cue to continue.

"Allors—" The German grabbed her arm as she stepped away.

"English?" he tried. He didn't wait for her to confirm. "He is injured?"

I groaned quietly, trying my best to come across sickly and bothered about being stopped.

"His arm was caught in some machinery on our farm. I hoped it would be better, but I fear it is infected," Gervaise said.

"And you as well?" the German asked. "Your hand."

"Desperation. I had to work the machine," she said with a hint of bitterness. My mind raced to the falsified papers I carried and to Jane. Had she kept walking as I'd asked? If I was detained, what would she do?

"May I see?" the soldier asked. Gervaise reluctantly stuck her hand out.

"Please, be careful. It took us much time to wrap things without so much pain."

The German gingerly unwrapped her hand and saw the angry

cut across the palm. His eyebrows furrowed with concern. The humanity of it transported me back to that night early in the war, the night I let a German go.

"His is worse?" he asked.

Gervaise swallowed and put on a brave face.

"We are going to a doctor inside the city," she said. He nodded and clicked his tongue again.

"German medics are better," he said. "Is your doctor far?"

She shook her head.

"He can barely walk," the German said. He eyed the motorcar. "I am done here. I will take you in my motorcar."

My heart pounded. If we went in that car, there was no telling if I'd ever see Jane again.

"That is not necessary. We can go on our own," Gervaise protested.

"Don't be dumb. He can't walk! Please, allow me to help." The German smiled sweetly at Gervaise, and I suspected he had more on his mind than simply driving us down the road. But our options were limited. We had already earned his attention, and to argue too much might kindle suspicion or anger. We didn't have the luxury of entertaining either.

I wanted to run. To push the German over and sprint into the city and find my friend. I'd made her a promise. How can you protect someone who is not with you?

Gervaise hesitated only as much as might be natural.

"Thank you," she said, inclining her head to the soldier.

"*Wunderbar*," he replied, motioning for us to follow him. I cast a glance behind me. Jane had melted into the crowd, disappearing into the slovenly street traffic of Ghent. She was gone.

I'd lost her.

We limped after the German sentry, who exchanged words with his partner. After much complaining, the other soldier threw up his arms and started walking into the city. The new sentries laughed and jeered after him.

Gervaise shuffled into the front seat of the motorcar, pulling me up behind her and cradling my head on her bosom. With my ear flush against her chest, her heart beat so loud I was afraid it'd give us away.

Understanding that Gervaise was as afraid as I was chilled and comforted me all at once. In the very brief time I'd known her, I hadn't ever imagined she could be afraid.

But if I had any hope of getting to that museum and meeting up with Jane again, I needed to trust her. If Gervaise thought submitting was best for now, I had no grounds to disagree, even if my heart begged me to.

The soldier clambered into the driver's seat and turned the engine over with a sigh before turning us down the bridge toward the heart of Ghent.

As we drove in, for the briefest moment, I saw Jane. Her wide eyes followed our car as we whisked around a corner and out of sight.

She clutched the marble around her neck. I did the same.

Chapter 26
Albert's Song
Jane

You are aware that once I sought the Grail,
Riding in armor bright, serene and strong;
And it was told that through my infant wail
There rose immortal semblances of song.
-Siegfried Sassoon-

Panic is such a weak word. What can five letters do to portray such helplessness and fear? If it were up to me, panic would be spelled with no letters at all, for when I saw Gervaise and Marcus driving away in a German soldier's motorcar, I wanted to scream but couldn't come up with a single sound.

My feet cemented me to the street despite how many "*Pardonez-moi*"s or "*Excuseer*"s tried to jostle me forward.

It took the loud blaring of a car horn to bring me to my senses. I stepped to the side to allow it passage, but though my faculties came around, my heart did not stop hammering.

What if that was the last time I would ever see Marcus?

I'd heard about the difficulty of intelligence gathering on the other side of the front line, listened rapt to the horror stories of how spies were questioned with chemical and physical persuasion before their eventual execution.

The soft angles of Marcus's expression hung themselves in the air where he'd just disappeared. His face wore not fear, but concern—worry for me. He always worried for me.

I stared ahead, the city split into several streets. Gervaise's words from the night before came to me: it was much easier to adjust action than to quit inaction. I had to do something. I had to trust that Marcus would do everything in his power to return to me, to carry out the mission.

The mission. I shook my head quickly, trying to shake the fright out through my ears. I had persuaded Marcus to come on this mission with me. I believed in it. Somewhere in Ghent, a magical device waited, and we needed to find it before the enemy.

But even if I found it, what then?

Gervaise had mentioned the name of the old museum, but I had little else to go on. It could be miles into the city, and the buildings stretched in every direction but the way I'd come.

I stared over my shoulder at the bridge. Where would I go? I could not fly the Albatross. But should I not wait at the Kasteel? Surely, if Gervaise and Marcus managed to escape, they would go back there to find me. Or would they rely on me to be a good soldier, to put aside my emotions and move forward? That's what Gervaise would do.

My stomach grumbled. My limbs hung from my torso, gutted and empty. I wanted to sit and sleep again, make up for the paltry rest we'd managed the night before.

I hugged my shawl closer and felt my smooth marble necklace beneath my blouse against my skin. The parcel of radishes ate into my back.

I breathed deeply, letting the cool morning air claw away at the nightmarish heat running up my spine and scalp, and my feet started into the city. At the very least, I could try to blend in with the passersby around me and not look like an Allied spy bothered that everything had gone wrong. Walk and think.

The Museum of Antiquities.

It couldn't be that far. But how could I inquire? If I attempted French, my accent would certainly give me away, and I didn't know who might be trusted not to turn me in to the Germans.

I passed an hour, wandering around, ignoring the pangs of my hunger and pretending to walk with purpose so as not to be stopped by the occasional patrol of German troops. I went by food stands and cafes, all with meager offerings. I was no expert on Belgian currency, but I had a feeling the listed prices for a bite of bread were significantly higher than usual. Several women cross the windows shook their heads and clicked their tongues. Still, I'd have paid it if I had the money.

Ghent's long streets stretched out as a beautiful labyrinth. The buildings had been erected with vision enough to tell the story of the city's rich history, but melancholy clung to their walls like coal dust. The clouds in the sky above did little to lift this mood.

Its maze of avenues and side streets spun me around, distorting my sense of direction. My hope waned with every new turn. The deeper my search took me, the more difficult it would be to find the path back to the Kasteel.

A sharp tap of a finger on the glass window of a bakery woke me. At some point, I'd sat on the ground against a wall to regroup my spirits. A grumpy man in an apron dusted with flour motioned for me to move along. I must have been blocking the window, deterring other possible customers, people with money enough to support his livelihood. Even from my walk of a couple hours, I'd seen who would be most likely to buy.

Germans.

"*Vous avez faim?*"

I squinted upward and saw a woman of about fifty years in a

long coat addressing me. She stood casually with gently set shoulders and relaxed spine, but her tone was conspiratorial.

I nodded. I was hungry, no point in hiding it.

She inclined her forehead, indicating that I should pay closer attention. In her hand, concealed among the folds of her coat, was a slip of paper, a newspaper.

"*Un journal?*" I asked.

"*Fermez la bouche,*" she hissed, checking carefully for eavesdroppers. There was no one. The way she held herself, the nature of the secret offer of the newspaper, gave me an odd sense of hope. I wondered if she knew Gervaise. But when I did not immediately take the paper, she started walking away.

"*Attendez-vous!*" I called after her, getting to my feet in hot pursuit. I doubted someone distributing clandestine newspapers would care if my accent were foreign. She pretended not to hear me. An elderly woman now made her way slowly down the other side of the street, but I risked a discreet offer of my own. "*Je suis Anglaise!*"

The woman's step faltered, and I caught up to her.

"Be quiet," she whispered.

"Please, I need help," I replied.

"I pass out newspapers, that is all," she said. The wrinkles on her face hung from her eyes and off the corners of her mouth. She increased her pace.

"Just some direction. Where is the Museum of Antiquities?"

She glared at me, eager to rid herself of the presence of a damning foreigner, attention that might get her caught.

"You're three streets over. It is north of Kasteel Gravensteen. Now leave me, please!"

"Gravensteen, thank you!" I marveled at the woman as she scurried off, at the immense bravery she had to go handing out papers. Who else in the world had the courage of Belgian women?

My eyes wandered to the towering gray stone of the castle

she'd indicated. It poked over the top of the brick facades next to me, and I hastened my step, hunger now forgotten. Thank heavens I had not given in and eaten the radishes. Thomas would need them.

And perhaps Thomas could help me liberate my friend.

I bounded confidently past other pedestrians and found the museum within twenty minutes, though I nearly walked right by it.

As museums went, its design was underwhelming, even if the large brick building sloped into a stately tower and parapet. The front door lay flush in a beaten wall, unassuming and quiet. I had the impression it wasn't heavily trafficked, especially in a time that could afford so little leisure.

I took a deep breath, said a quick prayer, and opened the door.

The entry was mostly vacant, with only an old man stooping over a broom in one of the corners. He picked his shoulders up briefly to assess me before deciding I was particularly uninteresting and going back about his work.

Before I'd managed ten steps forward, the clack of wooden shoes on the tile floor echoed in the stonework above, a messenger foretelling the arrival of the museum's curator. I could only hope it was the Thomas I sought.

But unless Thomas was a woman of my height with tightly bound raven hair, I was to be disappointed.

"*Bonjour, madame,*" she said formally, all proper posture and neutral expression. "*Comment pouvons vous aider?*"

"*Bonjour,*" I replied. My mind raced thinking of an excuse—any excuse—to be there. "*Je cherche un—*"

"But you're English?" she asked, startled.

I stuttered before nodding. It took no more than four words before she pecked out the source of my accent. A bothered British part of me wanted to continue in French to try and prove that I had studied the language.

"Pardon me, but we don't see very many English around here lately. They've all run back home or to France."

"And who could blame them?" I asked, smiling politely. This was normal. I was chatting with a lovely Belgian museum curator. What could be more typical than that?

"There are many who do," she replied flatly. "What courage has inspired you to visit our city?"

"I'm searching for someone, actually."

"You've found someone."

"His name is Thomas. My friend said he might be here with a present for me."

Her eyes narrowed.

"Which friend?"

I pursed my lips. Gervaise might very well be a code name, but I had enough sense not to throw it around to whoever asked.

"I'm afraid I can't say. I promised."

"I see."

The woman clasped her hands behind her back and walked directly past me toward the front door. She locked it and turned back to me, her shoulder blades resting firmly on what was now a sealed exit.

"What are you really doing here?" she asked.

My breath caught.

"It's as I've told you."

"Did the Germans send you?"

"Absolutely not."

"There have been whispers today of a German plane landing in a field nearby. Of a strange man in a German uniform wandering about the streets. Whispers that two people snuck into a house dressed in civilian clothes. But I have dealt with counter agents before. I'm not afraid to deal with more."

She approached slowly, every footstep filled with menace. Her hand slipped smoothly inside her shawl.

"I'm not German," I protested.

"No. Just desperate enough to accept their money. I've seen women like you within our own walls."

"I don't have time for this. I must see Thomas. My friends are in German custody. I'm the last hope for them, for Thomas—"

"Marie, please stop."

A crackling voice sounded from the corner. The man who had stooped so feebly over his broomstick stood suddenly tall.

"Are you certain?" Marie replied in a hushed voice. "This could be a trap."

"Look at her," the man replied. "Does she appear to be on the brink of desperation? Desperate enough to take German money? Her clothes fit too well, a sign that she hasn't missed many meals. Keep the doors locked, but I think she is from the network."

Marie inclined her head and retreated to the door, placing protective hands on either handle.

"Thomas?" I asked as the man stepped into a shaft of light from the windows high on the wall. His face was deeply creased under long strands of gray hair. Though he stood square and strong, his body reminded me of a skeleton. I clumsily retrieved the bag of radishes. "These are for you."

He smiled and bowed.

"What is the name of your friend?" he asked.

"Gervaise."

"Where is she? And were there not meant to be two of you with her?"

I clenched my jaw to stem the emotion his question inspired in me.

"They were taken," I said quietly. His face paled.

"Not Gervaise... captured? Discovered?"

"I don't know. I saw only that a German took them in his motorcar. I overheard them discussing medical attention for my companion and for Gervaise's hand."

"But they entered a German motorcar? Were the injuries substantial?"

"They were planned. Gervaise cut her hand to paint a sling we made for Lieutenant Jackson. He, though, has no injury. And if he's taken to any medic, it will be discovered."

His expression settled into the worn, worried grooves that lined his skin.

"I knew Gervaise was too reckless," Marie said from her position at the door.

"Her heart is in the right place, and I trust her judgment," Thomas replied sadly. "If she thought falsifying an injury was best to accomplish her mission, then so be it. I take it she tried this to explain Lieutenant Jackson's purpose for entering Ghent."

I nodded, eliciting a sigh from the old man.

"When the war finally runs its course, I wonder how long it will take the world to recover from losing a generation. Between service and deportations, how do nations cope with such loss? Widows. Spinsters. Women alone with shattered hearts. Daughters without fathers."

He looked at Marie, then smiled at me.

"And yet, the bravery and strength I've seen in the women of this war... It's in you I rest my hope."

If only he knew. There was powerful magic in the bonds between two people who suffered through trauma together. Powerful and sad magic.

"Come," Thomas said, "You did not risk so much to hear me rambling on."

He beckoned me to follow him. I glanced at Marie, but she didn't move from her post at the front door. I supposed someone had to keep up appearances in case someone came to visit.

I followed Thomas deeper into the museum, behind closed doors, into back rooms. The hallways were lined with sealed crates and sculptures covered by fabric. I wondered at the treasures that must reside in such a place, and part of me made a note to come visit if the war ended.

"The Germans have confiscated much of our collection. We've had to make some strategic decisions. What do we hide? What do we risk moving? How do we explain where such things went? At first, it started with the Germans laying their claim to disputed artifacts, mementos and treasures that changed hands during the Prussian war. They moved under the guise of righting past wrongs. Renaming their looting by saying they were returning treasures to their rightful place."

He took me into a small offshoot from the hallway into a large storage closet.

"But the spoils of war are too tempting even for disciplined generals. As surely as Belgian towns were looted by low-ranking officers and the foot soldiers drank the wine cellars dry, German High Command has its eyes on more lofty prizes."

I folded my hands patiently in front of myself. The storage room was dark with no windows. We were surrounded by hanging musical instruments, more closed crates, rolled up rugs and tapestries, an assortment of small chests, and tools needed for the cleaning and preservation of historical treasures.

"I'm afraid I know little of Belgium's great works," I admitted.

He smiled.

"I speak too freely, anyway. Forgive my excitement. You're here for something particularly special. But understand, it is not easy for me to part with it. The item you're here to collect is at risk in Ghent, yes, but we've successfully concealed other artifacts from the Germans until now. Is it not more dangerous to have you transport it?"

His mention of the magical device we sought woke me up. This was why we'd come. If Marcus was—well, perhaps the item could help me find him. I didn't know what power it possessed, but I hypothesized that Boelcke's goggles identified marks of magic, could locate other devices. I wondered if the device in Thomas's possession could do something similar.

Was it impossible that the magic latent in whatever I'd come to retrieve might open new possibilities in saving my friend?

"I've been ordered to retrieve the artifact, or device, or whatever you wish to call it. That is what I intend to do. It is not safe here, sir, despite what you may think. We've tracked these objects, and an unknown enemy does the same. You can't hide it the way you think. It gives off a signal, like a radio wave."

The old man stared at me intently, digesting the information and assessing my resolve.

"It's been here safely for a long time," he said.

"It is safer behind our lines, far away from enemy hands," I countered.

"And how do you intend to get it back there?" he asked, gently. "We've been instructed to trust no one in our network, never to attempt its export. What makes you special?"

Without Marcus, I didn't have an answer. I wasn't about to divulge our secret meeting at the farmhouse near Nancy. I wanted to say that we had the covert resources to get back, to fly over the front without intervention, but I could not.

"Perhaps if you show me the device, I can give you a better answer."

His eyes sparkled in the dark room, illuminated by an excitement from within his thin frame. Smoothly, he ensured the door to the closet was firmly closed. Then, he turned around, and quietly plucked a violin and its bow from the wall.

"Have you heard of the name, 'Albert Ball'?" he asked.

"Albert Ball? The pilot? He was all over the papers for most of the war," I replied. "One of Britain's top aces, but he died nearly a year ago."

"Yes, at the old age of twenty. A skilled pilot, but also a particular human being. One whose personality outshone even his formidable accomplishments. They say he kept a garden at his airbase, and that he slept apart from the rest of his companions."

I shifted my legs. I'd been standing most of the morning, and the fatigue gnawed at me.

"I'd heard he kept his hair long," I added, eager to get on with business.

"You could say he did things his own way. Even until the end."

"Yes." I nodded. "If I'm not mistaken, he was shot down by the Germans near Douai—"

"No. Not shot down. In fact, he scored a victory immediately before his demise. They say he forced Lothar Von Richthofen to ground, the great Baron's brother. Then flew into a dark thundercloud and plummeted from the sky amidst a trail of black smoke."

The hair rose on my neck. I'd flown through a storm cloud myself. It was terrifying, but I reassured myself that Marcus knew what he was about.

"Oil in the cylinders," I said, my mechanic's training diagnosing the problem. "What happened in that cloud to cause such a malfunction?"

"It is impossible to say. But it does seem a peculiar way for one of Britain's most accomplished pilots to go."

"I agree," I said.

Thomas didn't speak further, only settled the violin under his chin, tightened the hair of the bow, and started a tune.

At first, his playing kindled in me a sense of impatience. Was he being purposefully obtuse? Perhaps he found my insistence on taking the magical device with me back to France nothing but childish. Further, I worried that the sound of the violin might draw undue attention to the museum. If German soldiers walked outside near the building, I was nearly certain they'd hear the melody—he did not play it quietly.

But the connection between Ball and Richthofen didn't escape my notice. If we were looking for a chain in the magic, we had a connection here, albeit a labored one. It was a strange coincidence that Albert Ball tangled with The Red Baron's brother on the day of his machine's critical malfunction. The coincidence was attenuated still, knowing that we received news from Earnst and Lina so late after Ball had gone down.

But whatever magic device had materialized, it had some connection to the British ace.

Thomas's body swayed deeply with his haunting tune, the violin singing a nocturne more beautifully melancholy than I'd ever heard. The music pulled me in. As he played, I imagined I knew him better. This man, codenamed Thomas, used the music to open a window to all his fear, regret, longing for peace, courage, love—everything inside his heart slowly revealed itself to me as if they were dancers on a stage seen only by my eyes.

Yes. As he played, I saw him in so concrete a manner that I might have tracked him with my eyes closed. I knew who, where, and what he was without question.

But the music took me further still, and I appreciated all at once how unique and singular the man before me was. This understanding overwhelmed, sending gooseflesh all over my body. So powerful was the sensation that I feared I might lose consciousness. Yes! There were millions and millions of people out there, but there was only one Thomas. Irreplaceable. Though his existence might be cut short, it would not be denied. Even if he was not remembered, he would leave a mark.

The music stopped, and I found I'd closed my eyes. My breathing quivered. My heart hammered. His voice broke the darkness.

"I take it you believe in magic, madame," he said.

"I do. Since I was a girl," I replied, gulping as I tried to recover. The reality of our surrounding slowly slid into view. We were in the storage closet again, though we'd never left.

"Then I envy you. I wish I had never stopped believing."

I smiled gently. Now that I'd seen him so clearly, Thomas struck me as a friend, perhaps even a distant family member.

"You play well."

"You know what's interesting?" He grinned and looked at the violin in his hands. "I never knew how to play the violin. But the first time I strung this instrument, an overwhelming desire to play it came over me. I picked up the bow and played that song."

I stared.

"You'd never played before?"

He shook his head and reverently loosened the cords at the head of the instrument. I put a hand on his shoulder.

"And imagine I never will again."

"The violin?" I asked. He shook his head before he replied.

"These strings were discovered on the body of Albert Ball. He played, you know. Since then, we've risked much to stow them safely here. They are why you've come. Please, be sure they do not end up in the wrong hands."

I swallowed a nervous lump in my throat.

"I will do my very best."

Chapter 27
Make It Worth It
Marcus

Three lives hath one life—
Iron, honey, gold.
The gold, the honey gone—
Left is the hard and cold.
-Isaac Rosenberg-

"**D**on't forget your arm is injured," Gervaise said.
I winced and played the part of an infected loved one. But it seemed wrong to lie in a monastery.

Orderlies, soldiers, and a smattering of better dressed Belgians circulated in a small waiting area connected to the main wing of an old brick building in central Ghent. It was operated by a fair mix of monks and medical personnel. It was nowhere near as busy as some of the field hospitals I'd had the unfortunate chance of visiting, but even this far from the front, a healthy stir of activity kept people moving.

At first, Rupert, our dubiously motivated German soldier, had insisted he take us to the superior German doctors at the local barracks, a set of repurposed buildings near Ghent University. But

Gervaise was brilliant and bashfully flirted her way into convincing Rupert to bring us to the monastery a stone's throw from the Saint Stefanus Cathedral.

She had insisted that taking me to a German-run hospital, in my feverish state, would send me into confused fits and only aggravate my condition. After some back and forth, including stories of my existing relationship with a doctor who treated patients there, Rupert saw reason in her suggestion.

Of course, I didn't know any doctors, nor did I speak the language those doctors spoke. If Rupert tested her deceit, we'd be in a heap of trouble. And there was another cost of disclosing our alleged history with the doctor there. Rupert managed to wrangle enough courage to ask whether Gervaise and I were married.

I thought there would be protection for her in lying and saying we were. But she did not hesitate for a second before explaining that I was her brother, an answer Rupert liked very much.

From the moment he had approached to ask about our injuries, I recognized the gleam in his eye. I didn't need to speak French or German to understand what he wanted. I'd seen similar looks in the eyes of my own comrades going into town on leave. It was the wild luster of a soldier's lust. It instantly made me afraid for Gervaise in a familial, primitive way. And, if I was honest with myself, it even made me a little jealous. The Belgian spy had an attractive face and a contagious spark of passion in her eyes that lit something in me.

As if I needed more reasons to keep her from harm. Already I'd been tempted to fall in with Jane's line of thinking from the night before. Maybe we could fit her in the Albatross with us. It wouldn't be comfortable, but maybe...

At least imagining the impossible kept my mind off of Jane.

I had little time to wonder where Jane was, what she was doing, or if she was safe. Rupert kept me on my toes with his constant questions about Gervaise's wounded hand. She leveraged his interest to great effect. To him, the fever-inducing wound on my arm was but a second thought. Despite the maddening nibble of jealousy, I had to recognize that she was good at this. A couple of hours in, and she'd had Rupert so wrapped around her finger that I smarted at my own injury being ignored—my false one, that is.

When we had arrived at the hospital, Rupert set himself to the task of ensuring we received prompt medical attention. Thankfully, he wasn't an officer, otherwise he might have succeeded. Instead, the two of us had ample time to scheme some way out of our predicament.

"What do we do?" I asked Gervaise while Rupert all but slapped his military regalia on a receptionist's desk.

"You have to get to the museum. Jane cannot get back home without you."

"You mean we have to get to the museum," I whispered. She avoided my eye contact. "Gervaise? You don't expect me to leave you here with that Hun, do you?"

She swallowed and stared at Rupert. He was now pounding the desk with his fist. She measured her words carefully before speaking. When she did, it was as though she were swallowing a foul medicine.

"For someone like me, developing a close relationship with a German soldier might be productive."

I grimaced. A sickening fear in my gut already knew her plan.

"No, Gervaise. It's a higher risk. He will think he owns you. And he will watch you closely, jealously. Eventually he will notice that you do odd things like watch trains and leave little notes in boxes. He'll find out. It will end badly. That's not even mentioning the general moral wrongness in the idea."

She pulled my head to her shoulder under the pretense of comforting me. She used the proximity to whisper hotly, condescendingly in my ear.

"This is not my first soldier."

I shut my eyes. It was wrong. It was so wrong. Everything I'd ever been taught about virtue reviled against it.

"Judge me all you want, but women are not allowed rifles on the front line. We are not given planes mounted with machine guns or tanks or bombs. We are at war, and if I can provide the intelligence required to destroy regiments in exchange for welcoming a German soldier into the warmth of my affection, then the decision is made. You have done barbarous things as well."

She was wrong. I hadn't. All the terrible deeds she imagined at my hands were a myth I'd chased for years. But she was right, too. She was fighting. When it all ended, if she survived, these nightmares she walked through would be placed in a box of memories, stowed away somewhere, and left well enough alone. If she were anything like me, like anyone I knew, she was not immune to the terror of what she'd seen and experienced.

Still, I didn't want that for her. I didn't want it for Jane. I didn't want the war to ruin another human being. Something must change her mind. She scared me. In her quiet words, a hot, festering anger bubbled and brewed.

"But you would give that part of yourself up?"

She tightened her grip on my arm.

"Look at him, berating that receptionist. I will never say yes to him. I will even tell him no. Every inch, I will tell him no, but he won't listen to me. He will take and take. But I will take, too. From his lips, I will steal the details that will kill him. He will die on the front lines. Then, in hell, he will pay for all he's done to me, and all he's done to Belgium."

I swallowed, surprised to find a lump in my throat. I stammered. My protests coming out pitiful even to my own ears.

"But Gervaise, if he finds out..."

She shushed me gently, her rage dissipating at my concern.

"You and Jane must already be long gone, so that if they

manage to extract any information about your mission, it will be too late."

I shook my head.

"They'll kill you."

She put a hand through my hair. Her grip slackened on the back of my neck.

"They have killed better people than me." Our eyes met, and for a brief moment, she dropped the insurmountable courage she showed. I was overwhelmed by the sea of sadness flowing from within her.

The receptionist left her desk, and Rupert stood tall, straightening his uniform. He turned and waved gallantly at Gervaise. She donned her disguise again, smiled meekly back, then nodded toward the returning receptionist. Apparently, the girl brought bad news, for Rupert burst into another fit, tearing into the poor woman. I swallowed painfully.

"Gervaise, I can't let you,"

"You have no power to stop me, and if you refuse to take advantage, you will waste my sacrifice."

Was she searching for a way to die, or did she believe in right so much that nothing else mattered? I grasped at an explanation for such reckless courage.

I grabbed her hand and kissed it. Once. Twice. Again and again.

"I'm sorry," I said. She lifted my chin up and kissed me tenderly on the forehead.

"Pity him," she said with furious intensity.

Rupert turned now and approached us, closing any time left for conversation. She bent over and kissed my hair again, this time speaking quickly and fervently, the tenderness of understanding gone.

"They will treat us separately. Rupert will come with me.

When the priest arrives, leave immediately, do not wait for the doctor. The Museum of Antiquities, near Kasteel Gravensteen."

I had no time to disagree or ask clarification.

Rupert cleared his throat. "The woman at that desk is a witch, but I am persuasive. You will both be seen now."

Gervaise cast a wide-eyed glance in her direction, feigning that she was impressed.

"You mean before all these people?" she asked.

"I am persuasive," he said again, stepping forward and collecting her hands in his. He kissed her knuckles slowly. I set my jaw and turned away.

"Thank you, Rupert," she said with a grateful smile.

The receptionist crossed and collected us, her face still red and flustered. Just as Gervaise had said, they brought me to my room first, a sparse prayer room with a makeshift table and clean linens. I sat down and rested my head on the wall. The receptionist turned to lead Gervaise from the room.

"I will escort her," Rupert said, leaving little room for argument. Gervaise nodded her head in gratitude and looked back at me.

Make it worth it.

Shamefully, I admit that relief flooded me when the door closed. It came from escaping the claws of an enemy's custody. But it was more than that. Gervaise was too tremendous a person for me. I could not rise to her level of duty, nor could I save her from the terrors of war, and being dragged through the resistance she faced every day exhausted me emotionally and spiritually.

I was not ready to sacrifice everything as she was. I still had non-negotiables.

Jane was one of them.

The door opened again and an elderly priest in a plain robe entered with a small black kit. When he closed the door behind him, I removed the wrappings on my arm.

"Do you speak English?" I asked quietly.

If the priest was surprised by my language and accent, he didn't show it. He nodded.

"I have to get to the Museum of Antiquities," I continued. He set the kit down calmly and crossed to a framed map on the wall. He put one finger on the map. I peered over his shoulder.

"Us?"

He stuck another finger on a different spot on the map, not far from our location.

"The Museum," I confirmed.

He walked back to the bed and started unpacking some basic medical items. A thermometer, some bandages, a stethoscope. Then, he stopped as if having an epiphany.

"I forgot something. I'll be back in a moment." Then, he added in a rasping, tired whisper. "You can see the Kasteel from a few streets over. Leave through the back door. Do not linger in the open."

"Thank you."

"For what?" He left without another word. I didn't waste time. I slid through the door behind him and wound my way opposite the waiting area where we'd come from. The monastery's design was not complicated, and it took no time to find the back door, and spring out into the sunshine, leaving Rupert, Gervaise, and the hospital behind.

But I didn't make it far on the streets before my emotions caught up with me. I tucked into an alleyway and crouched behind a set of crates just before sobs wracked my chest.

I had gone so long without crying. But that moment with Jane in the wood near Callais unstoppered something, and now it was impossible to get the cork back in all the way. For several minutes, I fought to keep myself silent, but my throat ached.

I mourned for Gervaise, for the danger that had nearly claimed me, but it ran deeper.

I wept because my parents had allowed me to cart off to war. I wept because I'd never be a kid happy to work on Ford cars and bicycles again. I wept because so many men I admired so ardently had their bodies ruined, poked holes in, or blown up, and I'd never get to show any of them California.

I had no one. Only Lufbery and Jane.

Jane.

I shook my head, forced myself to stand, gulped in air to regulate what had become so unhinged. She was in the city. She needed me. Gervaise had laid down her sacrifice. It was up to me to make it worth something.

I acclimated to my surroundings as I regained my senses. Kasteel Gravensteen stood high above other buildings, and I scurried along the street. The silent, lonesome walk was more than ample time to turn over every concern I had for Jane. Had she tried to return to Kasteel Blaus Huys. No. She believed too strongly in our mission. She'd have found a way to the museum, assuming she didn't get picked up.

Please, don't let her be captured.

My hopes soured a little more every time I had to duck into an alley to dodge a German motorcar or a pod of soldiers patrolling the streets.

Rupert would not be the only soldier with a thirst for female company, and Jane was not unattractive. But even if soldiers on leave didn't stop her to try their luck, she'd stick out like a sore thumb wandering the streets without a map. And if she were stopped, all she had were false identification papers.

I clutched the marble around my neck.

The sun had passed its zenith, and the shadows ran long across the cobblestone streets, casting strange shadows on the canals that ran through the city. My panic swelled the more I walked. Shouldn't I have been there by now? What if one of the rogue flyers had found her instead?

My stomach turned as I considered one of those flyers might be in the city.

I heard the heavy plodding of military boots around the corner and ducked into an alleyway behind a box empty of all but a few rotting scraps of potatoes. Past the mouth of the alley, a small company of German soldiers marched by, an officer at their head.

I recognized the focus of movement. This was not a typical patrol. This group had somewhere to be and quickly.

I crept up the alley and looked up. Gravensteen was close, and in front of me the company rounded a corner headed just north of its location—exactly the direction I headed in.

Atkins's words floated back to me. We weren't the only ones searching for the devices. And as Gervaise had pointed out, this assignment was outside the usual activity of Ghent's spy network. Had someone talked?

I hastened my step. I could not close the gap between the column of soldiers and myself without raising suspicion, but I could not risk the possibility that this officer and his men chased the very thing I did.

Finally, a large brick building appeared from behind the facades of its neighbors. It's door flat against its own wall.

To my horror, the group of German soldiers approached that door. I stood dumbfounded in the middle of the street. There was no mistaking the building. Even my scant knowledge of the French language was enough to recognize the words above the door. But how could I have come so close only to fail now? And where was Jane?

If only I knew the city better, I might have taken a shortcut. Surely, even now I might find my own separate entrance into the building. And if I could do that, I might also succeed in finding the magic device before the soldiers. I still had Boelcke's goggles hidden beneath my jacket, after all. I slipped them on.

The museum lit up like a weak light bulb. The luminescent

thrum was different than it had been for the Sopwith Camel, less tangible, but it was undeniably shining in a way no other buildings shone.

I didn't know if Jane was inside or not. But something was.

I circled around the building, searching for another door, an accessible window, a vent to the exterior, anything large enough to shimmy through. My heart hammered. Just as I reached the corner of the museum, something caught the corner of my eye. A gentle pulse of blue, separate from the museum, far off, nearly imperceptible.

But before I had a chance to investigate, the sharp shock of a blunt metal tube poked me in the back.

I tried to turn my head to see but the gun dug harder into me, accompanied now by a thick German accent.

"Stay silent, or I will shoot."

My blood slowed in my veins. I clenched my jaw, every muscle in my body rigid and alert. I did not reply. What was there to say? I thought of Gervaise. What would she do? There were papers in my pocket. Don't panic. Continue the ruse.

In my very best French, I stuttered.

"*Les papiers?*"

"Don't bother with your papers. Your French is terrible. Start walking."

The gun directed me as if it were a bridle in my mouth. The German turned me away from the museum and marched me quickly down a street to the north. The man's breath crept across the skin on my neck, hot and suffocating. Could I turn and fight him? I'd have to prevent the gun from discharging if I didn't want any more attention, but from what I could tell, he was alone. How fast would I have to be to spin and grab his hand?

I'd never excelled at hand-to-hand combat, but desperation might bolster my weaknesses. And what other choice did I have? I couldn't wait until he'd marched me back to his unit. One on one were the best odds I could hope for.

"Stop," he said as we reached the middle of a street connected to the museum's plaza. "Turn. In there."

In front of me stood an old cafe. Nothing stirred inside. I assumed that the occupation had driven its owners out of business. Perhaps it was repurposed now as a ring for German intelligence.

In any case, I didn't want to go in.

"Walk inside." The command came again with more menace. I took one step forward, then spun round with a wide sweep of my hand.

I expected my arm to come in contact with his, but he anticipated the movement and had stepped back. My momentum only knocked me off balance. As soon as I recovered, I lunged at the gun. It hung limply by the German's side, the man evidently stunned by my boldness. Still, he pulled it back, and I connected with his midsection. A sharp pain came down on my back, the hilt of the pistol.

"You idiot! You stupid American! Go inside the cafe!" Every curse came with a blow, but I didn't think of the bruises. My legs pushed forward, and we both fell painfully to the ground, elbows and knees knocking against the stone.

The door behind us opened, and the fear of reinforcements pulled my attention.

But there were no German soldiers pouring out of the cafe. There was only a woman, vaguely familiar and extremely disgruntled.

"What are you two doing?" she hissed, looking both ways down the street.

Lina.

My mouth fell open. A vengeful knee closed it, snapping my teeth together hard enough to make me dizzy.

Marcus

"This idiot didn't follow directions," the man said. I finally eyed his face. Earnst.

"Well, come inside and stop drawing attention to yourselves. We'll be lucky not to have a whole Kompanie down on us."

I was too stunned to speak, mind still reeling from the blow, incapable of anything but following directions.

Chapter 28
Trapped
Jane

Since the poets perished
And all they cherished in the way,
Their thoughts unsung, like petal showers
Inflame the hours of blue and grey.
-Francis Ledwidge-

Any other day, I'd not have appreciated the proportion of water in my soup, but today, after all the shock and given how long it had been since I'd eaten anything, the flavor of the circulating juices from carrot, cabbage, and radishes made me close my eyes and hum with satisfaction.

After Thomas had finished his violin performance, he removed the strings and we quickly hid them in the lining of my boots. But before sending me off, he insisted I eat something—and perhaps stay the night. The meal, at least, was an invitation I could not decline.

They offered humble food, but by the reverence with which they ladled me the soup, I intuited that they had nothing greater to offer. If anything, they may have been pained to give me what they did. Their eyes lit up like children when they examined the turnips and radishes I'd brought.

Gratitude sharpened my taste buds and enhanced the placebic nutrition of the watery bowl we all enjoyed.

After some prodding, Marie and Thomas explained to me how the city operated under occupied German rule.

At first, looking at Ghent from an outsider's perspective, one might not have noticed much of a difference. Stores stayed open for business. People walked about freely, harboring bitterness for their captors but mostly unmolested. The border with France was, unsurprisingly, off-limits and subject to close scrutiny and regulation. But with Holland, the neutral neighbor to the north, commerce continued, albeit with modifications. Even Belgium's judicial system was left in place to administer Belgian laws. Such was German High Command's desire for the appearance of a benevolent, temporary occupation.

But it hadn't lasted long. The spirit of the Belgian people turned out to be unconquerable, and soon executions of suspected spies darkened relations. As more and more military-aged men tried to flee to neutral (and apparently spy-infested) Holland, the Germans installed a large electric-wired fence on the border with a current strong enough to cook a human being as throughly as a holiday goose.

Professors at the University of Ghent vanished overnight only to reappear in German labor camps. As Belgian judges had opportunity to adjudicate treason laws in cases of pro-German sympathizers, their jurisdiction came to an abrupt end. The mandatory monetary exchange in favor of German currency impoverished all but the wealthiest citizens. Food became scarce. More and more were deported. The German Secret Police clamped down on its investigations of espionage, shipping many discovered spies to Brussels to be interrogated and thereafter shot.

Trapped

In other words, the Germans realized that Belgium would not simply sit still and be quietly occupied.

Based on the Belgian operatives I'd worked with so far, the sentiment warmed a smile on my face. Thomas, Marie, Gervaise—all proved to be such tremendous individuals, one step ahead, clever, non-violent, but deadly all the same.

But thoughts of Gervaise turned my mind back to Marcus, and my mood dampened.

Was he alive?

"Your thoughts dwell on your mission," Thomas said as he cleared my empty bowl.

"Thomas, let me," Marie said. He waved her off.

"Let you dirty your hands with soup? And what if we have a late visitor?" he asked.

"When is curfew?" I asked.

"Dark," Marie replied. "Our days have been lengthening with spring. And we moved the clocks forward just the other week."

"Still," Thomas said, "if you're planning on leaving, it will be dangerous. Are you sure you won't stay the night? You could leave at first light."

I shook my head. Only one route led through fear, and that was moving forward. I had to continue with the mission. My instincts told me that Marcus would do the same, not even because he believed in the mission so much but because it was our only route back to one another and safety. If he and Gervaise escaped, they would either meet me at Kasteel Blaus Huys or else Marcus would meet me back in France. If it took days, months, even a year, he would find me in France.

And in the case that he—well, I'd accomplish something for both of us.

I swallowed and coerced hope to guide me onward.

I'd arrived here. The next step would be getting back to Blaus

Huys. If they weren't there, I'd leave a message for him in our cipher. But then?

"If my contact is not at our rendezvous, and I'm stranded, may I return here while I change plans?" I asked Thomas.

"Certainly not," Marie replied.

"Yes," said Thomas.

Marie craned her neck violently towards him.

"Don't worry, Marie," he said quietly. "We have enough rooms to hide her. And she can have my soup if it comes to it."

Marie's lips puckered as though remembering the taste of lemon.

"I'm not worried about my soup ration, Thomas."

Our conversation ended with an abrupt banging on the front door. We fell silent. I held my breath.

"Likely just visitors," Thomas whispered, but from the fear in his voice I knew he didn't believe it.

"Yes. At this hour, visitors trying to bang down the door in their enthusiasm for art and history," Marie retorted. "Hide her."

She stood and smoothed her skirts, put her hands on her head, then folded them in front of her stomach. In a moment, she transformed from the agitator and resistant nationalist to the demure and doting docent.

"I'm sorry for this," Thomas said to me. "It will not be comfortable. I hope it will be short-lived."

He led me back to the large storage room and gently pried the back off a crate half my height. A metal clasp and lock dangled on the open exterior. Inside, it was empty.

"Is it better if I run? Out a back exit or something?" I couldn't divulge to him the nature of my reservation, that I feared the magic of the violin strings could not be hidden. If it were one of the rogue pilots, they might have no difficulty sensing the presence of the device even if it were out of view.

"Against the German Secret Police? No. They have eyes all

over the city. If they see you running from here, they will shoot without a question."

"But the magic—"

"Has been hiding here for a long time without problems yet. Get in."

I was tempted to argue, but even if I wanted to explain all about the Boelcke's goggles and my suspicions of arcane traceability, there was simply no time. No time to run. Hardly time to get in a box.

I pulled my knees close to my chest, curled into a ball, and Thomas closed me in the dark. The padlock shut with a click.

"I'm turning you, to hide the stress on the wood," he said before rotating the box on its side. Now, I flopped ninety degrees, my face and knees below me.

Scraping on the floor. The whoosh of a heavy tapestry over me killed the last pinpricks of light, and I was alone. Even my hearing was dampened now.

Raised voices rang from down the hall, guttural German and desperate French, followed by boots clomping through the museum, through the doors, down the hall, stopping, finally, so near that I scarcely dared to breathe.

"*Messieur de Maere.*" The voice was clear, but it filled me with menace. "*Voici.*"

My French was inadequate to understand the conversation in its entirety. Ironically, I understood more of what the Germans said than I did Thomas, what with his smooth and rapid pronunciation.

Thomas said something about being surprised.

"Do not pretend to be dumb," said the German.

Thomas muttered something.

"We know you are hiding it."

"If you lost a piece of art, you should speak with the curator. I was removed."

"You still run this museum."

"I sweep floors. She runs the museum."

My neck cramped uncomfortably as they spoke, and the pressure on my hands and knees was quite painful. But I had no choice but to stay put and stay silent—claustrophobia be damned.

"She doesn't know where the panels are."

Thomas laughed.

"Something funny?"

"The Adoration? Still looking for those?"

"They belong to Germany."

"They were made in Ghent."

"They were purchased by the King of Prussia."

"No need to argue. They're not here."

"You're lying."

"Search if you want. They're not here. Germans have searched for the museum several times. Someone moved them to Great Britain long ago."

The German issued a quick command in his mother tongue, and my heart rate spiked as I listened to several heavy boots come forward. But Thomas did not resist.

"We will question you further. The panels are here. If not, you know where they've gone."

"No need for roughness. Information is old. Germans removed me as curator. Belgians trusted no more."

Footsteps and rustling clothes exited the room, but still I didn't move for fear that a German soldier had been left behind to conduct the search Thomas suggested. I continued my shallow breathing, working my lungs carefully so that they would expand only enough to sustain me, only enough to prevent panic and insanity from being confined in so small a space.

Silence assailed the minutes that passed. Gradually, time stretched like tar, oozing and sticky. Soon the confined space was more than a prison, it was hostile to me, and I marveled at how something as banal as sitting in a small box could untie my reason so quickly.

My wrists throbbed, set at ninety degree angles where my hands splayed out on the interior of the crate. Pain wracked at where my forehead met the wall, and my knees wanted to scream. Beneath it all built the conviction that I might implode, that the box shrank with every passing breath, that the cracks between wooden planks were insufficient to allow me oxygen.

I had no way of getting out on my own. And the Germans had taken Thomas. I fought to conquer the surging panic.

In a plane with Marcus, fighting one of the rogue pilots, I'd come so close to death. But there, its possibility appeared to me as a form of relief, a benevolent, uncontrollable contingency as part of playing the great aerial game. Here, there was nothing vast or open, just a space that would only shrink smaller and smaller until it crushed me into a cube no large than those meant for bouillon.

I clutched at my glass marble, but it could not save me. The marble was never designed to safeguard against insanity.

I began to thrash. Surely the Germans were gone by now, and anything would be better than this.

The rushing sound of fabric above me chased off the panic.

"They are gone," said Marie.

"Here," I croaked back. Pathetic tears wet my cheeks. Relief blossomed even at the hint of my oncoming liberation. "He flipped it on its side. There is a removable panel on the floor below me. It's locked there."

"I don't have the key," Marie said. "And there is no way I will succeed in flipping you again."

"Please, you must do something!" I cried.

I listened to rustling around the room, of the clank of tools while my reason simmered. It took only a moment before the scratching sound of iron disturbed the crate above me.

It took Marie several minutes to successfully pry the top off the crate and only after many jarring and painful blows to the top of the crate. I emerged at last, gulping for air and looking the worse for wear.

"Clean yourself up," Marie said. "You're a mess. You only sat in a box for an hour."

"An hour?" I wiped the tears from my cheeks with my sleeves. My legs ached, but now in Marie's stern presence, embarrassment took first place among my discomforts.

She turned a disdainful shoulder while I composed myself.

"They've taken Thomas," I said.

"Just barely. We spoke at length in the main room," she replied, reluctantly handing me a handkerchief.

"I'm so sorry, Marie."

She shrugged.

"It's not the first time they've questioned him. I expect he will return. He didn't lie when he said he knows nothing about the panels of the Adoration's location."

"The Adoration?" I asked. She glowered at me.

"The Adoration of the Lamb. Ghent's great artistic master-piece. They've been searching for it since the beginning of the war." She furrowed her brow. "I take it, then, that's not why you came."

I shook my head.

"Did Thomas not tell you what he kept in your storage?"

She eyed the various treasures, instruments, and laden crates littered around the closet.

"I make it a point not to ask. An information network does not thrive on needlessly spreading information. The less any of us knows, the better."

She stood stiffly and assessed me, sucking in air as if she had a question, but she didn't ask it.

"You want to know," I surmised.

"What I want is irrelevant," she said bitterly. "But it must be important. We used to do these types of things more, you know. Smuggling people and objects through the lines. It all changed last year. Everything is too high a risk. We watch and report now. That is all. For the network to have agreed to help you... We've put many lives at risk. Just tell me for what purpose? Money?"

I bit my lip. Marie couldn't hide the tremble in her voice or the shaking in her left hand. She was afraid in a way I'd not yet seen from her or Gervaise. Afraid for Thomas, yes, but a deeper fear worked inside. I knew it well. She was afraid that it would all be for naught. That the Allies would fail, and Belgium and Ghent would never return to the life she once knew and loved.

My father's rough and kindly face came to my mind. He always knew how to reach others. When I was little, he tried to teach me the magic of disguised encouragement. Marie would accept no bald reassurance. To acknowledge her fear would be to crystallize it.

"The less you know, the better," I said. Her expression melted into a twisted sense of relief. My answer confirmed that the system still functioned as she'd come to know it. If I had information too valuable to share, it must be too dangerous for the enemy to uncover. There was hope in that.

She squeezed my arm in the most congenial gesture I'd seen from her yet.

"You'll need to hurry to make it out of the city before curfew," she said gently. "I will not forget you, Miss Doe."

I wanted to thank her, squeeze her arm back and smile, but gunshots rang out.

Chapter 29
Wir Sind Stark
Marcus

But Death, who has learned to fly,
Still matchless when his work is to be done,
Met thee between the armies and the sun.
-Duncan Campbell Scott-

"What the hell was that?" I hissed across the room and took cover against a dining cabinet. Earnst flattened himself against the wall beside the front door while Lina ducked behind a counter.

"You're the one wearing the goggles!" Earnst called back.

Boelcke's old flight goggles hung around my neck. I'd used them an hour and a half ago to confirm that there was certainly some type of magic inside the museum. Since then, the three of us puzzled over the purpose of the German unit forcing entry. They might have been the German Secret Police hunting spies, a German patrol intent on requisitioning the building, or a cover for either the Blue Flyer's or Germany's own magic hunting company. By now, I doubted I could rule anything out.

I only prayed that whoever they were, and whatever was in the building, Jane wasn't with them.

The Germans stayed for some time, but finally they emerged with an old, plain-clothed man walking in the middle of their lines. Checking again with the goggles, nothing had changed, and the faint luminous blue around the edges of the building remained.

They had left with a prisoner, but if they'd sought the magic device, they either didn't find it or couldn't move it.

That's when the shooting started.

We had almost made up our minds to brave the streets and approach the museum directly, but the crack of a rifle echoed through the streets of Ghent, scattering the sparse passersby into nearby alleys, houses, cafes, or anything else with a solid door.

"Use the goggles!" Earnst cried.

"I told you what I saw with the goggles!" I called back. "Nothing changed. And you know what, it turns out the goggles don't tell you where random gunfire is coming from."

More shots continued, the sound ricocheting from different points of origin. But none zipped through the front window of our cafe, nor passed nearby outside from what I could tell.

"Earnst, poke your head out and see what's going on," I said, pushing myself out of my hiding place.

"After you," he replied.

"You have to be kidding me," I muttered, cursing my own cowardice at asking him to do what neither of us wanted to. I crossed the room and cracked the front door. On the front line, only dead men poked their head above the trench. But a battle in a city with a thousand doorways and a thousand windows was not like trench warfare. No one could watch everything all the time. So, slowly, I opened the door, hoping that the gradual movement attracted no attention.

I poked my head out and heard the cacophony of gunfire with

fresh ears. Somehow, the streets made them louder, each explosion ricocheting off the narrow avenues and echoing around corners. The shots seemed to come from somewhere beyond the museum, but the more I listened, the more I was convinced they sounded from every direction, as if this were a planned ambush.

Suddenly, a concentrated volley of gunfire shot off, disciplined and orderly. That would be the Germans, maybe from the small squad of soldiers marching away from the museum.

I reentered the cafe.

"I think we're all right. Looks like the Ghent resistance set up some kind of ambush. Rifle fire coming from all over the place. Not shooting at us, though. In fact, it could provide great cover."

Earnst and Lina exchanged nervous glances.

"What?" I asked. "Now you're upset that they're not shooting at us?"

"Belgians don't shoot back," said Lina. I scoffed.

"What are you talking about? Belgians aren't pacifists. There are entire divisions of Belgian infantry."

"She means," Earnst cut in, "that occupied civilians in Belgium don't do this. They take obnoxious pride in the fact that they don't put up armed resistance. But it is wise. Violent resistance leads to violent reprisals. Instead, they put their efforts into their information networks."

I bit my lip.

"Then what?" I asked. "You think these are our boys?"

Earnst shook his head.

"I didn't say that, but we aren't the only ones after the device."

I let out a strangled groan.

"We don't have time to decide who is shooting at the Germans. We just need to be grateful they're distracted. With this racket, the entire barracks will be on the streets in half an hour. This is our only chance to find Jane."

Earnst and Lina stared at me. Lina inclined her head know-ingly, almost embarrassed on my behalf.

"You mean to retrieve the device," Earnst said.

"It's the same thing." I turned to cover the red creeping into my cheeks. "I'm willing to bet anything she's already in there."

"Then by all means," Earnst said.

"You two can't be running around on errands," Lina said. "If the military sees two men out of uniform at a time like this, they'll shoot without question. A woman however..."

Earnst started forward.

"Lina, no! They will shoot you as well."

She shook her head.

"It is less likely," she insisted. "Sergeant, give me the goggles. I will find the device and return."

"I can't allow it," Earnst replied.

I didn't want Lina to go either, but for reasons decidedly different than Earnst. If Lina went alone to the museum and retrieved the device, I had no assurance that she would come back. I didn't doubt her competency; I doubted her loyalty. I'd met her only once before, beside Mustermann back at the farmhouse southeast of Nancy. She'd hardly said two words out loud, and those were not words pledging her allegiance to Mustermann's idea of joining forces to stop the rogue flyers.

She held her hand out to me, ignoring the protests of her husband.

"Boelcke's goggles," she said. "I found them first. You can trust them with me."

"I think Earnst is right," I hedged. "Sending you alone is dangerous, with the goggles more so. If you do get shot, heaven forbid, they'd be sitting in the open for anyone to take."

"A group of two or three is more conspicuous than one woman running for cover. If I go, and the Germans suspect me, I can explain that I was separated from my cook unit."

I bit my lip and tried to think up more excuses. The argument chewed up valuable time.

The rifle fire outside amplified, both from sporadic single shots and the return volleys. With all of the troops parading around the city, reinforcements didn't take long.

"You need to trust me," Lina said softly. "If Jane is there, I will bring her back. I promise."

I turned toward the window. Even if Jane weren't in the museum, with this activity going on, she was in danger. But it all fit too perfectly. Earnst and Lina were the ones who sent a message to Atkins about the location of this new device in the first place. Of course, they would have never found opportunity to retrieve it themselves. It was under the custody of resentful Belgian resistance. Under no circumstances would a Belgian intelligence operative deliver up anything of strategic importance to Germans operatives.

I was so close. It was a very brief walk to the museum. But the gunfire was loudest in that direction and increasing all the time. If there were troops within sight, and they saw me enter the museum —Lina was right.

But wasn't it too coincidental? I had arrived at the museum myself only to have Earnst put a gun in my back and pulled me out of harm's way into a cafe. And now, Lina demanded to retrieve the device herself.

Her eyes bored into the back of my head, as if she had her own gun pressed there.

I'd spent two years learning to hate these people, never to trust them, how to evade their bloodlust. I'd trusted a German once, a defenseless, harmless kid. I'd been paying it for since.

What would Jane do? I closed my eyes and imagined her face, felt the glass marble around my neck. I remembered how even at my most pathetic, she had cradled me and believed in me. She would have trusted them. Maybe it was time to try her way of things.

"All right," I said. "You go."

"She won't!" Earnst turned his pistol on me again, but I swung around and dropped Boelcke's goggles into her hands.

"Be quick. It's only getting worse out there. If you find Jane—"
Lina closed her other hand around mine.

"I'll bring her home." She faced her husband and growled. "Put the gun down, Earnst. What is the matter with you? This is a war. Men die every day. Do you think women will stop fighting? I'll be back in five minutes. You get the escape ready. Be careful."

"Lina," Earnst said shakily. He had always been hard, at least how I'd seen him. But now, he was a puppy.

"I'll be back, my love." She kissed him gently. "*Wir sind stark.*"

In a flash, Lina slipped out the door into the sound of gunfire. We absorbed the quiet for a long moment, letting the small ricochets and combustions from down the streets sink in, each saying a silent prayer for his wife.

"I'm sorry," I started. "I know it was dangerous but—"

"Do not talk." Earnst shook his head. "Come. We must move quickly."

I balked.

"Move? What are you talking about? Lina just went in there. There's a skirmish two streets away. We need to bunker down and wait for our women to get back."

Earnst disappeared behind the counter and produced a German Luger pistol. He placed it on the counter beside a handful of rounds and busied himself loading it.

"Your plane was found," he said. "Some hungry Belgian farmer exchanged the information for three sacks of potatoes."

My heart dropped. I'd been worried about how well we'd hid the plane, but it still anchored my hope of escape. Without a German two seater, how could we hope to get back to France?

"Is it still operable?" I asked. My mind already raced to put together desperate schemes to get back in the cockpit.

"It would be suicide to find out. The Geheime Feldpolizei will have it surrounded and watched. You won't get within two kilometers before they see you. You must now take a different route."

My limbs hung weakly at my sides. First, the Blue Flyer had revealed my most shameful secret to Jane. Now, Ghent stripped me of everything that made me strong. My plane, my friend, even the goggles. I was an unarmed American spy in occupied Belgium putting my trust in two Germans. This was not what I left my parents for. I would die without notice. My mother wouldn't even receive the satisfaction of knowing I was killed in action. I'd be one of the missing.

"Focus, Sergeant." The strange pronunciation of my rank pulled me from panic. He handed me the Luger, now loaded. "There is another plane. It's been sitting in a hangar at an airfield south of here, waiting for repairs."

I gripped the gun, a thin-barreled thing, and my thoughts raced back to our sortie near Clairmarais, then further back to the night I'd let that German go. What good did this pistol do me? I wouldn't shoot it, not when it mattered. But the plane, even the mention of another option brought me cautious comfort.

"What good does a broken airplane do us?" I asked.

"It is operable," Earnst replied. "It's just old. Many pilots would consider the model obsolete. That's why it sits unattended. The motor is tricky, and there are some unpatched bullet holes in the fuselage, but it will fly."

"What model?"

"I didn't look closely."

"Shut up, Earnst. We're both pilots. You know the model at three hundred yards. What is it?"

He paused, mouth turning down with consternation.

"It's a Rumpler. A.CI."

I buried my face in my unoccupied hand.

"This day can't get worse."

"It's not a bad plane," he insisted.

"It's slow. We won't be able to outrun anything. We'll either get spotted on this side of the line by some pilots wondering what an old Rumpler is doing in the air, or our new planes in France will blow us to bits before we can set her down safely."

"Maybe you should be showing some gratitude that my wife and I have risked so much to make up for your decisions about where to land the Albatross!"

"What decision? Atkins drove us to a barn, threw us into the plane, gave us a map, and wished us luck. There was no plan. We haven't had the luxury of planning. Your urgent communications about a magic device in Ghent in urgent need of recovery meant an urgent Command sent us out in a hurry, without proper briefing."

Earnst crossed the room to me in such a fury that I instinctively pulled the gun hip-side and backed against the wall.

"We are wasting time," he spat. "Soon the Feldpolizei and the infantry will be all over this part of Ghent. We are all suffering for this. The difference is that you and your companion have somewhere safe to return. We face the axe of German High Command every day. Do you know what they would do to us if they discovered our mission?"

I bit my lip, anger softening.

"Yes," he went on. "Now you begin to understand. But perhaps we could flee. Do you think we could find welcome arms on your side of the line? No? I didn't think so."

He turned and head toward the front door to glanced out of the window.

"Lina will expect us at the next location. We must beat her there to avoid her implementing another contingency of our plan."

"And what about two men our age running around together carrying pistols? Didn't Lina just say that we'd be shot on sight?"

"Yes, but we're not going toward the fighting. We're headed in the opposite direction. Come on."

He didn't wait for me to argue any further, and to avoid ending up alone in that cafe, I followed him into the street. We turned eastward, hugging the walls of the building beside us, abandoning any casual air of nonchalance in exchange for speed. Earnst walked forward boldly. I followed with head tucked down toward the ground.

If anyone saw us, I hoped they'd notice Earnst's German features first and pay us no mind. The shooting continued sporadically behind us. After a few blocks, we paused to catch our breath and assess our location.

"Have we been seen?" Earnst asked.

"I don't think so. If we have, no one's cared. That's something."

Around the corner, I could see Kasteel Gravensteen behind, tall and watching, but made smaller by the distance we'd achieved.

"What's the plan for getting to that airfield?" I asked, when we started moving again.

"It depends," Earnst replied.

"On?"

"If we can make it out of the city before curfew."

I nearly laughed.

"I think the whole concept of curfew just got shot up. You think they'll let people out of the city now?"

Earnst didn't bother turning around.

"They have no choice. The German army runs low on supplies and provisions. In the north, the British hope to block the mouth of the canal to Bruges. High Command must keep commerce running as smoothly as possible."

"Yeah, but what good does that do us? We don't exactly have a truck full of steel or rubber we're driving out of the city."

"We have something more valuable than that," Earnst replied grimly.

A chill ran through my blood before I even asked.

"What's that?"

"We have a truck full of Belgians being deported for labor."

Chapter 30
Shards
Jane

And the giant with his club,
And the dwarf with rage in his breath,
And the elder giants from far,
They are all the children of Death.
-Lord Dunsany Edward Plunkett-

A rifle shot rang out from a third story window above my head.

"Quickly, Jane." Lina had one arm around my shoulders and hurried me through the streets.

After the shots rang out, Marie had locked down the museum, sliding in place heavy metal bolts over the door. We waited inside, and I tried not to think about Thomas or Marcus.

Soon there was a frantic banging from outside. I looked to Marie, but she just shook her head.

But when a German's voice shouted my name, I stood and loosed the bolts myself, despite Marie's protests.

Lina.

Atkins must have sent word. I don't know why I hadn't considered it before. Earnst and Lina had notified us first about the device's location. Of course, they'd be around to see the mission through.

I flung the door open. When I saw Lina standing in the doorway wearing Boelcke's flight goggles, my heart soared anew. A gasp caught in my throat.

"The goggles? Does that mean? Marcus?"

"Yes. No time to explain. Do you have the device?" Shots rang out in the distance.

I extended a boot, where we'd hidden the violin strings inside. She glanced down at it through the goggles before pulling them down around her neck. "Come."

I took her hand, and we hurried off down the street.

It was nearly impossible to tell where the shots came from, but Lina didn't seem to care. She pushed forward like a tank.

"Quickly. Earnst and Marcus will be waiting for us at a small truck depot near the eastern edge of the city. There is transport there."

I fought back tears of gratitude. Marcus. He was alive. We might both still make it home.

"Lina, you've saved me. I was so distraught. I thought I was all alone."

"We are not safe yet."

Another shot fired from a window across the street. Instinctually, I glanced toward the source of the sound. I saw another muzzle smoking through the window. But something more peculiar gave me pause. The sun had already started its descent, and perhaps the long shadows played tricks on the eyes, but it almost appeared as though the rifle had no shooter. As if it were propped up on a stand and fired of its own accord.

"Jane!"

Lina tugged my shoulders down and forward. We scurried away from the fighting and swept around a corner.

"We didn't plan for shooting," Lina muttered to herself. "I hope it doesn't ruin us."

"We can overcome it. We've overcome everything thus far."

"This way." Lina nodded to another street, lined with old stone facades and large windows. All of Ghent's buildings blurred together. It wound in complex patterns, a never-ending labyrinth of mazes crisscrossed by alleyways and canals, topped over the horizon with the silhouettes of its magnificent churches.

At the end of the street in front of us lay an intersection with two options: right and left. We pushed forward.

"A right at the end of the street," Lina whispered. "Then we can move more slowly."

I patted her hand gratefully. Already, the exertion of our frantic escape from the museum had my breath racing, and as the shots became less frequent, my adrenaline wore off.

But after twenty paces toward the intersection, something stopped us cold.

Ahead, a lone man clad in a soldier's long coat and rifle appeared from around the corner. He was very far off, but he stood still and stared in our direction. Even at this distance, he had an odd demeanor, not tired or disciplined—almost amused. His head tilted slightly to one side, observing us like curiosities.

We froze.

"What do we do?" I asked Lina. She responded by turning us around and heading back the way we came.

"Another route," Lina mumbled through ragged breath. Already, our frantic escape started to wear on her, and the steady physical resolve she'd shown at the museum lagged. We walked with purpose back toward the shooting, and after a few moments, I glanced behind us. The man followed.

"Lina, he's coming."

She took an alley down a small opening between two stone buildings, and we nearly broke into a run. We were both winded already, and I didn't consider myself in excellent form, but the panic willed our legs forward. If Marcus was alive, I needed to find him, to show him the device, complete our mission, and go home.

How had he escaped? Did it require bloodshed? Between panicked steps, I thought of him, fragile and precious in the wood. He gave his vulnerability to me. If I died, it would wither.

No. No soldier would prevent me from fulfilling the promise I'd made to Lufbery. There were two things I had to do in this war. Protect magic and protect Marcus.

We came out the other end of the block and crossed a plaza. Its planter beds were vacant. Its fountain was dry. I glanced back again. We'd not lost the soldier yet. If anything, he was closing the gap between us.

"Lina..."

"I don't know where to go," Lina confessed, her voice trembling between lagging breaths.

"How far is the rendezvous?"

She shook her head.

"We can't arrive at the rendezvous with someone chasing us. We were to drive a truck east of the city. You and Marcus were meant to slip into the back of the truck among those being deported. But if a soldier is right behind us he will halt the truck. We will go nowhere."

We were to slip in amongst those being removed from their homes. A bitter swill rose at the back of my throat. I had yet to meet a Belgian coward. Of course, I knew that they weren't all war heroes, but to be deported from their home to work for the German war effort... No one deserved that. And to think we were to sit among them before walking free—my heart shrank at the thought.

And yet, we could not stop the deportations. All we could do was labor ourselves to hasten the end of the war. And that meant getting to him with Albert Ball's violin strings.

"So we lose our tail," I said. "Perhaps we can enter a building. A shop? A house? Anything to break line of sight and give us a chance to slip away."

"Who will admit us with the guns firing as they are?" Lina asked. "Not to mention my German features."

"Oh, your face doesn't look that different than the Belgians. Come now."

We crossed a bridge across a canal and resumed our hurried pace. I scanned the buildings around us feverishly. Every door was a possibility and a liability. We could not waste time trying to gain admittance somewhere that would not accept us. It would give the soldier opportunity to catch up. But then, we needed to hide somehow or at least take a shortcut.

My eyes caught a reflection on a cobbler's shop door. Framed in the wood lay a glass window. If it was locked, we could likely break the glass with a sharp kick and open it from the inside. Even if it were only temporary, a hiding place would give us at least a moment to catch our breath.

"Here," I said, now pulling Lina along behind me. We arrived at the cobbler's, and I rattled the doorknob. It didn't budge. "Stand back."

I withdrew, held Lina's shoulder for balance, and delivered the best chest-height kick I could to the window in the door. A sharp pain shot through the ball of my foot and up my shin.

"What are you doing?" Lina gasped.

"I thought I could break the glass." I limped to the door again and inspected the pane. It hadn't even cracked a little.

"You could have broken your foot!" Lina scolded.

"I think I broke my self-esteem. Come on!"

Our break had cost precious time, and when I glanced back again, the man was close enough that I could easily distinguish his features. Sharp eyes. An aquiline nose. A pointed chin and—

My knees grew weak. I nearly stopped running.

Shards

My memories rushed backward, into the air, into the storm. I fought for breath. The world turned around me. It couldn't be.

I'd seen his face before, though partly covered, under similarly strenuous circumstances.

It was the Blue Flyer who had stolen the Baron's scarf.

"Faster, Lina," I croaked.

"I'm trying. What's wrong?"

"Blue Flyer," I managed to say. Her eyes shot open, blood draining from her face.

"Run," she urged.

I didn't wait to be told twice. Lina bolted ahead, a new wind of energy powering her strides. I sprinted forward, ignoring the pain in my foot, to search wildly for some type of salvation. Endless stone and brick avenues. Endless locked doors.

As we reached the end of the city block and turned down another street, Lina slowed.

"I can't keep this up for long," she gasped.

But ahead of us, I found refuge. A literal refuge. A cathedral loomed, and I ran straight for it, persuaded easily by the echoes from childhood storybooks shouting sanctuary.

We pushed through the doors and burst into the chapel. Rows of pews stretched out before us, and a small handful of elderly worshippers turned to assess the commotion before returning their devotions to the candles and saints in front of them. I hoped one disgruntled worshipper could spare room in their prayers for Lina and me.

We didn't wait in the chapel, though, instead pushing through a door quietly set in the wall beside one of the altars. It opened into a stone hallway, tall thin windows in the walls beyond.

I closed the door behind us, and we paused to catch our breath. This would not do as a long-term hiding place. The flyer had likely seen exactly where we'd run. I shoved a small credenza from within the hallway in front of the door.

"We can lose him now," I said. "Just breathe and take a minute."

Lina shook her head.

"We can't." She fought to get the words between gasps for breath. "They know somehow. They can track the magic."

I stared down at my boot. It was a reminder more than a revelation. Hadn't I suspected the same?

"How?" The fear in Lina's eyes upon learning the soldier's identity spoke to her greater understanding of the situation. She knew more about the magic than she shared.

"I don't know." She spoke haltingly between recovery breaths. "But at the start, they came for Boelcke's goggles as well. They must have another device—something that lets them find the others."

I nodded. The goggles on her neck and the strings in my boot damned us, then. Yet, I couldn't abandon them, which meant we needed to incapacitate the Flyer or else stay far ahead of him.

"What happens if we don't arrive at the truck depot in time?"

"It will leave without us."

"Did you have another plan, in case things went wrong?"

She nodded.

"There's an abandoned bakery beside a park not far from the depot. We were to meet there."

I grabbed her wrist and led her down the hallway and up a flight of stairs.

"So we need to shift our plans. If we lead this man on a goose chase long enough, it will give Marcus and Earnst time to arrive at the bakery. Then, when we get there, the four of us can scare off the Flyer together."

I closed my eyes, convincing myself my idea would work.

"What you need is a rest," I went on. "And so we need is a building we can roam around well enough to get him all mixed up, and by the look of things, we've got it."

"Of course. We must not lose hope," Lina said. She squeezed my hand fervently. "Thank you, Jane. When I came to the museum, I felt so brave. Now look at me. I can hardly breathe for all the effort of our running."

"Nonsense, Lina. Don't get down on yourself. I've observed that the perseverance of courage has, at times, much more to do with how full one's stomach is and much less to do with some magical spark inside the soul."

The staircase was tall and winding, and it did little to help Lina catch her breath. I continually glanced behind us and strained an ear in attempts to identify our pursuer. But I heard nothing.

Eventually, we opened a door that led out onto a choral balcony, granting a sweeping view over the cathedral's interior. The scene took my breath away. The ceilings towered high above us in domed crisscrossing supports. Contrasting black and white marble designs varied the floor, and picture-perfect renaissance era statues stood as features in alcoves or tucked away in corners.

It was the most beautiful building I had ever seen.

And there, near the front of the room, the Blue Flyer waited patiently. I peered over the railing, and he gazed up at me with a sick smile.

A chill ran up my neck. If he wanted to catch us, why didn't he run? Why not sprint quickly and overcome us when he had the chance?

We sat on the balcony for a few minutes. Lina struggled to maintain her composure. The Flyer didn't move. He seemed perfectly content to wait until we left to resume his pursuit.

Either that or he wasn't alone. I knit my brows as paranoia smothered me, casting every shadow in sinister black. If he had companions, they could be surrounding every entrance to the church. Every window that might make for an escape.

But we had few options. We had to wait until our men

reached the rendezvous. At least in this building we had the benefit of hiding places. A small baker's shop would do little to conceal us.

"When does the truck leave?" I asked, trying to take my mind off the panic of hostile possibilities.

"About an hour before the sun sets," she replied. I peered out the stained glass.

"That's not far off," I said. She shook her head, and I noticed she'd set herself busy to praying. I softened my tone and continued. "Listen, in a little while, we will find a back door and pray we escape the Flyer's notice long enough to at least get a head start. Then we hurry to the baker's shop. You know how to get there from here?"

Lina nodded.

"That time of evening, we will need to be careful," she said. "The attack will make German soldiers strict."

"Then we'd best not stop to say hello to any," I replied as cheerily as I could. I didn't know why I now felt such a sisterly protection toward Lina. She was likely older than I was.

"It was very brave of you and Earnst to help us," I said. She opened her eyes, and a slight smile graced her lips.

"Earnst is brave. I'm very fortunate to have him. I—" She cut herself short. Her face was bright red and pale all at once.

"Go on," I urged, peeking back over the railing. The Flyer had taken a seat on one of the pews near the back of the chapel.

"In some ways, I'm happier that we're working for Mustermann now. The work is more dangerous, and we've been set against our own military. But at least I'm involved. There are so many widows. We weren't married long when war started. I didn't want to mourn someone I didn't know well."

I nodded, appreciating the fear of being left behind. I had no husband, but there was more to mourn than a loved one. The war had taken so much, had changed everything. And if it ended tomorrow, what could those who did not participate say to those who returned?

"Do you have parents waiting for you in Germany?"

She shook her head.

"My father died in service. They say an artillery shell landed on his platoon, and the crater spread fifteen meters in all directions. My mother never recovered."

I rubbed my temples, and my eyes lost focus as memories of my own family rose before me.

"My father wanted to serve," I replied. "He had no military experience when the war broke out. And he was older than the initial recruiting age. But that window has since expanded. My mother made him promise he would not volunteer."

"What does your father do for work?" she asked.

"He makes fish and chips." I smiled. The smell of his food almost tangible in my nostrils from how much I missed him. The recollection warmed me through. I could all but see the seats of his restaurant, mother chatting with guests, father laughing with his staff. "I think," I went on with unchecked emotion catching my voice, "he was concerned I would think he was a coward. When I volunteered, it was as if I'd slapped him across the face, as if I'd said, 'If you won't serve, then I will.'"

Lina put a hand on mine.

"One day, you will return and tell him the truth."

I wiped my eyes with my sleeve and cleared my throat quietly.

"Right. And you and Earnst will help bring a new age of peace to your country."

"Perhaps," replied Lina. The sadness in her voice struck me, and a great swelling of pity pulled at my heart. Lina still gasped for breath. "It's my lungs. I'm sorry."

I nodded and turned my head back to the Flyer. He tipped his head in challenge.

"Lina, give me the goggles."

"Why?" She asked, handing them over.

"I'm going to keep him busy. You stay here, catch your breath, and if he goes after me, meet me at the front door in thirty minutes."

"No, Jane. What if you're captured?"

The Flyer smiled and inclined his head again.

"I won't be. And you'll need your strength for our run to the bakery. This way, you'll be able to take the stairs calmly. Trust me, Lina. I think I can lure him from the entrance."

Lina screwed her face into a concerned grimace.

"Don't take any risks," she said. I gave her hand a squeeze, stood, and walked back to the door, glancing back just long enough to see that the Flyer stood as well.

I slipped through the door and worked my way down the stairs. From the outside, a tall tower had spiked into the air high above the rest of the city. But I knew the higher I climbed, the further I would need to come back down to get back to the entrance. Besides, there was less room toward the top of the tower, and I needed options.

So down I went. Mechanically, my legs took me through doors, down hallways, past the occasional priest who regarded me curiously or suggested I might not be allowed in a certain area. None of them chased after me, though. None of them seemed to have the energy.

Doors closed in the hallways behind me, and the paranoia that the Flyer came closer nibbled at my mind. But I embraced the dark, vast cathedral and made a knot of my path. In one door, down one hallway. Across the chapel, up a stairwell, down over a railing.

It went on like this for fifteen minutes or so until I recognized I'd run out of rope.

After following a stairwell down a couple of flights, I stumbled into a dark room, lit only by candles. Stone columns arched like trees to support the low ceilings, and dark recesses branched off from the main chamber. I realized with a chill that I'd found tombs. And seeing that there was no way out, perhaps my tomb.

Unhurried boots clacked on the stone up and behind me. I put on the goggles and glanced at the stairwell. A faint blue shone from the hallway. My breath caught. I closed my eyes and counted my options before hiding within the furthest alcove from the entrance.

I wished I had a weapon. A gun. A knife. Anything. Instead, I clutched my marble, back against the cold, deathly stone and prayed.

The boots scraped at the foot of the stairs and stopped.

Did he know I was there?

"Why did you leave your friend?"

The voice whispered its way into the space between my veins. The Flyer had a strange, soft accent, but the English was not labored. I wrestled with the decision to respond. He knew I was there, clearly, yet he did not come forward.

"I wanted to protect her," I called back. If there were no way out, perhaps my only strategy back to Marcus would be to talk my way through.

"So you left her all alone, winded, and wheezing?"

I strained my ears, waiting for the sound of boots coming forward. Still nothing.

"She doesn't have what you're looking for, does she?" I asked.

A step.

"No. She does not. Still, what if I had companions waiting to swoop in and snatch her?"

My heart pounded.

"I didn't think of that."

"You did." His voice was maddeningly calm. He might as well have been discussing the weather. "But you didn't care, did you?

Admit it. The notion of our meeting excited you. You wanted something almost as much as I did."

I scoffed. I wanted to get back to Marcus.

"And what might that be?"

A step.

"Answers."

My neck burned. I gulped silent, steadying breaths, but my heart only beat faster.

"Answers don't do much for the dead," I replied.

"Have you ever asked the dead that? You picked up the shards, knowing I'd be drawn to their magic, and managed to pin yourself in the catacombs below St. Bavo's. I don't care to presume, but it seems like something inside of you was dying to have this conversation. Didn't you see me nod?"

I clamped my teeth and shut my eyes.

A step.

"Go on," he continued. "What do you have? Something of Albert Ball's?"

I searched my wits. There had to be something I could do or say that would lead to my escape.

"Why do you want it?" I asked.

"Because I know what it is, though I must admit, when compared to its sisters, the relic Ball left behind has little use to me. Are you interested in its abilities? Or are you going around risking your life to collect things you don't understand?"

"I know about the magic," I said. "I know how powerful it can be."

A pause.

"I find that hard to believe," he replied flatly. "Tell me. What do you plan to do with the devices you hope to collect? Hand them over to your superiors? What will they do with them? Fight? Kill more people?"

"Oh, it's the devil you know, I suppose," I replied flippantly, buying time.

"And you think I'm the devil you don't? The devil you don't know know lives inside of you, young miss."

I snorted.

"What are you talking about?"

"Don't say you haven't felt it. I can almost smell it on you. There is a darkness there."

Unbidden, my mind raced back to those first flights with Marcus when I'd seen a German plane, the hunger to chase after it. Then again, when despite my best judgment, I'd emptied the the ammo drums of my Lewis Guns.

"I'm against the war. I want it to be over."

"I never suggested otherwise. You're the one who brought up devils, I'm just notifying you that a killer hides behind those eyes."

He was trying to get beneath my skin. I started rocking back and forth, clutching my marble in my hand. The goggles hung heavily around my neck, the strings pressed painfully against my foot in my boot.

"I don't know who you are. Are you British? Dutch? German?"

"No."

"Then why are you and your friends shooting down planes?"

Another step.

"That's simple. We're trying to collect the shards, before they fall into the wrong hands."

The shards? I almost laughed.

"That's all anyone wants, isn't it? Keep the magic from falling into the wrong hands. Whose hands are the right hands?"

"Exactly. I'm glad we've finally seen eye to eye. Now, let's talk about you. There aren't many options left, I'm afraid, and you have something I want."

I quietly bumped the back of my head against the wall several times, trying to dislodge some kind of genius.

"I can't give it to you."

"You're going to give it to me in one of two ways. The first way, you live. The second way, regrettably, you don't. But I do not enjoy taking the lives of human women, so please, let's not make this difficult."

"I'm on a mission to bring it back," I stammered. Tears were pooling in the corners of my eyes now. I didn't know if I could trust him to keep his word, but suddenly the bargain of seeing Marcus, and perhaps even my family again, in exchange for a simple set of violin strings was overwhelming.

"You can tell your superiors I overpowered you. That's not even lying. I'm being polite in offering you the option."

He was right. I stood little chance, and with the latter, at least I might live to fight again. We could regroup. Take what I knew about him back to Atkins.

"How about a bargain?" I tried. "I hand over Ball's violin strings in exchange for a few answers to my questions."

There was a pause. He may have been considering my proposal.

"Ah, well. Ball's relic would certainly be nice. But there's something I'm much more interested in at present."

I knit my eyebrows.

"Namely?"

"Must you ask? Weren't you taunting me when last we met?"

I looked down at the marble in my fist. That afternoon in the storm. He had pulled in right behind us, lined up a certain shot, but didn't fire. I'd held up the marble.

"Where did you come across that necklace?" he asked.

Suddenly, something woke up inside me—a deeper fear, a more animalistic desire to survive. If this man had followed me all over Ghent to get my marble, the one Aunt Luella had made to protect Marcus, then I was in even less control than I'd imagined. An instinct grew in my brain that I must not allow him to have it.

"It's just that it sings differently than the others. It sings differently than any shard I've found so far, in fact. It's a song I haven't heard in a long, long time. And it may just be the one I need. If I could take it without violence, that would be preferable. But if—"

Something snapped inside me. I twirled around the corner and ran. He stumbled, surprised at my choice, but recovered quickly and cut off my escape path. I stopped and put one of the stone pillars between us in the tomb between us. Awkwardly we danced right and left, each predicting the other's next move.

Finally he lunged, but instead of running away, I met him forward. The clash of bodies startled him, and I used the surprise to pull him by the wrist, turning his own momentum against him. His body fell forward, falling on me and then directly into the stone column. His face collided with the rock, and he slumped to the floor. I didn't wait to see if he would recover.

I bolted up the steps, closing the door at the top behind me and pushing a set of wooden shelves to block it. Then I sprinted across the chapel and found Lina by the front entrance.

Chapter 31
Motorrader
Marcus

The sun turns north, the days grow long,
Later the evening star grows bright—
How can the daylight linger on
For men to fight,
Still fight?
-Sara Teasdale-

W e watched a group of trucks pull out of the depot and sputter down the road east towards Germany. The back of each truck was crowded with Belgian deportees. An escort of motorcars flanked them.

"Frankly, Earnst, I'm actually relieved that your first plan didn't pan out," I said from our hiding spot across the street.

"It would have worked well. No one would have stopped us as we left."

"You know, leaving isn't what had me most concerned. When did you expect us to get off?"

"There was a plan."

"I understand that. I'm just asking to hear it."

"There's no time to explain. The sun will be down soon, and curfew will be in effect. Then there will be real problems."

I scratched my head with one hand, the other rested inside my coat on the handle of the Luger.

"Well, the gunfire in city central stopped. That's good, right?"

Earnst shrugged.

"Now our army will hunt who was behind the attack. It's been obsessed with rogue shooters since the beginning of Belgian occupation. They will take any excuse to search houses for insurrection. We hoped we would have the opportunity to hide for another day if necessary, but I don't think that will be possible."

"So we leave tonight? How?"

"Follow me."

He buried his gun in his coat, and we slid down the alley to a connecting boulevard. I followed him at a jog as we ducked around corners and cut across avenues. The city made me dizzy. I could hardly tell two streets apart. But soon we arrived at a wide stretch of canal. Across it lay a large, open park.

I stared. Years ago, before leaving home, I'd have killed to see a place like this. Ghent was beautiful even in wartime. The setting sun in the west silhouetted the distant steeples of countless churches and cast long, bright reflections on the water. Spring was right in the middle of summoning forth green patches in the trees vibrant enough to inspire artists.

I wished my mother could see it. The desire surprised me. I usually kept her locked safely away in my memory.

"Get over here," Earnst hissed behind me. I turned and followed him into a shop with a large boarded front window. He closed the door behind me quickly and settled into the dark. From the fading shafts of light coming through the planks of wood, I made out shapes. A store counter. A back room equipped with ovens. It smelled of dust and neglect. In a cleared space at the front, two large lumpy shapes rested under large canvas blankets.

"From one shop to another," I muttered as I felt around for a chair. "And Lina knows to come here?"

"It was our contingency if the trucks didn't work," he replied. "Now we just wait for her to come."

"Then what?" I asked. "I thought you said you wanted to leave tonight."

"I do."

"So, what? The four of us swim the canal?"

"I considered it."

"Of course you did," I replied brusquely. I wasn't happy to have handed over my only tool to Lina. I was terrified and all but certain I'd come so close to finding Jane. Instead, I sat waiting in a bakery, and our fates were out of my hands. Being personable was the last thing on my mind.

"We have another plan, but it's noisy. I want Lina's opinion first."

"And Jane's," I added.

"Yes. Everyone must be aware of the risk. The east border of Ghent is less patrolled than the west. There aren't canals to prevent land travel, either."

I found a chair and settled into it, hoping it would alleviate my nerves. Instead, my leg bounced incessantly.

"So what? We take these two Luger pistols and shoot up a checkpoint on our way toward Germany?"

"How are you so insufferable?" Earnst turned on me in such a fury that it stopped my leg from moving. "What do you want from me?"

I didn't have an answer, and getting called out for my insolence for the second time in as many hours only made me blush. But in that moment, I saw the real Earnst—not the German radical, not even the pilot. He was a man trying his best.

"Look, I'm sorry." My voice came out quiet and subdued. "I'm not used to sneaking around and hiding. I was an ambulance driver turned mechanic turned pilot. And Jane is out there, and I swore I'd protect her. So forgive me if I seem impatient."

Earnst's shoulders cowed, and he nodded.

"I understand. I'm doing my best to do exactly what you want. Our goals are the same. We all want to leave here alive."

"All right," I said, trying quickly to paint over the vulnerability that had left me so uncomfortable. "So if we're not emptying the Lugers like two cowboys riding off into the east, what's the plan?"

"Well, I didn't say anything about not riding off."

He yanked the canvas blanket back, and instantly I wanted to vomit.

He was insane—a mad German lunatic.

Glinting in the pale light sat two motorcycles and sidecars. Each sidecar had a metal shield in front. At the top of either shield gleamed the ever-so familiar cooling sleeve of a mounted Vickers machine gun.

"No," I said, dropping my face into my hands. "Tell me I'm dreaming. You can't be serious."

"This was not our first plan," he admitted sheepishly.

"Are these Enfields? Where did you possibly find these?"

"In Germany's recent offensive, it captured significant ground at surprising speeds. The German army was almost within artillery range of Paris and nearly captured Amiens."

I didn't open my eyes.

"Yeah. I get it. You closed a front with Russia and surged," I said. "But what of it? You didn't keep going."

"No. High Command was frustrated as it watched its infantry and stormtroopers outpace its artillery and infrastructure. And with outstretched infantry marching forward, the British managed to plug holes in their line with machines like this. Many were left in the wake of the retreat, and we requisitioned some that were headed to Brussels. They're highly mobile and can be very effective."

I dropped my hands between my legs.

"I don't doubt that. I doubt the wisdom in using this type of firepower in a city that just turned into a war zone from a few rifle shots. What do you think the German troops stationed nearby will do when they hear a Vickers rattling off five hundred rounds a minute from a motorcycle?"

I kicked the drum of the side car with a hollow thump.

"We're not going to shoot five hundred rounds a minute. First, we only have at most half an ammunition pan each. Second, it is obvious we want to be discreet, but if there is a need, I prefer having strength available than none at all."

I shook my head and let out a slow breath.

"I disagree. This far into German territory, excess firepower is conspicuous, loud, and—"

"Quiet!" Earnst held up a hand to shut me up and craned his head toward the window. We listened closely. I heard it only a moment after he did. Distant footsteps slapping the street.

I jumped from my seat, and we both peeked through the cracks in the boarded window. The sight nearly overwhelmed me.

Jane, the side of her skirt clutched in one hand, sprinted in our direction down the road coming from the right side of the bakery entrance. Lina did her best to keep up behind her. Sweet relief flooded my body. I almost fell over. Instead, I opened the door, unable to hold back an all-encompassing smile.

She was limping, but she was alive.

"Wait!" Earnst said, but he failed to stop me in time. I staggered out into the road.

If Jane was happy to see me, she didn't let it show. She shouted and waved, frantic and flailing, but I couldn't understand what she said. It wasn't until she reached me and fell into my arms, gasping violently for breath, that I put it together.

"He's following us," she coughed. Beside me, Lina collapsed

on the ground beside her husband. He kissed her passionately on the face.

"Who?" I asked. "You're all right. You made it back. We're all right."

"No," she stammered. Her forehead was slick with sweat, as if she'd been running for a half hour. "The Blue Flyer."

She pointed down the street behind her, and my eyes stretched wide. A hundred yards off, if that, a man in a German soldier's uniform hurried our way. The hair on my neck stood.

Earnst didn't hesitate. He raised the Luger, and shots exploded from the gun. We scrambled back to the bakery, Earnst strafing and firing all the way to the door.

At the first gunshot, the soldier ran for cover behind the corner of a building. But it took him no time to sling his rifle and return fire.

"What are you thinking?" I cried as we regained the shop. "We were just talking about keeping quiet! These gunshots are going to wake up the city all over again."

He shook his head.

"If this man is the Blue Flyer as Jane said, there is not time to be quiet. Lina, *die Motorrader!*"

A rifle shot ricocheted off the building outside. Another splintered a piece of wood barring the window. The shots came in from the right at a sharp angle. Earnst fired back almost blindly in the Flyer's direction.

"You think you're going to outshoot him with that pistol?" I shouted.

"I nearly got him!" he insisted, closing one eye and squinting down the sights of the gun.

I huddled with Jane in the corner. She shook. I'd seen her after a fight. The flying bullets didn't scare her. There was something else.

"I thought I'd lost you," I said.

"Marcus, I spoke with him. It's worse than we imagined. He's, he just—we need to end this," she said, eyeing the Luger.

"I know," I replied, helplessly. "I just— I mean I'm afraid I can't."

"It's all right. I remember my promise. I fire, you fly," she said, as she gently took the gun from my hands. My head hung in shame, but she crossed to Earnst and joined him in exchanging shots with our enemy through the boards. This was the deal we'd struck, but until this moment, I hadn't appreciated the burden it put on her.

But before I could mope about, distant shots rang out across the city again. Just as I'd feared, our commotion was restarting the violence. I needed to do something.

"Did you have a strategy for getting these things out of here?" I asked Earnst. Jane noticed the bikes for the first time.

"Enfields?" Her jaw dropped. "What are those doing here?"

"They're the only remaining option at this point," Earnst shouted. "The boards. We must kick down the boards for egress. The window is large enough, but we need to kick down the boards."

I gritted my teeth.

"That would have been a lot easier without someone shooting at us!" I cried. The window had been cast into a stone archway, and the planks boarding that archway had already taken a fair amount of damage on the left side, opposite the Flyer's position.

Earnst tossed me a cast iron pan from a crate on the counter and handed his Luger to Lina. She flattened herself against the front wall beside Jane and alternated returning fire from the pistol out the door toward our pursuer. The Flyer's shots came in deadly and sporadic. I wondered if he was taking the opportunity to get closer and improve his angle. Hopefully, the women could keep him pinned down while Earnst and I got to work forcibly removing the boards.

The nails gave easily, but with each successful plank we pried loose, we increased our enemy's visibility and made ourselves a greater target to him. One round struck particularly close to Earnst while he pulled a stubborn plank with his hand, triggering a whole stream of German swears.

Then, Lina's pistols went quiet.

"I'm out!" she growled angrily as she inspected the magazine. "I hope you're nearly finished."

We were, but as I leaned forward to pry another board loose, a string of machine gun fire splattered through the wood on the right side of the archway, kicking splinters everywhere sending me stumbling backward.

"Machine gun!" I shouted. "This guy's got more firepower than we thought!"

"You were right, Sergeant. We've drawn far too much attention!" Earnst said as he, too, fell on his back for cover.

Jane crept toward the archway bravely and returned fire in the direction of the machine gun. Then, her pistol clicked quiet, as well.

"That's it," Jane moaned. "There's a small platoon of German soldiers down the street on our left. We don't have any more bullets?"

Another rifle shot whizzed through the window frame as Earnst shook his head, and I shimmied forward to the boards, kicking at them with my feet. The final plank gave way. To my relief and horror, the bakery had turned into an open-mouthed cavern etched into the side of a brick wall. We'd be as easy to shoot as an observation balloon with no escort.

But then all was quiet.

"Do you have eyes on anyone?" I asked.

"Yes," Jane replied. "I can see the infantry. They're headed toward us now. Marcus, they're coming. We're trapped." Her voice wobbled with fear. But before desperation sank in, a new volley of rifle fire rang out on our street.

"What was that?" Earnst shouted.

"The infantry are taking cover! There are rifle shots coming from the windows," Jane replied. A terrible dawning fell across her features. "It's the Flyer, he doesn't want them to find us. He needs the devices for himself."

"Jane, give me the goggles," I said. She took them from her neck and slid them across the floor to me. I held them to my eyes and lost my breath.

Faint blue emanated from down the street to the right of the archway, similar to the burst that had distracted me at the museum before my German friends so kindly put a gun in my back. That must be the Flyer, just like how the goggles lit up his plane. But it was the other bursts of blue that surprised me.

With the crack of each rifle shot, I saw a small blue flash above us from the windows outside. They lit up the goggles like fireworks. Magic blossomed all around us, and a crazy idea hit me.

"The Flyers are controlling the rifles!" I cried. "He must have friends all over the city."

"We can't stay here," Lina said. I couldn't agree more. I didn't come all the way here to die pinned down by two different enemies in a Belgian bakery.

"Now or never, Ernie," I said. "Let's get those Enfields going while they're distracted."

I scrambled to a sidecar and lifted my leg to get in, but Jane grabbed my arm.

"You fly, I fire," she said, though she grimaced as she said it.

"No, Jane, we shouldn't be firing these guns much, anyway. As soon as we're free of the street, we need to be as quiet as we can. And you're more comfortable on the Enfield than I am."

"You fly," she repeated, and I knew there was no arguing.

"You fire," I confirmed.

She nodded and settled into the passenger car behind the Vickers, familiarizing herself with the gun.

"Just pretend it's an airplane," she said. Lina took the driver's seat of the other Enfield beside me. Earnst checked the gun and eyed me from his sidecar.

"Follow Lina. There's a path south on this side of the canal that connects to the road east. If we can disappear into the darkness between here and Lokeren, we will plan our next steps."

I nodded and settled my hands on the handlebars. Despite the impending chaos, there was something about having transportation under me that soothed some of the fear I'd suffered the past few days. The motor lay waiting to be ignited. Jane sat by my side behind considerable firepower. And unlike being in an airplane, the night would be on our side. Just as Earnst said, we just had to get past the boundaries of the city. The German front was far from here, along with the bulk of their manpower and resources. In some ways, we were safer deep into Belgium and enemy ground than if we were near France.

"Lina, I'm on you," I said. She grunted and assumed the same confident posture she'd approached me with when demanding Boelcke's goggles. "Jane, stay low once we're out. Then fire only if necessary. You've only got so many rounds in that thing right now. I'd love it if—"

"I'm not an idiot, Marcus," she said. "But if you do want me to hit something, be sure you point the Enfield in the right direction. This isn't on a ring like it is in the planes."

"Roger that."

Lina's engine roared to life, and I kicked my machine to follow suit. The sound in the gutted bakery was deafening. I wanted to time our exit between rifle volleys, but I didn't even get a chance to take a breath, Lina punched her machine forward like a rocket. I squeezed the throttle and followed after.

Several metallic pings resounded off the shield in front of the sidecar as we exited. I peeked to our right down to see the the Blue Flyer working the bolt on his rifle like the wheels of a locomotive. His shots zipped by us, close enough to sense their movement through the air.

It looked like we'd be outrunning him this time.

But when I veered left, away from him, to to follow Lina, my confidence wavered.

The squadron of German infantry was spread into the corners of the street, eyes wide. Two motorcars had stopped fifty yards off, each with a trio of soldiers lining up their rifles. But the machine gun between them was by far the largest threat. It swiveled on its stand to account for our movement as shots from the rifles in the windows kicked up bits of stone around us.

My heart skipped, but these Enfields had some attitude, and I was sure we could outmaneuver—

RAT TAT TAT TAT TAT TAT!

My sidecar came alive with explosive activity. Jane flooded the streets with Vickers' rounds. Numbly, I watched the men at the machine gun each take at least twenty of her rounds to the torso before falling to the ground lifeless.

Earnst followed Jane's example and let off a stream from his own Vickers gun that sent the Huns scrambling for cover behind their vehicles. Lina and I didn't wait. She leaned on the motor and zoomed right by them, me desperately following through the cloud of smoke and smell of sulfur in their wake.

We'd made it clear of the the street but would have precious little time while the Germans mounted their vehicle to come after us. And at this speed, the cobblestones under the motorbike jolted us uncomfortably.

We needed to cross the canal, but more German infantry had gathered on the closest bridge, eager to investigate the source of the new gunfire. So we lurched right and double back down a tight street lined by buildings with tall facades.

Those Germans weren't the only ones curious, either. The shots had perked up the remaining outfits in the city, and as we weaved through alleyways, attempting to navigate Ghent's maze, we bumped into more and more pockets of German resistance.

But worse than that, the rifle fire from the windows seemed to follow us somehow, and we were never free from the threat of rounds from above or across a plaza.

We pushed the engines so hard, I smelled the burning of oil and gas. But finally, we found a bridge over the canal that was not manned by soldiers. We bound across it and worked our way out of the city's center. The towering windows above us diminish quickly, and the random rifle fire faded in our tracks. Suddenly, I saw nature on the horizon, distant woods, gentle hills, not just building after building. My thoughts raced to Atkins's map. This view was a sign that we were almost free, almost to the city limits. As the buildings faded in prominence, our chances at freedom grew.

I couldn't keep down the relief bubbling up from my heart. We could do this. Jane was safe by my side. All that remained was getting to that airfield and flying that piece of junk Rumpler back to France.

But a minute later, I saw the road Earnst had mentioned to me growing ahead of us. A large intersection defended by a thorough checkpoint blocked our freedom. It was filled with several German cars, more sentries, barbed wire—all designed to make entrances and exits to the city awkward and time consuming. For us to get through, it would mean destroying the men that stood guard and carefully skirting defenses.

I glanced down at Jane. She had seen what I had and gripped the handle of her gun with cold fists. It only hit me then.

She had mowed down that machine gun. She had killed two men.

"Jane," I called. Glancing over to her, I hardly recognized the expression on her face. It was hard and dark. Her mouth drooped in grim resolution. My heart plummeted from my chest. I knew what went through her mind. It was the same thing that went through every soldier's mind when they had to prepare to do what must be done.

Every soldier but me. Somehow I'd been broken. Cursed. I never managed to cross that threshold. And to protect me, she'd crossed it herself.

Every human soul finds bloodshed reprehensible until a singular moment. There's a blip on the clock when the brain switches off the burden. It numbs the heart, desensitizes the conscience. It's willful blindness of reality or moral justification.

It was everything I didn't want for her, and already I'd failed. Despite my promise, I'd failed her.

I wouldn't do it again.

I pushed on my engine and cut across the front of Lina and Earnst. He waved wildly at me, pointing at the intersection, but I paid him no mind.

"What are you doing?" Jane called above the sound of the engine. Her tone was biting. She sounded angry.

"Jane, I'm so sorry!" I shouted. I drove the bike directly toward a wooden gate set in the fence surrounding one of the old farmhouses around us. It snapped on impact, granting admittance into a yard strewn with mechanical and agricultural tools. If I'd thought the cobblestones were uncomfortable, now the bumps of a rural work yard bucked the seat of my Enfield beneath my legs like a bull at the rodeo. We jumped, skidded, squeezed our way through the yard before slowly picking out a path to another that bordered the property. I paid no mind to the property we destroyed behind us.

There was a reason the allies used these bikes to plug up holes in the line, and it wasn't because they excelled at driving on roads. The highway was the escape route for Earnst and Lina's truck. It was the road any motorcar would take. But these were Royal Enfield Motorbikes.

We continued our way through properties, keeping the sun behind us. Eventually, work yards gave way to fields, then unfenced land. We'd already passed the last canal on the east of Ghent, and there was no thick city wall to overcome.

When we flew by our last farmhouse into open field, the sensation thrilled me.

"Watch for ditches and holes!" Jane called out, pointing ahead. She craned her neck backwards. "It's just Earnst and Lina behind us!"

"Yeah, well, the Germans don't have to follow behind us," I said, pointing to the main road far on our right. "Keep an eye on that."

A lethal zip cut the air around us as soldiers from the checkpoint at the mouth of the city hazarded rifle shots after us, but all of their shots went wide.

I took us across fields, up and down irrigation ditches, winding an impossible route through donkey trails and walking paths. The landscape was mostly flat and open, and were it daytime any Bosch with binoculars would be able to track us.

But the night came on fast, and it would stem even an effective search by plane for the time being.

After putting a gap between us and the main road, and fifteen minutes had passed without rifle fire in the air or any other indication of a pursuit group, I powered down the motorbike.

Lina pulled up beside me and did the same. After the roar of the Lugers, the rifles, the machine guns, and the motorbike engines, we might as well have been dreaming up the quiet field in Flanders where we sat now.

Earnst jumped from his side car and approached me.

"Crazy American!" He shoved me.

"Hey!" Jane scrambled to get out of her seat. I backed off the bike and grounded myself.

"What were you thinking?" he demanded, hitting me in the shoulder again. "A field? In the dark in the middle of nowhere!"

I put up my hands to defend myself, but a smile split his lips. He laughed. I glanced at Lina. She smiled as well, shaking her head as though we were crazy.

"Those sentries never expected that!"

He laughed like a madman and embraced tightly. We'd done it. We had escaped. I wanted to share in his enthusiasm, to let out a yell of victory, but all I could think about was Jane. Jane who hated the violence of war, the burden she carried now, what she had done for me. She wore a somber frown.

"He can still track us," she said. "We have to keep moving. We're not safe until we're back in France. He will come after us. And I don't know if he's afraid of flying in the dark." Her lip quivered. I wanted to wrap her in a large embrace, but found myself withholding.

"We'll be fine," I said, lamely. "We're miles ahead of where we were a while ago. We're back together. Earnst has got a plane at an airbase south of here. We can get home."

She shook her head and put a hand to her chest.

"I thought I'd saved it. He must have grabbed it when we collided."

"What?" I asked. "The device?"

"No," she replied. "My glass marble."

Chapter 32
Bleu, Blanc, Rouge
Jane

Again the guns disturbed the hour,
Roaring their readiness to avenge,
As far inland as Stourton Tower,
And Camelot, and starlit Stonehenge.
-Thomas Hardy-

We took our journey slowly southward on the motorbikes, opting for stealth. We didn't bother turning on our headlamps, instead allowing the waxing gibbous moon in the night sky to illuminate our way. The Enfields cut smoothly across the fields for a half hour or so, parallel to but distant from the main road exiting Ghent.

After some time, we connected with another, smaller country byway, and Earnst pulled a map and compass from inside his coat before directing us onward. Once we'd put enough distance between us and any possible German pursuer, we risked the headlights.

If the Blue Flyer chased after us, I doubted the headlights would make a jot of difference.

He hadn't needed headlights to find me in Ghent, after all.

While I bumped about in the sidecar, I turned over my encounter with the rogue pilot many times. I tried to scrutinize every word, but it was hard to focus knowing that despite my best efforts, I'd managed to lose the glass marble, the very thing the flyer admitted he wanted most.

Why?

Its loss weighed more heavily on me than perhaps it merited. But the marble had become a symbol of safety, a beacon that Marcus was still alive, that our connection made us stronger. Now, it rested in the hands of somebody who, evidently, understood a great deal more about the magic than I dared to expect.

I shuddered.

There was no method I was aware of to use the marble to harm Marcus, no reverse channels to send malicious enchantments upstream through the connection. But he certainly could invalidate its protections. I feared he might also use it as a more accurate method to track us.

It was well into the night, and we'd been following Earnst for a couple of hours before he signaled for us to turn off the road into a nearby wood by a small Belgian hamlet. We stashed the motorbikes and crept toward the town, where Earnst insisted he had support.

Marcus, Lina, and I waited in a barn, exhausted, while Earnst crept in.

"You doing all right?" Marcus asked me carefully as we leaned against the wall in the dark.

"As well as can be expected," I replied. "I can't believe I let him take my marble."

I couldn't hear Marcus breathe in the pause that followed.

"Right, that," he said. "I'm more worried about you, though, if I'm being honest."

"Me? Why? What's wrong with me?"

More silence.

"Nothing. Of course. Let's just get home, huh?"

"Out with it, Marcus."

"It's just—well, I don't know how to say it. But you shot someone."

My jaw went slack as the escape came back to me. He was right. I'd mowed down two men to open our route out of the bakery. He flew, I fired.

"You're right," I muttered.

"So, I just want to make you sure you are all right."

I was. I didn't know how to explain it, but it all made sense to me. They were trying to kill us. I did what was necessary.

"I don't think it's hit me yet," I said. Marcus grabbed my hand.

"I'm here when it does."

Earnst came back with a small truck. I was grateful for the change of transportation. I climbed into the back, leaned on Marcus's shoulder and tried my best at dreamless, restless sleep. But at every sound of an engine, or a distant artillery shell, I started.

It was a couple of hours still until Earnst shut off the head-lamps and indicated the familiar markings of airfield hangars dimly illuminated on the horizon.

"We made it," he said with a sigh of relief. "Now, we just have to steal an old Rumpler."

"Do you have a plan for that?" Marcus asked. Earnst smiled grimly.

"This is where my record as a German pilot will be useful. Mustermann has already arranged for orders to come through for the Rumpler's relocation." He checked his watch. "It's nearly sunrise. I will report and enforce those orders. They will equip me with the plane. I will fly it over that grove of trees. You will wait with Lina in the truck in a clearing there. Then we will make the switch."

Marcus nodded.

"I take it this is a pretty sleepy airbase?" he asked.

Earnst nodded.

"It is maintained, but there is much more activity closer to Brussels, and of course, closer to the front line."

"Then we just have to fly an old Rumpler though German and Allied airspace," I said.

A heavy silence fell on the cab as the gravity of the mission settled. It had been a terrifying pair of days, and though we'd escaped Ghent, we still had much to risk. I shuddered at visions of no man's land from our recent flyover. I could all but smell the exploding anti-aircraft fire bursting around me.

Crossing the the same way in an old, battered aircraft sounded like certain death. Marcus agreed with me.

"I think we'll fly south," Marcus said.

"South?" Lina asked.

"It's too hot here up north, and I don't know anything about the geography. If we set out early, we should be able to make it down to more familiar territory. If we could, I'd even go south of Croix-de-Metz. We should be safer in German skies for the bulk of the journey. Then, I know the patrols down there. I even know the pilots. Maybe they'll recognize me."

I lifted my head from his shoulder.

"And if the Blue Flyer chases us?" I asked.

He grimaced.

"I think we stand a better chance evading him down south than we do getting caught up with him as the lamest duck in a ten-plane sortie up here."

"Thank you," said Lina quietly. She grabbed my hand. "If you had told me two years ago that I would feel so warmly for a Briton and an American, I'd have never believed you. But this is a friendship I will never forget."

I patted her hand.

"It's funny what the war does to us," I said. "If you'd asked me five years ago if I'd ever have an issue befriending a German, I'd have thought you were crazy. I'm glad that in the two of you, I've seen some return to a normal heart."

"Come along then," Earnst said. "Let's get this plane."

Earnst exited the truck and set off into the fading night across the field. I grabbed Marcus's arm.

"We've nearly made it. Then, I will tell Command to find someone else for this mission. I can teach whoever they like about magic safely from behind our lines. They don't need me to go running around."

Marcus studied me with a gentle gaze. Boelcke's goggles hung loosely around his neck.

"Let's just get home. Then we can talk about the next mission."

Lina slid into the driver's seat and pulled the truck out on the road to wait at our rendezvous point. The sun rose on the horizon as we waited, and my beleaguered body wished we could stay in that moment until the war ended. I wanted to call someone and order a bed, have them come with a truck for us, each with a lovely mattress in the back, to cart us home and out of the war forever. I wanted my father's fish and chips. I wanted to hear my mother read a novel aloud to our family.

The sputtering sound of the Rumpler's engine cut through the Belgian peace. Earnst brought the plane down without much grace in the field ahead of us.

"Let's go," Marcus said. He kissed Lina on the cheek. "Keep an eye on the old boy."

"Of course."

We climbed out of the truck and approached the plane from behind. It really did look old. The simple vertical struts connected the bottom and top wings like toothpicks. The wheels were bulky, and the whole thing appeared as a long box with a propellor strapped on the front. Earnst didn't bother cutting the engine, and Marcus gave me a lift high enough so that I could force my tired limbs to search the gunner's bay. I found two flight suits inside. I hopped back down, tossed the larger to Marcus, and draped the oversized, full-length coat over my skirt and blouse. The warmth brought me so much comfort I wanted to cry.

Dressed for the cold, I scrambled back to the bay and found a rear-facing Parabellum machine gun standing tall on a ring mount that needed oiling. I noticed several shoddily patched bullets holes on the fuselage, and some that hadn't been patched at all.

Marcus climbed on the wing and exchanged brief words with Earnst that I couldn't hear well. Instructions on flying the old machine, no doubt. Then they awkwardly switched places.

"Jane," Earnst called loudly before stepping away from the machine. "In case you need some extra persuasion for those boys in your skies." He handed me an old, linen flag. I didn't need to unfold it to recognize the blue, white, and red of France. "If needs be, tie it to your gun mount and let the world see a captured German Rumpler."

"I've never been so happy to see the French flag!" I called back. He laughed, and his enthusiasm kindled the excitement of our journey in my chest. A new wave of adrenaline trickled in my veins. After all, I was about to go flying again.

Earnst shoved off and waved before retreating back to the truck.

"Does that gun have any ammunition?" Marcus called back to me.

I inspected a short belt in a small compartment in my bay.

"Not much," I replied.

"Well, here's hoping we won't need it! It's a race back to France now. If that rogue mongrel is chasing us, he's going to have to contend with an old, trusty, likely rusty, Rumpler engine."

He opened the gas, and we jerked forward. I felt the faulty

supports strain all down the bumpy field before we lifted off. While the speed dwarfed that of the Enfield and the motorcar we'd been driving, it didn't have the same gusto I'd come to appreciate both from the Salmson and the Albatross. But we were airborne, and despite the danger and the trauma I'd pushed down for days, the beauty of the rising sun on our tail, directly in front of me, took my breath away.

We left Ghent behind. Brussels, in the distance, shrank away off my right and we pushed on. We had several hours of flying ahead, and I busied myself searching the sky for other pinpricks, either against the clouds or the sun. That was the most dangerous attack position, so they said. Strike from the sun.

But the only planes we saw were a fair way off, and they didn't care to investigate. I closed my eyes and envisioned the pilots of the 94th. Some of them would be waiting at a small table by a telephone. I wondered if our plane would cause an alert.

After an hour or so, Marcus banked left, and I caught sight of a large city in the path we'd been flying. He cut the engine, then turned to shout to me.

"Luxembourg. We go around, then cut south until we hit the border northeast of Nancy. Never thought I'd have to be so worried about my own boys shooting me down."

"With our luck," I yelled back. "Lufbery will be stalking on this side of the lines and bring us down himself."

Marcus gave me a thumbs up and bobbed his head, signaling laughter.

"At least we'd go down at the hands of an ace."

I smiled. It would be an ironic end. I turned to scan the clouds. Soon we might be close enough to bump into one of the 94th pilots. Rickenbacker or even Huffer or...

I squinted. Behind us, a small black wasp followed. I blinked several times, for fear that I may have been staring into the sun for too long, but it did not go away.

"Marcus," I shouted with every attempt at professional calm. "Do you see him?"

Marcus pitched the plane gently and craned his neck, peering through the mystical goggles that had started our journey.

He didn't look for long before righting the plane's course.

"Well?"

He nodded.

"Blue Flyer."

My optimism dulled, a cold dread seeping through my flight coat as if we'd flown through a storm cloud.

"He is still a way off. We can outrun him," I said.

"We can try."

He gave new life to the engine, and the propellor cut through the air ravenously. Marcus tipped the nose forward into a gentle dive to give us more speed. We were so close. Part of me wondered if we should risk flying over Luxembourg, but I knew how many airfields on both sides of the line polluted that path.

We could do it. We just had to make it back to our lines. Then, I could let out the French flag, and nothing would rally our troops more than seeing a German plane pursuing a Rumpler flying a French flag. Every pilot and ground gunner within miles would want to take a shot at him.

We pushed west, making our way through the circumference of the city slowly. The pilot was gaining on us but still was well out of range.

I'd strained my memory for details of the maps that lay all over Gengault aerodrome. It would be perhaps a half hour to the border. It would take too long to get past Nancy. We would have to risk an earlier crossing.

Soon, I could make out the rough silhouette of the plane. How could it gain on us so quickly? Yes, the Rumpler was old, but it had been used effectively up until six or nine months ago.

"He's closing quickly!" I yelled. "I don't know if we're going to make it."

In response, Marcus banked to the right. And I saw the city behind us shrinking, just as Brussels had hours ago. The Flyer altered course to follow.

It was a losing game. He grew steadily closer. I craned my neck forward, and far in the distance I saw a bleak scar stretching across the earth. Another fifteen minutes may have been enough.

But the first shots rang out from far off. A tracer round whizzed by, and the zip of other bullets cut through the air. For the distance, the Flyer's accuracy was terrifying.

"Make your shots count!" Marcus screamed over the wind and roar of the propellor. The air tore the words from his mouth, and it was hard to catch them. Marcus tipped our wings in irregular patterns, shifting the plane back and forth. Scattered bursts of fire spewed from the plane behind us, but no rounds landed. The front line drew nearer.

He was on us all at once. We were minutes short of Allied lines, but now his plane was near enough to recognize. A terrible triple-winged monster with menacing black crosses on their canvas. It was a Fokker Dr.I—the same plane that the Red Baron had flown the day of his death. He made a pass across us. I heaved the Parabellum gun with all of my might, but it did not move smoothly on its mount. Lining up the Flyer with such equipment would be a terribly difficult task.

But I had no choice. Marcus broke right and corkscrewed us downward, sending my stomach reeling. He popped out from the base of the dive with greater speed toward our lines. The Flyer's triplane tipped over on its back and fell below us before righting and using the momentum to get at our underbelly.

I fired off a few rounds as it came up and across our tail—just a burst, but it ate up the ammunition belt. He went by unscathed. My fingers trembled. The anxiety was mounting, and I shoved down a persuasion of inevitability, the belief that all our roads led to this moment.

I struggled to pay attention, my actions becoming automatic, giving way to a dark, hungry subconscious. Brace for maneuver, settle in behind the gun, pray for a better angle, take a shot, watch the rounds go wide, watch the ammo belt shrink.

Perhaps it was foolish to tie myself to a pilot who couldn't bring himself to kill his enemy, but even if we died here, I stood by my belief in Marcus. I regretted only that my insistence had brought him to harm.

The Flyer came in on us from a high arc above, spiraling down, rattling its gun loudly. I cranked the Parabellum with exhausted arms and retaliated.

Click.

My gun stopped. The belt had run empty. I pounded on the fuselage.

"I'm out!" I shouted, fighting with everything left to keep the tears from my voice. As I yelled, explosive shells began to burst around us on every side, black smoke popping like balloons. Someone from the ground was shooting at us. I didn't care to know who. What did it matter?

"Send out the flag!" Marcus screamed. I followed his instructions as if he were my commanding officer. I didn't want to think about our friendship, not now—didn't want it to pull me to pieces. I carefully found the eyelet in the linen. I needed a cord, and mechanically, I bent over to undo my boot, struggling with the laces while Marcus continued his wide curving evasive tactics. Wind whistled through holes in the body of the plane. Had those been there when we took off?

My stomach somersaulted, but I managed to get the boot off and pull free some of the violin strings.

I looped it through the eyelet, wrapped it around the Parabellum's mount. It was slow going. My hands were freezing, shaking, and the force of gravity amidst the breaks and dives pushed me around the bay. I only managed knots in two of the strings before telling myself it would hold, but at least it was tied. I unfolded the flag, pushed it free, and the *bleu, blanc, rouge* caught in the wind, rippling awkwardly from its single anchor. Shrapnel battered it, but it was the best we could do to let anyone who saw us know that we were not as German as our plane appeared.

"Woooooo, Jane! We made it! Look at her fly!"

The bursts around us ceased almost instantly, and my heart soared. Those were our guns below, and even if the Flyer shot us down now, we'd be home. We'd made it to the line.

Marcus tipped the Rumpler's nose, unafraid now of fire from below, eager to give our gunners on the ground an easier shot on the triplane.

We pulled up, and in our wake, Archie's pops beleaguered our enemy's flight patterns. But he still pursued. We had the support. We might just make it through...

Marcus went straight into a bank of thick low-hanging clouds, trying to buy more time for the gunners. I held my breath. The bright linen of the flag appeared strange in such dense mists. When we burst through the other side, there was no stifling the budding optimism.

Perhaps we'd encounter one of our own planes to help, a morning patrol about to witness the strangest set of circumstances of their career. Or perhaps Archie landed a round on him. I stared at the bank of clouds, waiting for the German triplane to emerge.

But it didn't. Another did. A Nieuport 28. The plane flown by the 94th Aero Squadron.

"Marcus! A Nieuport!" I squealed in relief. I let out a holler of victory, premature as I knew it was. The momentum of the whole sortie shifted now, and the certain despondency that possessed my every feature fluttered away like the breeze.

Marcus craned his head back, and he even looked comical with the old goggles on his eyes and a smile alight on his face.

But in a moment, his grin melted into confusion, then grim resolve.

"What?" I cried. "What is wrong?"

The Nieuport opened fire.

Chapter 33
Ace of Aces
Marcus

The thundering line of battle stands,
And in the air Death moans and sings;
But Day shall clasp him with strong hands,
And Night shall fold him in soft wings.
-Julian Grenfell-

It couldn't be possible.

I wiped one glove on Boelcke's Goggles. They must be malfunctioning.

A Nieuport 28 had flown from the cloud bank, but the writhing blue tentacles that had marked the plane for the past hour remained unchanged.

But how could that be? I searched the sky in vain for the Fokker Dr.I that had been expertly blowing chunks off our Rumpler. I scanned the ground for its remains. It must have gone somewhere.

We should have had the upper hand by now. We should have been attracting allied pilots like fruit flies to a slice of summer melon. They should have seen our flag and gone after him.

But now, they'd only see a Nieuport 28 trying to shoot down an old Rumpler C.I. Whose side would they choose?

I was losing my mind. But I had no other explanations. The Blue Flyer had somehow transformed his airplane in that cloud bank.

But it didn't matter how the Nieuport got there. It fired off both Vickers guns like a trigger happy private on his first sortie. And I didn't have much maneuvering left in me. By now, he'd seen all my tricks, and my vision was starting to blur at the edges.

Our boys on the ground had stopped firing at either plane, letting the two warbirds decide the bout amongst themselves. The Nieuport gained on us quickly, leveraging its greater muscle to come close and bring us down.

It wasn't fair.

I did everything asked of me. I'd only come to this God-forsaken war to make something of my family's name. I didn't ask for this magical mission. I only wanted to protect Jane, and we'd come so close to getting back to Lufbery, back home.

I was flying so low now, and my instincts took the stick. Before I knew it, I was repeating the same break pattern I'd used in the storm by Clairmarais. Only this time, our Rumpler didn't have as much power. It was a losing game.

It wasn't a game at all. Wasn't that what Jane had been trying to tell me all this time?

Our plane jolted as one of the Nieuport's rounds connected with our landing gear. Another burst from the Vickers, and a fresh hole ripped through my left wing.

Another burst and I heard Jane scream in pain.

The sound penetrated my eardrums, drilled down to my heart, and shattered it.

"Jane!" I screamed. I couldn't look back to check on her. I couldn't cut the engine to ask if she was all right.

I yanked on the joystick, and followed the Nieuport. It flew from me well, back up and into the sun. I couldn't see much of anything just—

—just the wisps of blue in Boelcke's goggles.

Jane had gone to the dark for me. She didn't do it to keep score. She didn't do it for glory. She didn't even do it to prove something to herself. She did it for me.

I slammed down my trigger. The Spandau roared in front of me. I didn't let go. The gun continued, grew hoarse from so much shouting, until it finally stopped, out of ammunition or jammed, I didn't care.

I pulled my nose away from the sun and blinked rapidly trying to get my eyesight back.

"Jane!" I cried. "Jane!"

"I'm here!" she called back slowly. "I'm all right."

But something was wrong, I could tell. Even through the howling wind, I could tell.

"Just hang on," I shouted, eyesight returning to a workable state, enough to continue my maneuvers. I craned my neck backward and caught sight of our flapping French flag, and a melancholy void on Jane's face.

She only pointed.

I followed her finger and saw him. One Nieuport 28, losing altitude, smoke billowing from the engine.

I stared in shock. My wild spray must have caught him, and now he sank, slowly, gracefully from our low altitude.

"I don't believe it," I said, an entire cocktail of emotions bubbling in my chest. Pride, remorse, suffocating relief, joy, fear...

I'd seen my fair share of pilots go down for being stupid enough to circle back on their kills, to survey the crash site. Experienced pilots warned against the practice. After all, you never should be completely confident that you were alone in the air. I'd never understood the temptation until now. I banked around and followed. Presently, we relied on the flapping French flag behind us to ensure our own allies didn't shoot us down. But I had to see the remains.

The Nieuport finally went down on our side, miles from any base, in the middle of a farmer's field beside a dense wood. The wings broke on impact, and the body of the plane crumpled into a tangle of wooden debris. As I circled around it, a fire from the engine spread, and I watched numbly as the flames licked up at the frame.

My first victory.

After two years at war.

Some animal inside of me curled in on itself, defensive like a snake about to strike. I waited to fight off the specter my conscience prepared for these two years. I had shot the man down. I was a killer. I wanted to vomit.

At least it was right. He'd nearly blown us from the sky. I had to do it. I had to protect Jane. She was counting on me. Smith and Atkins and Dupont and Earnst and Lina and Mustermann and Lufbery and Gervaise and Jane's mother and Jane's father and my mother and my father and all of France and all of England and all of the world. They were all counting on me.

Suddenly, something died inside of me as I understood. The world expected men to do terrible things, relied on them to be broken. Honor was nothing but an idea, a meager currency to repay those for what they had to do.

Honor did not fix the holes.

I glanced about at our old Rumpler, shot to bits, and I remembered the jolt to our landing gear. I wasn't looking forward to trying to touch this thing down. But we could try.

"Jane, are you there?" I called back. Her scream still echoed in my ears.

"It's my foot," she said. "I'll make it back."

We could get home. Nothing blocked our way now. I'd dealt with the Flyer, and I was in familiar territory. The French flag should give our boys enough pause to at least let me land. By now, word would have already gone through the line. In a half hour, I could be hugging Lufbery, telling him all about my first. He'd be so proud. He'd never doubted, always gave me a chance.

I leveled us toward Gengault and was tickled with delight when I saw a Nieuport I recognized. Huffer's plane. He pulled up beside us, and I saw his mouth hang agape. I smiled and gave him a salute.

Then, the landing strip came into view, and I managed the bumps as well as I could, tried to give a little more power to the engine than usual to compensate for the holes in our sails, to avoid stalling right before our finally descent.

After a few bumps, and an awful dragging, scraping noise beneath us, the old Rumpler C.I came to a rest.

"Jane, your foot?" I asked shakily.

"You shot down the Flyer," she replied. Her voice shook.

"You shot down the machine gunner," I replied. Upon turning, I found her battling with a swell of varying emotions. I continued carefully. "I thought he'd got you."

"Just my foot," she replied. "But only a scratch from a bit of shrapnel. I'd taken my boot off for the violin strings."

"Violin stings?" I asked.

"Albert Ball's violin strings. That's the device we were sent to retrieve." She nodded glumly to herself.

I nodded. I'd never even cared to ask her about the device once we reunited in Ghent. An irrational part of me hated the magic for putting her in such danger. I hadn't expected violin strings.

"I'm sorry, Marcus," she said weakly.

"It's all right," I replied. "I'm sorry, too. But we're back. We're all right. We made it home. We can work through it together."

The boys arrived next. First, an investigative party from the French Army, weapons drawn, shouting commands at us in awkward German. But it only took a minute to clear things up, and before long, Campbell and Rickenbacker were the first from the 94th to arrive in a car to greet us.

Rickenbacker jumped out of the seat.

"Davis said he had the strangest call from alerts," he said. He was only half-dressed in his uniform but gaped like a boy seeing his first race car.

"How do you like my new ride, Rickie?" I asked proudly. My morale still soared. The adrenaline pumping through me hadn't been shut off yet, and I wanted to take on the world.

I helped Jane down. Her foot looked bad, but she insisted the cut was superficial. We helped her to the car and Campbell carted us quickly off to the medical tent.

She held on to my hand tightly, her eyes brimming not with pain but concern.

"What are you going on about?" I whispered.

"I'm sorry. I'm sorry you had to—"

"Jane, don't be sorry. I'm cured," I replied, trying to don the coat of enthusiasm I'd seen the victorious pilots around me wear for years.

She didn't appear convinced, and she refused to let go of me until the nurses pulled her on to a bed to examine her foot and shooed me off. When I turned, Lufbery stood beside the car waiting.

He smiled weakly, but his mind was elsewhere, his eyes filled with preoccupation.

"Luf!" I gave him a big hug, a gesture rarely shared between us. When I pulled back he smiled softly. "What's the matter? Aren't you happy to see me."

"Very happy," he replied. "Marcus, you're a brother. Of course, I am. Just worried, that's all."

"You and Jane both. Neither of you can take a win. What are you worried about?"

He sighed and shifted his weight. He seemed different than

the last I'd seen him.

"Nothing," he said. "You may have brought a German recon plane in behind you, that's all. You were quite the sight with that flag flying from your tail wing like that."

I deflated an inch.

"Oh, come on. I'm sure we can manage a little recon plane. What's the worse they can do? Take some pictures? As if the Germans don't know where we are—"

"Things have changed since you left," he replied. "We can't let them take any photographs right now. There's too much movement. Too much they can discover."

I swallowed. Luf's demeanor darkened. I expected welcome arms. Sure, I didn't expect him to stand there with a Vodka bottle in hand ready to have me take a shot for my first victory, but something at least a little warmer than this.

My hands found their way sheepishly to my pockets, and my shoulders hunched.

"We've got a lot to tell you," I said somberly. "You wouldn't believe what went on out there. The magic is real, Luf. The goggles work. We may have been all wrong about Boelcke, Richthofen, even some of the boys on our side."

"You will have to tell Smith. I'm not the officer in charge of your mission. If Smith wants me involved, he will ask me to be." He hardly paid me any mind, instead furiously taking a drag on a fresh cigarette. It did little to ease his uptight posture.

Despite all the wind he knocked from my sails, he was right. Luf always had a way of reminding me of my duty. I turned to go.

"Hey," he continued, "don't let my temper get you down. It just feels like something is changing. It's been a long time since I thought the war's end might be in sight. The thought makes me crazy, anxious to move it along. With the United States lending its strength to the Allies, victory seems inevitable. But recon planes like this one push it all back. Anyway, Huffer is up there now. He will shoot the Bosch down. Then, we can talk. I'm glad you made it. That German piece of junk looks plenty shot up."

I let him soothe away the low mood. Here he was, the Lufbery I knew so well.

"Well, when it's your time, it's your time, but I guess it wasn't my time," I said with a smile. "That reminds me. You won't believe it, I mean, maybe you saw it, but—"

"He's back!" A voice shouted nearby, one of the orderlies by the medical tents. Far off by the hangars, Winslow had a pair of binoculars in hand. Luf whirled with a start, hopped on a motorcycle, and sped over. I climbed back in the car with Campbell and we followed quickly behind him.

"What do you mean back?" Luf was grilling Winslow by the time we pulled up.

"Huffer. Coming in now."

"And the German?" Luf asked.

"See for yourself."

He seized the binoculars and swept the sky for all but a few moments.

"It's still in the damn sky!" he growled. "Where's my plane?"

I hadn't seen Luf angry like this in a long time. A sheepish mechanic replied.

"We're still working on it, sir. She's not flight ready."

"Well, whose is that one?" He pointed wildly to a Nieuport sitting in the airfield.

"Lieutenant Davis's, sir."

"You're with me."

Luf jumped into Davis's aircraft, and after a set of rapid-fire questions from the major, the mechanic admitted the plane could fly. Luf was airborne in a moment. Shrinking into the sky to chase after the recon plane.

"What is going on?" I asked Campbell. "I can't remember ever seeing Luf take someone else's plane unless it was an absolute emergency."

"There's a whole different mood around here now, Markie," he replied. "It's not just that old gentleman's sky game you used to talk about. Pershing is playing for keeps. They're pushing us to get this thing buttoned up."

"That means keeping secrets better. A recon plane like this is an emergency," Winslow added. "We should help him in case there are more. You never know. Get our planes ready!" He shouted to his mechanic and disappeared inside the hangar to prepare himself.

There was no telling who had my plane, or what state it was in. Jane was my primary mechanic, and she was in the medical wing with a busted foot. So I was resigned to spectate from the ground with the binoculars.

But after our escape from Ghent, part of me was glad for it. I always loved seeing Lufbery fly.

He climbed quickly after the recon plane. It was a German Albatross similar to the one Jane and I flew into Ghent. I couldn't help but reflect on how easily Luf caught up in a Nieuport 28. The state of the art planes the 94th flew outshined so many of the older models.

Soon, Luf was in range and dove down on the Albatross firing in short bursts. The German plan banked wide to evade him. The tactic surprised me. Was Lufbery toying with them? My thoughts drifted to Boelcke's goggles around my neck. I slipped them on and noticed with great concern that Luf's gun had jammed. Go figure. The man polished every round that went into his gun in a desperate attempt to prevent such jams. But this wasn't his gun. It was Davis's.

Luf's preoccupation about the recon plane getting away bit at the back of my mind. He seemed to be in a dangerous mood, breaking his own rules. If all the boys here were in such fits about it, there must be some sort of preparation going on. Something big was coming.

But after a wide circle over the top of the German bird, the impression through the goggles went away. Luf had managed to fix the jam. Leave it to experience to right mechanical failure, even when it wasn't his own machine. That was my Lufbery. My mentor and friend. My brother and—

My heart dropped from my chest.

Luf had come back round on the tail of the Albatross, and now his plane was on fire.

Flames in the sky.

The German gunner must have landed a round in his engine.

Luf sailed by his prey in a straight line, ignoring the combat altogether. With every second, the disaster picked up momentum. I couldn't turn away. Horror glued my eyes to the sight.

No. No. No.

This wasn't right. We'd made it back. We were safe. And that was a damn Albatross reconnaissance plane. He'd shot down a Gotha. He'd shot down scores of planes. He'd shot down six in one day. How? What right did they have?

Not Lufbery. Please. Please. Please not Lufbery. Anyone but Lufbery.

My nightmare intensified as I watched my friend desperately scramble from the flaming cockpit and jump from the burning plane.

He fell and fell and fell from view.

The Nieuport, without a pilot, barreled from the air and crashed out of sight.

Our entire aerodrome stopped and watched the tower of smoke billow up on the horizon. The whole world stopped spinning.

He had jumped. Maybe he'd survived. It was a long way down, but maybe he'd found a pool of water? Maybe his legs were broken somewhere, but he'd still come home. Maybe this awful war didn't just steal everything from you at a moment's notice at all the wrong times and for all the wrong reasons.

Pilots running. Jostling my shoulders. A terrible whistling noise in my ear. Gravity yanked me to the ground, overpowering my knees. I crumpled to the dirt.

Screaming and yelling. Someone barked orders. Huffer's red face.

I staggered looking for a plane. I needed to get in the sky. I fumbled to put the goggles on. Shouted the word "plane" hoarsely over and over. But everyone stared at me dumbly, as if I were crazy.

Now Jane was limping my way. They hadn't finished bandaging her. She collapsed on me. Repeated it would be all right. But she shook with sobs. How could she bring herself to lie at a time like this? It wouldn't be all right. This was new. I'd never held her so tightly. My stomach had never contracted like this before.

I couldn't sit up anymore, just fell, back in the dirt, looking up at the sky.

That was Lufbery's sky. His second home. The one he'd invited me to. But man never belonged there in the first place. We had ruined the sky. Lit it up with war.

So much movement. It yanked, stretched time like molasses. Jane and I lay there motionless, exhausted, empty. An island in a hurricane. Faceless heads trying to convince me to sit up.

Redundant and cruel confirmation then. A final blow to break whatever dam of fortitude I had left, coming in through the alert phone, whispers around me to cement in history what I already knew.

Major Raoul Lufbery, America's Ace of Aces, was dead.

Chapter 34
Nieuport 17
Jane

Drink sometimes, you whose footsteps yet may tread
The undisturbed, delightful paths of Earth,
To those whose blood, in pious duty shed,
Hallows the soil where that same wine had birth.
-Alan Seeger-

Marcus was never the same, indelibly altered from such a terrible end to our mission. He hardly spoke more than a few words for several days after Lufbery went down.

I wasn't surprised. To deal with the weight of his first kill and the death of his closest friend and greatest hero, all in a day, was enough to unravel any human being—even if my first kill didn't seem to have as strong an impact on me. I suspected it hadn't hit me yet.

We were no strangers to death. War acquainted all of us with the terrible specter, and we adjusted by holding even those whose company we enjoyed at arm's length.

And yet, because of the weakness in human nature, we all

succumbed to one bond that would break us. Each of us had someone who, in our deepest hopes, we believed we could save from the great calamity.

We all planted the seeds of delusion in someone.

But Marcus was special. He had allowed his heart to attach to two others. One, he nearly lost in the flight from Ghent. The other, immediately after.

Lufbery's funeral was unlike anything I'd ever seen. A full procession of hundreds of military personnel and many more French citizens in full mourning followed his casket, draped with a beautiful American flag. The procession started at the hospital where his body had been resting. Marcus walked alongside his brothers, as muffled drums played their way to a truck decorated with so many flowers I'd have thought spring awoke in 1918 solely to honor his memory.

But even with the lorry decorated as it was, the flowers, sent by countless admirers, were too plentiful to take a place of honor beside him. A river of French Foreign Legion personnel in red fez hats carried the remaining floral designs in his wake.

As the funeral party, now led by the commander of the French aerial corps, wound its way slowly to his final resting place, a small boy burst from the crowd to hand a bouquet to the lorry driver. Expressions in a crowd thousands strong ranged from reverence to despair, from grief to anger, from appreciation to ambition.

At the grave site, a chorus of white-robed nurses stood at the ready, and a full military band played a hymn, the words "Nearer, My God, to Thee" and the sounds of mournful brass breaking the spring tranquility of a buttercup-laden meadow. Then, we tilted our heads to the sky, as one Allied service plane after another flew above the spot, killed their engines, and tossed roses from their silent planes. The flowers fell on us like strange rain, flashes of green and red.

Where did all these flowers come from when war had made even radishes a precious commodity?

One of the generals shared glowing, respectful sentiments, ending with fitting words, "Rest peacefully, Major Lufbery, close by the martyrs to our great cause. Your glorious example will inspire in us the spirit of sacrifice, till the day when humanity's enemy shall be finally vanquished."

Then came the ceremonial firing of rifles, and the bugle farewell, echoed far off by a second bugler hidden in the woods.

The crowds took their time dissipating. Marcus was among the last to leave the site. I had to pull him away gently by the hand.

Days later, I found myself eating alone in the mess, struggling to keep my composure. The past month had been nothing short of a series of nightmares, and they haunted me even while awake. Any moment my thoughts were not occupied with some pressing task, the ghosts of our adventure harrowed me. I relived that moment when a Nieuport 28, our own model plane, opened fired on us. I could feel the Blue Flyer's fingers groping at my neck.

By night, I woke in cold sweat from dreams of being stuck in a crate with Johann's body, deprived of life at the farmhouse, only to break free to see Marcus and Gervaise carted away in a German car.

All the while, I waited for the impact of my first kills to settle on me. It did not come.

Is there a floor to grief, a place where even the numb sensation of pain goes numb? Or is the capacity of human loss evidence that we are more than our mortal shells?

A handful of unopened letters lay beside my bowl of soup. I had no stomach for either.

"Jane?"

I turned my head up, and to my annoyance, Flora, queen of the cackling hens took a seat across from me. I didn't bother answering.

"I just wanted to say it's nice having you back."

I examined my letters. I dribbled soup with my spoon.

"Some of the ladies and I," she went on, "well, we were just wondering if you'd like to come into town with us tonight. It might be good to clear your mind a bit. No? Perhaps we can work on getting that smile back. A woman has no defense like a good smile—"

I pushed my chair from the table with a scrape, gathered my letters and began walking away. She called after me in just a few short steps.

"I'm sorry. I know how much he meant to you. He meant so much to so many of us."

I didn't turn around.

L ater, I busied myself by working on Marcus's plane. As of yet, Major Huffer hadn't had the courage to give him any new assignments. In fact, Huffer hadn't found the courage to speak with him at all. Chatter was already circulating among some of the pilots that he should not have landed without shooting down the Albatross first—that his decision to turn in started the chain of events leading to Lufbery's death.

Guilt for the dead was so strange, a commodity the honorable fought over and the weak refused to touch. Marcus was all too ready to add Lufbery to the list of names he'd doomed with his negligence and cowardice.

I didn't know what to make of that, myself. Cause and effect were strange cousins with a complicated relationship.

My work gave me something to busy my hands and mind with. It was familiar and safe. The magic I used for plane repairs was simple and helpful. It didn't threaten lives or incur the interest of warring nations. Beatrice, my step ladder with low self-esteem, wobbled beneath me as I worked on the top wing of Marcus's Nieuport.

"Come now, Beatrice. Don't be cross with me. I was on assignment."

Our turbulent relationship would need some mending of its own, and I was about to descend and tighten her screws when a sound across the hangar pulled my attention.

I put down my wrench and walked past some of our other planes to an old Nieuport 17, the model flown by so many of the early Lafayette Escadrille. The sight of it disturbed my mechanical state of mind, sparking recent memories of our flight in the Rumpler. Old planes. How many Rumpler C.Is had the Nieuport 17s shot down?

I pushed the thoughts away, ran from the trauma.

Marcus sat in the cockpit.

"Should I be working on this one instead?" I asked, wiping my hands on my jumpsuit.

He rested an elbow on the top wing, just below the Lewis gun.

"Seventeen," he muttered.

"A Nieuport 17," I replied. "One of the best."

"No," he said. "That's the count they're giving him. Seventeen victories."

I leaned against the plane and shrugged.

"Does that include the Gotha he shot down to save us at the farmhouse?" I asked.

"Of course not," he said bitterly. "It doesn't include any kill that couldn't be officially confirmed."

"It's just a score, Marcus. He wouldn't have cared—"

"But I care," he said. "They're grouping him with the wrong crowd. He was more than a good pilot. He was an incredible pilot. He was the best."

"He was more than a pilot," I said quietly.

Marcus looked at me, the pain in his eyes more real than any magic.

"You know they're not counting my victory, either," he said.

I closed my eyes and swallowed.

"I had assumed that would be the case." When I opened my eyes, I noticed a machine gun round in Marcus's hand. "What's that?"

"It was from Luf. I made a promise to myself that my first victory would be on his bullet." A bitter scoff escaped him.

"That's mighty difficult to do when a round that size doesn't fit into the machine gun on a Rumpler C.I."

"Yeah," he agreed. "But we were never supposed to fly that Rumpler. I should have been here. We could have had my plane ready, and I could have gone up beside him to take down that recon plane. I could have—"

"Marcus, stop."

He set his jaw and dropped his face into his hands.

"We can't let ourselves into such dark corners," I continued. "We must take from our friends the virtues they possessed, carry them forward like a torch to light the way for those who never knew them. Right now, it's the examples of others that keep me going. I think of Lufbery's humility. I think of Gervaise's passion. They inspire me."

"Don't," Marcus replied. "Don't let them inspire you too much. Lufbery's gone, and Gervaise is probably following after him soon, the way she's carrying on. If you get to inspired, you'll join them. You got a taste of that sense of victory in Ghent. Do you want to talk about it yet?"

I swallowed and shook my head. For years, the concept of killing another human being had paralyzed Marcus. How could I tell him that despite all of my talk of non-violence, I'd yet to experience the fallout?

"I don't want to be here anymore," he moaned.

I pulled my mouth into a tight frown. It wrinkled my chin.

"You'd leave me here alone? Come now. You didn't let me go off to Clairmarais or Ghent by myself. You certainly won't leave me to fend off Flora and Major Huffer."

"They're reassigning Huffer," he replied calmly. "They've got some liaison post for him at First Army Headquarters. It's hard to lead when you've lost the faith of your men."

"Do you blame him for what happened?"

He shook his head.

"I blame myself." He buried his head into the bay, out of my view. I retrieved Beatrice, with some coaxing, and set her up beside the plane. I only needed a few steps to get closer to him. This was the closest he'd let me come to him since we'd collapsed on the floor of the hangar in a broken heap. I put a hand in his hair.

"What else could we have done?" I blinked away the fear. The despair of our return flight that fateful morning stabbed through my defenses. But I would go there for him, if he needed. He had gone to hell for me. "We could not have gone further south. We were just trying to survive."

"We brought that recon plane in. Our flashy sortie with a French flag flying behind us, we may as well have handed that German pilot a map to the airbase."

His stare was hard, glowering a hole in the wooden panels inside the cockpit. He sheltered from the rest of the world under the sturdy canopy of the top wing.

"We had orders to come back with the violin strings and the goggles," I replied. He let out a slow breath.

"Orders. I know. We had orders. Who were our orders from? Smith? Atkins? An anonymous German operative named Muster-mann? The mission smelled funny from the beginning."

I bit my tongue, trying not to take his words as a critique upon me. But it wasn't easy. I'd already spent so much time the past week berating myself for my insistence that we go retrieve the magic.

"What have they done with the strings?" he asked.

"Nothing yet," I ruefully admitted. "I retrieved them from my boot, and I managed to untie the flag from the Rumpler with pliers.

"When did you do that?" Marcus asked roughly. I understood the accusation beneath. I hadn't unfastened the flag when we first got out of the plane. Then Lufbery went down.

"When you all went to find him. I had to keep myself busy," I admitted sheepishly. "And it's a good thing. The Rumpler disappeared. I asked around, and some of the mechanics knew what I was talking about, but not many. So I took up the issue with Flora. She told me it had been claimed, quietly, during the night. I kept expecting a newspaper report or gossip or something, but—"

"But Luf's death overshadowed all of it."

I wrung my hands. Outside, a Nieuport rolled by the mouth of the hangar. One of the 94th boys headed off to battle, eager to avenge his fallen brother, eager to take the fight to the Kaiser again. The cycle continued as it had for years.

"You don't think—" Marcus began.

"No, I don't." I cut off the thought. Even with their obsession with secrecy, I was not ready to believe that any Allied government would take down one of its brightest simply to cover up our mission in the press. "I think it was just his time."

Somehow, that brought a small smile to Marcus's drooping features.

"And when it's your time, it's your time."

I reached into the cockpit and grabbed his hand.

"Thank you," I whispered shakily, forcing him to stare me in the eyes. "I didn't think we were going to make it back, and I know what it cost you."

"I don't know if you do."

I blushed, ready to concede to his point. The first kill affected people in different ways. Marcus had seen death in the ambulances. Before I took down the machine gun, the closest I'd come to death was that night when Mustermann executed Johann.

"Of course, I only meant—"

"No," he insisted with a sigh. "I've been debating telling you. You think I had to kill a man to save us."

I nodded carefully.

"I needed my first victory, and I got it. But—" he pulled the glass marble from his shirt. A single crack ran down one side, the same crack he'd received what felt like months ago after his sortie across lines with Winslow and Campbell. My hair lay inside the marble, frozen in space. "Look."

"What about it?" I asked.

"I think it's still working. I think the Blue Flyer was wearing it when he came after us. That's why he couldn't shoot us down."

I examined the marble, straining my memory for everything Aunt Luella had mentioned about it.

"But you shot him down," I replied.

"Yes, but the other night, I woke up from a nightmare. I was back in the ambulances, showing up to that platoon my negligence had gotten shot up. But Luf's body was there. And yours. I woke up sweating, and this marble—well, it was glowing a faint blue."

Beatrice wobbled beneath me.

"Why are you still wearing it?" I asked. He looked me dead in the eyes, our faces close to one another.

"I promised you I wouldn't take it off."

"Marcus, Jane! You've got a visitor."

One of the orderlies called to us from the hangar entrance. Sergeant Smith stood beside him.

"There were some comments in your report I wanted to follow up on," Smith said. We sat in the office at aerodrome headquarters. Marcus and I each slumped into our own seat. We had expected Smith's visit sooner or later.

"I don't know what else you'd like us to add," I said. I had submitted a full interview with Lieutenant Atkins, in which I detailed all the specifics of our time in Ghent, my understanding of the effect of Albert Ball's violin strings, my conversation with the Blue Flyer, and our tumultuous flight home. "Atkins's questions were thorough."

"Yeah, I listened to the report. But your description lacked some particulars. You said the violin strings did what exactly?"

I glanced at the door, unconsciously concerned about confidentiality.

"It's as I said. The strings somehow showed Thomas how to play a song on the violin. And, when he played that song, he gave off this sort of impression. I don't know how else to explain it. As a spectator, suddenly I understood who he was. Not an agent for intelligence. Not a name. In fact, I didn't understand any concrete details in particular, but I saw who he truly was, as if he would never compromise the things he loved most about himself."

I massaged my temples, wishing I had a better explanation.

"I apologize. I really only had one interaction with him. I wish the strings' effect were as simple as turning someone invisible or something, but magic doesn't work that way."

Smith stroked his chin.

"And the other thing? Dewar?" Smith asked.

"What other thing?" Marcus replied.

"The thing that doesn't make any sense at all."

"What about it?"

"Do you stand by Jane's explanation?"

The muscle in Marcus's jaw pulsed with irritation.

"What do you want, Smith? A Fokker Dr.I pursued us into a cloud. We came out pursued by a Nieuport 28."

Smith cocked his head to the side.

"You were flying a Rumpler. It could have been one of ours—"

"It wasn't one of ours!" Marcus shouted, leaning forward in his chair and putting a finger into Smith's face. "Put whatever you want in your report. That triplane changed into a Nieuport, and I shot that abomination out of the sky. And stop looking at me like my judgment is compromised, sir."

Marcus folded his arms and fell back into the chair. Quietly, I attempted to fill in the gaps.

"Had it only been a matter of a Nieuport appearing, we would be more amenable to your suggestion. But, the Flyer's plane vanished. The sooner Command embraces the nature of this enemy the better. Phantom shooters in Ghent. Inexplicable damage from aircraft machine guns. Changing planes. We have no idea what they can do."

"What they could do," Smith replied.

"I beg your pardon?"

"There haven't been any more sightings of those rogue flyers since your escape from Ghent. And that's on either side of the line. Whatever you did scared them good."

"We didn't do anything," Marcus said.

"You shot one down," Smith countered. I nearly spoke up, but Marcus sent me a warning glance and put a hand on his chest where the marble lay under his shirt.

"We found the crash site," Smith added, noting the exchange without comment. "We thought that perhaps Richthofen's scarf might be on the body of the pilot. There wasn't much left of the plane."

"And the scarf?" I asked. Smith clenched his jaw.

"You didn't find any human remains, did you?" Marcus asked. Smith shook his head, and a curious smile adorned

Marcus's face while his head drooped back toward the floor between his knees.

"What will you do with the violin strings? And the goggles?" I asked.

"For the time being, I will take them from you," Smith said. "Now that we have two devices, we will have the eggheads analyze them to see what we can find out."

I leaned back, unsure if I'd been insulted.

"I was under the impression that you chose me for this mission because of my knowledge in the extraordinary. Why not have me on a team to investigate our findings?"

Smith opened a drawer on the desk and peered inside nonchalantly.

"We mean no offense, Private. I don't need to remind you that those goggles made a believer out of me. But I'm not the colonel or the general or the Commander in Chief. The United States military likes to be thorough. When the eggheads fail, I suspect they'll come knocking."

I wanted to protest, but Smith shrugged in such a way to suggest he had no control over the decision.

"I see," I replied. A hint of remorse cracked through Smith's detached features, one of the rare glimpses he offered of the man beneath the uniform. Perhaps he wasn't all bravado and resolve.

"I was so sorry to hear about Major Lufbery," Smith said quietly. "I know your victory came at a great cost, but I hope you're aware what good you've done. The whole of the Allied forces appreciates what you two did in tracking down the mission objective and bringing it home."

"Do the Allied forces know they're so grateful?" Marcus asked with a sullen and upturned chin. Smith smiled evasively, glancing at a hat he had placed on the desk.

"What happens to us now?" I asked.

"I'm putting you both on leave. Go to Paris or to England if you're brave enough to sail or fly the channel. Go do what you have to do to become mission ready again."

I folded my hands in my lap and tried to hide my relief. I didn't want Marcus flying back into combat in his current state. Grief led to poor choices, and the air was not forgiving of poor choices.

"And if I don't want to become mission ready again?" Marcus asked.

Smith stuffed his hands into his pockets. I'd have expected Marcus's continual insubordination and candid melancholy to anger the sergeant, but Smith's countenance shared in his defeat. A compassionate curl to the sergeant's shoulders made me think he might reach out and embrace Marcus like a brother. He pulled a chair from behind the desk and slid it beside us.

"I know you're in the dark right now, son. I wish I could turn on a light for you, but I can't. War has asked so much from so many that it's not easy to remember anyone's name anymore. But this war will end. And when it does, it will be important that it didn't beat you. Defeating the Kaiser will mean little if we bring home nothing but defeated soldiers to show for it. This feeling you've got right now, that's them winning. We can't let them win. I won't let them win.

"You may never again find a friendship like you had in Lufbery, not in your whole life. You might even be mad at him for dying. But sooner or later, you'll hear him whispering to you. And I don't have to know the man as well as you did to know what those whispers will sound like. You still have people to honor and protect, and you can let those people honor and protect you as well, even from yourself."

Marcus didn't meet the sergeant's gaze at all, but after a prolonged pause, he nodded his understanding. Smith grabbed him by the wrist, opened his hand, and placed a large bullet in his palm.

"Remember how he always polished his rounds before he went up? I swiped one once, to see if 'polishing rounds' meant doing something special to the bullet. But it wasn't the polish at all, it was the man polishing them. I want you to have it."

Marcus stared at the large machine gun round in disbelief.

"I have one already."

Smith smiled.

"Of course, you do. Well, in that case, maybe Jane will hold on to it. After all, she is your gunner." Smith stood and made his way toward the door. "Enjoy your leave. I'll be in touch soon."

"Sergeant, might I ask what you did with the Rumpler?" I called after him. "I heard that it had been claimed."

He paused in the doorway and gave me a knowing smile. "What Rumpler?"

"Quite right. What Rumpler?" I replied.

Chapter 35
Upward, I Fly
Marcus

Take up our quarrel with the foe:
To you from failing hands we throw
The torch; be yours to hold it high.
If ye break faith with us who die
We shall not sleep, though poppies grow
In Flanders fields.
-John McCrae-

I looked at my trunk sitting on the rickety bed. By necessity, a soldier's life was portable. All that I owned fit inside the trunk easily, ready to move at a moment's notice.

"That's a big suitcase for a week's leave." Douglas Campbell, one of the first heroes of the United States Army Air Service stood behind me with his hands stuffed in his pockets.

"It felt strange to pack half a trunk. Besides, I'd rather be prepared," I said.

"Prepared for what?"

"Reassignment."

Smith's words from the day before wouldn't leave my head, and strangely enough, they gave me hope. The world turned dark after Luf went down, the way it does in a nightmare. Even though some of the terror ebbed as time marched on, the fog did not.

I recognized Campbell's plays at manly affection, showing his remorse that I might be putting the 94th behind me through short, punchy remarks. But even recognizing the attempt, I could not connect with it.

I could hardly connect with anything anymore. I wandered around like an actor who could not persuade his fellows to break character, as though I was the only one who noticed the movie camera. Everything seemed scripted. Everything was staged.

"For what it's worth, I truly hope you don't get reassigned," Campbell said. "You're a swell pilot, Markie. Even if the record doesn't show it."

The record. I struggled to grasp its importance anymore. The record had failed Luf. It had failed me. For so long, I'd worried so much about the record. But now I saw it for what it was, something to distract us from what we did, what we faced.

And yet, all that the world saw was the record. It was the only currency on which a soldier could trade beyond his reputation. It was all I had to send back to my parents in California to share with their friends.

That maddening grin Lufbery always had on his face finally made sense—the way he paraded around in his uniform, flaunting the medals, the *Croix de Guerre* with its palms, like he knew a secret. I was in on the secret now.

"Thanks, Campbell," I said rotely. "You just remember me when you make ace."

He shuffled his feet.

"Don't pretend like it's some far out possibility. You only need, what, one or two more?"

He lifted his head and met my eyes. I wanted to shrink from the exchange. I wasn't ready for that kind of intimacy again. I didn't want anyone to see my eyes—anyone, maybe, other than Jane. She was all right.

"The title doesn't really mean anything. Not really," he said.

"As long as you know that," I replied. I took a deep breath. That morning, the squadron was scattered, some pilots on assignment, others in town, others at work in the hangar trying to honor their late Captain by learning a few things from their mechanics. "Campbell, would you do me a favor?"

"Anything."

"Would you tell the boys goodbye for me? I don't think I can do it." My voice broke. Once, I'd dammed my tears up so well that never a trickle came through. Now, it seemed I was always one rain away from breaking down.

"They'll understand," he said. "Besides, you'll be back in a week."

I smiled sadly.

"That's right. Back in a week."

Campbell put a hand on my shoulder and lowered his voice.

"I don't know where they sent you or why, but it took a special kind of bravery. You'll always have my respect. Know that."

I took his hand off my shoulder and shook it firmly.

"Thanks. If we all make it out of this, maybe I'll come knocking your way for a letter of recommendation."

He laughed. I smiled, trying my best.

"Take care of yourself, Markie, and Jane. Weird as she is, she's lucky to have you."

I slung my trunk over my shoulder and walked from the barracks.

France waited outside. The world was green around the aerodrome. The sun was shining gently, and I could almost smell summer coming on the breeze.

Upward, I Fly

Once, the scene would have been a beautiful promise, a dreamy getaway. Then came war, and the smells were the opportunity of a blank canvas, ready for pilots to make a name for themselves.

But now, when I closed my eyes, I saw the roses raining down on Luf's final resting place. I heard the band playing the hymn. The words of that song had echoed in my head over and over since the ceremony.

O r if on joyful wing, cleaving the sky,
     Sun, moon, and stars forgot, upward I fly,
Still all my song will be,
Nearer, my God to thee;
Nearer, my God to thee, nearer to Thee.

L ufbery would never be forgotten. The history books would remember his skill in the air to the tune of seventeen victories. But more importantly, when I saw the air above France, I'd know that he believed in something. He believed in me. And if magic was real, maybe he wasn't gone. Not really.

Maybe none of them were gone.

The breeze pulled at my shirt collar. I breathed in through my nose, let it out slowly, and opened my eyes.

Jane waited for me at a motorcar near the mouth of the aerodrome, just beside the office where it connected to the road off to Toul or Nancy, depending on which fork you took. The sight of her reminded me of all those evenings when I came back from a patrol and she waited by the mess for me to come in and catch up.

She smiled gently. The smile was the signpost. It said she was there, that she cared. I found joy in her concern.

"You ready?" she asked as I came near.

"I guess. You?"

She bit her lip.

"I wish we could bring my Enfield."

I smiled, genuinely this time, not the way I had with Campbell.

"You don't want to write off the motorbike? After Ghent, I'm not sure I'll ever ride one again," I said.

"That's because you have planes to fly to satisfy the urge," she replied, settling into the driver's seat. I threw my trunk in the back and slid in beside her.

"Well, you'll get another chance on the Enfield when we come back in a week," I said.

"Right."

We both stared at Gengault. A Nieuport 28 was running down the airstrip to take off for a patrol. The French army ran drills out of view. The buzz of activity hummed in our ears. To me, the site would always be sacred, both because it was Luf's last aerodrome and because it was where I'd made a home cradled in the magic of a new family.

And despite the shadowing despair that blanketed the wake of Luf's loss, that was one ember that could not be extinguished. It took an overwhelming night to recognize the fire that fueled me, but that was a gift the dead could leave behind.

"Take a good look," Jane said, "then, off to new adventures."

I nodded solemnly.

"Did you say goodbye to Flora?" I asked.

"Incredible. A touching moment absolutely ruined. You have a gift, Marcus, an astounding gift. Why on Earth would I want to think about Flora at a time like—"

The sound of the car's engine sputtered to life, and Jane pulled us onto the road leading from Gengault. She hadn't told me where we were going on leave, and I didn't need to know.

There's magic in the horizon for those who know to find. I didn't know where to look, but Jane sure did.

And I was ready to learn.

END OF BOOK ONE

Gervais Raoul Lufbery
March 14th, 1885 - May 19th 1918

Gervais Raoul Lufbery was an American aviator in World War I. He volunteered to fly for the French Foreign Legion with the Lafayette Escadrille and eventually became one the United States' greatest influences when it formed its first air service. He was known for his mechanical prowess, aviation wisdom, and uncanny knack for going across lines to fight German planes. Officially, he was credited with seventeen victories, leading the new American Army Air Service as its Ace of Aces. But the estimated total of his downed enemy planes is much higher.

When I started researching for The Shards of Lafayette, I bonded with this fallen hero. Firsthand accounts of those who flew with him rarely had poor things to say about his character. His determination, bravery, and prowess continue to be an inspiration to me. He will live on in memory as one of the United States' greatest combat pilots of all time.

For anyone interested in aviation or military history, I highly recommended spending time to learn more about Luf.

Review

Dear reader,

Thanks for spending so much time with Marcus and Jane.

If you enjoyed the book, I'd really appreciate it if you took the time to leave a review to let others know. A simple review or rating on Goodreads, BookBub, Amazon, or any other book outlet goes a long way in helping readers take a chance on new authors.

Thanks again.

Sincerely,

Kenny

About the Author

Kenneth A. Baldwin spent childhood in his California backyard concocting magical potions from mosses and shade-loving plants. Through his youth, he toiled away at piano and computer keyboards going nine rounds with creativity. After graduating from college in 2013, he fought through law school by turning outlines into card games. Now he lives nestled under the Wasatch Mountains where he spends his free time writing stories that blur the lines between history, magic, dreams, and reality.

f facebook.com/kennethabaldwin

🐦 twitter.com/kennethabaldwin

📷 instagram.com/kennethabaldwin

Ingram Content Group UK Ltd.
Milton Keynes UK
UKHW011909110623
423271UK00005B/16/J